NIGHT OF RAPTURE

The soft click of her door handle made her breath catch in her throat. Lydia turned her head very slowly.

In the faint light from her window she saw the shadowy figure move toward her bed. Her breath was constricted in her throat. She knew she should cry out, protest, scream . . . but her mouth was so dry she did none of those things.

Vincent stood by her bed a moment, a dressing robe covering his body. She wondered wildly if he was naked beneath it, and the thought caused her to be even more breathless.

"Are you afraid of me?" he asked softly.

She shook her head, her eyes wide. "I knew you'd come," she whispered.

His response was to untie the dressing robe and let it fall from his shoulders, and she knew she had been correct. He wore nothing beneath it, and his powerful body was lean and broad in all the right places. She ran her tongue around her dry lips, and at the small movement, Vincent reached for the bedcovers and pulled them back . . .

SECRET TOUCH
JEAN INNES

ZEBRA BOOKS
KENSINGTON PUBLISHING CORP.

ZEBRA BOOKS

are published by

Kensington Publishing Corp.
475 Park Avenue South
New York, NY 10016

First printing: May, 1992

Printed in the United States of America

Chapter One

Lydia Grey drew a deep breath as she reached Greystone Manor that morning, preparing to meet the habitual irritation of her cousin, Audine. The far more attractive of the two young ladies arrived that blustery Monday morning at the solidly built house in the most fashionable part of Bath, mentally armed to continue tutoring the difficult younger Grey children, Audine's two sisters.

Lydia knew quite well that the haughty Audine, like the rest of her family, never considered it patronizing to offer such a post to their impoverished kinswoman. When Lydia's parents had died from a fatal attack of cholera during the voyage bringing the family back from India, Lydia had been fortunate to have generous-hearted relatives to take her in, as her Uncle Percival still reported loudly to anyone who would listen.

He had done so from the outset. Lydia could still recall the exact way he had looked her over on her first arrival at the house, as if she were a piece of meat on a slab. And she could still feel the chilly hostility of the family as a whole . . .

"So you're my foolish brother's child, are you?" Lord Grey had said abruptly, the cruelty of the phrase putting Lydia on the defensive immediately, although she tried very hard not to let him see how his insensitivity upset her.

"I'm your niece, Lydia," she said, as evenly as she could, remembering that she had finally chosen to come here, as her parents had urgently requested.

She noted how the three girls of the family had drawn together, as if to remind her that here was an already established family, who didn't take kindly to an outsider. And if she had expected the older girl, about her own age, to become a friend, then one look at Audine's tightly pressed lips soon told her otherwise.

Lydia had glanced toward her aunt. Surely, her Aunt Maud, of whom her mother had always spoken with affection, wouldn't be so unwelcoming. But though the lady smiled diffidently at Lydia, it was clear that she was very much dependent on her husband's whims as to how she should react to the newcomer.

"My mother spoke kindly of you, Aunt Maud," she said directly, deciding it was best to be straightforward. "She told me to come to you if anything happened . . ." her voice had faltered, and she had looked down at her trembling hands. Something terrible *had* happened, and she still had not quite recovered from the shock of losing both parents so tragically.

"My dear—" her aunt began gently, but her husband stopped her with a wave of his hand.

"Yet it took you all this time to come to us, when family hospitality was obviously to be offered. After the tragedy you chose to spend an entire year in the country with strangers rather than come directly to see your own family."

6

Lydia decided he was ruthless, and surprisingly irritated with her. He obviously didn't want her here, yet he took it as a personal affront that she hadn't arrived at his home tearfully and abject, pleading poverty.

If he expected that, then he didn't know her, she had thought indignantly. But that was the truth of it anyway. He didn't know her at all.

"I stayed with friends. They were not strangers," she replied with some spirit. She stared him out, with the unblinking stare that she had begun to realize infuriated him so. She dared not say that these newfound relatives were the strangers, but it was true.

"Is she going to live with us?" one of the younger girls said resentfully.

Lydia looked at her, and her heart sank. There was no welcome here, not even from the smaller children.

Her uncle had spoken with some finality then, pompous to the last.

"Since you preferred to stay with these 'friends' and until now you've declined to get in touch with your family since you informed us of your parents' demise, I felt it perfectly legitimate to absolve myself of any further responsibility toward you, miss."

Lydia had felt herself grow cold inside.

"Uncle, I'm not asking for charity. I felt it my duty to come and see you. And you must understand that it has taken me all this time to come to terms with what happened to my parents. Surely you have some compassion, and some fond memories of your brother and his wife?"

He had snorted derisively. "If the pair of them had taken my advice, they'd never have gone haring off to India chasing impossible dreams in the first place."

Lydia had stood there, fuming inside, her hands held tightly together inside their thin gloves. If she hadn't held on to them tightly, she was sure she'd have hit him, and that would have done nobody any good. She drew a deep breath.

"The fact is, I can't stay with friends forever, and I need to find a good position to support myself. I . . . I wondered if you could help me to find something respectable."

"Surely you can think of something, Percival?" Aunt Maud had said encouragingly. "What about the plan we were discussing a few weeks ago? And after all, Lydia is our blood relative. We could do far worse."

Lydia had looked at them suspiciously.

"I daresay it would do no harm," her uncle had said slowly. "Can you read and write, miss, and do you have some understanding of simple arithmetic and the social graces?"

"Of course," she had said indignantly. "Didn't I write to tell you about—?'"

"Yes, yes," he'd said testily. "Very well. We'll go into the study and I'll put a proposition to you."

She followed him, her head held high, feeling more humiliated than ever as she heard the titters of the three Grey sisters. Once in her uncle's study, she had been told to sit down while he eased himself around the other side of the great oak desk.

"I can offer you a post here, as tutor to my young daughters. You'll be paid accordingly, and you'll occupy quarters in the west wing."

"That won't be necessary. I'm not asking for a roof over my head. I have already obtained lodgings

8

in the town with a milliner and his wife, and I'm very happy to stay there. If I accept your kind offer, Uncle, I would much prefer to remain there and come to Greystone Manor daily."

She thought he would have a seizure at that moment, from the angry reddening of his face and neck.

"You young chit! *If* you accept my offer, indeed. You should be damned glad to get it. A pauper could easily find herself out on the streets begging, or selling herself." His gaze wandered over her shapely figure in the blue visiting dress, and a narrowed look had come into his eyes. "A niece of mine would be well-advised not to take to the streets of Bath and cheapen the reputation of the family."

"I assure you this niece would never demean herself so," Lydia replied stiffly and furiously, hating him more every minute. If it had not been for her promise to her parents to be sure and make contact with the family, and to repair the old breach between them, she would have stormed out of there at once.

"Very well then. So what do you say to my offer?"

"What I said before. I'd like to think about it, Uncle. May I come back tomorrow and tell you of my decision, please?"

"Good God, miss, I begin to deeply question the way you've been bred. I always thought my brother entirely irresponsible in his futile dream of making a fortune in the tea plantations of India. It seems his head was completely turned with all the fantastic tales he'd heard, and he's brought you up to be quite ungrateful. And what of the Mutiny?" he said, with a quick change of mood. "What kind of fool was he to keep you all there, when you could all

9

have been in very real danger, by all accounts? Any Britisher who remained there, when he had the chance of getting out, must have been mad in the head."

"We were in no danger, Uncle. We lived in the hills, many miles away from Delhi."

With the pomposity of those who knew little of the true facts, it was clear Lydia would never persuade him of that fact. During their stay her uncle's letters from England had impressed on her father the madness of his decision to remain in India.

Percival had never thought they'd get out of what he called the melting pot alive. And it was clear that he considered his niece to be as irresponsible. The final straw, in his opinion, was that the girl had not come to him as soon as she arrived in England, as good as penniless and alone. And Lydia knew he was wishing very hard that he could simply wash his hands of her.

But in the end, she had agreed to tutor the two small girls, praying that in time they could get along reasonably well. They were her family, after all.

And so the arrangement had begun.

Once inside the manor house, Lydia shook out the folds of her serviceable grey dress and tidied her glossy dark hair, trying vainly to push it back into the pins from where it inevitably slipped in wayward fashion to curl about her face. The milliner thought it a charming trait, but she knew her uncle had very different ideas about her appearance.

Lydia sighed, knowing how far short she fell in gaining his approval. She did try, but at eighteen years old it wasn't easy to conform to the boredom of life in an English gentleman's house. Once she had had the freedom and color of all India at her disposal—or felt as if she had.

She bit her lip guiltily, knowing she must be grateful. She was startled at that moment to see her older cousin Audine come flying down the curving staircase of the austere house, and knew something must be amiss. Young ladies of Audine's upbringing *never* flew down staircases except in cases of dire emergency.

"What's happened?" Lydia said uneasily. "I know I'm late, and I'm sorry—"

"Never mind all that." Her cousin was as impatient as ever, drawing her into the library and away from servants' ears.

"Mother's not feeling well, and you know she was going to accompany Father and me to the Hotel Splendide today to meet Lord Montagu. You'll have to come with us instead."

Lydia stared at her, her heart beginning to thud, her palms beginning to feel uncomfortably damp.

"But I can't . . . the children are expecting me for their lessons—"

"For heaven's sake, Lydia, can't you see this is more important than giving spelling lessons to infants who aren't in the least interested in such things? Lord Montagu will almost certainly offer for my hand in due course, and Father insists on another lady being present at this first meeting. It's the done thing; not that you'd know anything about that, I suppose. Heaven knows what kind of people you were in the habit of consorting with in that heathen country."

"If you mean India, I've told you often enough we lived a comfortable life and were acquainted with princes."

11

As she was stung into her reply, a swift vision of that lovely, mysterious country with all its smells, its vibrant colors and blistering heat, sprang into her mind with a mixture of pleasure and pain. She heard her cousin's contemptuous laugh.

"You surely don't expect us to believe all that nonsense, do you?" Audine said.

Lydia looked at her silently and unblinkingly, in the same way the dark-eyed Indian women stared their unfathomable stares. It was something she had developed almost unconsciously over the years, through her friendship with some of those lovely doe-eyed women. She had also acquired the lovely honey-colored skin that no longer looked quite English, yet could never be termed foreign, and contrasted so dramatically with her vivid blue eyes. Compared with her cousin's narrow face and sharp features, she was undoubtedly the beauty in the family, a fact that had infuriated Audine from the moment they met, and began the antagonism between them.

It was one of the reasons Lydia had tactfully insisted that the easygoing milliner, who had known her parents years ago, should still be her benefactor in terms of living accommodations.

Audine looked away first. "Must you stare at me like that with those cow-eyes of yours?"

"Cows don't have blue eyes," Lydia said, with the unconsciously tutorial habit of correction, which she knew annoyed her cousin even more.

"Very well, schoolmarm," Audine snapped. "I'm not so well acquainted with bovines that I care to know about such things. But enough of that. You may spend the morning with the children, but immediately after lunch you'll have to borrow one of

12

my gowns to make yourself look presentable for the meeting with Lord Montagu. He has an entire suite at his disposal in the Hotel Splendide, and we're invited to take tea with him."

"Must it be me?"

Audine looked at her with an almost active dislike.

"For someone who professes to have consorted with princes, Cousin, you seem irritatingly coy about meeting young men. Is it not your wish to be married if anyone will have you, that is?"

Lydia felt her cheeks go hot. "Of course it is, when I find the right one—"

Audine's hooting laughter stopped her, "Good Lord, anyone would think you had a *choice!* Think yourself lucky you have a roof over your head, girl, and don't go filling your head with nonsense about the right one. I suppose that's more of this Eastern way of thinking."

"It's not, as a matter of fact. Most Indian women have their marriages arranged for them, especially those of a higher caste." She tried to keep her voice even, so as not to irritate Audine still more by her superior knowledge of such things.

It had been obvious to her from the start that Audine was a dullard with no inclination for learning. Her sole occupation was in following the dictates of fashion, and being seen in all the best places, of which the beautiful Georgian city of Bath excelled. She had all the confidence of a young lady born to riches, but to her fury Audine discovered her younger cousin had all the beauty and gentleness she lacked.

"I know nothing about castes," Audine said now. "It all sounds hideous to me. Do you mean a woman

13

has to marry whomever her parents choose for her?"

"I do, and sometimes she doesn't even see his face until after the ceremony," Lydia said, thankful that the conversation had taken a less personal tone now, and wondering just when Audine was going to let her attend to her duties.

"Well, that wouldn't suit me," Audine said, with an aristocratic toss of the head. "I intend to look Lord Montagu over very thoroughly before I decide whether to accept him or not."

Lydia kept her gaze on the well-stocked bookshelves of the library, so rarely used by the inhabitants of this house. She had to hide a smile, wondering if Lord Montagu was going to have the same reaction when he met Audine. The situation was not so very different from the Indian arrangement, she thought, since neither party had met before, and it had been her uncle who had instigated the meeting with this most eligible suitor. She caught Audine's suspicious look and composed her face quickly.

"Wouldn't you rather I wore my working dress, rather than borrow one of yours, Audine?" she queried. "I could always appear as your maid if you'd prefer it."

"I would not. Have some sense, girl. Your name is the same as mine, and I've no wish to begin my acquaintance with Lord Montagu with a falsehood. Once we're married, you and he are bound to meet on future occasions. Now get along up to the nursery, and I'll see you again at lunchtime, by which time I'll have chosen a suitable gown for you to wear."

Lydia was dismissed. She let her breath out in a long sigh as she mounted the staircase toward the nursery, aware that this was the way an encounter with Audine often left her. They were at loggerheads most of the time, which was why she avoided her cousin's company as often as possible. She knew Audine was bitterly jealous of her, which was a situation that seemed quite ludicrous to Lydia herself.

Audine was a rich man's daughter, living in a house that had been in the family for generations, and which she would eventually inherit.

Lydia had nothing in the world but the small annuity her father had provided for her, and her looks. And a lifetime of wonderful memories, she reminded herself swiftly. And nothing, not even Audine, could ever take those away.

Lydia looked in on her aunt. She was becoming quite fond of her now, and really, Aunt Maud was the only one who gave her any real sympathy in this household. But today, the lady looked pale and drawn, lying in bed in her darkened bedroom.

"I'm so sorry to see you like this, Aunt Maud," Lydia said at once. "Is there anything I can do for you?"

"Nothing at all, my dear," she replied, her voice thick with the effort of talking. "It's no more than one of my miserable migraines, but the only remedy for it is to take powder and lie here until it's relieved. But I thank you for coming to inquire, which is more than my daughters have done."

"Audine has gone out riding, I believe, and the young ones are getting ready for their lessons," Lydia said swiftly.

Her aunt gave a half-smile. "You're more generous than Audine, to forgive her so readily. I can only wish that her temperament was more like your own. But with any luck, some of your sweetness will

15

rub off on Frances and Davinia. Leave me now, there's a good girl, and let me rest."

Lydia went out, closing the door quietly behind her. She didn't particularly look forward to the Monday morning sessions with her young cousins. Mondays were always the worst days of the week, when the weekend influence of time spent idling had persuaded them it was a waste of time to bother about their letters and sums.

In the schoolroom, Lydia looked at them with growing exasperation as they sprawled in their chairs and refused to do the simplest of spelling tests.

"How do you think you'll ever be able to write an intelligent letter if you can't spell?" she demanded.

"Who should we want to write letters to? *We* don't need to apply for positions. *We* shall marry rich men and never have the need to write anything more than a dinner invitation," Frances said airily.

"And even then we shall get our secretaries to do it for us," Davinia added, having just learned the word for the first time.

"All right, we'll forget the spelling test for today, and do some sums instead."

"Daddy says it's vulgar to discuss money," Frances told her. "He says the only people who do it constantly are bank managers because they have so much, and poor people who don't have any."

She stared insolently at Lydia, who stared steadily back. Frances was no match for her, and she was the one who blinked and looked away first.

"That's an incredibly silly thing to say, Frances," she said coolly. "I think you're going to grow up into a very narrow-minded young woman if you don't change your ideas. Don't you want to be educated?

16

Most girls of your age are eager to learn all they can."

Frances was a gawky twelve-year-old, and Davinia, at eight, was as aggressive and stubborn as her elder sister. The older one shrugged, and the younger one followed suit, parrot-like as ever.

"The last tutors we had were all so boring, they never stayed long," she said pointedly.

"Have you had many?" Lydia asked casually.

"About five. They were all old, until you. Tutors are usually old, aren't they?"

Lydia smiled faintly at her rudeness, and the implication that she, too, would probably end up as crabby as the rest.

Davinia spoke importantly. "I want to be a duchess when I grow up, and Daddy's promised to find me a duke to marry."

Lydia almost laughed out loud, except that she could see that the child was deadly serious. It was all so sad, she thought suddenly. These two were conditioned to the kind of life society demanded of them. Because of their wealth and fine home, they thought they were cushioned against the vicissitudes of life, yet they had no conception of the wider world. Like their older sister, the assurance of introductions into society, followed by good marriages lay ahead of them, and apparently nothing else mattered. To Lydia, it all sounded so stifling.

"I think we've had enough learning for today," Lydia said, knowing they had learned virtually nothing, and hearing their whoops of joy.

"Tell us about the princes instead," Davinia demanded, as plain and narrow-faced as all the Grey sisters, and destined to remain so, Lydia thought with swift sympathy.

"You know I'm not supposed to talk about them," she said with a smile. "Your father doesn't approve."

"But did they really ride on elephants?" Davinia insisted. "And were the elephants really covered in jewels?"

"It's all true, every bit of it. India had so many princes at one time. It's not quite the same now, but when I was a small girl the country was divided up into little states, and each one ruled his own little principality and had his own palace and many, many servants—"

"More than we have?" Frances wanted to know.

Lydia smiled slightly. These two had no conception of the glory of those elegant princes and their wondrous array of jewels. Gems that glittered in the sunlight to dazzle the eyes until they hurt, whenever one of the princely processions went by . . .

"Far more. They also had their own astrologers to advise them every day on what they should do. Many of the high-born people in India consult such men, believing that everything is written in the stars, and that our destiny is prearranged for us, even before we're born."

Without realizing it had happened, her voice had softened and become almost singsong, like that of her old Indian nurse, who had enchanted her with exotic tales of folklore and mystery.

"Father says such talk is wicked," Frances said, jumping up suddenly. "And you're not to say such things to us in that funny voice."

Lydia started, knowing she had been caught up in a past that would never completely let her go, even though she lived a conventional life now, in a country ruled by a dignified and sorrowing queen after her beloved consort's tragic death. Three months later now, it was said the queen was still distraught with grief, and would probably never recover.

Like their queen, Lydia's own heritage was here in England, yet in her heart she was far more in tune with that hot distant land in which Queen Victoria too had such a deep interest.

She shook herself, telling the girls they should wash their hands and go downstairs in an orderly fashion to the dining room for lunch. Lydia knew the time when she must accompany Audine and her uncle to the Hotel Splendide was fast approaching.

When they had gone from the schoolroom, chattering like magpies, Lydia gazed out the window beyond the manor grounds and across the green meadows toward the beautiful soaring turrets of the Abbey, still hazy in the crisp March morning.

Bath was a splendid city, Lydia conceded. Since Roman times, it had been famed for its natural springs and their health-giving properties. The social scene was becoming ever more a rival to London as the many visitors arrived, eager to take the waters for medicinal purposes.

The Abbey's history reached back through the ages, being built and rebuilt on the same spot; the wonderful Pultney Bridge in Florentine style that spanned the river Avon was a marvel of elegant arches and shops across its width, a credit to its designer, the famed Robert Adam; the elegant Assembly Rooms were there for social activities, together with the inaptly named Pump Room where one could take the mineral waters and enjoy a concert or other form of social amusement; there were so many cultural delights brought to the city by the celebrated dandy, Beau Nash, as an alternative to fashionable London.

But for Lydia it still wasn't home. And the piquancy of it was, she didn't even know where she truly wanted to call *home*. For despite her memories of India and her childhood there, she knew in her heart she could never go back. It was one of the things she felt very deeply. You could never go back. . . .

Once the meal was over, Audine instructed Lydia to accompany her to her bedroom, where several afternoon gowns were laid out on the bed.

"We're about the same height, but you're considerably fuller than me in places," Audine said almost accusingly, eyeing Lydia's rounded shape, "so I'd ask you to choose the gown that's less likely to split when you wear it, if you please."

"I'll do my best," Lydia said sternly, imagining the horror if the bodice suddenly burst open, revealing the luscious curves inside. Without warning, she felt a dart of pleasure somewhere deep inside as she visualized the scene, sensing the shock of Audine, her uncle, and the unknown Lord Montagu.

But perhaps he wouldn't be shocked. She knew nothing about him, save that Audine had been almost animated as she told her how Lord and Lady Grey had met the charming young man in a theatre party, and the acquaintance had grown from there. She knew nothing but her uncle's description of someone tall and dark-eyed, with an abundance of black hair, and altogether a very handsome countenance.

And Lydia had half-closed her eyes, as if she could conjure up an image of the man out of curiosity alone, and the image she had created in her mind was of someone impossible to live and breathe. She had conjured up the man of her

20

dreams which was the main reason she dreaded this afternoon so much, knowing that Lord Montagu would surely fall far short of her fantasy. It would be a very good thing if he did, she admonished herself, since he was destined for her cousin Audine . . . and not for her.

But what if he matched her fantasy exactly? The little devil inside her wouldn't let the thought go. What then? Lydia shunned from the answer, knowing it only too well. Knowing she would want him desperately for herself.

"Well?" Audine snapped. "Which one are you going to try, ninny?"

Lydia forced herself to look at the gowns. There was a clear azure blue with tucks and pleats, with a looped up broderie petticoat effect at the hem, with a matching cape and bonnet. And there was a fussy deep violet affair, which although being altogether richer and more dramatic, was a dress she knew had never done much to enhance Audine's appearance. Lydia suspected it would also do nothing for herself, and chose the blue.

"Fancy!" Audine sniffed. "I'd have thought you'd want the other, being more to your exotic taste."

Lydia turned on her in exasperation. "Why do you dislike me so much, Audine?"

She saw her cousin color, unused to such directness from other people, despite her own rudeness.

"I don't dislike you. I have no particular feelings about you at all."

"Don't you? Then at least tolerate me, as I have to tolerate you. I didn't choose for my parents to die, nor to feel beholden to relatives I never even knew. We both have a cross to bear, Audine."

The girl's mouth gaped open at this, and Lydia

guessed she rarely met such opposition, and knew she had held her tongue far too long. In her attempts to fit in with this awkward family, she had appeared far more docile than she really was, and knew it was high time she asserted herself before she was swamped by them. She picked up the gown and accessories while Audine was still trying to find a suitably cutting reply.

"I'll take these to my room and get ready," she said pleasantly. "And I thank you for your generosity, Audine."

She went out of the room with her head held high, but her hands were shaking when she reached her own room and leaned against the door for a few minutes. Mention of her parents had reminded her poignantly of all she had lost, all the lovely days in India that Lydia had confidently expected would never end. She assumed that her future would be rosy until her father's business ventures had so drastically failed, and they decided to set sail for England again, with such disastrous results.

Lydia swallowed, resolutely putting the memories behind her for now. She must make herself presentable for this afternoon's meeting.

She smiled faintly as she removed her plain dress and slid the soft blue afternoon gown over her shoulders without bothering to ask for the assistance of a maid. Audine presumed too much. In her friends' house where she resided, there were trunks of lovely gowns made from beautiful Indian silks, the likes of which Audine had probably never seen. Sensuous, stunning creations which were worn by the high-born Indian ladies in their palaces; gowns guaranteed to stir desire in all the gentlemen present.

22

When she was ready, Lydia went downstairs to join her uncle and cousin, already waiting for her in the drawing room. Lord Grey was a portly, florid-faced man, but he smiled generously when he saw his niece.

"You look very comely, my dear. It's not every day a man has two pretty young ladies to escort about town. The carriage is already outside, so let's waste no more time now."

Audine was wearing a soft cream gown, which was probably meant to soften her angular face, but actually drained it of all color, Lydia thought. If only the girl had been more friendly toward her, Lydia would gladly have advised her, but there was little warmth from any of the inmates of Greystone Manor, she thought sadly. She felt little more than an encumbrance, and was eternally thankful that she was housed with the Claremont family.

The day was chilly, spring not yet having arrived. The ladies were glad of the rugs inside the carriage as their driver began the journey along the cobbled streets toward the Hotel Splendide, situated near the river and with a panoramic view of the city from its windows.

As the journey progressed, Lydia realized that Audine was becoming quite agitated, fidgeting with her gloves and fichu. She felt quite sorry for her as the nervous blotches in her neck became apparent, assuming that even someone as unemotional as her cousin could be affected by the prospect of meeting a young man who was probably destined to be her husband.

"I'm sure everything will be all right," she murmured under cover of the clattering carriage wheels, as her uncle leaned out to see if they were approaching the hotel yet.

"Of course it will be all right," Audine snapped. "What an idiotic thing to say, Lydia. Do you think I haven't held a conversation with a titled gentleman before?"

But never one like this, with whom, if things went according to Lord Grey's plan, Audine would share more intimacies than she had ever done in her life before.

Wanton images that shouldn't appear in any young lady's head were instantly in Lydia's at that moment. She knew all about the intimacies of the marriage bed. She was aware not from personal experience, but from the simple way her old *ayah* had explained it all to her. She had wanted her young lady to be well prepared for the eventuality, and saw it as her duty to explain everything in detail so that she would be unafraid when the time came.

"He will love you in a way you have not known before," the wise old Nadima had said in her lilting voice. "He will know your body as well as you know his, as intimately as you may touch a flower and break its petals. If you yield to him, he will break you just as gently, my Lydia, and even though there may be a little pain at first, it will be followed only by intense pleasure."

Lydia had listened, wide-eyed and dry-mouthed, as the calm and patient explanations had gone on.

"He will want to touch every part of you, to feel that you belong to him, and he will expect the same ritual from you. It is all a part of love, this expressing by touch. Don't be afraid of it, when it comes. Don't succumb to the restrictions of your English upbringing, but be generous and welcoming in love, and love will be returned to you a hundredfold. You have become almost one of us over the years, my young one, and you see many things that the Indian sees. I beg you not to turn from love when you find it, for love is the most precious gift we have."

Lydia gazed out the carriage window, lost in remembering that magical day when she had learned more about the beginnings of life and the wonders of creation than she had ever known before. Would Audine be generous in love, in the touching and yielding rituals? she wondered.

"We're here," Lord Grey said briskly, and Lydia realized the horses had stopped, and so had the rocking movement of the carriage. She waited until her uncle and cousin had alighted, and accepted the hand of their driver with a swift smile of thanks. She followed her relatives into the elegant interior of the Hotel Splendide, curious to see this paragon of a man who apparently wanted to marry Lady Audine Grey.

They were approached by a stiffly formal majordomo who waved to an attendant to take their outer garments. They were allowed to compose themselves before being shown into the main foyer of the hotel, where fashionable people milled about in their afternoon finery to a background of muted chamber music. Recognizing a gentleman of quality, the majordomo himself took Lord Grey's name, bowed, and went away to instruct the gentleman concerned that his visitors had arrived.

And then, as if she was seeing a dream awaken before her, Lydia saw someone rise from one of the velvet-covered sofas in the foyer, and walk toward them. Tall, lithe, his features strong and darkly

25

handsome, he moved with the confident ease of a man well assured of his masculinity. Lydia knew without a moment's doubt that this was Lord Vincent Montagu. And just as certainly, with that presentiment old Nadima had always said she possessed, she knew she wanted him for herself.

Her senses swirled for a moment, as if experiencing something far more mystical than the prosaic meeting of four people in a city hotel. She had been too long immersed in the old tales of astrology and fate learned at Nadima's knee, and all her senses were crying out to her that here was her destiny. This man, out of all the world, who was here to press his court to her cousin Audine. . . .

That realization rudely shook her out of the trance that seemed to almost paralyze her. She heard Vincent Montagu speak for the first time. It was a richly textured, cultured voice that sent her pulses racing and her nerve ends shivering. She wondered fearfully if she was in the grip of some madness, and only her cousin's simpering reply to the introduction made from Lord Grey, reminded her of where and who she was.

"And this is my niece, Miss Lydia Grey," she heard her uncle say brusquely, after apologizing for his wife's absence, as if Lydia's presence was of no real consequence at all.

Lydia looked up into the stranger's eyes, and felt a tremulous frisson of recognition, as deep and primeval as the ancient rivers that ran through India's cities. They had never met before, but it was as though a moment out of time burned between them in that glance. Their brief exchange assured Lydia that they had indeed met, and loved; not once, but often, in the beyond that was the past, and in the

26

future that was yet to come.

"I'm delighted to meet you, Miss Grey," the stranger, who was never a stranger, said gravely. His fingers touched hers for a moment and held them captive. The fine leather of her gloves did nothing to lessen the warmth of his skin against her own. If anything, it added to the awareness of sensuality she felt emanating between them.

Lydia removed her hand quickly, knowing it was shaking. Audine would put her discomfiture down to nervousness at being in this situation, and would dismiss her haughtily as some little ingenue. But Lydia knew it wasn't so.

In those moments, when all her senses seemed to be heightened nearly beyond all endurance, she knew she was more of a woman in the truest sense of the word than her cousin would ever be. Mentally, she was aware of her own blossoming, experiencing all of a woman's physical needs and longings and desires that could only be matched by one man out of all the world. *Her man. Vincent, Lord Montagu.*

"I've arranged for a quiet corner of the sitting room to be put at our disposal," he was saying now. "Tea will be brought to us in about half an hour, if that suits you all."

"That will be admirable," Lord Grey said. "And it's very good of you to arrange this little tête-à-tête, my dear Sir."

It was hardly a tête-à-tête, Lydia corrected silently, that delightful French phrase that implied something far more intimate for two, than a public meeting between four people. And suddenly she felt very much the outsider. She should not be present, at what was obviously meant to be very much an initial inspection of a man and woman with a view to marriage. To Lydia, it was the only way to regard this marriage market.

She had more sympathy with the Indian culture, where a man and woman first beheld each other at the ceremony itself, when there was no turning back. She had seen so many successful marriages result out of what seemed a heathen ritual to Occidental eyes. But wasn't this just as big a gamble? Wasn't her uncle going to have the last say in the end, as to whether or not he wanted his daughter to marry Lord Montagu?

She kept her eyes lowered as the formal talk went on all around her. They were fencing with one another, she thought suddenly, each trying to assess the other's feelings and thoughts. And Audine, who never had any perception of anyone else's thoughts, would be floundering inside.

"I understand you've only recently come to live in Bath, Miss Grey," she heard Vincent Montagu say, and she looked up quickly.

He was watching her steadily, and she sensed the unbidden, unspoken communication between them. He knows what I'm thinking, she thought, just as I can read his thoughts. It may be all imagination, but I know he's as bored by these people as I am. She felt instantly ashamed, knowing that neither Audine nor her father could help being the people they were.

"I've been living in the county of Devonshire for the last year," she informed him, "but before that I had lived with my parents in India since I was two years old."

"Really?" She felt and saw his interest quicken.

"You must find life here very different indeed from that hot clime."

"Very different," she said, trying not to let herself sound too regretful, and knowing she must sound as if she owed her uncle every gratitude.

The hotel maids hovered near them with the afternoon tea and biscuits. Conversation was halted until it was served, and then Lord Montagu spoke thoughtfully.

"But you've adjusted, I take it, Miss Grey? You don't find the English winters too cold and miserable?"

"A little," she said with a wry smile. She became aware that Audine was flashing her furious looks now, and she took a few sips of her tea to indicate that she had nothing more to say on the subject.

"I, for one, would simply hate to live in a hot climate," Audine said loudly. "It must do hideous things to one's complexion, and dry the hair abominably, and don't they say the women grow old much earlier in hot climates?"

She was being appallingly rude, and only the fact that Lydia knew very well that the blistering heat of India had done nothing disadvantageous to her own appearance, prevented her from commenting. But not so Lord Grey.

"My daughter has the typical English peaches and cream complexion that young women rightly try so hard to preserve," he said heartily. "Wouldn't you agree, Lord Montagu?"

Lydia avoided looking at him as he observed quietly that Audine's pale features were indeed typically English.

"Then you would not be happy in a more southerly climate, Lady Audine?" he inquired.

"I would not," she said stoutly. "I don't believe in people dashing about the world like gypsies, except on a tour, of course. That's quite different, as long as one can return to one's roots without being affected by the natives in any way."

"Really, Audine!" Lydia had to protest at the insufferable remark, but Lord Montagu gave an easy laugh.

"Then you would hardly be willing to accompany me to my Greek island, my dear lady."

Audine stared at him, clearly unsure whether or not he was funning with her.

"Your Greek island?" she said in a stupefied voice.

"Did I not mention it to you, Lord Grey?" Vincent turned to his guest with an apologetic gesture. "If I did not, it was very remiss of me, although we had so little time to talk at our earlier meeting. Please forgive me if it slipped my mind."

"I don't recall hearing about any Greek island. Perhaps you could explain yourself, my dear Sir?" he said, an edge to his voice now, and Lydia knew him well enough to guess that his hopes for Audine were already slipping away.

"Of course. A relative of mine actually bought the island many years ago. It's quite remote and without any of the amenities of a fashionable city like Bath or London, though remarkably self-supporting, aided by supplies from the mainland every few months. I myself intend to make my permanent home there. It's not exactly tropical, but with an idyllically hot climate that suits me very well. I shall return before the end of the summer."

He wasn't looking at Lydia. All his attention was centered on the other two: her Uncle Percival's disappointed face at realizing he wasn't going to be rid of his irritating daughter so easily after all, Audine's furious one, seeing all her hopes dwindling away by her own vindictive words. Yet, uncannily, Lydia felt that his words were meant solely for her.

She realized she must have made some small sound, because without warning, Vincent turned his gaze directly toward her. She felt the heat in her face, and then the heat spread, filling every part of her body at that nakedly desirous look. It was a look that was at once an invitation, a need, and a certainty. He was as sure of her as she was of him.

Chapter Two

"Lord Montagu has invited us to a concert in the Pump Room," Audine announced to Lydia the following week, looking remarkably animated, considering her pale face and normally sullen features.

Ever since the meeting at the Hotel Splendide, Audine had been at her worst, and Lydia had naturally borne the brunt of it. Audine had accused her vociferously of flirting with a gentleman above her station, of flashing her cow-eyes at him, and of trying to instill a sense of familiarity with him, just because he'd mentioned a near tropical Greek island, and Lydia herself had lived in a dreadful tropical climate.

"I don't know why you all seem to think it so wonderful, anyway," she had gone on at length. "I can't imagine anything more disgusting than spending the day avoiding the heat and its effects on your skin, and trying to appear a lady at the same time. Not, of course, that that would bother some people."

"I assure you there were many genteel ladies in the part of India where I lived," Lydia was stung into replying. "And you really know so very little about it Audine. I've tried to explain to you that we lived in the hills, and some parts of the year were blissfully cool and refreshing—"

"I don't want to hear it. I've no interest in such things. I'd advise you to stop filling the girls' heads with all that nonsense, too. Father doesn't like it. And you needn't think all this worldly-wise talk is going to make you appear more attractive in Lord Montagu's eyes, either. Pushing yourself forward in the way you did is hardly the manner of a lady."

Seething, Lydia answered her shortly. "I did not push myself forward, and I resent the accusation that I did. I was merely being polite to the gentleman when he spoke to me. Would you have had me stand there like a dummy and say nothing?"

That would probably have pleased her, Lydia thought dryly. To be the center of attraction, as had been intended, was just what Audine had expected. Guiltily, she accepted that Audine had had every right to feel affronted at being upstaged by her cousin since Lord Montagu had apparently come to Bath with the sole intention of seeking out Audine Grey for his bride. Though, her own feelings aside, Lydia couldn't see what possible future there could be for two such unlikely partners.

So she went on strenuously denying all the bitter accusations, knowing only too well the truth of the attraction between herself and Lord Montagu. How could she fail to know it? It was as strong as if an invisible cord was drawing them together. It hadn't been sought, nor had she tried to charm her cousin's suitor. But there were some things under heaven and on earth far stronger than anything mere mortals could invent, and she doubted very much if someone as insensitive as Audine could ever understand such things.

Once, Lydia had tried to explain the pull of the moon on the tides, and it had been like talking to a blank wall. So, even if she had wanted to, how could she ever hope to explain that the pull of Lord Montagu on herself was as forceful and inevitable as the moon on the tide? Even she was shocked by the force of her own feelings to a man who was a virtual stranger.

None of them had seen him since that day at the Hotel Splendide, though Lydia admitted that he had hardly been out of her thoughts and her dreams for a single instant. In fact, she had begun to wonder if the whole episode had been a dream, so this concert invitation Audine was announcing had come as a complete surprise. Her cousin had been so bad-tempered since that evening, smarting at having been forced to be so vocal in declaring that she would most certainly never agree to going off to live on some obscure Greek island. She still meant it, but it didn't do her self-esteem any good to know there were such conditions attached to her possible marriage, and she had lost a most eligible suitor.

"It's probably all for the best," Lord Grey had said loudly, once the family was alone that evening, and they were discussing the turn of events. He had a clumsy way of trying to comfort his daughter, and did more harm than good in Lydia's opinion. "These fellows who take their women away from England and all that's familiar to them have a great deal to answer for. You'd never have been

34

happy with him, Audine, for all his good looks. He may well have allowed his eyes to wander after a time, and then where would you have been?"

Lady Maud had murmured something in sympathy, but with a quick glance at Lydia's burning face. Unable to leave it there, Lydia had quickly sprung to her own father's defense.

"It never did my mother any harm to be taken away from England, Uncle. We had a wonderful life in India, and my mother would never have had things any different."

"I thought we were discussing Audine's future, miss, not something that cannot be changed. If this outspokenness is what happens to young ladies in hot climes, then I begin to see that the possibility of a marriage with Montagu was all a ghastly mistake and Audine is well out of it."

Lydia wasn't so sure that Audine still felt the same way. She had rejected the very idea of Vincent's proposal, but that didn't mean she wasn't furious about the whole thing. Audine may still have hopes in his direction. Somehow this fact did nothing to disturb Lydia. She felt herself drifting off in reveries of Vincent.

She felt in her soul that she only had to wait for events to take their own course. She recalled her *ayah's* mysterious words that a woman's destiny may not come readily to her in this life. That she may have to wait until the next, or even the one after that, to recognize her soulmate again . . .

"But what if I want him *now*."

On the evening after she had seen Vincent for the first time, Lydia had whispered to herself in the confines of her bedroom. "I want to know a

35

man, in the way Nadima told me. I want to feel his touch, and to learn his body as intimately as he learns mine."

The words were almost drawn from her soul. She hardly knew she said them, or imagined that she would ever have voiced them. She had looked at herself in the bedroom mirror at the milliner's house, and seen that her eyes were almost feverishly bright, the pupils large and dilated with desire. She hardly recognized herself. She was someone else, because of him. She was a wanton, a concubine, a harlot. All the forbidden words slid through her mind, exciting, shaming, and finally exulting.

For hadn't Nadima told her that nothing was wrong between a man and woman who truly loved. It was written in the stars. In the eyes of God, nothing was forbidden . . .

Tentatively, in the soft darkness of the night, she had run her hands over her own body, touching herself as if Vincent touched her, seeking out the erotic places Nadima had instructed her about, and discovering that there was more to learn about herself, before she learned about a man.

"So, what do you think about that?" Audine was saying triumphantly, deciding that Lydia had been dumbstruck for long enough. "You were so sure I'd lost the chance of my handsome husband for good, weren't you? But it seems most likely to me that he's given up this foolhardy idea of living on some Greek island, and will decide to settle down in England instead. It'll be right here in Bath, I shouldn't wonder."

"You're quite sure of that, are you?" Lydia said

evenly.

Audine tosse her head. Her pale hair was life-
less that day, as it always was when she was out of
sorts with her monthly flow. Her face resembled a
suet pudding, and despite all her viciousness, Lydia felt quite sorry for her. She had always been
unconcerned about her own vivacious looks, taking
them for granted. But now she could see just why
a plain girl like Audine, two years older than herself, would be so desperate to find a husband.

"Of course. Why else would he ask us to the
concert? He wants to continue our acquaintance,
and he didn't include *you* in the invitation. It was
sent to Lord Grey and family."

"I was under the impression that I was part of
this family," Lydia said mildly.

Just why she felt so calm, she couldn't think.
She had never felt particularly psychic before, despite the influence of Nadima and the fascination
of the fabulous Indian princes and their astrologers, and she was becoming slightly alarmed at the
way those feelings were intruding now. She didn't
want these fey sensations that sometimes flooded
her mind. But if they had been bestowed, how
could they be refuted? And, more pertinently, did
anyone have that right?

As if to underline her calmness, Lady Grey,
hearing their last remarks, spoke sharply to her
daughter.

"What are you saying to Lydia now, Audine? If
you're implying that she's not to attend the concert
at the Pump Room with us next week, you can
think again. Of course Lydia's included. I'm sure
Lord Montagu would be very distressed if he

37

thought we assumed she wasn't included in his kind invitation."

"Thank you, Aunt Maud," Lydia murmured, seeing her cousin's flashing eyes, and knowing she would be in for even more scolding because of her mother's support of the underling.

But none of it really mattered, with the concert at the Pump Room to look forward to. And this time, she wouldn't be wearing borrowed plumes, but one of her own beautiful gowns, lovingly stitched by Nadima, one that hadn't even been brought out of the trunk yet. Suddenly, the memory of Nadima's voice was very powerful in her mind:

"Whenever a special event occurs, cover yourself in perfumes and silks, my young one, to make you feel secure in your own being. You will send out whatever messages you wish from this simple subtlety. And for good fortune and harmony, and as an added talisman, wear the color of Islam when you find your heart's choice."

Later, when she had left Greystone Manor and was in her own small room at the milliner's house once more, Lydia thought ruefully that it would take more than a gown of emerald green to stave off the disharmony between herself and Audine. But, still drawn by something stronger than herself, she looked through her trunks and drew out a brilliantly hued gown of pure Indian silk.

The emerald color glowed and gleamed in the lamplight as though it had a life of its own as she slid the sensuous fabric over her bare shoulders, and felt its caress against her skin. The ripples of silk rustled very softly, enticing and provocative. The deep décolleté neckline revealed the upward swell of her firm, creamy breasts. The tightly sashed waist and billowing skirt with its layers of supporting underskirts alluringly accentuated the feminine shape of her body.

She felt the aura of Nadima very strongly as she twisted this way and that in front of the mirror, assessing herself as if through someone else's eyes— Vincent Montagu's eyes.

"This is a very special gown, little missy. I stitch it with love and with wishes. Long after I am gone, you will wear it and remember the love, and you will make your own wishes."

"I wish," Lydia said softly to the image in the mirror, "for a true love of my own. For the happiness and cherishing my parents knew. For an end to waiting."

The words seemed to be hardly of her own making. They were a litany, a prayer, and she closed her eyes for a moment as if to shut out everything but the solemnity of the wish.

She heard a tap on her door and she blinked, needing to drag her thoughts back to the present, almost as if she had been halfway into another world. And then the very practical shape of the milliner's wife appeared around the door, gasping as she saw the vision inside her modest home.

"My Lord," she said, obviously moved. "I never saw such a beautiful gown, Lydia, nor such a beauty wearing it. You'll stun every man in sight when you appear in it!"

Lydia laughed at the uninhibited praise from the

rounded little woman.

"There's only one man I want to stun, Mrs. Claremont," she said mischievously. "And I'm not sure that I'd want to render him too dumbstruck!"

"So there is a gentleman, is there?" the woman said with satisfaction. "I thought there must be. A lovely young lady like yourself wouldn't be without suitors for very long, now that your period of mourning is well and truly over.

A small shadow passed over Lydia's lovely face.

"I don't forget though," she said slowly. "I loved my parents dearly."

"Lord a' mercy, I wasn't meaning to suggest that you should forget, my dear. You've too generous a spirit for that, and it's obvious to anyone that you come from a good and loving home. We can't forget our loved ones even when they've passed over, and nor should we. To forget them is to deny they ever existed. But the pain lessens, and we must go on living however we can until we all meet again."

Lydia felt her heart warm to this tribute from such an unexpected quarter.

"Thank you for that. Not everyone understands the way you do, Mrs. Claremont."

"I believe in letting everyone live their own lives, no matter where it takes them. And there's no sense in fretting for ever over what can't be changed," she said. "So let's stop being so morbid, and tell me about this young gentleman who can put such a sparkle in your eyes, and who's obviously inspired you to wear this lovely gown."

She sat down on the bed, clearly meaning to stay until she had heard whatever tidbits of gossip Lydia would impart. So far, Lydia had said nothing about Vincent, except that she had been obliged to attend that first meeting at the Hotel Splendide, where Vincent was residing while in Bath.

"He's very handsome," Lydia said, smiling at the memory of that wide, sensual mouth, and those dark eyes that she sensed would darken with passion even more than their natural color. She felt a small shiver run through her at the thought, aware that a woman had the power to arouse such feelings in a man. But it had to be the *right* woman.

"Is that all? He's very handsome?" Mrs. Claremont encouraged. "Does he have a name, this wonderful man?"

Lydia laughed, knowing she had been lost in her own dreaming, and feeling her cheeks grow hot.

"It's Vincent. Lord Vincent Montagu," she said dreamily, as if the very name was a caress on her tongue. "He's very tall and dark, and he came to look over my cousin Audine—"

"My dear girl, what an unladylike way to put it," Mrs. Claremont laughed, too. Though having seen the haughty m'lady Audine, Lydia knew Mrs. Claremont would be aware of the unspoken reaction when Vincent first saw Audine, and compared the two cousins.

She shouldn't have been present at that meeting, she thought, with a small pang of remorse. Perhaps she had ruined all Audine's hopes of marriage simply because of her own appearance, which she couldn't help, and which had been a mere accident of birth and inheritance. And if she hadn't been there, the small insistent voice whispered inside her, she and Vincent might never have met, at

41

least in this life . . .

She gave another unconscious shiver, thinking how often the course of destiny was held by a thread. A chance meeting, a forgotten letter, an unfortunate demise or a change of fortune . . . kings had been dethroned, kingdoms lost, because of destiny . . . and Lydia Grey had found hers through being in the right place at the right moment in time.

"So you think this is the right gown for the concert at the Pump Room, Mrs. Claremont?" she asked quickly now. "It's not too ostentatious, is it?"

"It certainly is not. And if it makes some of the ancient biddies look to their laurels, so much the better," she said irreverently. "When you're ready, you give the gown to me, my love, and I'll see that it's pressed and hung for you well before the night."

When she had left, Lydia removed the gown almost reluctantly, holding the sensuous silk to her face for long moments, and breathing in the faint scents of her own body that lingered in the shimmering jewel-bright fabric that was the color of Islam.

But she couldn't stand here all night, dreaming. Mrs. Claremont would have prepared supper, and the smell of her excellent cooking was wafting up the stairs. Her husband was away on business for a few nights. Since his millinery was attracting attention far and wide, he was often called away to present a selection of his wares in the best houses. So there were just the two of them to enjoy the rabbit pie and fresh vegetables, and to sit and talk by the fire in leisurely womens' fashion until it was time to retire to bed.

The following evening, Lydia left Greystone Manor after a particularly irritating day with the two younger Grey girls. They had obstinately refused to pay attention to anything she said, and were clearly determined to disrupt every lesson. She had withstood it all, but by the time she left, her patience had been running out, and she felt distinctly ruffled. And then Audine herself had kept her talking, wanting her opinion on which gown she should wear to the Pump Room, and inevitably arguing with everything Lydia said.

She breathed a deep sigh of relief as she finally walked briskly away from the big house and into the busier streets of the city toward her lodgings. Her Uncle Percival had shown his disapproval when she had insisted on walking the distance to and from his home, rather than taking a hire carriage. But she enjoyed the exercise, and especially the chance to fill her lungs with the crisp fresh air after the stuffiness of the classroom.

The main streets were fairly well-lit by now, the lamplighter having already done his duty, but the narrow twisting alleyways through which Lydia had to walk were dark and a bit alarming.

The March winds were still sending leaves and rubbish scurrying about skirts and ankles, and Lydia gave a small shiver, pulling her cloak more tightly around her as she entered one of the dark alleyways. She tried not to notice the sounds of muffled laughter and other guttural sounds, knowing that many of the city lightskirts followed their trade in these alleys with their hidden nooks and

43

doorways.

Her shoes echoed on the cobbled surface, and then her heart missed a beat as she realized that hers were not the only footsteps. The hand on her shoulder would have sent her racing on, screaming for a constable, had it not been for the softly rich voice that accompanied it.

"Hold still, my lovely. It's not safe for a young lady to be out walking after dark without an escort."

Lydia turned, and was immediately held close in the embrace of Vincent Montagu. Her heart was racing now, part of his heart, his body . . . her face was uplifted to see her rescuer, if such he could be called. The next moment she felt the warmth of his mouth on hers, demanding and ruthless, and promising far more than this first hungry contact between them.

She gave herself up to the magic of this first romantic kiss, savoring the difference with a sensual awakening as Vincent's arms held her captive, her body molded to his.

"So," he said softly, when he finally released his mouth from hers, but keeping it so close that she could feel as well as hear the words. "I was not wrong about you, Lydia Grey. You put your pale cousin in the shadows—"

Lydia gave a small moan deep in her throat, wishing he hadn't mentioned Audine just then.

"She expects you to make an offer for her, Vincent. She has every right—"

"She has no rights," he said, his voice fiercer now. "Nor does any woman but the one who captures a man's heart. Your pale and aggressive

44

cousin with the vinegar tongue has the power to render a man impotent. While you, my beautiful one . . ." he gave a small laugh, and without warning, he caught at her hand and ran it down the length of his body to his breeches. Through the soft, sleek fabric, Lydia felt the swelling hardness there, and gave a small gasp in her throat. This then, was what Nadima had mysteriously called the source of all power.

"You see what you do to me, Lydia Grey?" Vincent said softly, his voice oozing with desire. "Would you not wish to ease this affliction?"

His hand still covered hers, and she realized he was moving it gently, so that she was unwittingly caressing the hardness of his erection. Her mouth was dry, and wild, wanton sensations were beginning to fill her body; taking control of her, making her weak and helpless. The feeling suddenly frightened her. She snatched her hand away, her heart beating sickeningly fast now.

She could hear the evidence of others farther along the alley, and her mind didn't want to accept what she was hearing, nor to include herself in these nightly rituals that attracted neither complaining constables nor respectable folk.

"You forget yourself, Sir," she gasped out. "I'm the niece of a gentleman, and my parents brought me up decently."

"Your parents brought you up in a hot climate, and allied to a different culture. That makes you inescapably different. You can't change what you are, Lydia," Vincent said lazily, his arms still encircling her, not letting her go.

And where would she run to? she thought desperately. Away from him, shouting for help that wouldn't come, while she endured the cat-calling of the lightskirts who weren't so fussy over where and when they gave their favors.

"And what am I?" she said bitterly. "Do you presume that because I'm the poor relation, I'm fair sport to be ravished in an alleyway?"

His voice changed. "I do not. I've no wish to take you here and now. If I had wished it, it would already have happened."

She gasped again at his arrogance. But the potency of his desire couldn't be denied, and she knew his words were true. If he had wanted her minutes ago, he would have taken her. So obviously he hadn't wanted her enough, and the humiliation of that vied with her fury at being accosted like this.

"Don't doubt my needs, Lydia," he said softly, as if he could read all that was in her mind. "Or my intention of having you beneath me. But not here, not like this."

Even as he spoke, and she was registering all that he implied, a painted and scented lightskirt lurched past them in the arms of a roughneck, both giggling and mouthing obscenities as they went on their way.

"Make 'im pay 'is whack, ducks," the lightskirt screeched back to Lydia. "A shilling's not too much for a dandy, 'specially if 'e wants special favors!"

Lydia turned her face into Vincent's chest, knowing she must be scarlet-faced at this assumption that they, too, were here on the same sordid business. She felt Vincent's finger gently lift her chin. In the moonlight she couldn't see his face

46

properly, only its planes and shadows, and the dark glitter of his eyes. But she could feel the throbbing of his heart, matching the erratic beat of her own.

"That's not for us, sweetness," he said softly. "I have no wish for a quick lift of your skirts in an alley, delightful though the prospect might be. I contemplate a much grander bedding for you and me."

"You mustn't speak to me like this," Lydia said hoarsely. She knew it was wrong . . . and yet it was so wickedly exciting, like nothing she had ever experienced before.

"A man can speak to his woman any way he chooses," Vincent said, male arrogance edging his voice again. "It's all a part of the loving process, into which I intend to initiate you most thoroughly, my sweet one. But as I said, not here, and not now."

She swallowed dryly. She shouldn't ask. It was foolish to ask, to allow this conversation to continue a moment longer, but she had to know. She was too naturally curious, burning with an inner heat that was almost consuming her to know.

"Where then?" she said in a cracked voice. "Where do you intend this loving process to take place? I'd like to know, just so I can be sure to avoid it at all costs!"

She was being perverse, having no intention of making it all too easy for him, nor of letting him think she was so dazzled by his masculinity that she was almost drowning in her own pleasure as the wanton sensations ran through her body at his every touch.

He gave that small sensual laugh again, sending the shivering pulsebeats into her loins.

"You cannot escape your destiny, sweetness. I know something of the Indian culture, and I'll wager you were indoctrinated into the mysteries of destiny and fate and all the other fantasies."

"Do you question them then?" she demanded, seeing his words as a mockery of all that her dear Nadima had told her.

"I do not," he said, his voice suddenly rough. "And how quickly you become defensive, Lydia. It's something I shall have to watch against when I make you mine."

"Don't avoid the issue, please."

"What issue? There is no issue. You and I were always destined to be together. You knew it the moment we met, the same as I did. Deny it if you can."

She was helpless in denying it. How could she, when she had felt it, too? When she had spent the last days dreaming of being held like this, and wanted like this? So why was she now being so obstinate in refusing to accept his desire?

She answered her own question. It was because of her very Englishness. However deeply Nadima had instructed her in the ways of the East, and however attractively her skin had deepened to that rich honey color that Audine scoffed at so frequently, she was still essentially English. Her heritage was English, and she wouldn't allow herself to be swayed by all this talk of hot climates and the hot passions that went with it. She was quite ready to rebel against the very idea.

"Perhaps I go too fast," Vincent had leaned toward her again, whispering against her mouth. "It's no matter. Now that we've found one another, I shall never let you go."

"I'd be obliged if you would let me go right now," she said, shriller than usual, and deliberately turning his meaning. "I've had a very tiring day, and Mrs. Claremont will be worrying about me if I'm too long delayed."

"Then on no account must we allow Mrs. Claremont to be worried," he answered with a smile in his voice. He offered his arm, and when she refused it, he simply tucked her hand in his arm and held it fast as he started to walk along the rest of the twisting alley with her held tight to his side. Only when they reached the end of it and emerged into a better lit street, did Lydia manage to extract herself.

"I prefer to walk the rest of the way alone, if you please. There's absolutely no need for you to accompany me any further."

And in future she would choose another way to return home, she added silently, so that there was no possibility of being caught up in this embarrassing situation again. She dare not be, with the specter of her cousin's hopes always looming over her shoulder. She was guilty of knowing Audine had been Vincent's first choice, and that Audine was preening because of it. Despite her cousin's rudeness, Lydia wasn't so callous that she couldn't imagine the humiliation Audine would feel at knowing of this encounter tonight.

With this in mind, she spoke more boldly.

"Please don't bother me again, I beg of you, Lord Montagu. My uncle can make things very difficult for me if he chooses."

"Your uncle's opinions would no longer be of any consequence on my island. I've never found anyone I wished to share my paradise with until now."

She was at a loss how to answer this, when to her intense relief a passing hackney carriage came into view, the horses' breath steaming in the cold air. Impulsively, she waved out, ladylike or not, and the driver stopped at once.

"Where to, lady?"

She clambered inside quickly and gave him the milliner's address, thankful that at least Vincent made no attempt to stop her. The last thing she wanted was a scene in public, or the coziness of having him climb in the hackney after her. She leaned against the hard backrest, closing her eyes, and wondering just what was happening to her.

She hardly understood herself. She wanted him so much, and yet, when he'd followed her like that, she had rebuffed him totally. But in those circumstances . . . that was it, she thought suddenly. Despite all the erotic things he had said about initiating her into the loving process, she had still felt like a whore. Being pressed up against the dank walls of the alley, where the street women earned their pennies or their shillings, according to whatever special favors they gave. Lydia had felt like a whore, about to be taken against her will, and she resented it totally. She had once consorted with the little Indian princesses, and shared their *ayahs,* and no one should treat her any less civilly now.

At that moment into her mind came Audine's

haughty words the first time they were alone together.

"Don't think that just because you had servants in India, you're in the least important here, Cousin. You're a poor relation, that's all, and just you remember to be grateful to my family for taking you in."

And her own pointed reply, implying whatever her cousin made of it. "I always understood that gratitude has to be earned, and I give it freely to your parents, Audine."

Lydia smiled ruefully as the hackney clattered along the darkened streets. She was certainly fond of her aunt, and could tolerate her uncle, but her cousins were a different matter. But did she consider herself overly important? she wondered. Was she unconsciously too awash with that sinful pride in her own exotic upbringing to be able to fit into the English way of life ever again?

An English lady would surely have been scandalized at the way Vincent Montagu had pressed against her in that dark alley tonight. She should have shouted for help, screamed rape, alerted the constables. Lydia knew she had not reacted in the way of an English lady, however much she had protested. And certainly Vincent Montagu would not have acted the way he had, had he thought her a truly prissy English lady.

Lydia felt the pleasurably wanton feelings rippling through her again at the memory of all that had passed between them. And instead of trying hard to stifle the feelings, she allowed them to flood through her, lulled by the clattering motion of the hackney.

And, yes, there had been an undeniable wild excitement in the whole encounter. She was honest enough to admit that. She remembered the forbidden moment when Vincent's hand had grasped hers and she had felt the hard potency of his desire, throbbing with life beneath her fingers. Shamefully now, she knew she had felt an almost irresistible urge to move her fingers, to know more about this unknown phenomenon. An organ that could apparently surge from a flaccid creature to a monster, pulsing with life . . . such had been Nadima's awed description of this part of the male anatomy that had stunned Lydia into a frightened silence.

At the time she had questioned no more about it. She had been a child then, and this thing that was a man's source of life had been like the stuff of nightmares or legends. But now she was a woman and it was real. It was inescapable, like the fury of the wind and the might of the sea. It was Vincent Montagu.

"Is this the place, lady?"

The driver's prosaic words broke into her dreaming, and she started, realizing they had drawn up outside the milliner's house. All was as it should be, and in front of her was a solid stone building with smoke rising from the chimney, and fantasy and illusion should be put far from her mind.

"Thank you very much," she said quickly, fumbling for some coins as he alighted from the driving seat to assist her. "I'm sorry it was such a short journey," she added, feeling obliged to apologize at the meagerness of the fare.

His weathered face creased into a smile, his

broad country accent gentling the voice.

" 'Tis no trouble to take a pretty young lady any distance at all, m'dear, and safer for you to be riding than walking the streets these dingy nights. You never know what rogues and pickpockets be stalking the dark alleyways."

"That's true enough," she said solemnly, and opened the door of the Claremonts house, thankful that no one could know just who she had encountered in the alleyway on this dark night.

Mrs. Claremont greeted her with a smile of relief.

"I was just thinking of sending out someone to look for you, Lydia. You're very late this evening. Is everything all right? You look rather flushed."

"I'm perfectly all right," Lydia said. "I was delayed with my young cousins, who were even more impossible than usual today. I've been rushing, knowing that you'd be worried."

To Lydia's relief, Mrs. Claremont seemed quite satisfied with the explanation, sympathizing with Lydia over her irritating young cousins.

"It's a shame a lovely young lady like yourself should have to deal with such contrary young misses," the woman said. "You should be thinking of marriage and having children of your own, and I daresay this would have been the proper order of things had your parents still been alive."

"I'd really rather not talk about it if you don't mind, Mrs. Claremont," Lydia murmured.

"Of course, and I'm sorry for reminding you of your sad loss, my dear."

"If you'll excuse me, I'll go upstairs and get ready for the meal," Lydia said, knowing she hadn't been confused by the woman's reference to her parents, but by the image of marriage and children, and thoughts of the man she would want to father those unborn children. *Vincent Montagu.*

"I must be going mad, to have such reckless thoughts about him," she said to herself once she was alone. "The sooner he either makes a declaration toward Audine, or gets out of our lives forever, the better it will be for my peace of mind."

But in her mirror she could see the feverish color in her cheeks and the burning lights in her eyes as she splashed cooling water onto her face. She dabbed her skin dry with a rough towel, knowing there would never be any peace of mind for her as long as Vincent Montagu remained on earth. Time and distance were of no consequence, for he was already in the heart and soul of her, and there was no getting him out.

Chapter Three

By the time she went downstairs to dinner that evening, Lydia was determined not to let these new feelings disrupt her enforced new life. She discovered that Edwin Claremont had returned from his sojourn to London with his collection of hats and accessories. He brought with him his usual whiff of enthusiasm.

"Well, and what have my two favorite ladies been about while I've been away?" he said heartily, encompassing them both in a wide smile.

They looked at one another. Visits to the local parks and cozy chitchats over an evening cup of cocoa hardly seemed the most stimulating topic of conversation with which to regale a traveller like himself. And Lydia felt that the further doings in the private world of the Grey family was best left undiscussed for the present.

"Nothing very exciting, my dear," Mrs. Claremont said mildly. "We leave all that to you."

"Then you should not. Especially a pretty young lady like Lydia. It's time we began looking around to find you a suitable beau, my dear. I know my wife and I will be delighted to act as your chaperones whenever necessary. We must all put on our thinking caps and see what can be done."

He was more expansive than usual since being in the capital city, where life was lived at a much faster pace, even than in fashionable Bath. Lydia laughed at his teasing.

"Please don't put yourself out on my account, sir! I assure you I'm not wilting away for want of a gentleman friend!"

"That you're not," Edwin said thoughtfully. "In fact, now that I take a good look at you, you're positively blooming. Perhaps you've already met someone, and are reluctant to confide in us." His voice dropped to a new seriousness. "If that is so, my dear, please look on us as your confidantes. There are too many scoundrels in the world ready to take advantage of a young and beautiful girl—"

"But not one who is virtually penniless, I think," Lydia said swiftly. "And really, you have no need to worry about me at all. I can't think why you should be so concerned, but I thank you for it all the same. I would much rather hear about London!"

She knew very well it would not take very much for him to be diverted into talking about his craft and his business. His small factory in Bath was thriving now, and Lydia had been privileged to be taken on a tour of the premises behind the shop.

She liked the couple enormously, in spite of, or perhaps because of, Mrs. Claremont's inevitable wish to mother her, and Edwin's almost childlike enthusiasm for his work. It was always a pleasure to hear of his doings in the big houses, and the sometimes comical ways he described the aristocratic ladies trying on hopelessly unflattering styles for their ages and appearances. She had discovered that Edwin had to be more than a diplomat on such occasions, in persuading the ladies to try on something more suitable.

"Please, stop talking about me, and tell us who you've seen in London this time," she begged now. "You're keeping us in such suspense, and you know we're longing to hear if the day will come when Queen Victoria becomes a patron of Claremont's Millinery!"

"I'm not sure whether that's meant to be a compliment or not, you young tease," he said, laughing. He was not the type of man to take offense, as she well knew. He was dapper, with enormous energy. He was neatly moustachioed and refreshingly frank in manner, and on several occasions he had generously offered Lydia imperceptibly faulty models from his factory workshop at no charge.

"But has it happened yet, Edwin? Do stop prevaricating, and tell us!" his wife added, as impatient as Lydia now. They both knew it was the man's dearest wish to add a sign over his shop that he was now under royal patronage.

"Alas, not yet," he sighed elaborately. "But since I live in hopes, it is perhaps opportune to inform you, my dears, that I've decided to open up a new business in London very soon. I've seen suitable premises, and the time seems ripe."

57

Lydia was alarmed. "But you wouldn't want to live there, would you?"

Mrs. Claremont was only half reassuring. "It wouldn't be my choice, Lydia dear, but if Edwin thinks it advisable, then naturally it would have to be. One would be very foolish to flaunt such opportunities when they arise."

And the very last thing they would want was for an encumbrance such as Lydia hanging on their coattails should they decide to remove to London, which had apparently been discussed fully by the lack of surprise on Mrs. Claremont's face. This would mean the only option left open to Lydia would be to move in permanently with her relatives at Greystone Manor. Her face drooped at the thought, and Mrs. Claremont interpreted it correctly.

"Now then, Edwin, see what you've done in even mentioning London," she said, overlooking her own sparkle at the thought. "I'm sure such a move isn't imminent, Lydia dear. Most likely, you'll be happily wed long before that happens, and not in the least interested in where we two ancients live!"

"Is there someone in the offing then?" Edwin said, his eyes brightening like the old gossip Lydia affectionately thought him to be. She gave a forced laugh.

"There is not!" she protested. "The only gentleman I've met of late is the one destined for my cousin Audine, though I don't think there's such a possibility as my uncle had hoped. But we're all to attend a concert at the Pump Room on

Saturday evening, so perhaps things will have taken a turn for the better by then."

She didn't really know why she was championing their cause, when it was what she wanted least in the world. But the thought that it was so unlikely to happen made her feel more sympathetic toward Audine than she might otherwise have done. The girl had a really spiteful tongue, and Lydia thought privately that any prospective husband would be wise to take that into account. She listened idly to all that Edwin was relating to his audience now, his wife agog and adoring at hearing the names of the gentry trip so easily from his tongue. And then Lydia herself heard a name that caused her heart to skip a beat.

"There was a gambling party at the Fitzherberts a few evenings ago, and Lord Fitzherbert lost quite heavily. Not that it made much difference to his fortune I daresay, but he was bemoaning the fact that his old gambling partner Montagu wasn't there to back him up, and how he still missed the old roué even after all these years—"

"Montagu?" Lydia echoed without thinking. "Did you say Montagu, Mr. Claremont?"

"I did, m' dear. Why, do you know someone of that name?"

"Yes, although not very well."

Just well enough that his image seemed to fill her waking days and all her sleeping dreams, so that she only had to close her eyes and he was there . . .

She swallowed, willing the thought away.

"It can hardly be the same," Edwin chuckled. "The gentleman I refer to bought up some tiny Greek island many years ago, and lives in splendid seclusion. The island's quite off the beaten track, as they say—"

"Lydia dear, you've gone quite pale. It's a mere coincidence, I'm sure. It can't possibly be the same man you met recently."

"Good God no, begging your pardon, my dears," Edwin went on breezily. "Lord Vincent Montagu must be eighty years old if he's a day, and rumor has it that he's ailing fast now, and rarely moves away from his house, let alone the island. But in his day he was a gambler of notorious proportions. He'd put a wager on anything at all, and rarely came out the loser."

Lydia was trying hard to compose herself all the while he was talking. She shot a warning glance at Mrs. Claremont at the mention of the gentleman's name. *Lord Vincent Montagu, eighty years old!* When the man she knew of the same name was young and aggressively virile, and all she had ever dreamed of in a man.

"Lydia, didn't you tell me?" the milliner's wife said hesitantly, a worried frown between her eyes.

Lydia tried to think sensibly. Hadn't she seen the gilt-edged visiting card that Vincent used, the name flamboyantly and elaborately sculpted? Would he have gone to so much trouble if he wasn't who he said he was? But perhaps such things were all part of a rogue's cunning. She had had nothing to do with tricksters in her life before, so how could she tell? She forced a small

60

laugh and tried to sound nonchalant.

She shook her head quickly at Mrs. Clare-mont's half-query. The last thing she wanted was to arouse suspicions in these kindly folk. There were suspicions enough inside her own head.

"It was a similar sounding name, that's all. For a moment, I wondered too, but it must have been someone else."

At Edwin's puzzled look at this piece of apparently disconnected conversation between the two of them, Lydia looked at him quickly, clasping her hands together in eagerness and forcing a look of intent interest on her face.

"I'm far more interested to hear about the fashionable ladies and their choice of hats. And you know I was dying to know if anyone purchased the beautiful peach silk with the veil and feathers that I admired so much!"

Edwin laughed at her quick questions, flattered that she took such an interest in his wares.

"Then you'll be glad to know I persuaded the Honorable Eloise Tankerton *not* to buy it."

"Is she the lady you've mentioned before, with the build of a fairground wrestler?"

"Edwin," his wife protested mildly. "You really shouldn't say such things about your clients, and Lydia, dear, I'm not sure that you should repeat them!"

"I would never do so outside these four walls," she assured her. "You have my word on it."

"And it's only a bit of harmless fun," Edwin added. "If we can't trust one another in this house, then we can't trust anyone."

61

Lydia kept the smile fixed on her face, wondering just how unwittingly prophetic his words could be. She wondered just how far she could trust Vincent Montagu.

"Could you imagine that beautiful peach silk creation sitting on top of that outrageously mannish head?" Edwin was warming up nicely now, chuckling at the memory of the masculine lady.

"So what did you persuade her to purchase?" his wife wanted to know. "Or did she go off in a huff and buy nothing?"

"My dear, when have I ever been tactless with a client and sent her off in a huff?" he smiled without rancor. "No, I coaxed her into the wide-brimmed purple, to match many of the outfits in that dreadful color she prefers. She was so pleased with the effect that she has ordered a dark green in the same style."

The small triumph in his voice was one of the endearing things about him, Lydia thought. He was so artless in the pleasure his work brought him. So at ease with royalty and commoners alike, and in the company of gambling Lords like the Fitzherbert of whom he spoke.

At the memory of his name, Lydia felt the chill run through her again. Even while Edwin rambled on happily about the people he'd met, and the orders for hats that had been taken, and his undoubted success as a salesman as well as a professional man, her heart was racing. Her mind was seething with possibilities and suspicions, and all were directed at Vincent Montagu.

She tried desperately to believe it was all an

62

innocent coincidence. There must be some explanation. It *could* be coincidence, and everyone
knew such things happened in life. There was no
reason on earth why two men shouldn't have the
same name. It certainly happened in families all
the time. Or it could simply be a choice of parents at a child's birth. Sometimes people gave
their children the names of prominent people
they admired, and titles could be bestowed or in-
herited for any number of reasons.

But there was the unlikely fact of the island
. . . it was the mention of the Greek island that
filled Lydia's mind with the deepest suspicions of
all. It seemed hardly likely that two completely
separate men named Vincent Montagu lived on
similarly remote Greek islands.

She seemed to hear Vincent's voice in her head
right at that moment. It was strong and vibrant,
and filled with unmistakable passion.

"Your uncle's opinion would be of no consequence on my island. I've never found anyone I
wished to share my paradise with until now."

She ran her tongue around her dry lips as
Edwin Claremont's voice drifted in and out of
her head, and she made appropriate replies without knowing what she said.

My island. My paradise.

Disjointed thoughts, and remembered phrases,
swirled about in her head while the Claremont
couple chatted on at the dinner table about the
renewed possibility of their move to London,
which Lydia began to realize now was far more
than an idle dream.

Was Vincent a complete charlatan, disguising himself as the unknown Lord Montagu, being quite sure he wouldn't be discovered down here in fashionable, but still rural, Bath? Did he truly share the same name as the other one that Lord Fitzherbert had mentioned so casually to Edwin Claremont? Had he suddenly seen a scheme whereby he could cash in on the old gambling roué living on his faraway Greek island? Presumably by marrying a rich heiress, such as Audine Grey, and eventually obtaining her father's fortune . . .

Lydia caught her breath at the thought, and Mrs. Claremont looked at her sharply.

"Are you quite well, Lydia dear?"

She spoke hurriedly, "Yes, thank you. I just swallowed rather too quickly. I'll take some wine and I shall be quite all right. Please go on discussing London with your husband. It's all so fascinating to listen to, and I don't want to miss anything."

Thankfully, they returned to their discussion, leaving Lydia to ponder on this last thought regarding Vincent Montagu. If it were true that he was no more than a fortune hunter, then somehow the events that followed didn't quite ring true. Surely a rogue wouldn't have balked so obviously at marrying a shrew, and would have continued with his ruthless plan.

Nor would he have been diverted by the sight of a penniless cousin such as herself, and risked thwarting his chances with the other one. He'd certainly not have accosted her in a dark alley with the clear intent of ravishing her, when she could have gone crying rape to her uncle. Which it hadn't even occurred to her to do, of course, and she felt the slight stain of heat on her cheeks, remembering the occasion and the thrust of Vincent's leg between hers, and his hands on her breasts.

He had been so sure of her then. And even she, innocent as she was, had had the strangest sensation about the two of them. As if the fact of their mating was inevitable . . .

She willed the crude phrase out of her mind, but had to accept the fact that whatever the explanation to Edwin's meeting with Lord Fitzherbert, there might be far more to Vincent Montagu than was apparent. She should obviously go straight to her uncle and confront him with all she knew.

But what could she actually say? And how ludicrous it would all sound, even if anyone believed her at all.

"Oh, by the way, Uncle, I think you should check Lord Montagu's credentials, since I've reason to believe he's not all he says he is." Would she have the nerve to be so accusatory?

She could just imagine his reaction! How dare she, a little nobody, dare to accuse a nobleman of treachery and deception! If Vincent got to hear of it, and all was above board, she would be most likely thrown out by her family, and even worse, put straight into a womens' prison for her wickedness. It was far better to wait and watch, and see what happened.

And after all, since Audine was obviously not going to be his wife, there was no obligation on Lydia's part to denounce him. She was uncomfortable at the thought that some other young lady might well be taken in, but for the time being, she would say nothing.

And after all, what did she actually *know?* It was all hearsay, nothing more, and she was the only one in the world who suspected anything, she reminded herself. And the moment she put the thought into her uncle's head, then if he believed her, Vincent would be banned from the Greys' acquaintance forever. She didn't want that. She couldn't *bear* that. She bit her lips, knowing herself to be weaker than she had ever imagined herself to be where Vincent Montagu was concerned.

Lydia began to feel as if she didn't know anything any more. She was thoroughly out of sorts because of Edwin's innocent comment, and her head ached with the anxiety that if things had gone according to Vincent's plan, then Audine might have been cheated out of her money. Audine could change her mind even now, but Lydia doubted that she would. The thought of leaving England and home was too strong a deterrent for Audine, and Lydia was fervently glad that such a trait would prevent her being duped.

She smiled slightly at the thought of being so defensive on Audine's account, when the girl had done her no favors ever since they had met. But family blood did count after all, she thought, despite all Audine's vindictive ways.

And if Vincent was truly an adventurer, he would obviously pursue Aúdine in the end, once his dalliance with Lydia was over. It was a cruel smart to her self-esteem, but it was a fact to be faced. Perhaps it would even be better to allow herself to be wooed, to take the stars from her cousin's eyes and reveal him in his true light of philanderer, seeing just how far Vincent would go in his pursuit of the penniless cousin.

If she was a gambling person, she would wager heavily that he wouldn't go as far as to propose marriage. She would sacrifice herself to her uncle and Audine's wrath by letting Vincent flirt with her, and responding outrageously. It would be for Audine's benefit in the end, she thought, ignoring just how bittersweet the performance would be.

"Lydia dear, would you like some more syllabub?"

She heard Mrs. Claremont's voice as if through a fog, and shook her head quickly.

"Thank you, no. It was delicious, but I've had quite sufficient. I think I'll go to bed if you don't mind. You and Mr. Claremont obviously have much to talk about."

"As you please, but I'll bring you up a hot drink in a little while."

Lydia might have guessed that the hot drink was an excuse for Mrs. Claremont to question her on the extraordinary coincidence of the names. She appeared in the bedroom while Lydia was still half undressed, apologizing for her intrusion.

"It's quite all right," she said, quickly pulling a

dressing gown over her bare shoulders.

"Now then, my dear, what do you think of it?" she said without further explanation. "Will you inform your uncle or the constables? The man's obviously an imposter."

"Oh, not the constables, Mrs. Claremont, and I beg you to say nothing to your husband until I've thought what to do. It could be all so innocent, and you can't condemn a man just because he shares the same name as another! You must see that."

She thanked heaven she had never mentioned the Greek island to Mrs. Claremont, for that would surely have damned Vincent completely. She was ashamed of herself for even defending the man, when in her heart she knew something was badly wrong. But until she knew the truth of it, she had no intention of surmising anything. And the only way to discover the truth was to face Vincent himself with it when she could catch him off guard.

"So you'll go to your uncle? Don't let the man's charm sway you, my dear. Many a villain has been godlike in appearance, and such an attribute can be to the dire cost of the poor victims."

"I'll do what I think best," Lydia prevaricated. "At least I'm alerted now, and can think more clearly about the man. But I can hardly think him a villain, Mrs. Claremont. If you had met him, you would agree, I'm sure."

She saw the woman's pitying look, and knew she was being seen as completely besotted. She drew a deep breath.

"Anyway, it's Audine who Vincent came to see, not me. And since I'm quite sure he's not as enamored as my cousin thinks, nothing will come of it, so there's nothing to worry about."

"You're quite sure of that, are you? You don't think he's after her fortune?"

"Quite sure," Lydia said steadily, although she still wasn't at all sure. But it was certainly a prize of a very different kind he had been seeking in the dark alleyway, and she resolved that she must confront Vincent Montagu, or whoever he was, with her knowledge the minute she was able. She owed it to her family, and to her own self-respect.

"Please, Mrs. Claremont, leave it to me to do what I think best," she said now. After a few moments, the woman nodded slowly.

"Very well. If it's your wish, I'll say nothing more about it. Since it seems we have some big decisions of our own to make at present, my mind will be fully occupied. But I'd be failing in my duty if I didn't beg you to be careful, Lydia."

Lydia assured her that she would, and continued undressing quickly when the woman had gone from the room. Just why she was defending Vincent Montagu so vigorously was a mystery, even to herself. But perhaps, after all, that was part of the fatal attraction. Growing up in that mysterious land of India, she had always been fascinated by intrigue and danger; there had been plenty in her young life. She loved a good mystery. And she was more than halfway toward loving the man.

* * *

"What on earth are you dressed like that for!" Audine said rudely as soon as she saw Lydia wearing the beautiful emerald gown. "It's a concert we're going to, not a fancy-dress ball. Haven't you got something plainer?"

Lydia stared at her blandly, refusing to be rattled. On instruction from her aunt, she had brought her clothes to the manor, so that she could make herself ready for the Pump Room concert in one of the guest bedrooms. It was decided she would stay the night, and the family could all make the short journey together. She found that Vincent, too, had been invited to stay overnight, since it would be late when the concert ended, and he had accepted the offer.

Audine had appeared in the room without bothering to knock, to stand and gape at the vision her cousin made.

"I wear plain clothes every day, Audine. Why shouldn't I allow myself the luxury of wearing one of my finer gowns when the occasion arises? And this is one of my favorites."

"Do you mean you've got more of the same?" Audine said incredulously, obviously well aware of the cost of such garments. "Anyway, it's . . . it's brazen, that's what it is. The color's gaudy, and the material's too shiny and brash. And it clings far too tightly in certain places."

"You mean here?" In a moment of sheer mischief, Lydia pressed both her hands firmly to her breasts.

70

"You're shameless," Audine snapped. "The sooner father gets you married off to some suitable young man who'll tame you, the better, and then we'll be rid of you forever."

Lydia's hands dropped. Considering she was about to do her best to preserve Audine's fortune for her, the girl's reaction was more shrewish than ever. But Audine didn't know that, of course. And of more concern to Lydia were the rest of her words.

"Is that what he has planned?" she exclaimed.

"Well, what else did you think? We didn't ask you to come here," Audine said rudely. "And you said yourself you want a husband. That much is very evident," she added darkly.

"I didn't ask for my parents to die either, nor for my father's business to fail, and to be obliged to leave India when I fully expected to spend the rest of my life there," Lydia said, the painful memories suddenly overcoming her.

Audine had the grace to look embarrassed at the raw emotion in her cousin's voice.

"I can't think why you'd want to," she muttered. "Anyway, father's begun thinking of suitable young men for you to see. As soon as my own affairs are settled, you're next. Not that it really matters which of us is first, since you're hardly considered *real* family." She put in the final acid, as if to compensate for her momentary softening toward her cousin.

And since Lord Percival Grey's word would seem to be law in this household, Lydia knew that eventually there would be a bevy of young

men paraded for her to see. And if the Claremonts left town, she would be obliged to move
into Greystone Manor and be even more beholden to her uncle. And why should they care
just who they married Lydia off to?

Even if Vincent Montagu didn't turn out to be
the catch for his daughter he had envisioned,
Audine's marital stakes were of the first priority.
She was twenty years old now, and an unmarried
daughter attaining much more than that age was
a slight on a gentleman. But right now Lydia
refused to rise to the bait of her cousin's words.

"You look very grand this evening, Audine,"
she said generously. For once the girl had chosen
to wear a gown with more color in it, even
though a rather violent purple seemed to accentu-
ate the sharp angles of her face and scraped-up
hair.

"I know how to dress for an occasion," Audine
answered. "And if you're quite determined to
wear that green affair, I suggest we go downstairs
to join the others. Mother's fretting that we'll be
late, and I know Vincent arrived some time ago."

Lydia's heart leapt. She hadn't realized he was
coming here. She had assumed they would meet
at the elegant Pump Room itself, not to sit in
the confines of the largest Grey carriage for the
twenty minutes or so it would take them. She
reached for her matching silk cape with shaking
hands, sliding her fingers into the long evening
gloves that finished the ensemble. With a final
twirl in front of the mirror, she saw that her eyes
were already feverishly bright.

72

They went down to the drawing room together, where the other three members of the party were waiting. Lydia looked anxiously at her aunt, hoping she wouldn't see disapproval in her eyes for the emerald gown, and saw nothing but the admiration that was echoed in her voice.

"My dears, how splendid you both look," Lady Grey said, including her daughter in the praise. "Come along and have a warming glass of punch before we leave for the Pump Room."

The weather was becoming too mild to really need the cordial, but Lord Grey always observed the nicety before going out on any evening excursion, pouring the hot punch himself while Vincent Montagu handed the glasses to the ladies.

He was darkly handsome tonight, Lydia thought, her throat catching. He had voiced his own admiring approval of the younger ladies' attire as etiquette demanded. When he handed her the glass of punch, their fingers touched, his eyes looked deep into hers. All the unspoken tension was instantly between them once more. To him, Lydia knew she looked stunning and infinitely desirable, and she had to look away to stop the trembling in her limbs. And she wondered how she could bear it if he were truly as wicked as she half believed him to be.

"I think we should leave as soon as we've all finished," Lord Grey said, when the obligatory small talk had been exhausted. "Montagu, you shall sit between the young ladies in the carriage, if you please, and my wife and I will suffer the rigors of our backs to the driver."

"It's not necessary for Lady Grey to do such a thing," he said at once. True etiquette demanded that the gentlemen should sit with their backs to the driver in case of a sudden lurching of the carriage, in order to steady and prevent any accident to the other passengers.

"But I insist, dear Lord Montagu," the lady said, smiling. "Our driver is well-trained, and I don't anticipate any mishaps on this short journey."

So Lydia found herself pressed quite tightly between Vincent and one side of the carriage, with Audine on the far side of him. She couldn't tell how closely the other two were seated, but she was shiveringly aware of Vincent's body close against hers. She could feel the strength in his thigh, the nearness of his arm. And the warmth of his skin was so evident, it was almost as if the fabric of their clothes was nonexistent.

When they reached the famous Pump Room, where crowds of elegant folk were milling excitedly about before entering, Vincent stepped down from the carriage, ready to help the ladies alight. Lady Grey first, then Audine, and then herself. For a brief moment, she was held close enough to him to hear the whispered words he spoke to her.

"You're the most ravishing woman I've ever seen. I mean to have you, Lydia, take my word on it."

His word? And just what was his word worth?

Still trembling at the effect he could have on her emotions and her very self-confidence, she reminded herself of her plan to flirt with the man, to make Audine so angry that she would dismiss the two of them completely. But was that so wise after all? Wouldn't Lord Vincent Montagu, or whoever he was, simply see this as an open invitation to seduce her whenever he got the opportunity? And with his expertise, Lydia had no doubt that he would very soon make the opportunity.

She decided she should have exposed him to her uncle before now. Or at least told him all that Edwin Claremont had said, and let him draw his own conclusions and deal with the man in his own way. As it was, she would be obliged to sit through this concert, only too aware that Vincent's eyes would rarely leave her.

And even when they did, his presence would still be there, powerful and potent, and undermining everything honorable she had ever thought about herself. If her suspicions were true, she had become as deceitful as he, as devious as he.

She gave up the effort of trying to think clearly about the man at all, and entered the elegant Pump Room, forcing herself to take an interest in her surroundings. She hadn't actually been here before, and was unprepared for the beautiful Spanish chandelier in the ceiling, the elegant columns around the huge room, and the rout benches for the comfort of its patrons. At the east end of the room was a very large and impressive clock, attracting much attention, which her uncle informed her was made in the early eighteenth century by Thomas Tompion, the most famous of all clockmakers.

But the guests were assembling now for the occasion for which they had come. The concert programme consisted of a string quartet and various acclaimed singers, including a puffed-up lady contralto and a very short basso profundo, whose exquisite harmonies belied the almost comic appearance they made together. As well as the solo artists, there were poetry readings and finally an excellent rendition of well-known songs by a choir of unaccompanied male voices.

The concert lasted for two hours, after which Lord Grey announced that he was taking them all to supper at a little establishment in the city. This was a surprise to Lydia, but she could see that Audine was preening herself on the prolonged length of time they were spending with Vincent. Throughout the evening, he had paid equal attention to them both, Lydia acknowledged. And still she was totally unsure whether to denounce him or not. Once she did, he would be gone from her life forever. And the guilty shame of it was, that she couldn't bear that to happen. Whoever or whatever he was, she wanted him.

The party arrived at the discreet establishment her uncle had chosen, and where he was obviously known. They were shown to the best table on a little dais, where they could see and be seen, as was their right. The meal was ordered, and the sparkling wine poured into the finest glasses. Above the rim of hers, Lydia met Vincent's dark eyes, and felt her heart begin its usual rhythmic clamoring at his every glance. She forced herself to look away, but his sensuous voice still sang through her mind like a recurring refrain.

". . . I mean to have you, Lydia . . ."

And then her attention was caught by the approach of someone who was walking toward them across the dining room. A respectably middle-aged gentleman whose delighted smile and outstretched hands were centered directly on the man who could arouse all her churning emotions so easily.

"Vincent, my dear boy. I had no idea you were in Bath. How goes everything?"

Lydia's gaze flew toward Vincent, her thoughts in turmoil. For unless this were a prearranged meeting, the action of the stranger was entirely unforced. And he had called him quite naturally by the name by which the Greys knew him. There was no reason why it should be prearranged, Lydia thought swiftly, since Vincent could have no idea that anyone was suspicious of him, which left her more confused than ever.

"It's good to see you again, Sir Howlett, and my fortunes are as ever," Vincent answered ambiguously. "May I introduce my party to you?"

When the introductions had been made, Lord Grey immediately invited the silver-haired stranger to join them, but he declined with a smiling shake of the head.

"Thank you, but no. My wife and son are waiting for me, but I couldn't resist coming to

77

say hello to an old acquaintance. I hope we'll be seeing you in London, Vincent. You'll be sure to call on us before you return home, I trust."

"I shall make a point of it whenever I'm in London, Sir Howlett," he replied.

"Good. Then I'll bid you all good evening," the man said, and departed to rejoin his family.

Lydia hardly knew what to think now. She concentrated on the food placed in front of her on delicate china dishes, and tried to reason things out. That the newcomer's name was Vincent, there seemed to be no further doubt. That the stranger had known him for a long time, also seemed certain. But if she examined Vincent's replies analytically, she could still see the prevarication in them. He had been vague about his so-called fortunes; he hadn't exactly said he would be in London, but had left the response to the invitation quite open.

And she was probably seeing too many things that weren't there, Lydia thought severely, ghosts on the wind, fleeting and ephemeral. She had, at least, to accept that his name was Vincent, or that his masquerade had preceded this visit to Bath to whatever previous times he had spent in London, making the acquaintance of Sir Howlett and others.

She passed an uneasy hand across her forehead, wondering if she had gone pale since she felt faint. There seemed no answer to the questions that nagged her, other than to ask Vincent outright just who he was. But this was neither the time nor the place. She could never do such a thing in public. If she was wrong about his credentials, her uncle would never forgive her.

"Are you feeling quite well, Miss Grey?" she heard Vincent say quietly.

"Quite," she murmured. "It's just rather hot in here, that's all."

"I would have thought you welcomed the heat, coming from that infernal climate," Audine couldn't resist saying. "Actually, I find the atmosphere quite refreshing in here, but perhaps your gown is too sheer for you to feel entirely comfortable."

Whatever her snide remark was meant to convey, it had the opposite effect on Vincent Montagu. Lydia saw the way his gaze lingered on the shimmering emerald silk of the gown, especially where it swelled so voluptuously over her breasts and revealed her smooth-skinned shoulders and her honey-gold arms.

She remembered the way her own fingers had caressed the peaks of her breasts into sensual arousal, and for a second she found it impossible not to imagine Vincent's long sensitive fingers following the same trail. She felt her cheeks go hot, where moments before they had been so pale.

"I think we've all finished, anyway," Lord Grey said briskly. "The hour is late, and I've a longing for my bed."

Again, Vincent's eyes met Lydia's, and she could read their meaning as if they were written in the stars. Lord Grey's was not the only longing around this table. Even before she could lower her eyes, she heard him speak quietly.

"I hope you'll allow me to have words with you when we return to the house, Lord Grey. There's a matter I very much wish to discuss with you, and I would wish all the ladies to be present, if they would be so kind."

He was so formal now, and Lydia felt a frisson of presentiment. Either he was going to declare his identity, whatever that was, or he was going to profess his intentions toward Audine. And that young lady would certainly be assuming it was to be the latter.

Lydia couldn't rightly think what his motive would be in offering for Audine now that he had made his desire for herself so blatant. Except for Audine's fortune, of course. That would be the real motive, and presumably, once in the family, he would think it no great hardship to engineer clandestine meetings with the impoverished cousin whenever he chose. Lydia burned with mortification at the thought, and sat stiffly in the carriage, as far away from Vincent as was possible, until they reached Greystone Manor once more.

Audine caught up with Lydia as they put their evening cloaks in their rooms, her eyes stormy, her lips pursed into an even thinner line than usual.

"Do you think he's going to make a public offer for me, as if I'm some prize animal in a show? I begin to think our Lord Montagu is more uncouth than we supposed, Lydia. And I've certainly got no intention of marrying a man who wants to live in some remote Greek island! I shall flatly refuse him."

"Aren't you in the least attracted by him then?" Lydia said cautiously.

She gave an unladylike snort. "Oh, I grant you he's personable enough, but I'm not sure I like that dark countenance of his. Well, it's almost un-English, and I've no wish to marry a man who may father dark-skinned children!"

She colored slightly at her own words, and Lydia had a job not to show her impatience at the stupidity of her narrow-minded cousin. Vincent was no more dark-skinned than she was, and it was only the time spent in the hot sun of more southerly climes that had produced the healthy glow in both their skins. But once Audine had got an idea in her mind, there was no changing it. And it seemed she was totally adamant now about not marrying Vincent Montagu.

They went down to the drawing room together, where Vincent and the older Greys were already deep in conversation. Lord Grey turned to them, an air of surprise that was akin to shock, evident in his voice.

"Well now, my dears, since you've been upstairs a considerable time, Lord Montagu has already made his suggestion to my wife and myself. He wants to make an offer of marriage, and since my daughter's made it quite clear she wouldn't want to make her home on any Greek island, the offer is for Lydia. So what do you say to it, Niece?"

Lydia's thoughts were in such disorder that she couldn't say anything at all for some minutes.

She could only register the impossible. Vincent had offered for her instead of Audine, and her cousin's face was contorted with fury at not even being given the chance to refuse her suitor. She heard Audine's shrill laughter, and the vicious abuse hurled at her.

"Yes, just what *do* you say to it, cousin, since you've been angling for this moment ever since you began making those great cow-eyes at Lord Montagu?"

Lydia still couldn't answer. She seemed momentarily to have been struck dumb. She could only think of Nadima, and the love and wishes she had sewn into the gown that Lydia was wearing, the gown that was the color of Islam. And she knew now that sometimes wishes and destiny were one and the same.

Chapter Four

Lydia was still speechless as Audine's venom was directed at her, as if Lydia had deliberately enticed Vincent away from her. As far as she was concerned, that certainly wasn't the truth of it. The seduction had been wholly on his part, mentally and physically, if not in the full meaning of the word, yet. She forced herself to look at the man in question.

He stood tall and motionless, watching her reaction with enigmatic eyes, awaiting her reply. He was so sure of her, Lydia thought swiftly. So sure that no woman with fire in her belly could refuse him, which was why Audine was able to do so, because she was a cold and frigid woman, with no perception of what loving between a man and woman could mean.

But was love what Vincent Montagu wanted, or expected of Lydia? And was he truly the rogue Edwin Claremont had unwittingly suggested him to be?

She felt the stab of tension between her eyes, wishing she'd never heard the milliner's description of the real Lord Montagu. If she had not, then she might have gone into this marriage only too willingly. Vincent crossed the room to her, to take one of her cold hands in his own. She felt the warmth of his fingers curl around hers, and she swallowed dryly.

"I beg you to take my offer seriously, Miss Grey," he said, softly and formally. "You'll have a good life on Kurnios, and I know that the climate will suit you admirably."

And what of the man? The *husband?* Would he suit her admirably, too?

"I think there's more to marriage than being suited to a good climate, Sir," she said, her voice higher than normal, and still totally unable to think sensibly.

"There is indeed, and I promise you'll not find me wanting in any respect," he spoke far more softly and seductively now, half-turning away from her family so that only she could hear the words.

The clasp of his fingers was harder, reminding her that here was a man of strong passions, who would want a full and loving relationship with his wife, no matter what the initial circumstances of their union. Exactly what those circumstances were, she was still at a loss to define. That he'd come here seeking a wife was obvious, but for what devious reason, she still wasn't sure. And she was in no doubt that she hadn't been his first choice.

"Well, cousin?" Audine spoke up spitefully from the far side of the room. "Are you going to reply to Lord Montagu, or are we going to stand here in suspense all night?"

Her mother intervened, placing a gentle hand on her daughter's arm. "Audine, my dear, you must

84

remember that this has been a shock to Lydia. She won't have expected a gentleman to have offered for her, and needs a little time to consider it. Though I must say, Lydia," she looked directly at her niece now, "you would be very foolish to refuse such an offer from a gentleman of means. You cannot rely on charity for the rest of your life."

Lydia felt her cheeks burn. Aunt Maud's meaning was abundantly clear. The Grey family had no intention of being indefinitely responsible for a wayward niece they hadn't really wanted here at all. They would certainly not want her now, when she had clearly taken the place of the Grey daughter in the suitor's affections!

Her uncle nodded in agreement with his wife. "I strongly advise you to accept, Lydia," he said. "And since I understand Lord Montagu wants an early settlement, I shall insist that you move your belongings back to Greystone Manor right away until we make the arrangements for the wedding."

Lydia drew her breath. "Please understand that if I accept, I'd have no wish for flamboyant wedding arrangements, Uncle. It would hardly be the most regular of unions, would it?"

"Well, really, my dear," Lady Grey said, affronted. "For a well-bred young lady, you speak far too frankly—"

"I doubt that Lydia need worry about any irregularity in the wedding arrangements," Audine said, as frank as her cousin, and ready to snipe at every opportunity. "She's been filling the girls' heads with nonsense about the arranged marriages in India, instead of teaching them their letters. It would seem to be perfectly normal to someone with her background."

"So does this mean that you accept, Lydia?"

She heard Vincent's quiet voice through all the babble of her family. She realized he was still holding her hand. The warmth from his skin was beginning to fill her with reassurance, and a feeling of certainty that, after all, this was the only man in the world for her. Whatever the future held for them, the only thing that mattered was that she wanted to share it with him. She became recklessly sure of that.

"I believe it does," she murmured, realizing that the others had gone silent, waiting for her reply.

"Thank God that's settled, then," Lord Grey said with a hearty bluster. "We'll all have a glass of champagne to celebrate, and then we can get off to our beds. It will be time enough to begin making plans tomorrow."

"May I be permitted to kiss my betrothed?" Vincent asked, with a grave formality. Without waiting for more than a nodding answer, he drew Lydia into his arms, and she felt the sweetness of his kiss on her mouth.

Obviously it wasn't to be a lengthy kiss, nor one that could be misconstrued as the prelude to passion. But as she dutifully raised her face to his, she saw the hot passion in his eyes and felt the tip of his tongue force itself between her lips, lingering there just long enough to savor her taste before he turned away to receive the congratulations of his hosts.

"Well, you managed all that very successfully, didn't you, Cousin?" Audine sauntered over, almost hissing the words, while her father was ordering the champagne to be brought up from the cellar and her mother was already asking Vincent if he had any ideas as to when and where the ceremony should take place. The two girls had automatically moved away from the others.

"I didn't manage anything at all," Lydia said, calmer now that things were settled, and there was no going back. "All you had to say was that you were happy to live on Kurnios, and none of this would have happened. You would have been the one Vincent married, not me."

She caught his glance as she spoke, and felt a small shiver run through her. Had it really been mere chance that out of all the world, he should have come to England at this time, when circumstances had decreed that she herself should be so dependent on her English family? Had the gods ever really intended Audine to be the one for him, or had it been mere capriciousness on their part, teasing Lydia Grey before this inevitable moment occurred?

"If you don't stop staring at him so indecently, mother will be outraged," she heard Audine say now. "You look like a besotted cow, and at least once the thing's done, I shan't have to look at your stupid face any more."

"Nor I yours, Audine," Lydia said, looking steadfastly at her cousin now. "And I truly thank God for that."

Her uncle came across the room to where the

two of them wrangled, a look of slight surprise on his face.

"Vincent suggests you may like the wedding to take place right here at the manor, Lydia. I daresay the minister will have no objection to it, unless you're going to allow your aunt to make it a big affair in church—"

"No, I'd prefer not to have a church wedding," Lydia said quickly. "I would feel uneasy, making vows I didn't mean—"

"You'll still be expected to make your vows, miss," Aunt Maud said sharply. "Your parents would think it very remiss of us if the ceremony wasn't conducted correctly. You'll promise to love, honor and obey your husband, and to adhere to the meaning of the marriage service. You'll still be married in the sight of God, no matter where the wedding takes place, and I hope you understand that fully."

"Of course I do," Lydia muttered. To love, honor and obey her husband in all things, and he would promise to love and honor her too . . . forsaking all others, until death did them part. The words were beautiful and sacred, and only those who truly loved should say them. It was going against God to do otherwise.

But by now her thoughts were taking her to other directions. What was she going to say to the Claremonts tomorrow? Both she and Vincent were staying here tonight, but when she returned to the milliner's house, she would be obliged to tell them she was going to be married, and that would involve the name of her future husband. Lord Vincent Montagu, whom Edwin Claremont had already described as being an elderly eccentric gentleman with a penchant for gambling.

As if following her train of thought, Aunt Maud approached the two girls now.

"Are there any friends you wish to invite to the wedding, Lydia? Your parents wouldn't wish it to be 'a hole in the corner' affair, and there's no reason why there shouldn't be a small reception afterwards. Your hosts, perhaps?"

"I'd prefer it to be kept as quiet as possible, Aunt Maud. I really don't want any fuss. You've all been kind enough to me already," she said quickly.

Lady Grey shrugged. It was obvious to Lydia she thought the whole affair was odd. However, what could be expected from the strong-willed daughter of an adventurous father who'd consorted with Indian princes and astrologers and the like. The sooner the conventional Greys of Bath could wash their hands of their responsibilities, the better.

"Just as you like, my dear. It will be just a quiet family wedding. You and Vincent must set the date between you."

By the time the champagne had been handed round, Lydia began to feel a little light-headed. So much had happened so soon, and she could still hardly believe she was to be Vincent Montagu's wife. She couldn't cope with making any more formal plans that night, and pleaded for any more discussion to be left until morning.

"A very good idea," Lady Grey said, with some relief at seeing her daughter's scowling face. Reaction was setting in as far as Audine was concerned, Lydia realized, and the sooner they all went to their separate rooms, the better.

She and Vincent were shown their rooms, strategically at opposite ends of the guest wing of the manor. After wishing everyone good night, Lydia all but wilted against the door of her room, before going to the washstand and splashing cold water onto her heated face. One of the maids had already turned down her bedspread invitingly, and she unhooked the back of her gown with shaking fingers. She slid out of its soft folds and let it drop to the floor in a rustle of silk, breathing deeply, as if unable to get enough air into her lungs with the enormity of all that had happened this night.

Hearing soft sounds from other rooms, she picked up the gown quickly, draping it over a chair for the maid to attend to its laundering in the morning. She stripped off her undergarments and slid her arms into the nightgown she had brought in her overnight bag. She took the pins from her hair and let it fall freely onto her shoulders, foregoing the usual nightly brushing, then climbed into the unfamiliar bed, blew out her bedside candle, and lay back between the cool sheets.

But it was quite impossible to sleep, just as she had known it would be. She was too overawed by this evening; too acutely aware that Vincent was a few doors away from her in the lengthening darkness of the night; too sexually aroused by his presence, and the knowledge of what marriage to him would mean.

A long while later she wondered if she was still dreaming. After all the turmoil of her thoughts, she had finally drifted into a lethargic half-sleep, where all the worries and suspicions had disappeared. All that remained was the glorious fact that she and Vincent were soon to be man and wife.

Into that treacherous half-sleeping state had come the abandoned sensual images of lying in his arms, of being warmed by his body and aroused to heights she couldn't yet imagine by his passion. She wanted him so much. She freely admitted it now, when there was no reason to hide her feelings from herself. But she would hide them from him, she vowed. He mustn't know just how vulnerable Lydia Grey could be.

The soft click of her door handle made her breath catch in her throat. She turned her head very slowly. Was it Audine come to spite her with more verbal abuse? Was it Aunt Maud, deciding it was an appropriate time to instruct her wayward niece into some of the proprieties of an English lady on the brink of marriage? Or even in the way a wife should conduct herself in the marital bed? Was it whom she knew it had to be, whom she had been waiting for and wanting so much?

In the faint light from her window she saw the shadowy figure move toward her bed. Her breath was constricted in her throat. She knew she should cry out, protest, scream . . . but her mouth was so dry she did none of those things.

Vincent stood by her bed a moment, a dressing robe covering his body. She wondered wildly if he was naked beneath it, and the thought caused her to be even more breathless.

"Are you afraid of me?" he asked softly.

She shook her head, her eyes wide. "I knew you'd come," she whispered.

His response was to untie the dressing robe and let it fall from his shoulders, and she knew she had been correct. He wore nothing beneath it, and his powerful body was lean and broad in all the right places, the gleam of his sun-bronzed skin darkened by the generous covering of hair on his chest. She had never seen a man's body before, and as he stood by her bed, she let her gaze drop to the potently jutting evidence of his desire. She ran her tongue around her dry lips, and at the small movement, Vincent reached for the bedcovers and pulled them back.

"Dear God, but you don't know what you do to me, Lydia. If you want to shout for help, you'd best do it now," he said, his voice rough with passion. "For I mean to seal our bargain this night, and you still have the means to prevent it."

She shook her head mutely, her own awakening needs dictating all thoughts of common sense or decorum. This was her love, her destiny, so soon to be her husband, and wrong or right were just words.

She felt him cover her body with his own, and the heat of his kisses on her mouth left her weak with renewed desire. His tongue forged into her mouth, a prelude to other pleasures, and then he leaned up, slightly away from her, tugging gently at her nightgown.

"A husband and wife have no need for modesty, my darling girl. Knowing something of the Indian *ayahs,* I'm sure you were wisely taught as much."

She nodded again, seemingly mesmerized by his seduction, and completely unable to resist as he removed the remaining garment between them with dexterous ease. She wouldn't let herself think how skillful he was in the bedroom. She didn't want to wonder how often he had done this before. She was the one he'd chosen to be his wife, and that was all that mattered.

She felt his gaze on her body, uncaring now whether or not he could see the heat in her cheeks, and wanting only to be perfect for him. She felt his hands circle her breasts, palming them until the pleasurable tingling became almost unbearable, and the nipples peaked under his touch, followed by the warmth of his lips. His kisses trailed over her body, slowly and lingeringly, as if he had all the time in the world. She became helpless with desire, allowing it all to happen, wanting it with primitive ferocity.

She felt him open her with his fingers, and her hands were in his hair, unconsciously kneading it. Little moans escaped her throat at the ecstacy he aroused when his tongue penetrated her most secret place.

"I must have you, Lydia," he said, suddenly hoarse, and her answer was just as erratic.

"Yes . . . oh yes. Do what you will . . . only do it *now* . . ."

For a second, a small lance of sanity seemed to make her stand back and gape at her behavior. She was a crazed woman, writhing on the bed in her uncle's house with a stranger. She was shocked, but only for a second. For in the next, Vincent's body was heavy on hers again, and she felt the sweet stab of pain as he entered her, filling her. Then he remained motionless for a few moments while he kissed her lips. She felt him murmuring what seemed to be endearments in a language she didn't understand. And then she was conscious of a heat inside her that she had never known before as he began to move gently and slowly, seductively initiating her into the art of love.

Lydia clung to him, her fingernails digging into his back, their crescents unconsciously marking him, as the abandonment went on. She was almost delirious with the new sensations and by the powerful response of her own body. It seemed to have a will of its own now, exquisitely pulsating. Finally, she felt Vincent gather her into him, twisting against her as the gush of his seed spilled into her.

He said nothing for a few moments, and she could hear his ragged breathing against her cheek, his rapid heartbeats against her breast. It endeared her to him even more, knowing now the power of a woman over a man. Universally acknowledged to be the strong one, the hunter, a woman could still make a man vulnerable.

Vincent touched his lips to hers, and whispered against her mouth. "You and I are as married now as if any churchman had already joined us. We're joined in the eyes of God, and the rest will be a mere formality."

Lydia's eyes prickled at the simple statement.

This was no charlatan, wanting her for her body and then abandoning her. This was a man of true faith, and she still couldn't believe he was as devious as Edwin Claremont had hinted. She simply blocked the thought out of her mind, and held him closer to her, feeling the inevitable dwindling of his passion.

"You see what you've done to me now," she heard him say ruefully, the hint of laughter in his voice. "I think I must go back to my own bed and start to conserve my strength, since I'm obviously going to need it in our marriage, my sweet."

She looked at him, a little startled. She often spoke frankly herself, but never in such a context. But then, the whole shrouded mysteries of married love, as intoned by Nadima, had always seemed such a serious business. To hear it spoken of so lightly, and so naturally, was a delight in itself. She felt a small gurgle of laughter in her own throat.

"Does it wear out so easily then?" she heard herself say, to her own amazement. Vincent laughed back, kissing the tip of her nose. She could see the lights of mischief dancing in his eyes as he looked down at her, passing his hands lightly across her breasts in a way that made her heartbeats quicken at once.

"It does not, you witch. It renews itself with amazing fortitude, as I shall have great pleasure in proving to you on our honeymoon. Until then, we shall not lie together again, and tomorrow you and I will be as circumspect as ever. It will be our secret delight to gaze at one another across the dining table, and know how much we have pleasured

95

each other."

His words shivered through her senses. Yes, they had pleasured one another. And yes, already she ached for it to happen again. Already he had discovered the woman in her, the latent desire of which she had always known, deep down, that one day she was capable of knowing.

Vincent bent to kiss each of her breasts once more, and then his mouth moved upwards until it reached hers. Still dazed and enchanted with the realization that lovemaking had been a sensuous, wondrous experience, she reached for him, holding him to her, unconsciously yearning upward toward him.

"No more, my love," he whispered softly against her lips. "Though God knows it wouldn't take long for my loins to recover with your sweetness beneath me. But we'll have the rest of our lives to make love, and the prospect of that alone gives me the strength to wait. You dazzle my senses, Lydia, but I intend to leave you tonight with the pleasure of this first time still warm within you."

She was too inexperienced to know whether this was arrogant masculine talk or not. She neither knew nor cared. With a new maturity that seemed to be borne of this night, she accepted everything he said as the way she herself felt. She still felt that they were truly one. Male and female personalities no longer mattered.

They had shared the most intimate of experiences, and the magic of his body filling hers was still there. Even though the physical part of him was gone for the moment, the essence of him remained. She was truly whole, as she had never felt in her life before.

"You did pleasure me, Vincent," she said huskily, the words almost drawn from her. "I want you to know it now, in case I never have the courage to say it again. I just want you to know that I feel no regrets."

She stopped, embarrassed at being so frank. But if two people couldn't be frank with one another now, she didn't know when they could. He was still heavy on her, and she gloried in the weight of him, his breathing feather-soft on her cheek now.

"I hope I shall hear you say those words many times in our marriage, my sweet. There's no need for reticence between husband and wife. It's a poor marriage where one partner can't convey his innermost thoughts and feelings to the other."

It trembled on her tongue then to beg him to tell her she was mistaken in her suspicions of him. The little devil of suspicion pushed its way into her consciousness, just when she least expected it. She bit her lips hard. Not for the world would she spoil these moments, for they would never come again. Nothing would ever be so sweet, so perfect, as this first time that she lay with her man and felt so cherished and so loved.

She was only vaguely aware that Vincent had never said he loved her in the heat of passion. But for her, the act of love conveyed everything she had wanted to know. The euphoria of it was still with her now.

"I'm going to leave you now, my love," he said gently. "It would be wrong of me to remain here all night, though I would dearly love to do so. But your aunt and uncle would be scandalized, and I dare not risk gossip among the early-rising maids. You have a reputation to maintain. But we'll only be parted for a little while longer. Soon you'll belong to me for all time, and there'll be no need for partings."

He kissed her once more, and rose reluctantly from the bed. She watched from her love-drugged eyes as he covered his nakedness with his dressing robe, her body still warm from its contact with that magnificent, virile flesh of his. She still marvelled at the way they had fitted together, as if God had intended each for the other. In her innocence she thought it must surely be providence that had sent him to her, out of all the world.

She watched him languorously as the dappled moonlight from the window threw soft shadows around him as he moved quietly toward her door. He gave her one last lingering glance, and then he was gone. Lydia closed her eyes blissfully, still wrapped up in the magic of this special time together.

Only slowly did she begin to feel as if she was coming back down to earth again. Colder without his presence, the slow reaction to all that happened began to seep into her brain. She was still bemused that he had actually come to her bedroom, here in her uncle's house, to seal their marriage bargain by making love to her.

He had been very sure that she would want him, she thought, the hot color rushing to her face. And so she had. She had wanted him so much . . .

without thinking what she did, and as if to hide the memory of her wantonness for a moment, she covered herself with her hands in the place where he had so recently lain. How abandoned she had been. . . .

Slowly, she began to fret that she had been too abandoned, too eager to share the pleasures of the flesh. She wondered just what he must have thought of her. They were not yet married, yet she had welcomed him without question. She could still feel the damp heat of his seed inside her. All the conventions said that what had happened between them without the sanctity of marriage was so very wrong. But as she closed her eyes and felt the weak tears trickle down her hot cheeks, Lydia was unable to resist the memory of how glorious it had been. In his own words, at the height of their passion, Vincent had made everything seem right.

"We belong together now," he had said thickly against her skin. "Nothing and no one can take this away from us, Lydia."

She remembered the words so clearly. They belonged. He was hers, and she was his, for always and beyond time. In her innocence, she truly believed it to be so.

When Lydia awoke the next morning, she felt as if she was a different person from the one who had gone cheerfully to bed the night before. She was no longer the virginal Lydia Grey. She was a woman, knowing now that a woman's needs could match those of a man; knowing too, the way that a man could fulfill those needs.

But in the midst of her new euphoria, she had glanced with some dismay at the evidence of Vincent's visit last night. She had been thrown into a small panic by the slightly bloodstained sheets and rumpled bedclothes. Then she reminded herself that the housemaids would see to everything. If any curiosity at all was aroused, it would be put down to the normal monthly occurrences all women had to endure.

She descended the stairs for breakfast with a quaking heart at the thought of seeing her lover again. How would they react to one another? Discretion was to be observed at all costs, but how could she help the rising color in her face and the trembling in her hands at the thought of all they had done. She was saved the necessity by Lord Grey's first words to her.

"Vincent has gone into the town in order to obtain a special marriage licence, Lydia," he said, somewhat sternly. Lydia guessed that he was still secretly affronted that this upstart relative should have got such a prize as Lord Vincent Montagu.

"I see," she murmured, not having thought of such a thing at all.

"He's also going to see the minister to make the necessary arrangements for the wedding."

Lydia stared at her uncle, feeling her hackles begin to rise. This was not what she had expected to hear at all. This should be an occasion for loving discussion between the two parties concerned.

"Without consulting me?" she began heatedly, and her uncle held up a hand to stop her.

"He's suggested that the ceremony should take place one week from today," Lord Grey went on, his demeanor clearly showing that he thought the whole world had gone mad. "It seems to be indecently hasty, miss, and if I didn't know that you and he had never met before—"

Aunt Maud spoke to him sharply. "I don't think we need have any of that kind of insinuation, Percival. We're all perfectly well aware that Lydia had never met Vincent until recently."

Even though it seemed to her as if she had known him for all time.

"And Lydia, dear, I really think it would be nice for all of us if you were to move in with us for the rest of the time you're to be in England. I never did like the idea of your living with strangers, and I really feel it's what your parents would want us to do for you now, so I hope you'll agree. And of course, there's no question now of your tutoring the children. I shall look around for someone else right away."

"Thank you, Aunt Maud. I accept your offer with pleasure." And especially the thought that she need no longer tutor the girls, even though the relationship between the three of them had become so much easier of late.

But there was so much else of more importance for her to think about now. She kept her gaze on the plate of food in front of her, and tried to stop her whirling thoughts taking her in all kinds of unwilling directions. One week from today she was to be married, and apparently she was to have no say in the arrangements for her own wedding.

For a moment she bristled, quite furious at the way everyone seemed to be taking charge of her life. For an even briefer moment, she felt quite ready to storm out of Greystone Manor and tell her uncle in no uncertain manner that the marriage was off, and that Lord Vincent Montagu or whoever he was, could take himself back to his island and good riddance. And then she paused.

For where was the sense in rejecting the very thing she wanted most in all the world? To belong to Vincent, and to live with him for the rest of her life.

And wasn't it to her advantage that events were moving so swiftly? It meant she could return to the Claremonts' house and collect all her belongings, merely informing them that her aunt and uncle wished her to move into Greystone Manor, and that she had accepted. She need make no further explanation. She needn't mention the fact that she was to be married, nor to whom, and Edwin Claremont would have no reason to voice any suspicions about the identity of her future husband.

If she was being a "head-in-the-sand fool," Lydia thought wryly, then she probably deserved all that she was about to get. But she knew in her heart that it was simply beyond her to betray all her suspicions to her uncle. If she did so, she would probably lose the thing she wanted most in all the world. Whatever the outcome, she simply couldn't do it.

Vincent still hadn't returned to Greystone Manor

by the time she left there for the Claremonts'. She was alternately glad and frustrated. She needed to hear his voice. She needed the timbre of it, richly vibrant to her senses, even if he was saying the most prosaic things. She ached to see him again, and yet she was half afraid, too. She was afraid of what she might see in his eyes. In the cold light of day, there were those black moments when she faced the fact that he had used her, and she had been his willing slave. He had made certain she would not back out of their nuptial arrangement, and she had given in to his seduction so very willingly. And if he despised her for it, she didn't know how she was ever going to bear it.

Mrs. Claremont welcomed her back with an excitement that seemed over excessive, and before Lydia could say anything at all, the lady had blurted out her own news.

"Oh, Lydia love, Edwin has had word of the establishment in London he wants to buy, and he's been offered it at a fearfully good price. We'd be just too foolish to let this chance slip by, and he's going to take me up to town to settle things this very day."

"That's wonderful—" Lydia began, knowing how much Edwin had wanted this, but Mrs. Claremont rushed on.

"I doubt that we'd be leaving Bath immediately, but we're to stay in London for two weeks right away. Naturally, you're very welcome to remain here whilst we're gone, and to treat this house as your home, but I'm afraid it does mean you'll have to find other accommodation eventually, my dear."

"It's perfectly all right, Mrs. Claremont," Lydia said as soon as she could decently break into the excitement. And secretly wondering just how far the gods were on her side after all. "My uncle has finally persuaded me that I should go and live at Greystone Manor with my family, and it was what I came back to tell you. I'll be collecting my belongings today, so please have no fears on my account."

Mrs. Claremont hugged her in affection and relief.

"Then it's all settled. We can close up the house, and I shan't need to worry about you, Lydia. I confess that I was a little concerned that you might be distressed at our leaving, but this solves everything. All the same, we shall both miss you."

"I shall miss you, too," Lydia said with honesty. "But I do have a duty to my family."

She felt her face go warm at the small lie. After their hostile welcome, she had never felt she owed the Greys anything, but family loyalty would never let her say as much.

She saw that Mrs. Claremont was studying her carefully.

"You are quite sure it's what you want, my dear?"

"It's everything I want," she replied, but not exactly in answer to the question.

For a moment, she was almost tempted to confide in this generous hearted woman about her wedding, but she managed to resist it. It was too fraught with risks. The hospitable couple might well be hurt that they weren't to be given a token invitation to the wedding, even though they would be far away in London. Mrs. Claremont would be sure to blather on about it to her husband, and both would want to know the name of the bridegroom, and wonder just how Lydia had conducted a secret engagement without telling them.

It was impossible to reveal anything. Especially Vincent's name. The moment he heard it, Edwin would think it his duty to tell Lord Grey all he knew about the false identity of her lover.

Lydia still thought there had to be some kind of mistake. After all, hadn't some old acquaintance greeted Vincent at the restaurant by his name? And she was sure that Vincent was no fortune hunter, since he knew very well that she had no fortune to offer. If that had been his initial purpose for coming to England, then there was no sane reason why he should have offered her marriage in place of her cousin.

Unless . . . her breath caught in her throat . . . unless the impossible had happened, and he had fallen in love with her. She dismissed that unlikely idea as soon as it entered her head. It wasn't love. It was lust. She felt a surge of depression sweep over her, wanting his love with all her being.

"Here now, you mustn't look so downcast, love," she heard Mrs. Claremont say at her sudden change of expression. "You must come up to London once we're settled and visit us. Edwin will like that. He's always liked having your pretty face around."

Lydia murmured something suitable, thinking privately how unlikely it was that she would ever be in London again. She'd never wanted to come to England at all, and now that the day was coming when she would be leaving she was beset with ragged nerves and self-doubts. Though it was far more likely it was pre-wedding nerves than any other kind, she told herself fiercely. Even more so, the nerves brought on by the thought of going off into the unknown with a stranger.

"Well, if you'll excuse me, I have to get our things packed for our trip. Edwin will be back for me in an hour," Mrs. Claremont went on.

"Of course. I want to get my things together, too," Lydia said quickly.

"You'll wait until he returns, won't you? He'll want to say goodbye, and perhaps take you to your uncle's house."

"That won't be necessary. I can easily take a cab, and besides, you'll be anxious to be on your way. But of course I'll want to stay and say goodbye. You've both been very kind to me."

"Nonsense. It's been like having a daughter in the house," the lady said briskly, and then they both went their separate ways before the conversation became too maudlin.

In just under an hour, Lydia was hugging them both and wishing them well in their new venture. Unknown to them, she would probably be already on the Greek island of Kurnios before they returned to Bath to settle the house and business here. It was better this way. It was unlikely they would meet her uncle in their various social circles, and if they did, then it would be left to them all to make what sense they could out of what had happened to Lydia Grey.

By the time she was seated in a hansom cab and on her way back to Greystone Manor with all her worldly possessions, Lydia felt a real pang at losing the friendship of these genuine people. She didn't imagine life would be easy for the next week, with Audine in particular, and beyond that . . . she gave a sudden small shiver. The seductive memory of last night seeped into her mind again. Beyond everything, there would be Vincent.

She discovered he had returned to the house when the hansom cab drew up at the door of Greystone Manor. He had obviously been watching for her, because he appeared almost at once, lifting her hand to his lips as the maids scurried away with her baggage.

"I missed you this morning," he said softly. "You haven't changed your mind, I trust? I'm told it's a lady's privilege."

He spoke lightly, confidently, as if sure that no lady in her right mind would retract a promise made to such a magnificent, virile man. For a second Lydia imagined herself throwing his proposal back in his face, challenging him with suspicions of his false identity. Over her raised hand, her eyes met his, and she was lost.

"I haven't changed my mind," she said huskily.

"Good. Because all the arrangements have been made," he said more firmly. "One week from today you will be my wife, and we sail to Kurnios from Tilbury the following evening. We shall stay at a decent hotel en route to London for our wedding night. It won't be the Ritz, my sweet, but I doubt that you'll be overly interested in the decor of the place."

His male arrogance was obvious, but her mouth was too dry for her to answer. Everything was moving ahead so rapidly, and she seemed to have little say at all.

"Come now. Your aunt and uncle have something to say to you, and are waiting in the drawing room."

"You've been discussing me then?" she felt bound to say.

She heard him laugh. "Why would we not? A bride is of the utmost importance at her wedding, wouldn't you say?"

To her relief, only the older Grey members were in the drawing room. Audine and the younger girls were nowhere to be seen. Lydia sat down on a sofa, and Vincent immediately sat beside her, as befitted a newly engaged man.

"Did you conduct everything satisfactorily, Lydia dear?" her aunt said automatically.

She doesn't really care, Lydia thought. She doesn't care a jot what happens to me as long as I'm out of her sight. She nodded briefly.

"The Claremonts are setting up a new business in London shortly, so this couldn't have happened at a more opportune time. Not that I knew that beforehand, of course—" she stopped abruptly, appalled that Vincent should think she'd accepted his offer as the lesser of two evils. Staying here or marrying him.

"Of course you didn't, girl," her uncle said testily. "Now then, your aunt intends taking you to her dressmaker this afternoon to have a wedding dress made for you, and the younger sprogs are agog at the thought of being bridal attendants. You've no objection to that, I take it? Audine has declined, naturally."

"Naturally," Lydia managed to say, wide-eyed. She hadn't expected any of this, but clearly the family honor was at stake, no matter how quickly the wedding had been arranged.

"And in place of your father, I will of course settle a marriage sum on you, Lydia."

Her shame at her own thoughts in the face of all this generosity was suddenly halted. So Vincent was to get something out of this alliance after all.

"I don't want anything," she stammered.

"It's traditional," he said sternly. "I wouldn't have it said that I didn't do the right thing by you. Besides, what kind of a gentleman would send his only niece out to foreign parts without the security of her own assets? You may even want to come home again one day," he added, in what was meant to be a tone of heavy humor.

"I assure you Lydia will want for nothing, sir, but I thank you on her behalf for your generosity," Vincent was saying evenly, his hand closing over hers when she seemed too tongue-tied to say anything.

"Yes, of course. Thank you both so much," she said finally. "But I thought it was to be a quiet wedding."

Aunt Maud gave a small laugh. "So it will be,

my dear, since that's your wish. But you must be dressed properly for the occasion, and the girls are so eager to attend you I couldn't disappoint them. Even the servants are quite thrilled at the thought of a ceremony in the house. They'll all be permitted to watch, of course."

Good God, Lydia thought, with total irreverence. Was all this pomp and circumstance as much for the benefit of the younger Grey girls and the servants, as for herself?

She hardly dared look at Vincent, feeling the small squeeze of his hand, and shrewdly guessing that he was as aware of her aunt's snobbery as she was. He was inwardly laughing at it, too, she was sure of it. She relaxed suddenly. Whatever else occurred between them in the future, they shared a kind of mental link that was sweetly comforting. And recklessly, she knew she had no objection at all to her aunt's decision to dress her in silks for her special day, whatever her reasons. As long as it resulted in looking beautiful for Vincent, then nothing else mattered at all.

"I thank you both," she said, still in that oddly husky voice. "And I know that my parents thank you, too."

Her uncle rose immediately, any hint of the supernatural putting an end to the conversation, as Lydia had known it would.

"Then if that's all settled, I suggest we all meet again at luncheon. In the meantime, Lydia, Frances and Davinia are waiting for you in the nursery, and could still benefit by a lesson to keep their minds properly occupied."

And if anything was destined to remind Lydia that she was not married yet, and still had her duties to fulfill, that was it. But not for much longer. Soon she would be Lady Vincent Montagu, and nothing could quite take away the glory of that.

Chapter Five

It was one of the oddest weeks of Lydia's life. She saw little of Vincent, who had returned to his hotel, as the conventions demanded.

Audine was completely distant toward Lydia and anyone else who spoke to her, as if denying to herself that anything unusual was taking place. The two younger Grey girls, meanwhile, did a complete about-face. Their growing affection for Lydia bloomed into full-grown worship. From the moment they knew they were to accompany Lydia and their mother on dress fitting excursions, and that they were to play such an important part in their cousin's wedding day, they became Lydia's willing slaves.

"I never knew weddings could take place in peoples' houses," Davinia said, clearly enchanted by this fact. "I've only been to one wedding before. It was the daughter of one of father's acquaintances, and we had to sit in the back of the church and couldn't see anything."

"That's because you were so small at the time," Frances said loftily. "I could see perfectly well."

"Well, you'll see everything even better this time,

112

because you'll be standing right behind Vincent and me," Lydia said swiftly, before the inevitable sibling arguments began.

A shiver of excitement ran through her at the words. It still didn't seem totally real. Very soon now, she was going to be Vincent Montagu's bride. And these two children were going to be a part of the ceremony that would bind her to the man she loved. However many times Frances and Davinia had irked her in the past, she felt warmed and glad that she had a real family of her own to share the day with her.

Involuntarily, she gave Davinia a little hug as they prepared to go to the final dress fitting session.

"You're both going to look enchanting," she promised them, "and everyone will say how lucky I am to have two such pretty attendants."

It might have been three, she thought swiftly, if Audine had been a different kind of cousin. But under the circumstances, it would have been like rubbing salt into the wound to even suggest that Audine be the chief attendant.

"I love my pink dress with the roses on it," Davinia said, childishly thrilled at being made to feel important. "And Frances says we shall be able to wear them both for the next ball father takes us to."

"How grand that sounds," Lydia said, smiling. "Are you in the habit of being taken to balls?"

"Sometimes," Frances said. "Though we usually have to go to bed before it's halfway through. I

113

shall be allowed to stay up longer once I reach thirteen, though."

Lydia could see a protest coming up very quickly from Davinia at this, and she quickly turned the conversation. She wanted no squabbles to disturb the serenity of her thoughts in these last days before the wedding. Thankfully, she heard her aunt calling to them that the carriage was ready to take them to the dressmaker's.

Nothing was going to ruffle her now, she thought, with a lift to her heart. The dresses were in their final stages of completion, and her aunt had done her very best to give her a fine farewell. The wedding gown was superb in its simplicity, the creamy silk folds caressing her shape, and giving her an ethereal look. She caught her breath, momentarily seeing a stranger gazing back at her in the dressmaker's long mirror.

All brides were beautiful, Lydia told herself. But even she, modesty aside, knew that she looked sensational. And then the thought whispered sweetly through her senses that as long as Vincent thought so, she cared nothing for anyone else's opinion. That thought was with her almost constantly now; she only wanted to be beautiful for him.

That evening, he was to come to Greystone Manor for dinner, and the children had been sworn to secrecy about the wedding finery the bride and her attendants would wear. This only added to their excitement and the adoring looks they occasionally threw to both Lydia and Vincent.

"I'm beginning to realize how very fickle children

114

can be," Lydia commented to her betrothed as they strolled together in the gardens later that evening.

"And just what prompted that remark?" he said, though he had obviously guessed from the chuckle in his voice.

"Those two, of course!" She motioned to the house, from which the sounds of the girls' screeching could be heard as they repaired for bed. "When I first came here, they were so hostile toward me, and so resentful of everything I tried to do for them. And now . . ."

She felt his arm close around her waist, and she thrilled to the fact they need no longer hide the fact. Everything was official, and she was soon to be his wife. She still had to keep repeating the phrase in her head, finding it so unbelievable and beautiful.

"Now they see what I see," Vincent said softly. "You have an inner beauty and goodness about you, Lydia. However irritating those minxes may have been at first, they couldn't fail to love you in the end."

As you did? she so badly wanted to ask. And if so, why do you never say it to me?

"You make me sound like a saint," she said instead. "And you and I both know I'm not!"

His arm tightened still more around her waist.

"I never wanted to marry a saint," he said dryly. "Yet sometimes I wonder if the glow on your lovely face is quite of this world, my darling."

She wriggled uncomfortably. "Please don't say such things! All the time I lived in India I was immersed in the ways of my old *ayah*, and almost persuaded that the finality of astrology ruled everyone's lives. But I don't want to think so. I want to believe that I make my own choices, Vincent. And I especially don't want to be thought fey or out of this world, as you call it! I just want to be like everyone else!"

Her voice had become more impassioned than she intended, and she felt his arm tighten around her.

"But that's something you can never be, my darling. Each of us is unique, and one of God's creations, since we're being so serious about it. But you can't deny that fate brought us together. Why else would you be here in this city at the exact time I arrived? If fate had decreed differently, your parents would still be alive, and I would never have left Kurnios to come looking—"

Her customary pang at any mention of her parents' deaths was stilled by curiosity as he stopped abruptly.

"Come looking for what? A *wife?* That is what you were about to say, isn't it? And since your first choice didn't accept your proposal . . ." she heard her voice grow bitter. However much she denied the fact, it was true. She hadn't been his first choice. And if Audine had accepted him . . . she shivered.

What value would the famous astrology have then, if things had gone according to Vincent's plan? Unless fate had already marked them out for one another in whatever ancient master plan was dictated in the heavens. Even to choosing the moment when her parents died so that she had to rely on her English family's charity. Even to decreeing Audine's cold character, so that she would be bound to refuse Vincent, and he would then turn to *her*.

She realized she was breathing heavily as these fantastic thoughts raced through her mind. She was beset with nerves, almost with a kind of terror at the speed with which events were overtaking her. She didn't want to believe in the influence of fate or coincidence, she told herself desperately, but there were times when such things were too strong to deny any of it.

"Hold fast, my love," she heard Vincent's calming voice, and realized she was almost gulping for air. She felt as if she was drowning, and she clung to him as though a lifeline. She felt the beat of his heart, rhythmic and strong, like the pulse-beat of the universe. She willed the unbidden fantasies away as she looked up into his dark eyes.

"I'm frightened," she whispered.

"Of me?" he said softly. "I promise you there's nothing to be afraid of, Lydia. I would never hurt you, and as for not being my first choice . . ."

Slowly, he bent his head and kissed her upturned face. Gently at first, on her closing lids, on the tip of her nose, her moonlight-pale cheeks, and finally her waiting mouth. And her heart was finding its haven in his arms as she kissed him back with an almost desperate fervor.

"Nothing can come between us now, Lydia," he

117

murmured against her mouth. "Whatever else you believe, believe in what your heart tells you. And you should know that when you find your soulmate, the gods smile kindly on you."

She looked up at him, startled. The voice was different, and this warm night was filled with the fragrance of an English summer, yet it could almost have been Nadima speaking, in words that boded no denial. She gave herself a little mental shake, and the images cleared.

"I think it's time we went indoors," she said tremulously. "Aunt Maud insists on my having early nights all this week to be sure to get my beauty sleep."

He laughed, and to Lydia's relief the mystical mood was broken. It had become far too intense for her peace of mind.

"You know very well you have no need of such ploys. But we'll go inside, as you wish, and obey the English rules. I've no desire to annoy your aunt at this late stage. But I'll make a prediction here and now, that after our wedding you'll be ready and eager for early nights."

The teasing innuendo in his words was obvious. Lydia felt her face burn, remembering that one night of passion they had already shared. And while she made reproving noises in her throat as they neared the house once more, she knew that what he said was true. The die was already cast, and she was irreparably lost.

The morning of the wedding was bright and

warm and sunny. Nadima would have said it was a good omen. Lydia had been helped into the creamy silk wedding dress by a sighing maid, openly envious of the young lady's beauty and good fortune. She adjusted the circlet of flowers on Lydia's gleaming hair, and arranged the short piece of veiling around her shoulders and over her face. Her aunt and uncle had presented her with a pearl necklace on her wedding day. It lay like purity against her throat where a pulse beat steadily.

"You may leave me now, Rose," she said huskily to the maid, gazing at the ethereal vision in the dressing-table mirror.

"Yes, Miss Lydia." The girl hesitated a moment, her round face red with embarrassment at speaking up. "If you don't think it's a liberty, Miss Lydia, all the other servants wanted me to tell you we're pleased for you, and we all think you and the gentleman are well matched."

"Thank you, Rose," Lydia said evenly. The girl bobbed and fled from the room.

Lydia turned back to the mirror. Rose was not as talkative as usual, though not quite dumbstruck at the sight of the bride in all the finery that set her slightly apart from everyone else.

"It's ridiculous," Lydia told her reflection quietly. "I haven't changed. I'm still the same person."

But she knew that she wasn't, and it had nothing to do with the costly gown Aunt Maud had so generously bought for her. It was more to do with the fact that she had already laid with the man who was soon to be her husband. She was not as pure

as the pearls around her neck. She was already
Vincent Montagu's woman.

Her aunt came bustling into the room, her eyes
suspiciously damp at the sight of her.

"Well, I must say you do us credit, Lydia. If
you're quite ready, I'll send your uncle in to you to
escort you downstairs. The girls have taken up
their positions and the minister is here. So is Vincent, of course," she added, almost as an after-
thought.

"I'm glad of that," Lydia replied dryly, but as
usual, her aunt failed to see the humor in the remark. "Will you give me a moment before Uncle
Percival comes for me?"

"Very well, just one minute." She paused, and
her voice became more flustered. "Lydia, my dear,
I feel I've neglected my duty somewhat, and it's a
little late in the day to be thinking of it now. But,
well, are you prepared to do your duty by your
husband?"

"Please don't concern yourself, Aunt. Nadima instructed me long ago in the needs of a husband.
In India, it was all part of a young girl's educa-
tion."

"Good gracious me!" Her aunt was clearly scandalized at this revelation. "Then since you obviously think you need none of my warnings I will
leave you to your moment's contemplation, and
send your uncle in to you directly."

Lydia smiled slightly when she had gone. *Warnings* was a strange word to ascribe to the consum-
mated love that flowed between a man and a

woman on their wedding night. But then, Aunt Maud thought in the dutiful way of a proper Victorian English lady.

She caught her breath, seeing her eyes darken behind the translucent veil. For all its tradition, it managed to transform her into a hidden Eastern beauty. Maybe that was why she had unwittingly instructed Rose to cover her face with its gossamer softness, knowing that her heart really lay in that mysterious, far distant land. She blew a silent kiss to a place far beyond the mirror image of herself.

"You instructed me well, Nadima," she said very softly.

For a second she thought she could see the hazily blurred shapes of her beloved parents in the glass, smiling and approving of what was happening today, and her throat thickened. She still missed them so much, and it should be her father placing her hand in Vincent's on this special day.

The knock on her door was immediately followed by her uncle's efficient voice as he entered her room.

"Are you ready, Lydia? Your aunt was right. You do indeed look like a picture. But come along now, we can't keep the minister waiting any longer. He has other duties to attend to."

And that was all the praise she would get from *him,* she thought. But in a way his prosaic manner was just the antidote she needed as she rose from the dressing-table stool and left the images behind her.

Slowly, Lydia descended the curving staircase on

her uncle's arm. The silken train of her dress caressed the carpeted stairs, and through the misty veil she caught sight of Vincent's face as he awaited her. She could see the enthralled faces of Frances and Davinia in their pink flower-sprigged dresses, ready to walk behind her into the drawing room, where the minister was waiting to perform the ceremony. Everything was ready, and in a very few minutes from now she would become Lady Vincent Montagu.

The realization of the title struck her anew. She rarely considered the fact that on their marriage, Vincent's status would become hers. Perhaps it was because of the uncertainty she still felt, deep down, that he had any right to it. But now was not the time to start pondering, and she quickly put the thought away from her. Besides, by now, she had come to accept the fact that in manner and deportment he was so very much a gentleman, and the person who had spoken to Edwin Claremont must have been mistaken after all.

She could see right into the drawing room now, and her uncle was fussing around her, arranging her train. It must have just occurred to him that after all, he was acting out the role of father of the bride, and had better be seen to be attentive. Aunt Maud awaited her arrival misty-eyed, and Audine stood beside her, sullen-faced and unsmiling.

There, too, were all the servants. Some of them were pop-eyed at the bridal vision about to come toward them; others openly wiping away a tear.

The surroundings might not be as sanctified as a

church, Lydia thought swiftly, but there was all the solemnity one could wish for. As she reached Vincent's side, he looked deep into her eyes, and gave a small nod, as if to say, "It's all right. From now on, I'm here to take care of you and cherish you."

And *love*, the unbidden words came into Lydia's head. *What about love?*

She felt Vincent's hand close over her own. He leaned toward her, ignoring anything else for the moment. There might have been only the two of them in that hushed room, as she looked up into his eyes.

"You look very beautiful, my love. And I want you to know, before the ritual begins, that your future is safe with me," he said softly. "I would never let any harm come to you."

It was a strange thing for a man to say to his bride, when such thoughts should never need to enter a bride's mind at all. But since this had been no ordinary courtship, and the circumstances of the marriage were less than normal, she could only nod dumbly, her throat tight with tears. The words were as solemn as a vow, but if only they had been the words she so longed to hear. Even if a lie, she longed above everything else, to hear him say that he loved her.

"Are you quite ready, Sir?" she heard the minister say quietly, and she turned quickly toward him, as Vincent gave a brief nod.

And then the minister began intoning the words that would bind her to Vincent forever, and she heard her beloved repeat them in that rich deep voice she loved. He spoke as if he truly meant every word, Lydia thought, with a catch in her throat, and she had a job to hold back the tears as she listened.

"From this day forward to love, honor and to cherish . . . in sickness and in health . . . forsaking all others . . . until death do us part . . ."

She glanced up at him as his part in the ceremony ended. He was looking into her eyes again, with an undefinable expression. Seconds later, she felt the coldness of the gold ring on her finger as Vincent slid it gently over her knuckle. He held her hand tightly as she made her own low responses, unable to stop her voice from quavering a little.

And then, as the minister pronounced them man and wife in the eyes of God and the assembled company, Vincent's hands were lifting the veil from her face to kiss her lips as a seal of the marriage. His mouth was gentle on hers, as befitted the formal occasion in front of witnesses. The time for passion would be later.

"Congratulations, my dear Sir, and to you, Lady Montagu," she heard the minister say, the formalities over. She felt her hand being pumped by the cleric, and smiled her thanks. It was all a dream, she thought mistily. She almost wished it could be all gone over again, so that she could remember it more keenly.

"My dear," Aunt Maud said, stepping forward to take her shoulders and peck her on the cheek. "You made a most lovely bride, and I wish you every happiness for the future. I'm sure you and Vincent will be very happy."

And if she didn't sound quite as certain as Lydia would have liked, Lydia guessed it was because her aunt was having some qualms about allowing her niece to go off to yet another remote part of the world.

"Can we please see your ring, Lydia?" Davinia was asking eagerly now. Vincent stood a little way back, smiling as these family congratulations went on. Even so, Lydia was so very aware of him, watching her, owning her, even if he didn't yet truly love her.

There were no congratulations from Audine. Lydia anticipated that eventually she would have to face some caustic comment from her cousin. Presumably she knew better than to break into these first moments when everyone was so pleased for the happy couple. Even the servants made their awkward congratulations, and then melted away to prepare the wedding breakfast.

Soon afterwards, the couple was to begin their journey to London, and then to their island home. And if Lydia paused to think about it at all, she admitted that it still seemed like the continuation of a dream begun long ago.

"Well, cousin, how does it feel to be married?" Audine's sneering voice said in her ear as they reached the dining room. She looked at Audine with her long, cool stare, exhilaratingly aware that this girl could do nothing to her now. She was free of her at last.

"I might have answered that more intimately after tonight, if I ever had the misfortune to see you again," she said sweetly, and saw the other girl blush a furious red.

"That's just the sort of coarse remark I might have expected from someone brought up in heathen parts," she snapped. "I thank the Lord I shan't have to converse with you any longer."

"And I say amen to that," Lydia retorted. "Now why don't we just stop pretending to like one another, and go our separate ways? My husband has need of me."

She moved across the room to where Vincent's eyes were seeking her out, as if he couldn't get his fill of her in her bridal attire. Or as if he couldn't wait to see her divested of it. Lydia shivered, already so perceptive of his moods, and feeling that right now she could read every nuance of expression in his dark eyes. Daringly, she linked her arm in his, as if to show the world where she now belonged. His hand went protectively over hers, and she knew he was aware of all her insecurities. But with him, she always felt safe.

The wedding breakfast was a determinedly bright affair, many toasts were drunk to the happy couple. Finally Aunt Maud escorted Lydia upstairs to assist the maid in removing the bridal dress, while Rose folded it lovingly and packed it with the rest of Lydia's clothes for travelling. Every time she wore it she would think of this day, Lydia thought dreamily, the day when all her hopes and dreams came true.

126

"You're quite content in all this, aren't you, Lydia?" Aunt Maud said suddenly, when the maid had taken some of the travelling bags down to the waiting carriage.

"Of course," she murmured.

"It's just that . . . well, I don't want you to think your uncle and I pushed you into this to get rid of you, my dear. You're part of our family, after all."

"Please rest assured that you did your honorable duty by me, Aunt Maud," Lydia said, melodramatically. Despite all the familial strain, she had a soft spot for her aunt, and gave her a warm hug. "I do genuinely thank you, Aunt Maud, and I promise you I have no regrets."

Her aunt was brisk again, clearly not wanting any uncontrollable shows of affection.

"Well, I should think not on your wedding day! If you're quite ready then, dear, I'll go and tell Vincent you're about to join him for the journey."

Even now they were not to be allowed time together in a bedroom, Lydia thought with a faint smile. Aunt Maud would never wish to know the finer details of how another married couple deported themselves, even fully dressed and about to leave the country for their new life together. Some things were never discussed, nor seen to happen, and therefore, in Aunt Maud's eyes, simply didn't exist.

Lydia felt a brief pity for the lady, wondering if she had ever really known the full joys of love. Had the consummation of her marriage always been a duty, followed in due time by the arrival of their three daughters. As if drawn to it, Lydia's own hand passed across her abdomen, wondering how soon it would be before a child of her own and Vincent's passion would be growing there.

And just who would that child be? The sudden question came hurtling into her mind without warning. She had managed to put to the back of her mind the suspicion that Vincent was not whom he said he was. Now, suddenly, at the worst possible time, it was back, nagging at her consciousness. She brushed aside the gush of angry tears that filled her eyes.

"I won't believe it," she vowed, twisting the new wedding ring that felt so strange and heavy on her finger. "No man could be so devious for no reason at all."

Unless he was a fortune hunter. . . . She had been dismayed at the lavish settlement her uncle had finally promised her, but she was reasonably sure that Vincent didn't know of it. So it certainly wasn't her fortune he was after.

And if he was, it was too late now. She was his wife, and had vowed to love, honor and obey him, sharing her life with him, as well as all her worldly goods.

She heard her two small cousins shouting excitedly for her to come downstairs, and to toss the posy of flowers. Frances was clearly hoping to catch it, her head full of adolescent dreams. Lydia caught up the fragrant posy of summer flowers and buried her nose in it for a moment. She took one last look at her room that had never felt like hers except for one glorious night. Then she turned her back on it forever.

By the time they were sitting back demurely in the carriage that was to take them to London, Lydia began wondering if all of this was a continuing dream. Was she really here, travelling across the world with a man she hardly knew, having promised to love, honor and obey him? She wondered just how foolhardy she had been to bind herself for life to a stranger. A stranger, moreover, whose identity was still cloaked in some secrecy.

They made one stop on the journey, in order to take a brief lunch and to water and feed the horses. To Lydia, Bath already seemed a very long way away, and the heat of the day was lessening.

Vincent seemed more silent than usual, seated beside her in the clattering carriage without attempting to touch her in any way. It might have been better if he'd done so, Lydia thought, keeping up the pretense that he wanted her for herself, and not for some dark reason she couldn't yet guess. As it was, she felt more and more afraid as the miles passed.

When they did speak, it seemed they had instinctively decided to break the silence together.

"What time do you expect us to reach the hotel, Vincent?"

"Your small cousins were in fine form today, Lydia—"

"It's the first time they've been bridal attendants,

129

so they were naturally excited—"

"I wasn't criticizing, merely making a comment. Why are you so nervous, my love?"

He took her cold hands in his, interlacing her fingers in his own. Now wasn't the time for making accusations, for finding herself in some impossible situation from which she couldn't hope to escape. The heaviness of the gold ring on her finger made her irrevocably his, and whatever hazards lay ahead, it was surely better not to know. She was burying her head in the sand and she knew it, but she still couldn't bear to have all her illusions shattered about this man.

She gave a small forced laugh, saying the first inane words that came into her head. "I've never been a married lady before. I'm not sure how to behave."

"I've never been a married man before either, so our pleasure will be in learning together," he said gravely.

Lydia looked down to where their hands were interlocked. His strong fingers wound about her own small ones, keeping them safe . . . or captive.

"But a man knows about the ways of a woman, and I shall disappoint you," she hardly knew why she was saying these things, but somehow the ragged words just kept coming.

He laughed softly, releasing her hand and tipping up her chin so that she met his understanding gaze.

"Did you think I would want my woman filled with expertise in the art of loving, Lydia? I love

130

your innocence, but I know it belies all the fire of a sensual woman. It will be my greatest pleasure to unleash all that fire. And in case you've overlooked the fact, I have already sampled your treasures."

She blushed furiously, moving slightly away from him.

"It's hardly gentlemanly to remind me of that night. It should never have happened like that in my uncle's house."

She heard the edge in his voice as he replied, "Good God, are you going to go all coy on me, like that frigid cousin of yours? It doesn't become you. And since you're my wife now, don't hide behind some silly pretense that we've never made love. I hardly intend to announce the fact to the world, but I don't forget a single moment of it. And neither do you." He finished with some arrogance.

And of course she didn't. How could she, when it had been the most sensual experience of her life? She smarted at the way he made her feel foolish for her earlier haughtiness.

"No, I don't forget," she said in a muffled voice.

"Then I suggest you calm your nerves and try to sleep for a while. We have a long way to go yet, and I shan't bother you with small talk."

He could be as distant in his way as Audine, she thought tremblingly. He made her even more nervous as he sat resolutely beside her, his arms folded. Beneath her half-closed lids, she studied his strong, handsome profile as the carriage thundered steadily toward London.

She hadn't really intended to sleep, only to close her eyes for a few minutes, but when she felt Vincent gently nudging her, she discovered that the shadows had lengthened and the sun was fast going down. The carriage was slowing and they had arrived at their destination.

"We're here, Lady Montagu," Vincent said softly.

Lydia started, finding a piquant pleasure in hearing her new name, whether she had any right to it or not. She smiled quite naturally for the first time since leaving Greystone Manor. Refreshed now, she knew it hadn't boded well to begin her married life with such doubts and fears, and she resolved to put them all behind her.

She peered outside the carriage at the ivy-covered stone frontage of the hotel. It looked solid and respectable, adding to her feeling of reassurance. Vincent's hand in hers did the rest. He was once more her beloved, her knight, her husband.

She allowed him to help her down from the carriage, where the driver was already unloading their baggage and a porter from the hotel was emerging from the reception hall to take them inside. The two sets of baggage placed close together gave an added air of respectability to their cause, Lydia thought fleetingly. They were man and wife in God's eyes, and the world's, and nothing could take that away from them.

While Vincent registered their names in the hotel register, she looked around her with interest. It was every bit as grand as the hotel in Bath where Vincent had stayed, with deep carpets and oak furnishings, and a plethora of potted palms and exotic plants. Somewhere in the background a small orchestra played discreetly, and the music floated upwards on the summer night as the new arrivals were shown to their suite. The valet escorting them threw open the various doors from their lounging room to the bedroom and adjoining bathroom with as much pride as if he had personally built them.

"Dinner will be served in an hour, Sir and Madam," the man said politely. "If you require any further assistance, or need to know the way to the dining room or other facilities the hotel has to offer, please ring the bell."

"I'm sure we shall find our way perfectly well, thank you," Vincent told him, somewhat impatiently.

When the valet had gone, Lydia gave him a reproving look. "You were a little short with him, weren't you? He wasn't to know how adept you are at living in hotels, Vincent!"

Vincent laughed, and as she saw the dancing lights in his eyes she felt her heart leap. He moved toward her and took her in his arms.

"Nor was he to know how impatient I am to lie with my wife in that inviting bed," he said blatantly. "Or do I have to break down that irritating coyness all over again, my sweet tease?"

His fingers lightly touched her breasts and they both felt their ready response. Lydia looked up into his face, and became at once the coquette. She met his teasing with teasing of her own.

"Do we have time? Dinner will be ready in an hour, the man said—"

"Then we shouldn't waste any more time by needless discussions," he said, as he swept her up in his arms and carried her bodily into the bedroom, kicking the door shut behind him.

He lay her on the bed and proceeded to unfasten every one of the irritatingly long row of buttons on her gown, while the laughter bubbled up inside her at his muttered oaths. Her fingers brushed against his as she assisted him in his task, and she trembled inside, knowing this freedom was theirs for the taking from now on. They had every God-given right to know each other's bodies, and the intense pleasures each could give the other.

Finally there was nothing left to remove, and Vincent stood looking down at her for a long moment before he covered her with himself.

"You're so beautiful," he said hoarsely against her throat. "You're so much more than I ever expected to find. Someday I must tell you—"

To Lydia's own surprise, she found herself putting her fingers against his lips. Whatever it was he had to tell her, she didn't want to hear it. Not now when he was awakening all the pleasurable sensations inside her, just by the naked feel of his skin against hers. Everywhere they touched, a new and erotic sensation seemed to spring into life.

"I didn't think we had time for talking," she said provocatively. "We mustn't shock the hotel staff by appearing late for dinner."

Vincent chuckled, clearly delighting in this newly

abandoned manner, and responding by putting his greatest desires into action. Lydia found herself gasping as the few preliminaries were quickly over, and he was forging into her body with long and powerful strokes. She clung to him, her fingernails digging into his back as she arched toward him.

"Do I hurt you?" he murmured, pausing for a second.

"No . . . you don't hurt me, Vincent," she whispered raggedly. Rather he filled her with a primitive need to thrust against him, to be a pulsating part of this rhythmic writhing that made them one. There was no longer any sensation of knowing where one ended and the other began. They were wholly one entity, one being.

Exactly one hour later, the young and beautiful Lady Lydia Montagu demurely descended the stairs to the hotel dining room on her husband's arm. Only the faint flush still staining her cheeks betrayed the memory of a passionate interlude. To the other dinner guests it could merely have been due to the strangeness of staying in a hotel that caused the added charm of the lady.

Vincent ordered a bottle of the finest champagne to accompany the excellent meal of tender veal and young vegetables.

"You know it will surely go to my head, Vincent," Lydia murmured, as the waiter filled their glasses again and again with the sparkling and heady liquid.

135

"It's no matter. Your husband will be the only one to see it," he said meaningly. "And if it has the effect of even more abandonment than I have already seen, then drink up, my darling girl! Inhibitions were meant to be lost on your wedding night."

"I thought I had lost them a long time ago," Lydia said, and then blushed, remembering the first time he had come to her room at Greystone Manor and seduced her. He had left her after their passionate session, but tonight she would sleep in his arms, and he would never leave her again. She blinked through the small rush of tears at the thought.

"There's no cause for tears, my love," Vincent said, seeing them. "You'll not find me wanting in any department, and your life will be a serene one from now on. I can't promise you India, but you'll be better served than a life with a dreary husband of your uncle's choosing on some stuffy English estate."

She looked at him curiously. "Why do you dislike England so much? It's your natural home, isn't it?"

She wasn't so dizzy with champagne that she couldn't see the guarded look come into his eyes.

"I don't dislike England at all," he parried. "It's just that I find Kurnios so much more likeable, and so will you. The Greeks are a particularly outgoing and friendly people."

"And are there any other English people on the island?"

"There are some with whom I have contacts.

Don't worry, you won't be entirely isolated from the rest of the world, whatever your family may have thought. Much as I'd like to keep you all to myself for obvious reasons, I shall also want to show off my lovely wife. Now then, shall we have some dessert, or would you prefer to go straight upstairs?"

He was prevaricating, Lydia saw at once. He didn't want to give her any definite answers, and conversely, she didn't yet want to go upstairs to their suite. He couldn't always lull her suspicions with these darkly seductive hints. In a sudden mood of defiance, she said she would like to go into the public lounge and listen to the orchestra for a while.

Vincent refused to rise to the small challenge in her voice. He spoke laconically. "Very well. After all, we have the rest of our lives to be alone together."

He stood up and came around to hold her elbow as she put down her dinner napkin and rose from the table. His grip was firm, and in her heightened state, she could have fancied it was almost cruelly so. Her head spun from the champagne, and she walked with some deliberation to keep her footsteps steady, so as not to disgrace herself as they went into the brightly lit public lounge, filled with background music and genteel chatter.

But the shivery feeling that ran down Lydia's spine at that moment wouldn't go away, nor was it entirely in keeping with the way a new bride should react to her husband's touch on her wedding night. It was more a feeling of apprehension, and

137

a wild wish that she really could see into the future, to be absolutely sure she hadn't been reckless in rushing headlong into marriage with Lord Vincent Montagu.

Chapter Six

Lydia awoke slowly. Her head raged and throbbed, and through it all she became gradually aware that someone was watching her. She managed to open her eyes a fraction, unable to remember just where she was for a few seconds, and wincing at the brightness from the sunlit windows of the hotel bedroom. She turned her head the merest fraction, and saw Vincent standing by the bed, his dark eyes studying her.

"You let me drink too much champagne," she said thickly, the first words to enter her head.

"So I did, and I was the one to regret it," he retorted.

She gave a low groan. "What do you think I'm doing now!"

Vincent spoke with more sympathy, stroking her forehead with cool fingers that gave blissful relief to the fire inside her head.

"My poor love. I should have realized you weren't used to it, but I have an antidote which will cure you in no time. I intend ordering breakfast to be sent up to our room, and the powder in your morning tea will soon clear your aching head."

"I can't eat breakfast." The very thought of it almost made her retch.

"You can and you will. It's the best thing for you," Vincent told her. "You can't possibly embark on a sea voyage without some food inside you."

His words clarified everything at once. She had temporarily forgotten the sea voyage that lay ahead to the unknown Greek island of Kurnios. She gave a sudden shiver and pressed her hands to her chest. As she did so, she realized at once that she was naked, and she felt the slow dull color fill her cheeks.

"Last night, you didn't . . . surely you couldn't have been so base," she stammered, and he gave her a brief cold smile.

"No, dear wife, even *I* couldn't be base enough to take advantage of you whilst you slept. That *is* what you were trying to say, isn't it?"

Her fury at his condescension was made more marked by his accurate assumption. She struggled to sit up, ignoring the wild hammering at her temples, only to slide back quickly beneath the bedcovers as his gaze fell on her full white breasts. She clutched at the sheet to cover herself. In her confusion, Vincent's sardonic smile was an insult, as if to say he could easily overpower her if he wished, and she would be helpless beneath his lust, as a dutiful wife was bound to be.

"Could you not at least have helped me into my nightgown, since I presume it was you who removed all my clothes?"

"Would you have preferred a hotel maid to do

it, to witness your inebriated condition?" he said blandly.

Lydia glared at him. "And whose fault was that, may I ask! And you still haven't answered my question! Why couldn't you have made me decent in my nightgown?"

He looked at her steadily, the glint of exasperation in his eyes reminding her that here was a man who didn't suffer fools gladly, nor the petty pouting of flirtatious young women. Since Lydia considered herself to be neither, her anger was increased tenfold.

"I did," he said briefly. "Only to have you disgrace yourself all over it. I rinsed the worst of it off, and the garment is drying in the bathroom to save you embarrassment. Now, while you decide whether or not you're going to remain in bed all day and shock the hotel staff still further, to say nothing of missing our embarkation time, I shall go downstairs and order our breakfast."

He was so damned pompous! Lydia seethed, wishing she had something in her reach to hurl after him. But guiltily, she also had to appreciate all he had done for her, bringing her to bed and tidying her up after she had disgraced herself. Even if the champagne and its aftereffects had been all his fault, it took a rare man to bathe and tidy a woman, and apparently leave her to sleep off the effects of too much champagne in peace. To her shame, she remembered nothing of it at all.

But she heard the click of the door as he left the bedroom, and carefully, Lydia put her feet to

141

the floor, feeling the room swim for a moment. Then she determinedly walked toward the bathroom. The hotel was well-appointed, and she vaguely remembered Vincent telling her that the luxury of a bathroom in its most expensive suites was a recent addition.

She looked longingly at the painted rose-flowered tub in the heavily decorated room. She had forgotten that she was naked, until she suddenly caught sight of herself in the large angled mirror above the washbowl. Her hair was tangled and unkempt, lying loose against her bare shoulders. She blushed wildly at the sight of the dipping curves and hollows of her own body, the rosy-peaked breasts and the rich triangle of curling dark hair at her groin.

Without thinking, she touched herself there, remembering instantly the way Vincent had touched her. She cupped her breasts, remembering how he had cupped them, her eyes glazing slightly as if to conjure up the magic of Vincent's hands on her soft flesh. She realized she was panting slightly, wanting him with a suddenness that stunned her. Wanting him desperately to lie with her and make love to her, to master her . . . her limbs seemed to be turning to jelly, and a deep insistent throbbing in her loins was making her weak. . . .

Quickly she turned on the tap over the washbowl and saw the gush of water spurt out. Without bothering to insert the plug, she splashed the cold water quickly over her burning cheeks and let it trickle over her breasts, wondering almost fearfully just what devil was possessing her. She resisted the lure of the tub, telling herself there would be no time for such luxuries. She swathed herself in the large towel put at her disposal, before returning to the bedroom to hastily don her clothes for the day.

As if to deny the fact that Vincent Montagu had unleashed in her a sensual and passionate woman, she dressed in the plainest dress in her wardrobe, buttoned high into the neck and with bodice frills that partly disguised her voluptuous shape. By the time Vincent returned to the suite, she was sitting demurely by the window, her hair neatly coiffed, hands folded in her lap.

He glanced over her thoughtfully, as if seeing right through the reasons for her transformation.

"So the wanton gives way to the virgin queen," he said laconically, reading her perfectly correctly.

"I would prefer it if you didn't make that kind of remark," she whipped back. "It's indecent, and in any case I don't care to be described as either person."

For two pins she'd hurl an accusation at him here and now. If there was any doubt as to her identity, how much more was there in reality to his! She should denounce him here and now, before it was too late. Once she was on board the ship with him and en route to Kurnios, there would be no turning back. But she knew full well that it was already far too late. She was his wife in the eyes of the law, and she belonged to him even more spiritually and emotionally.

She got up from her window seat, her blue eyes blazing. Before she could think what he intended

143

to do, Vincent was striding across the room and snatching her up in his arms. His kiss was brutal on her mouth, bruising her lips. She fought to remain passive in his arms, as if to prove to herself as well as to him, that she could resist him whenever she chose. It was the most difficult thing she had ever tried to do.

"Your attempts at masquerading as the virgin queen do you little justice, my dear," he mocked her as he let her go. His fingers insolently caressed the peaks of her breasts that were straining against the soft blue fabric of her day dress. "However much your mind tells you to protest at your husband's kisses, your delicious body tells me otherwise."

"I find such remarks insulting," she said, almost weeping with rage and distress. "Why do you humiliate me so? Or was it your intention all along to find a bride for some devious reason of your own, knowing you would only despise the woman foolish enough to fall for your charms?"

"I could never despise you. And humiliating you is the last thing on my mind," Vincent said evenly. "If I've upset you unduly, then I apologize, Lydia."

He spoke with unquestionable sincerity. He was a mixture of tenderness and ruthlessness, and she never knew quite where she stood with him. Uncertain quite how to accept this apology, she resorted to more mundane matters.

"Perhaps you'd tell me at what time our ship departs," she muttered.

"Three hours from now. Breakfast will be arriv-

144

ing any minute, and once we've eaten, we'll see about leaving in good time for the docks. I want us settled in our cabin before she sails. How is the headache, by the way?"

Lydia gave a small start. She had almost forgotten the way she had woken that morning, and in the flurry of activity since then, the pain had diminished to a dull ache at the back of her neck.

"It's much better," she said.

"Good. I don't care to see you unwell," Vincent said, a remark that she found oddly endearing by its very simplicity. "Though I suggest you still take the powder in your tea, my love. It will also act as a sedative in case you fall victim to the *mal-de-mer.*"

"I doubt that I shall," she replied brusquely. "You forget that I've travelled to and from India several times, and I consider myself a very good sailor."

"I don't forget." He smiled at her. "The golden tint to your skin is testament to your life in warmer climes, and in case I ever omitted to tell you, it is far more attractive to me than that of your pale cousin. I sometimes wonder what perversity of fashion makes young women want to keep that unearthly pallor, and resist allowing the sun to warm their skins."

His compliment sent an even warmer color to her face.

"You hadn't forgotten to tell me," she murmured, remembering other times when he'd complimented her on her healthy appearance. "But I promise I won't disgrace you by falling prey to

145

mal-de-mer. And I really prefer not to take sedatives unless it's absolutely necessary. A powder in the daytime is one thing, and I'll do as you say this time, but I don't care to feel drugged at night, especially—"

She stopped, realizing she had been thinking aloud, and that he would surely think she was referring to all the nighttimes ahead that they would share so intimately. So she had, she thought guiltily, but she hadn't wanted him to realize it quite so obviously.

"I didn't mean to sound quite the way it did," she began in confusion. He stopped her with a laughing kiss, his voice teasing.

"Did you not? Then you disappoint me, my love. I had hoped it was my passion that was the reason you didn't care to be drugged at night. Your sweet responses gave me every reason to believe it was so."

His fingers curled leisurely around her breasts in a very proprietorial manner and Lydia knew that nothing in the world was going to restrain their ready reaction to him. Everything about him had the power to arouse her. A look, a touch, a caress . . . she shivered, feeling for a moment as if she were truly under a spell, and no longer in control of her own destiny.

"Have no fear, my darling," Vincent went on softly. "In time you'll come to accept that loving and giving are ours for the taking. There's no need for embarrassment in words or deeds. Don't tell me your Indian nurse didn't instill that in you."

146

"I'd already begun to believe it," Lydia said. "It's just that—"

"Just that you've never had a husband before," he finished lightly as she floundered. "Well, since I've never had a wife before, that means we're both on the brink of a new discovery, doesn't it?"

But that didn't mean he'd never had a woman before, the insidious thought ran through Lydia's mind. And she couldn't imagine a virile man like Vincent being totally celibate until now. A crazy, unreasoning stab of jealousy for all the women he'd known in his life before her, hit her between the eyes, as cruel as any headache.

"Vincent—" she began, and then a knock on the door stopped her. Vincent strode across to usher in the waiter with their breakfast trolley.

The man hovered about, checking that everything was to the couple's liking. It was clear to see that Lord Montagu commanded respect and good service, no matter where he went.

By the time he had given the man a coin for his services, Lydia was quelling her stab of jealousy. For there was no sense at all in being jealous of something that was past and that could never be changed. In any case, how could she ever have asked him? The humiliation if he'd admitted having many women before her would have been simply too much to bear.

They dined on kippers and toast. By the time the meal was finished, the tea and stomach-calming powder had done their work, and Lydia was feeling more like her usual self again.

"If you would care to repack our overnight

bags, my love, I shall go down and settle the hotel account, and arrange for a cab to take us to Tilbury Docks. Unless you prefer that I request a maid to do the packing for you?"

Lydia laughed at the absurdity of the query.

"Good heavens, no! I'm quite capable of placing clothes into bags, Vincent! I'm not entirely helpless, and I haven't been living the life of a lady in the Claremonts' house all these months."

"Well, you'll have no need to do any of the menial things once you reach Kurnios," he replied. "And then you will most certainly be living the life of a lady. But it's good to know I haven't married a helpless individual. I'll be back in ten minutes or so. Once we're on board ship we'll really be starting on the first part of our honeymoon."

He left the hotel room then, and Lydia felt a thrill of excitement run through her veins. Not just at the thought of sharing a honeymoon with Vincent, but with the thought that whatever the future held, this was an adventure. And she dearly loved adventure.

Life would have been so dull in her uncle's care, despite his dutiful intentions toward her. The times she had spent at Greystone Manor had already shown her what a strict regime his daughters underwent, and she thanked her stars she'd decided long ago to remain with the more liberal-minded Claremonts, where she had had space to breathe and be herself.

But if she was never meant to be a children's tutor, neither was she born to be a mere lodger in a milliner's house. She had been born the child of loving and adventurous parents with a style and flair all their own. And as the wife of the dashing Vincent Montagu, she would surely fulfill her potential once more. It was a facet of their relationship she hadn't even considered, until now. There was nothing conventional about Vincent, and unconsciously, she realized it was one of the things that had drawn her to him.

By the time he returned to the room, she was ready, her eyes bright, her face filled with anticipation at the thought of the voyage ahead. As if he recognized some change in her, he came and took her in his arms.

"You look different. And much more elated than when I left you. Has the headache completely gone?"

"Completely," she said. "And, Vincent . . ."

"What is it?" he asked, smiling down at her parted mouth.

"Oh, nothing."

"You can't stop there," he said relentlessly. "Don't bottle up your feelings from me, Lydia. I demand that we have no secrets between us."

She almost said that was rich, coming from him! But then, perhaps there were no secrets. As yet, she didn't know, and she dare not accuse him. She feared losing the magic.

"All right," she said shakily. "This might be a quite unnecessary and embarrassing thing to say to you, but I do thank you, Vincent, for the offer of marriage. And for allowing me to live out a different kind of dream in getting away from England and finding my new horizons."

The words just tumbled out. She hadn't meant to say any of them, but they wouldn't be halted. For a horrible moment she thought he might be insulted, as if he thought she was merely grasping at the chance to get away from England and her family.

"You don't need to thank me for anything," he said softly. "I should be the one to give thanks for finding you."

It was almost as good as saying that he loved her, Lydia thought weakly. The air seemed so charged with emotion that she was sure she was going to cry and blurt out that she loved him so much. As if he were aware of how tense they both were, he gave a teasing laugh.

"This must be a day to remember. My bride is admitting that she's grateful to me, so I must have done something right at last!"

"Am I usually so contrary then?" she said, a little uneasily, and taken aback at the comment.

"Only sometimes," he said, taking her clasped hands in his and kissing them both. "But it's no matter, and I've certainly no wish to dampen that bright spirit of yours. God preserve me from a wishy-washy wife!"

The pressure of his hands holding hers, took any sting from his words, and she felt oddly comforted. In any case, this was no day to be gloomy, and the elation was quickly returning to her senses. This was the start of a new life for them both.

They went downstairs to where the cab was already awaiting them, and Vincent helped her inside. As they went steadily toward Tilbury Docks and the ship, Lydia felt her spirits rise with every corner they turned. The chill in the air and the briny scents told them when they were nearing the docks. At last they were within sight of the jostling ships at the quayside, and her excitement ran amok.

"I never realized just how much I was looking forward to this," she breathed involuntarily. "I adore the sea air and the strange sense of isolation on board ship, no matter how many other passengers there are. It's that piquant feeling of freedom away from sight or sound of land that is so exhilarating to the senses. That feeling that you're in another world!"

Vincent laughed. "And I never realized how much of a gypsy I had married! Perhaps we should simply obtain a ship of our own and sail the world forever, just the two of us. What would you say to that?"

She looked at him candidly, unsure whether or not he was quite serious.

"I think we'd very soon get tired of each other's sole company. We'd probably find ourselves talking to the fishes."

But, for Lydia, the image of the two of them voyaging into the unknown like two intrepid sea-going discoverers of old was suddenly very sweet. She turned her face away so that he couldn't glimpse the emotions she was sure she betrayed. To Vincent, this was surely a game. He had needed a wife, and he had got what he wanted. Her need for him was as primeval as the moon's pull on the tides.

At last they were stepping aboard the ship that was to take them to Athens, where a smaller boat would take them on to Kurnios. The captain welcomed them, showing enough deference to Vincent to make Lydia well aware of his status, whether it was genuine or not. They were shown to their cabin, as luxurious as the ship could provide, and with one large bed in place of the expected two. She stared at it in surprise. To her knowledge, few ships provided marital beds. But she guessed that if Vincent Montagu had wanted to arrange this, then it would be done.

"Is it everything a bride could wish for?" Vincent said softly in her ear, then twisted her into his arms. He kissed her with far more gentleness than he'd done that morning in their hotel room.

"It's beautiful," she said sincerely.

There were two large portholes in the spacious cabin through which the midday sun was already high in the sky. The ship bobbed gently on the dockside swell, and she felt a strange sweet lethargy. It could have been attributed to acceptance, or fate, or preordained destiny. And with it came a need to be sure she hadn't been incredibly foolish in accepting a proposal of marriage from a man she hardly knew. Still enclosed in his arms, she spoke hesitantly.

"Vincent, everything will be all right, won't it? For us, I mean? My family wanted to be assured that I'll have no regrets about our marriage. But what about you? I know so little about you, while you know all there is to know about me."

152

His answer was a second kiss, as gentle as the first. As if knowing that this was always going to be the most effective way to stop her words, she thought fleetingly. And then she gave up fretting for the moment, surrendering to the sensuality of his kisses.

But kisses couldn't go on forever, and a marriage was made up of far more than intimate embraces, however ecstatic they might be. Lydia knew that, and even through the magic of Vincent's caresses, there was still a sensible corner of her mind that questioned.

"No one ever truly knows another person, my love," he said softly. "But that only makes the learning so delightful. There was no great mystery in my travelling to England, which I do on occasion. This time I had the luck to find a beautiful wife and take her back with me. And I promise you there'll be a fine old celebration on Kurnios when I present my bride to my friends."

He had a sure knack of deflecting her thoughts, she acknowledged. But mention of a celebration aroused a different kind of curiosity.

"A celebration? A party, you mean?"

She was patently skeptical, still imagining Kurnios as a bleak place where nothing happened, and even the few English folk who lived there virtually reverting back to nature. Vincent laughed at her words, moving away from her to answer the knock on the cabin door, and admitted the steward with their baggage.

"Why not?" he answered when the man had gone. "I don't know what you expect, Lydia, but

I've already told you I don't live in total isolation, and people will be eager to meet you. As for a social life, I admit the island is remote, but the people on it have mastered the sea, and there are always boats going to and fro between Kurnios and the mainland. The ladies, in particular, occasionally visit Athens for the fashions and to restore their wardrobes."

"I see!" These were the most detailed comments he had made about his island, Lydia thought. It was as if he'd wanted to keep it a closely guarded secret until she could finally see it all for herself.

"You never tell me anything about your life there," she persisted. "How many people live in your house? Or what kind of a house is it? Are there industries on the island?"

He gave a short laugh. "I deliberately didn't want to spoil your illusions, my sweet. I want you to see it all with fresh eyes, to draw your own conclusions. Can't it suffice that I refer to it as my paradise?"

She was in the mood to be contrary, as he'd so often described her.

"Sometimes I wonder if Kurnios really exists at all."

"Oh, it exists all right. And, as I've already indicated, there's quite a social life. You won't be short of friends."

"I won't have to learn to speak Greek, will I?"

"Not unless you want to," he said, taking her seriously. "Most of the islanders can speak our language to some degree, some far better than others. There is also a considerable number of

English people living there. Surely I've told you?"

If he had, she hardly remembered it, and in any case, she wanted to drag it out of him now.

"You know very well you've said precious little about Kurnios at all. It's no wonder my uncle wondered if you were planning to carry off his daughter to some fearful mythical land."

"And instead, I carried off his niece, and I assure you she'll find nothing but pleasure in my island," he retorted.

Somehow she couldn't think of a single answer to that.

"No more questions now," Vincent said briskly. "We'll soon be under way, and I'm sure you'd prefer to be up on deck to say goodbye to the shores of England, rather than through the portholes. It can be an emotional time, so it's often better to be jostled in the company of the other passengers than to mope alone."

But Lydia wasn't alone, nor was she intending to mope! England had been but a passing interlude, she thought, in some surprise. She felt no deep attachment to it, save that it was the land of her ancestors. Her real love had been India. It had been her world for so long that she had found it very hard to adapt to the damp chill of English winters. Even the warmth of the delicate English summers disappointed her, simply because they were still so pale in comparison to the exotic color and heat of India.

Leaning on the ship's rail, with Vincent's arm loosely around her shoulders as the ship slid gently out of Tilbury Dock, she gave an involuntary sigh. As Vincent heard it, his arm tightened around her.

"I promise you everything will be all right, Lydia. And if you wish, we'll come back to England for a visit to your family in a year or so."

She gave a rueful laugh. "I'm hardly going to be homesick for my English family! It wasn't for them that I'm sad, nor even for England. I was just wishing that things never had to change, that's all. I wish I could turn back the clock and find everything as it was before I left India, so that I never had to leave it at all!"

Her voice choked a little, and she swallowed. It was no time to be getting so maudlin, when she was on the brink of a new life. She couldn't understand why her feelings seemed to seesaw between excitement and gloom.

"Nothing ever stays the same, sweetheart. Everything changes. We're born, we grow old, and we die. It's what happens in between that counts. We all have to make the most of what time we have. I'm sure your parents would have wanted a full rich life for you. That's just what I intend to give you."

He spoke so seriously that Lydia turned her startled gaze on him, ignoring the other passengers all around them.

She ignored the panorama of the London landscape sliding past them, and was comforted by the clasp of Vincent's hand in hers.

"I do believe you really mean that," she murmured.

"Why should I not?" he said, amused. "Did you

156

think a marriage of convenience is so doomed to disaster?"

His words sent her spirits crashing at once. *A marriage of convenience!* She must never forget that this was exactly what her union with Vincent Montagu was. Her cousin Audine had left her with no doubt that Vincent had come seeking a wife, and while she had thought she was to be the one, she had been ready enough to accept the idea. Once Lydia had taken her place in Vincent's plans, Audine had been scathing about the kind of woman who married on a whim, and with high hopes of a fortune. In her secret heart, Lydia still dreamed that this could be a marriage for love. But with his own words, Vincent had made it plain he saw it in a far less romantic light.

For a cold-blooded man, Lydia thought bitterly, even the act of love, and the words of love, meant less than nothing.

"Why did you marry me, Vincent?" she blurted out.

He glanced about, as if to ensure that people around them shouldn't hear such a blatant query in public. But no one was bothering about them right now. Most were too busy watching the hazy outline of England fast disappearing as the ship moved out into the middle of the English Channel and began its voyage.

"You can hardly expect me to answer that adequately in public," he said teasingly. "But as well as the obvious, perhaps for a kind of continuity. Every man wants a son, and you would seem to fit the requirements of my son's mother admirably.

You have beauty and brains, far more than your insipid cousin, and you strike a chord in me that I find impossible to resist. Our children will be well blessed, I think."

She heard little of the end of his words, being too incensed by the first part. Was she being brought to Kurnios as some kind of breeding mare! As she opened her mouth to speak angrily, he caught her to him, his dark eyes alive with mirth at her obvious outrage.

"Oh Lydia, I thought you more capable of hiding the expression in those beautiful blue eyes! I've seen the way you squash your cousins with that special look you give them. But right now anyone can see how furious you are, and it was never my intention to offend! It was a compliment, you ninny!"

"Expecting me to be a brood mare was a compliment?" she said baldly, voicing what was in her head. Several ladies nearby glanced their way, and she bit her lip, angry that she had been goaded into being so crude in public.

Vincent stood behind her, his arms around her now, as if to allow her to watch the coastline more clearly, while he protected her from the wind. His voice was right in her ear.

"Hush, love. I think this is a conversation best kept for the privacy of our cabin, though I doubt that I shall be in the mood for talking once we retire for the night. I shall have far more interesting things on my mind, and so will you."

Lydia shivered at the meaning in his voice. She could feel the strength of his body, warming her, and the erotic memories of their times together were scattering her resolutions to confront him. This *was* her honeymoon, she thought weakly, and whatever confrontations there had to be could surely wait.

He was her husband, and he wanted her. Even standing here on the gently rolling ship, his arms enfolding her, she could feel the evidence of that wanting. She'd be a fool to throw away the pleasures that this voyage would bring. She argued vainly with her conscience, and her conscience lost.

Later, with the evening darkness settling all around the ship, Lydia surrendered to her destiny. Vincent undressed her slowly, savoring every instant, and kissed each new area of bare flesh that was exposed to him. Lydia was in the thrall of excitement as he touched and caressed, aroused and seduced. He never failed to give her exquisite pleasure, she thought faintly. And when the moment of his release came, she couldn't have said who clung to the other most desperately. As though the very life source was wrung out of him. As though she yearned to receive it.

"No matter how unconventional our beginning, or what the future might hold, my lovely Lydia, we always have this," he murmured into the wanton spread of her hair when they finally lay apart, all passion spent.

She felt the soft slow trickle of tears on her cheek. Passion was wonderful, powerful, even awe-

some, but was it enough to bind two people together for a lifetime? Lydia was brutally aware of
the fact that Vincent had never said he loved her.
He lusted for her, but that wasn't the same thing.
And because she was too afraid of his answer, she
couldn't bring herself to ask him outright. For the
moment she must let things remain as they were,
having his protection and his name — whatever that
was. She shivered at that thought.

"Are you cold?" he asked, pulling the covers
more securely around their naked bodies. Lydia
shook her head.

"Not cold. Just apprehensive of the future," she
said in all honesty.

"There's no cause to be apprehensive, since the
future's what we make of it, Lydia. I wager your
old Indian nurse told you otherwise," he said. "I've
heard about these people and their astrologers and
how they lay great store by what's written in the
stars."

"Why should we scoff at such things?" Tired as
she was, she was suddenly ready to argue. Safe in
his arms, cocooned in their cabin, they could have
been on another planet entirely. Who was to say
whether things beyond their knowledge of earth or
heaven decreed anyone's future?

"Are you telling me you really believe in such
things, my quaint little wife?" he said, patently
amused.

"Don't patronize me, Vincent!" she was stung
into replying. "I've heard predictions in the past
that have been amazingly accurate, and I don't
discount anything. I doubt that anyone brought up

160

in India ever could."

"And just what was predicted for you?"

He spoke so softly she could barely hear him. His voice was seductive, waiting, just as if he knew. She felt transported back in time and distance to her old room in the white-painted bungalow outside Delhi. She could hear Nadima's singsong voice in her head.

"You will travel far, my little one, for India is not your final destiny. Fate may play games with you before you realize your true dreams."

And she had scoffed at the old woman, confident in her comfortable security.

"Those words could apply to anyone, Nadima! And I assure you I'm never going to leave India, or Mama and Papa, or you!"

But Nadima had looked at her pityingly, as if she was a foolish young thing to think she could defy the fates. And Lydia had left them all, or had them taken away from her. . . .

"I don't want to talk about it any more," she said crossly to this man who was now her husband, and for whom fate had surely never intended her. He had been intended for Audine, perhaps.

"Neither do I," Vincent said, his arms enfolding her more closely. "We should both try to sleep now, for we have far to travel."

She started, hearing the echo of Nadima's prediction in his words, and wishing these dark images didn't keep filling her mind. Desperately, she tried to stop worrying about anything and let the blackness of sleep envelop her.

161

The voyage was a singularly uneventful one. Days were spent watching the ocean until they were mesmerized by its spell, or chatting with fellow passengers who were clearly enchanted by the handsome picture they made. They were invited to dine with their travelling companions and sometimes the captain. On the evening they were to tie up on the coast of Spain for a night ashore, Lydia became the toast of the ship in one of the spectacular Indian silk gowns she had never worn before.

It was a riot of color, rich scarlet blending through all the colors into palest lemon, and edged with gold, almost in the style of a sari, but with the conventional European tight waist and billowing skirt. The fabric alone made it a sensational garment, and it turned heads wherever Lydia went.

"You look like an Indian princess," Vincent murmured when he first saw her in it. "I hardly know you."

"I'm still the same," she said decisively. "You're the one I don't know."

The words were blurted out before she could stop them, and he stroked her cheek for a moment.

"I wonder why you feel obliged to say such things, when you know me now as intimately as any woman ever knew a man?"

Lydia blushed. "I didn't mean in that way! I meant—"

It was on the tip of her tongue to say exactly what she did mean, that Edwin Claremont had described Lord Vincent Montagu as an elderly recluse, and her virile husband was nothing at all like that! But the moment she denounced him, perhaps discovering that he was a charlatan, she would lose him. Rightly or wrongly, it was what her sixth sense was telling her, and she simply couldn't risk that.

"My poor darling. Despite your upbringing, there's still a strong sense of the English in you, isn't there? I presume you feel you've missed that interminable tradition of wooing before being rushed into marriage, is that it?"

"That must be it," she muttered, knowing she was being weak, backing down, and unable to stop herself.

"Then just for tonight we'll pretend we're not married, and begin the wooing process all over again. We're all scheduled to go to a hotel for some Spanish entertainment when we disembark, and some of the passengers have chosen to remain there instead of going back to the ship tonight. I thought we would do the same, but I shall ask for separate rooms, and say good night at your door. How will that suit your prudish little mind?"

She gaped at him, unsure if he was teasing or not. She was suspicious of everything he did, she thought miserably. This was no way to begin a marriage. Her silence went on too long, and Vincent shrugged.

"So be it," he said shortly. "For this one night, at least, you may preserve your chastity."

"It's a bit late for that, isn't it?" she was stung into replying, and was immediately hot with embarrassment at her own blatant words.

Vincent smiled slightly. "Physically, yes. But in a European's eyes a bartered wife can remain mentally chaste however long she's married. It's not what a man looks for in his life's partner."

Lydia gasped. A *bartered* wife! Is that how he saw her? Bought and paid for, without having the benefit of a normal courtship? However much she might have accepted such things in India, when they were applied to herself, she was completely mortified.

"Have I disappointed you so badly then?" she stuttered, hardly able to speak.

She didn't know how they had got into this argument. She only knew she felt bitterly hurt at his sudden coldness, and increasingly fearful that she had jumped into a situation with a man she didn't really know.

He spoke more gently. "You know you have not. But I'm aware that everything went too fast for you, and I'm offering you the chance to take things more slowly. On board ship, we're bound to be in close contact, but in the Spanish hotel, we can behave in a more civilized fashion. It will help to calm your nerves."

Lydia wanted to scream at him that she didn't want her nerves calmed! The only time she felt at one with him was when the intimacy of lovemaking removed all the barriers of strangeness and mistrust. But she wouldn't beg for his favors! She nodded fervently.

164

"I agree. A more civilized relationship would be very acceptable."

And if he thought her pointed words meant she abhorred the animal lust with which he made love to her, she wouldn't disillusion him. Even though she felt the loss of his closeness as keenly as if he had cut her with a knife.

Chapter Seven

As if in defiance of Vincent's decreed celibacy on their sortie to the Spanish mainland, Lydia chose one of the exotic gowns of shimmering Indian silk to wear that evening. They had disembarked early in the morning with the rest of the passengers going ashore, to a brilliant blue sky and welcome Mediterranean sun. They were taken by specially arranged carriages to the hotel high in the hills, travelling up tortuous mountain roads in a dry and dusty atmosphere. While many of the English passengers were distressed by the heat, both Lydia and Vincent gloried in it, easily adapting to it.

Their baggage was stowed behind them in the carriage they shared with an older couple for the overland journey. In Lydia's carrying bag was the seductively sensual gown in shades that merged from softest green to brilliant gold, carefully folded between sheets of soft tissue paper. Vincent had never seen it yet, nor many of the similar garments that Lydia adored so much. Wearing them, she felt halfway between one culture and the next, with past and present intertwining. Since that was also the way she felt in her sojourn to Kurnios, it seemed an apt choice of evening wear.

"I don't believe we've met before," the portly gentleman opposite them said. "Our name is Fitzwarren, and we're from Berkshire, travelling to Athens."

Lydia smiled at the friendly couple. Until now, she and Vincent hadn't mixed with many of the passengers at great length, but now she was glad to have these others to keep her mind off the uneasy relationship with her husband. She heard him give their names abruptly, and knew he wasn't so pleased.

It could be, of course, because he was ever alert that someone might know of the real Lord Vincent Montagu, she thought suddenly. However much she tried, she still couldn't shake off the nagging doubts, only kept at bay by the memory of the friend greeting him so naturally when they had all been out to dinner that evening in Bath. How long ago it all seemed now . . .

"My wife, Lady Montagu," she heard him say gravely, and she gave a little start, still taken by surprise when addressed in that way. She gave the couple a warm smile, seeing the sudden reaction on the lady's part at realizing that their companions were titled.

"Are you doing the Grand Tour, Mrs. Fitzwarren?" she asked to put her at ease.

The lady sounded regretful. "Not in the accepted sense, unfortunately. We had intended going to the subcontinent, but Athens is as far south as we go. We intend to travel back overland through Germany and France."

"I'm sure that will be very pleasant. They say the Black Forest and the wonderful castles in Germany are very romantic. But you would have loved India," Lydia said, not bothering to hide the dreaminess in her voice.

"Have you been there, Lady Montagu?" the other woman said, clearly thinking Lydia was very young to have travelled so extensively.

Vincent answered before she could. "My wife was brought up in India, Ma'am. It was only when her parents died that she was obliged to return to England to live with family connections."

Lydia glared at him. What right did he have to tell her life story to these people? She would probably have done so herself without much invitation, but it irritated her that Vincent did it so casually. She sensed that he did it to end the conversation, but she had been in a perverse mood ever since he'd decreed that they would stay in separate rooms this night. She didn't let it rest there.

"I'm English by birth, of course," she said, smiling at the other lady. "But I've lived most of my life in India, and now I'm going to live in an even more remote destination."

"Then this isn't just a tour for you?" Mrs. Fitzwarren said, clearly enchanted, and wanting to know more.

"Oh no. I'm going to my husband's home on Kurnios."

"And where might that be, Lady Montagu?"

The gentleman had joined in the discussion with his wife now. The horse-drawn convoy of carriages twisted and turned around the mountain roads, and the conversation was clearly keeping their minds off the barren precipices on either side of them, and the plunging valleys far below.

"It's a very small Greek island that's thankfully not on the tourist itinerary, nor ever likely to be," Vincent told them briefly in a tone that Lydia considered very bad manners.

She was all too aware of how tense he was. She could feel it in the rigidity of his arm next to hers in the swaying carriage. The other couple could easily have taken offense at this apparent snubbing, but obviously neither saw the irony in his words and Mrs. Fitzwarren spoke teasingly.

"Ah, I see, Lord Montagu! You've found your own island paradise and want to keep it all to yourself! Am I right?"

He smiled faintly. "I'm very much afraid you are, Ma'am."

"Then we won't pry any more," the lady said. "I declare this carriage is in danger of giving me the *mal-de-mer* more violently than the ship! I hope it won't be too much longer before we reach the hotel."

Thankfully for them all, it wasn't much longer. The road levelled out considerably before they reached a plateau on which a small town of whitewashed houses and cobbled streets unexpectedly thrived. They could see the massive circle of the bullring on a nearby hill. The center of the town itself was dominated by an enormous church in the town square. The town was built on either side of a deep ravine that had once kept out marauding invaders, their driver yelled back to them.

"And now we're the invaders," Mrs. Fitzwarren commented. "But better tourists than a bloodthirsty army, wouldn't you say so, Lord Montagu?"

"I would indeed," Vincent said gravely, as impervious to her gentle barbs as she had been to his.

The long trail of carriages drew up at the two hotels the town boasted. Rioja was obviously part of the tourist itinerary already, Lydia thought cynically, seeing the posters on every possible background advertising the bullfight tomorrow afternoon. The passengers got out stiffly, and Lydia shook out the folds of her travelling skirt, longing for a bath and some refreshment.

She followed Vincent into the hotel, and was pleasantly surprised to find it cool and fragrant. The floors were tiled instead of being carpeted, the walls were white-painted and hung with wrought iron containers filled with brilliant red and purple flowers. The whole interior was spacious and airy. Vincent signed the register for them both, and in a very little while they were shown into a suite of rooms.

"It's better this way than arousing curiosity," he told her when the man had brought their baggage and left them. "But there are two bedrooms, so we've no need to change our plans."

It was on the tip of Lydia's tongue to say it was his plan, not hers. She managed not to say it, but moved to the long open windows and the small balcony outside, again embellished with tubs of the brilliant Mediterranean flowers. The inside walls of the rooms were again white-painted in a kind of rough stippled look, in an authentic Spanish manner, and it took nothing away from the luxury of the furnishings. The hotel was placed in an advantageous position, high above the surrounding hills and the cubelike houses of the town. It was a fabulous view, and Lydia exclaimed with delight at the panorama spread out before her.

"It's good you're not afraid of heights," Vincent observed dryly, behind her.

"Why do you say that? We're only here for two nights, aren't we? And the mountain roads didn't frighten me unduly—"

"I'm glad of that, because they're a foretaste of what you'll find on Kurnios. The only similarity to India will be the hot climate, though of course we don't have India's steaminess."

"Do you realize that's practically the first real information you've given me about the place, Vincent? I begin to believe it's just as Mrs. Fitzwarren said. You've found your island paradise, and you don't want to share it with anybody!"

She was half-teasing, half-belligerent, but her breath caught in her throat at the look he gave her, deep and penetrating and enigmatic.

"But I'm going to share it with you, and that will be enough for me."

She felt the prickle of tears in her eyes as he turned away and began investigating the various rooms in their suite. Sometimes he could be so terse that he unnerved her, and at others so gentle she felt completely at one with him. Even if he didn't always mean the words in the way she'd prefer to interpret them. She wondered why it couldn't always be that way. Why did she have to have these doubts and anxieties, instead of just accepting things as they were? Nadima would have told her not to fight against fate. She should flow with the tides, to be carried along on the breeze, and to believe in the ultimate goodness of karma.

"Are you feeling quite well?" Vincent's voice broke into her dreaming thoughts.

She unconsciously clasped her hands together, and stared him out.

"Who are you, Vincent?"

If she had expected to get a guilty reaction from him, she was disappointed. He gave a short laugh.

"What an absurd question. I'm your husband, my dear. Have you forgotten our wedding vows so quickly? I'm the man you promised to love, honor and obey until death do us part."

Did his words have an ominous ring to them? Was there a warning in that last phrase, so beautiful in the correct context of the wedding service, so lethal in another interpretation?

Still mesmerized by his returning stare, he came to her and took her in his arms, and his voice was more gentle.

"Lydia, my darling, I've told you we'll take things more slowly. For tonight at least, we'll be as we were before we made our vows. I'll be as attentive as an ardent suitor who knows he hasn't a hope of holding the girl he loves in his arms all night. We'll pretend we're still at the beginning, still getting to know one another, by decorously parting company at the bedroom door."

She was certain he didn't mean to imply that she was the girl he loved. They were just words, platitudes, as he sought to calm her. She wondered why he bothered. She was his wife, and he had every right to storm down her door if he wished.

But to Lydia's sensitive nerves, it seemed he didn't wish it enough. He was content to carry out this charade without ever asking if she wished it, too. And she was still woman enough not to go to him. The man always had to make the first move. With an effort she tried to push old Nadima's whispering words out of her mind.

"Nothing between a man and a woman who love, is wrong. For the man to make the first move is natural, but for the woman who is sure of her man to do so is to awaken an exquisite sensuality between them. It is not only a woman who needs the caresses of a lover. Remember this, my young one . . ."

Lydia remembered it now. But such intimacy would only seem to apply to a woman who was sure of her man, and as yet she was totally unsure of Vincent Montagu.

He moved away from her, brisk now.

"I suggest we each take a bath and a rest before dinner this evening. The entertainment promises to be excellent, and if you've never seen Andalusian Gypsy dancing before, you're in for a wonderful evening."

"I have not," she murmured, presuming that

they were to go to their separate bedrooms now, with the bathroom linking them. What a farce their marriage was becoming.

"Tomorrow morning we will explore the town, and in the afternoon we will go to the bullfight," he went on. At this, Lydia flinched visibly.

"I don't think so!" she said quickly. "I've no wish to see the wretched animals killed in such a humiliating fashion."

"You know what happens then?"

"I've heard of it," she nodded. "The so-called brave *matadors* play with the bull, while the poor thing is stuck with lances until it's so weakened it offers no resistance before it's finally killed. It's barbaric."

"But a national sport, and as such, we will not offend our Spanish hosts by not attending," he said calmly.

"You may go, but I will not."

"And as the wife who promised to obey me, I say that you will." His voice was ruthless now, as if this was of vital importance to him. Lydia couldn't see why it should be, but other than feigning illness, which her pride wouldn't let her do, she couldn't see how she could get out of the occasion.

"Very well. I'll come, but I don't have to watch, nor to acknowledge what's happening. You might control my movements, but you can't control my mind."

He gave a brief nod and strode away to his bedroom, closing the door with quiet deliberation behind him. It was impossible to judge what his feelings were at her words. Like her, his thoughts were his own, and she gave up worrying and fretting, and turned instead to her bedroom and the luxurious invitation of the tub.

There had been a time when she would have expected Vincent to come to her, revelling in the pleasure of attending her, but she knew that wouldn't happen today. Somehow, they seemed to be drifting ever further apart, and they hadn't even reached their island yet. It was a chilling thought.

Lydia decided against the Indian garment for the evening. It just wouldn't feel right, with all the growing hostility between herself and Vincent, and she chose to keep it for a less turbulent time. Instead she wore a soft blue dress, demure enough for an English lady, but caressing to her curves and low enough in the neck for her soft golden skin to be the envy of many a dowager Englishwoman or swarthier Spanish maid. Against her throat lay the seductive creaminess of a single rope of pearls, matched by the pearl drops in her ears.

By the time they went downstairs to the hotel dining room, they appeared to be a glowing, attractive young couple, who turned heads wherever they went. Against the fussiness of some of the older women and their escorts that evening, the Montagus were strikingly understated. Vincent, in dark clothes and white shirt that complemented his bronze skin and dark eyes; and Lydia, the

175

perfect English rose with the alluring honeyed skin.

"You look quite stunning, my dear young lady," the elderly Mr. Fitzwarren said gallantly when they first encountered them. Lydia heard Vincent's little sigh as he realized they were to be stuck with the other couple for the rest of their stay in Rioja, but Lydia didn't object to their company. It was better than enduring the prickliness that seemed the only hallmark of the relationship between herself and Vincent right now.

"You do indeed, Lady Montagu," his wife exclaimed, unconsciously patting her own elaborate grey coiffure and openly admiring Lydia's glossy dark hair.

"Thank you," Lydia said, smiling at the frankness of these two. They reminded her of the Claremonts, which made her warm to them all the more. She wondered briefly how the milliner and his wife were faring in their new establishment, and felt a brief pang for yet another life she had left. She was something of a nomad, wondering with a kind of fatality just where her final home was to be.

"Wherever you've gone, come back to me, Lydia," she heard Vincent say softly. She felt his hand close over hers, and realized her vision had blurred for a moment, and she must have been staring into space. The warmth of his hand seeped into her.

"I'm right here," she said softly.

But she couldn't bear to look at him for long, seeing the beginning and end of all her dreams in his eyes. What had gone so wrong between them? She was bewildered and upset, and if she appeared to be serene and well-adjusted, it was all due to Nadima's teachings to maintain calm thoughts at all costs. This would help overcome any trauma, no matter how great.

She hardly noticed what she ate or drank, although the tastes were quite new to her, and the food was well spiced and heavily oil-based. But she was well used to exotic flavors, and although Mrs. Fitzwarren grimaced at some of the dishes, Lydia ate it all without question.

"Your travelling has given you a strong stomach, Lady Montagu," the other woman observed. "I fear my digestion will be complaining very soon if I take more than small quantities."

"That's the correct thing to do," Vincent told her. "Little and often is a good rule when travelling abroad, and never to overload the stomach with strange tastes."

"Remember that, my dear," her husband said sternly. "You don't want to be ill on these few days in Spain, and you'll need a strong stomach for tomorrow afternoon."

"You're going to the bullfight then?" Lydia asked.

"Good Lord yes, begging your pardon, Lady Montagu," he went on enthusiastically. "We wouldn't dream of missing it! It will be something to tell our grandchildren when we go home, and we've promised to take them a programme to prove we saw it."

And if Lydia had hoped to provoke a sympathetic glance from Mrs. Fitzwarren, she was disappointed. For all the lady's delicate digestion, she was obviously as keen to see the bullfight as her husband. Was it only Lydia who viewed the whole prospect as barbaric and distasteful, akin in violence to the hideous cockfighting outlawed in England now? There was just no accounting for peoples' tastes.

The large semicircle of tiled floor in front of the diners was where the dancers would perform. Excitement grew as the meal came to an end, and the waiters were flurrying about, removing dishes and cutlery for what was evidently an important part of the evening. The two days' stay in the Rioja hotel was part of the ship's regular itinerary for British visitors en route to Athens, and the Spanish dancing was very much a cultural occasion. Lydia had never seen it before, and was totally unprepared for the proud elegance and precision that followed.

There were four young women and two men. That in itself was a surprise. Somehow she had not expected to see men dressed in extremely tight black trousers that hugged every part of their figures, the white shirts topped by figure-hugging black waistcoats, their feet gleaming with shoes that seemed to have a life of their own as they tapped relentlessly on the tiled floor. Lydia was completely fascinated by them as they twirled and postured with hands clapping high above their heads, their taut bodies rapturously embracing the music that seemed to be almost a part of them.

178

And then the girls took their places. They wore exotic, low-necked dresses with flounced red skirts, with wildly clattering castanets on their fingers. Their long black hair bounced with health on their bare shoulders, and each wore a brilliant red rose tucked behind one ear. Their feet were as full of rhythm and fire as that of the male dancers, and the entire audience was captivated by them.

By the time the performance was at an end, Lydia was leaning forward in her seat, almost unaware at how fast she was breathing from the sensual excitement the dancing was generating. As a finale, the dancers split up from their tight formation in the semicircle, and came around the audience, threading their way through the tables, still tapping their feet to the music. Somehow it was impossible to resist joining in, the British visitors applauded and swayed to the music. As they passed, the dancers tossed their roses at a gentleman of their choice, to the amusement of the onlookers.

As one of the beautiful girls reached their table, Lydia saw her look deep into Vincent's eyes; her red, pouting lips smiling a blatant invitation, her dark eyes flashing, her voluptuous breasts heaving with the exertion of the dance. She pulled the rose out of her hair and threw it into his lap, then with a swiftness that took everyone by surprise, she bent forward and kissed him full on the mouth. Then she twirled away to roars of laughter and applause.

"My word, Lord Montagu, you charmed that one all right," Fitzwarren chuckled. "Would that

I'd been thirty years younger!"

"Oh, you mustn't take it seriously, sir," Vincent said with a smile. "I assure you it's all part of the act. These dancers are real artistes, and they're experts at knowing how to reach an audience's heart. The next time they perform, some other fortunate gentleman will be getting the favors."

Not until then did he glance toward Lydia, who had been sitting, stunned and silent, at the dancer's blatant kiss. It was madness to feel such keen jealousy rip through her, but she felt it, and still did. He was her man, she thought, with a quite irrational primitive feeling of possession, and no other girl was permitted to touch him in any way.

"Perhaps I should have warned you, darling," he said lightly, seeing her frozen look.

She forced a laugh to her lips. "Good heavens, it's of no matter to me," she said, as carelessly as she could, considering the way she was seething inside. "I'm not foolish enough to feel jealous of such a person."

As soon as she had spoken, she felt the deep color stain her cheeks. She had sounded appallingly snobbish, and if the Fitzwarrens didn't notice it, Vincent certainly did. His stare was as insulting as her own words had been.

"It can be very foolish indeed to be so patronizing when one is a guest in another country," he said quietly. "You of all people should know that. Though from all that I've heard, the British in India always thought themselves a very superior race."

Lydia was aware of the older couple glancing at one another now, as if realizing that all was not quite right between their companions. Knowing that she had better back down, at least for the moment, if she didn't want this evening to end in a highly embarrassing scene, Lydia gave an acquiescent sigh.

"You're right, of course, darling. It's an unfortunate trait we all have to watch very carefully. And no one could deny that the Spanish Gypsy dancing is of the very highest quality. I feel privileged to have seen it. Don't you, Mrs. Fitzwarren?"

She turned to the other lady, not wanting to linger on Vincent's sardonic look at her endearment. It was the first time she had ever called him darling, though it hadn't been said with any loving intent, and they both knew it.

"I do indeed, Lady Montagu. Though I confess it makes me weak even to think of all that energy."

Lydia could see that the lady was thankful the awkward moment had passed. Lydia was even more thankful when the evening came to an end, and they could retire to their separate rooms. They had been silent all the way upstairs to their suite, and hardly looking at Vincent now, she said good night quite coolly, and made to walk past him into her designated bedroom. He caught at her arm.

"I trust that your little show of pomposity wasn't a true indication of your character, Lydia. Have you been playing me false all this time?"

She caught her breath between her teeth. Any

softening of her attitude and a vain hope that this silly farce of separate bedrooms would end when they returned to their suite, vanished immediately.

"How dare you ask such a thing of me!" she spluttered. "I have not played anybody false! I assure you *I've* kept nothing hidden from *you!*"

If she hoped to goad him into betraying some unease at her words, she was unlucky. He spoke coldly. "Then please remember that we're the foreigners here, and that the Spaniards are our hosts. Remember too, that when we reach Kurnios, the islanders are to be accorded every civility."

She bridled at the very idea that he thought she could behave in any other way. She was never normally rude to people, or scathing about other nationalities. She knew very well it had been searing jealousy at the sexual invitation from the Spanish dancer that had made her speak the way she did. But that was something she was never going to admit, especially to this hard-faced man with whom she didn't have the remotest wish to consort at that moment.

"I promise I shan't let you down," she said icily. "Now, if you will please let me go, I'm tired and I want to go to bed."

He released her at once, and strode away from her. Lydia turned on her heel and went into her own room, totally unable to resist slamming the door behind her. Only then did the sting of salt tears run down her face.

"I *hate* him," she raged at the four walls, and then, less forcefully, "I hate him."

She wilted a little, knowing it wasn't strictly true. She hated the feeling of being manipulated, of letting herself be bundled into this marriage before she had time to think. She was the foolish one, and how he must be crowing to think he could win her over so easily. It was herself she hated, for being so weak, when she had always thought herself so strong.

But it was even more foolish to stand here complaining at her lot. Swiftly, Lydia undressed and lay down in the unfamiliar bed. The night sounds of revellers had long since ended, and only the crickets and the whispering of the soft night wind in the trees outside disturbed the silence. She closed her eyes tightly and willed sleep to come, trying to forget that Vincent was so near, and yet so desperately far away.

They enjoyed a walking tour of the town the next morning with the Fitzwarrens. Far from resenting their company now, Lydia was glad of it, and she suspected Vincent felt the same. It gave them both breathing space, after the unpleasantness of the previous night. Lydia sensed that each of them was set on pretending it had never happened, and the Fitzwarrens probably thought they had imagined the sudden antipathy of the young couple last night.

"I particularly want to explore the ancient church," Mrs. Fitzwarren announced. "But if you two young things prefer to go elsewhere—"

"Oh no, I want to see it, too," Lydia said quickly, and Vincent echoed her sentiments at once. It wasn't that she didn't want to be alone with him, but being in the others' company certainly made the transition from anger to serenity somewhat easier. Besides, ancient churches held a strange fascination for her.

"I like to imagine how many feet have trodden these floors," she said in a suitably hushed voice, once they were inside its vast musty interior. "It always intrigues me how huge these churches are for such tiny villages, yet they must have been built for hundreds of people. How often has it been used for sanctuary, I wonder? How many people have just come in here for strength and to absorb the peace of the atmosphere? How many have found solace and comfort for their ills?"

"My word, but I never realized what a deep thinker you have for a wife, Lord Montagu!" Mrs. Fitzwarren said admiringly.

"My wife's philosophies probably stem from her years of living in India, where everything in life is questioned, and possible explanations are sought for everything under the sun," Vincent told her quietly.

For a moment Lydia wondered if he was mocking her, but she could detect nothing untoward in his voice. And what he said was true, although she had never defined it so accurately before. The old astrologers and thinkers did question everything, and those seeking knowledge paid handsomely for their services, whether they were rogues or not.

The scent of incense was almost overpowering in the church. Although she was not of this particular faith, Lydia felt a strong urge to light a candle, to place alongside the endless rows of others. It gave her an odd sense of companionship with all those who had gone before her to do so. She cared nothing for the thoughts of those with her as she lit her candle and left it wavering in the small breeze from the great wooden door.

But it was good to be outside again and into the clear air of the mountain region. One of the town's nearby attractions was a deep gorge in the mountains that had long given the town its impregnability against invaders. After they had driven the short distance in a hired carriage to view it from the dizzying height above, the ladies clung to their menfolk gladly.

"I never thought I should be grateful to a mere cleft in a rock," Vincent said in dry amusement.

Lydia looked at him. "Grateful?"

"For the pleasure of having you cling to me," he said softly so that the others wouldn't hear. "I'm assured that it's quite safe for us to stand here, but please don't let that deter you from your dependence on me, my darling."

She might have shrugged away from him then, but he was holding her too tightly. It was very pleasant to stand in the sunlight with his arms about her, listening to their carriage-driver act as a guide and recount the various times the townspeople had fought off their enemies. Most of the invaders had fallen to their deaths in the depths of the gorge, he finished with great relish. Lydia shuddered, and felt Vincent's arms tighten around her.

"Don't fight me, Lydia," he breathed into her ear. "You and I have too much life ahead of us to waste it in futile arguments."

She wasn't sure how she would have answered that, had not Mrs. Fitzwarren declared she couldn't remain here for one more minute, because the blood was rushing to her head and she felt positively faint. She only knew she didn't want to fight with him either, and she allowed herself to be led back to the carriage, where the driver was clearly ready to be their escort for however long they wished.

"We should see the bullring next," Fitzwarren said suddenly.

"Ah yes, for the *corrida!*" the driver said, smiling widely. "The ladies and gentlemen wish me to get them tickets for this afternoon's sport?"

"No, thank you," Lydia said quickly.

"Oh, but we must go! I thought it had already been decided," Mrs. Fitzwarren said excitedly. "Lady Montagu, dear, you truly shouldn't miss the spectacle."

"Of course we shall go," Vincent said. "If you dislike a thing, it's always best to face it head-on, to rid yourself of your fear. Lydia can always close her eyes if necessary, but I doubt that she'll want to miss any of it when the time comes."

Which just proved to her how little they knew of one another, she thought, as her aversion to the so-called "sport" threatened to send the bile to her mouth. But as Vincent looked at her steadily, she tilted her chin, and agreed to whatever they all wished to do.

186

For now, they merely drove around the huge circumference of the bullring, and listened to their driver's enthusiastic snippets of information about the brave *matadors* and their various injuries. Lydia was already wishing she was feeble enough to invent some indisposition by the time they returned to their hotel, but her pride simply refused to let her do so. She gritted her teeth, knowing she was going to see this through.

But all too soon, it seemed to her, the traditional time of five o'clock in the afternoon came around. By then, they were all seated in one of the rows of tiered seats at the *plaza de toros*. It was packed with spectators now, so that there was little chance of her getting out, even if she had wanted to.

They and the Fitzwarrens were seated on the side marked *el sombra*, which was thankfully the shady side, for the brilliance of the afternoon sun would have dazzled the eyes and burned the skin. Even so, Lydia would almost have risked the burning skin for the chance to have her sight blurred from all that was about to happen in front of her in the sawdust-covered ring below.

As it was, before they left the hotel to come here, she had seen in the bedroom mirror that her face was much paler than usual. She was truly dreading this occasion, and Vincent had finally seen how distressed she was.

"I'm sorry, love. I hadn't realized. If you want to remain here and rest, I shall quite understand. I've a curiosity to see the entertainment myself, so you'll forgive me if I accompany the Fitzwarrens."

"It's all right. I don't want to stay here alone," she said blandly. And since he obviously didn't want to remain with her. . . .

So they went to the bullring, and the *matadors* entered the arena, to the wild roars and cheering adulation of the vast crowd that must have come from miles around, to greet their heroes.

"It will not last very long," Vincent whispered in her ear, in what she saw as a gesture to her unusual pallor. "Concentrate on the spectacle at first, and then on the bravery of the *matadors*, and try to ignore the rest."

It was easier said than done, though Lydia couldn't deny there was a kind of fascination at the strutting parade of the *matadors* in their tight-fitting garb, encrusted with red and gold and silver that gleamed in the sunlight. They were a proud race, she acknowledged, and probably never more so than when facing a bull. It didn't make the unequal fight any more palatable in her eyes, but she could grudgingly admire their courage.

She kept that thought uppermost in her mind as the young *picadors* first teased and goaded the bulls with their lances, piercing the vulnerable muscles in the bull's shoulders to the roars of excitement from the crowd. Again and again they attacked until the animal resembled a pincushion, albeit a far more sinister one; blood dripped from the wounds as the barbs bobbed about in its back as he alternately charged and pawed the ground.

When the *picadors* retired from the ring, the gruesome teasing continued from the *matador* until the final thrust, as he went in for the kill. At that point the once powerful beast fell to its knees and then collapsed lifelessly in the sawdust to roars of approval from the crowd and an upsurge of triumphant music from *la musica*. It thoroughly sickened Lydia. Only by concentrating on the thought that the bull was out of its misery now, could she try to ignore the bearing away of its carcass by the *plaza* attendants and their mule team, and the brushing clean of the sawdust, in preparation for the next.

Later, the thought of an evening meal was enough to make her want to retch. She could still imagine the smell of hot blood in her nostrils, and the anguished look on the animal's face as it breathed its last gulp of air.

She clung tightly to Vincent's arm, marvelling at the way the Fitzwarrens could chatter so enthusiastically about the carnage they had just witnessed.

"You did well, my love. I was proud of you," he said quietly to her surprise.

Lydia felt her eyes prickle. They were among the first gentle words he had spoken to her since last evening. Now that they were out in the open again and she could breathe clean air, her nerves began to relax.

"What do you young people say to an innocent game of cards before we go in to dinner?" Mr. Fitzwarren asked them as they reached the hotel. Lydia agreed at once, if only to put off the moment when she would have to eat whatever kind of meat the hotel served up. If it was going to be beef, she simply wouldn't be able to face it.

As it happened, it was a light fish dish on the menu that evening, as if the hotel management was sensitive to British stomachs. By the time they retired, Lydia was feeling more like her old self. Again, Vincent said good night and let her go to her bedroom alone. But tonight, sleep wouldn't come. And when it did, she awoke in a fever, crying out as she dreamed of the barbarism of the bullfight.

Almost at once, Vincent was there, slipping into bed beside her and cradling her in his arms as he murmured soothing words to ease her out of her nightmare. She sobbed against his powerful chest, her frustration at the fate of the doomed animals still overwhelming her. And gradually, as Vincent's arms held her and his body warmed her, she became aware of a feeling of great calmness, like that of coming home to a safe harbor.

He didn't make love to her that night, nor did she want him to. It wasn't the time. But in the morning he was still beside her, and the feeling of serenity hadn't left her.

Chapter Eight

Even with her meager knowledge of men, Lydia wouldn't have expected a virile man like Vincent Montagu to forego the pleasures of the flesh indefinitely. And once they had returned to the ship and continued on the last part of their voyage to Athens and thence to Kurnios, she was assured that none of his passion for her had abated.

Each night in the closeness of their cabin, he reached out for her, certain that she would respond, as she had been responding so helplessly and wantonly since the first day their glances locked.

But on her side there was a definite reticence now. She began to feel piqued that he assumed he was in such total control of her life that he could either be with her or leave her alone whenever he wished. Complete male domination was a facet of family life she had always abhorred. It had never been evident in her own family, where she still regarded her parents marriage as being a perfect one.

"Marriages may be ordained in heaven, but they're made on earth," she recalled her gentle mother saying once, commenting on some marital disaster between acquaintances. "When two people love each other to the exclusion of all else, and enter into the commitment of marriage as a fulfillment of that love, then it cannot help but succeed."

Lydia bit her lip, remembering those words now. How short of her mother's ideal had she fallen! In her worst moments she admitted that it was lust, not love, that had drawn Vincent Montagu to her. On her part, it had been a need to escape, though coupled assuredly with the secret love she harbored for him that had made her accept him. They were not the perfect partners.

She was unable to submit to any kind of servility to a man. Not even in her English relatives' household had her Aunt Maud been completely under her uncle's thumb. The friendly Claremonts, too, had seemingly enjoyed a blissfully harmonious relationship. And Lydia Grey had too much spirit of her own to be unquestioningly subjected to the whims of a man, however charismatic he may be. He may own her in the eyes of the law, but he didn't yet own her spirit.

The nearer they got to Athens, the more uneasy she felt about what she had undertaken. On the night before they docked, Vincent took her in his arms in the confines of their cabin and ran his palms sensuously over her breasts. That they responded at once was more a natural reaction, Lydia told herself, than for any real wish to submit to him once again.

She was shocked at her own thoughts. He was her husband, and she loved him. Yet at that moment she felt totally isolated from such emotions, unable to relax and allow the delicious sexual tingling to envelop her body and mind.

"What's wrong?" Vincent said quietly. "Has my wife gone cold on me so soon?"

She felt the sting of tears behind her eyes. "Sometimes I still don't truly feel your wife," she mumbled, aware that his hands had stopped their gentle palming now.

He gave a short laugh. "Do you doubt that the minister who preached over us was genuine? Or do you suspect me of abducting you for my own gain, and that you'll eventually end up in the hands of white slavers?"

"No. Of course I don't think anything like that," she said, half cursing herself for her weakness at that moment. She assuredly did suspect there must be some gain in the arrangement for him.

He tipped his finger under her chin. There was a full moon that night, and although there was no other light in the cabin, the brilliant moonlight flooded the room and she could see his face as clearly as he could see hers.

"There's something troubling you," he insisted. "Are you going to tell me what it is?"

She felt a frisson of anger. "Are you going to make me? I've never doubted that you're strong enough. What hope would a mere woman have against any man who forced her into doing whatever he wanted?"

He looked down at her silently for a moment. "I've never seen you in this mood before, Lydia. Do you really think I want to force you into anything?"

She turned her head away from him, not wanting to see his unblinking stare.

"I don't know," she said softly. The heartbeat throb of the engines beneath them was strong and unending, and far less erratic than her own.

And when Vincent continued to say nothing, she became unnerved and bitter, knowing he still studied her intently in the moonlight.

"What defense would I have against whatever plans you have for me, anyway? A wife promises to obey her husband, doesn't she? Marriage is a trap for women."

She heard herself saying these things with something like horror. It was as if she stood aside and listened to someone else. They weren't her words, nor her sentiments, but somehow they were coming from her lips; Vincent's cold voice told her only too well that he was anything but pleased.

"So that's what you think, is it? That I trapped you into marriage? If I was the mistrusting kind, I might throw a few accusations back at you, my sweet."

She turned sharply to look at him again. His face was icy above her, as if it was carved out of marble.

"What kind of accusations!"

"Just think about it. Here you were, living a life of luxury in India, with doting parents, and servants to wait on you. Suddenly, everything changed. Your parents died and you were obliged to return to England to live with strangers, and under the patronage of a loveless family. Even more, you were at the beck and call of three mis-

194

erable sisters, one of whom was seething with jealousy at your beauty. Don't deny that you were aware that I wanted you from the moment I saw you. What normal young woman in those circumstances wouldn't jump at the chance to get away from a life of drudgery to new horizons?"

Lydia gasped. She shook herself away from his embrace, though there wasn't very far she could go in the confines of the small double bed.

"Is that what you really think of me? That I chose to marry you as a kind of escape route from a life of *drudgery?*" It was too close to her own uneasy thoughts for her to do anything but bluster.

"Well, didn't you?" Vincent said coldly. "I hardly think it's because you discovered some instant passion for me. I'm quite a realist, Lydia. Even though we've spent some delightful hours together when I could almost imagine your feelings were real and not pretense, I believe differently."

She was more shocked and wounded than she could dare to let him see. Of course her feelings were real! Of course her throaty murmurs when he pleasured her were not faked! She had no experience of knowing how to pretend to a lover.

Abruptly, she pushed at his rigid body and sat bolt upright in the bed. Her hair fell about her face and shoulders, hiding her expression from him as she folded her arms tightly about her. She had never felt more like crying. Even through her blazing anger, she knew there was a semblance of truth in what he said. She *had* wanted to get away from her uncle's household. She *had* married a virtual stranger. What he didn't know, and must never

know, was that she had also fallen headlong and ir-
reversibly in love with that stranger. She spoke now
with great bitterness.

"I'm obviously not the right sort of wife for you,
Lord Montagu! Since you made it clear you went
to England to find anyone to fit the role, I'm surprised you didn't pick up the first comely street girl
you saw after my cousin rejected you."

Too late, she saw how she had taunted him.

"Indeed? But I thought I had done just that. Do
you forget how we met in one of the poorly lit alleys on your way home from your uncle's house?"

No, she didn't forget. It had been her first real
encounter with him, when he had made his feelings for her perfectly clear. They had been those of
a man lusting after a woman, she remembered
with growing humiliation, and she had almost been
foolish enough to mistake them for love.

"I don't forget. You treated me like a whore."

He gave a soft laugh. "I still wonder whether I
should have been glad or sorry when you reacted
like a lady? A whore would have been far more eager for my advances, and welcomed my sixpence.
As it is, I've paid far more dearly for you!"

All of a sudden Lydia realized how heavily she
was breathing. And Vincent, too, was no longer in
such iron control of his breathing. Somehow he
had pinned her arms back on the pillow, and his
eyes glittered as he saw her breasts heaving beneath
her thin nightgown.

"Why don't you take me then?" she said hoarsely,
hardly in control of her own speech any more. "I'm
bought and paid for, just like a whore, aren't I? So

196

you have the right to treat me any way you like. Isn't that what a man does with a whore?"

She half expected him to push her aside in a fury, and yet some devil inside her was reacting in completely the opposite way. She *wanted* him to take her, to ravish her . . . again, it was as if she stood aside from the scene being enacted on the bed in the ship's cabin, and watched another side of Lydia Montagu . . . the sensual, wanton side of a woman hungry for her man. She was horrified at her own unbidden reaction, and furiously she knew she mustn't give in to him, no matter what he did. She was still in control, and she must stay in control now or she was lost forever.

Before she could get her scattering thoughts together, she felt the push of his hands on the hem of her nightgown. Before she could even think about crying out in protest he had parted her and was inside her, filling her. He still had her pinned on the bed, and his weight was heavy and damp on her body. She had goaded him into this and she knew it, but somehow she made herself lay inert, unmoving, as if this thing that he did meant nothing at all to her.

It *should* mean nothing, Lydia told herself dazedly. This was rape, despite the fact that she was his wife in the eyes of God and man. He violated her, and as if to impress that fact on him, she lay motionless and limp and let him do it.

When he finally realized that there were no sounds coming from her lips, no involuntary cries of joy or pleasure, and that her arms made no attempt to cling to him, he slowly rose above her and stared down into the eyes she deliberately kept blank. He hadn't yet moved away from her when he spoke harshly.

"So. Perhaps without knowing it you've already learned one of the ways of a whore, my darling. The quickest way to dampen a man's ardor is by total indifference. You see what you do to me now."

He withdrew from her quickly, and thrust her unsuspecting hand downward onto him. She flinched back at once from the contact, somehow shamed that her determination to be unaffected by this invasion of her body should have diminished him. There was no earthly reason why she should be the one to feel shame, when he had perpetrated the rape. It was simply instinct telling her it was wrong to demean a man so.

"Vincent, I'm sorry if I've hurt you in any way," she found herself muttering, snatching her hand away and tugging down her nightgown in hot embarrassment.

"You haven't," she heard him say.

Amazingly, she thought she detected a touch of amusement in his voice now. "I assure you I'll be as good as new the next time, and as a dutiful wife you'll oblige me by being more responsive so that we can finish the job properly."

He turned away from her then, stretching out languorously in the double bed, apparently unconcerned and still confident of his own prowess. And it was Lydia who still felt humiliated, vowing resentfully that she wasn't even sure there would be a next time, yet as his wife, there was little she could do to prevent that.

The day the ship docked at the busy port of Athens, it was steamingly hot, with the sun almost directly overhead as the morning neared midday.

Although she was well used to the heat, even Lydia was affected by its dryness. Her eyes were assaulted by brilliant images of blue and white, as sea and sky and buildings filled the horizon, relieved only by the tall ships of many different nationalities vying for space in the safe harbor.

The Fitzwarrens were clearly sorry to part company with Lydia and Vincent, and were obviously charmed at having been in the company of the newly married couple.

"I do so hate goodbyes," Mrs. Fitzwarren said, fanning herself furiously in the blazing sunlight.

"I always tell my wife she shouldn't make such a production of it if she hates it so," her husband put in meaningfully, and Lydia heard Vincent give a small sigh. It was obvious that although Mrs. Fitzwarren may profess to hate goodbyes, she certainly meant to relish every moment of them, especially this one with her newfound friends.

She hugged Lydia to her ample bosom, and Lydia let herself be clutched for a moment, feeling half-stifled by the contact, and finally managing to wriggle free.

"Our paths may cross again one day, Ma'am," she said vaguely, fairly certain that such an eventuality was never likely to happen, but feeling obliged to make the platitude.

"Oh, I do hope so, dear Lady Montagu! In fact,

the very next time you and your husband visit England, we would be so honored if you would come and stay with us."

"That's very kind of you," Lydia murmured. "But we have no plans for returning to England in the foreseeable future."

"Oh, but of course you'll be back sometime! My husband will give you one of our visiting cards, so I do hope you won't take this as an idle invitation, my dear. I hope you'll remember us as we shall certainly remember you."

She glanced at her husband for confirmation, and after some throat clearing, he affirmed the invitation.

"We shall always think fondly of our time spent together," Mrs. Fitzwarren went on gaily. "And you would both be so welcome at our home in the Kent countryside."

"Then we both thank you, Ma'am," Vincent put in firmly, sensing that this conversation was in danger of becoming an extensive one and wanting to put an end to it. "Though, as my wife says, we have no plans at present for visiting England."

"But you'll never desert English shores forever, I'm sure. The two of you are as English as summer roses, and no one ever truly forgets their roots, do they? You'll want to return to your homeland to live one of these fine days, mark my words. And when you do, my husband and I will look forward to hearing all about your travels and adventures."

Lydia gave up trying to explain that she was just as sure that neither she nor Vincent had the slightest intention of returning to England again. She had never felt that her roots were there, and she was reasonably sure that, for whatever reason, Vincent had settled for good on Kurnios.

They were both nomads, she thought suddenly. In that respect, if in nothing else, they were well-matched.

But Vincent was accepting the gentleman's gilt-edged visiting card now, and assuring him that if the occasion arose, they would certainly make a point of calling on them. She wasn't sure if there was an edge to his voice or not. Certainly Mrs. Fitzwarren's effusiveness was in danger of wearing his patience very thin.

They finally parted company from the pair, glad to get away from Mrs. Fitzwarren's flustering and fussing over her baggage. They waved them off, and returned to their own cabin for the few bits and pieces still to be collected, feeling somewhat wilted.

"I'm quite sorry to see them go," Lydia admitted. "In many ways Mrs. Fitzwarren reminded me of my aunt, a sort of comforting presence, despite all her panicking. Like a little bit of old England, I suppose."

She surprised herself by her own words, but truly, the older lady and her husband had seemed like a little link with a past she hadn't even been sure she wanted to remember. But she had long accepted that blood ties would always have a certain tug on the heartstrings, no matter if they were welcome or not.

"That was a very profound remark, coming from

201

you, Lydia," Vincent said. "I thought you couldn't wait to get away from England."

Again, she couldn't be sure if he was mocking her or not, but she refused to be goaded into an argument.

"I know," she said. "But I couldn't help noting what Mrs. Fitzwarren said about our past always pulling us back. Does she have a point, do you think? Can we really never escape it?"

In answer, he pulled her into his arms. They really should have left the cabin by now. Most of the passengers were already milling about on deck, eager for departure from the ship that had been their home all these weeks. But suddenly it seemed as if this was a moment out of time, Lydia thought with a catch in her breath, as her husband held her close in his arms.

"Whatever the past meant to us, it's time to look to the future, my sweet. Look to the future and our life together, for it's the only thing that counts from now on. The past is dead and gone, and should be left to memory."

"I suppose you're right," she said slowly. "But the past has made us what we are, Vincent, and memories are all we have left of it."

"Then from now on, we'll make more memories together."

He gave her a long slow look before he bent his head to hers, and she felt the sweetness of his kiss on her mouth. And hadn't they already made memories to share? The words of her marriage vows slid into her mind, for perhaps never quite so poignantly had she felt so truly cherished as she

202

did at that moment. And then the mood was broken as he released her.

"We must go, love," he said briskly. "We have more travelling to do yet before we reach Kurnios, and I don't want us to risk missing the day's boat."

In minutes, it seemed, they were on deck, and joining the other passengers still departing. And then it was all hustle and bustle until at last they were seated precariously in a mule-driven cart, moving at an appallingly slow speed to a much smaller quay away from the main harbor.

"Is this where we find the boat for Kurnios?" Lydia inquired.

"It is," he said tersely.

His mood had changed so swiftly, she realized again. Such a short time ago she had felt that they were so close in mind and spirit, and now he was far away from her again. They were obliged to be touching one another in the close confines of the cart, yet in spirit she knew he was gone from her. Probably he had fled to that place he knew so well, and which was still an unknown to her.

Kurnios. For some reason she felt suddenly shivery, despite the burning heat of the day, which was made even more oppressive by their slow progress in the mule cart.

What did she know of anything there? Vincent had told her nothing to allay her fears or to ensure her interest. It didn't seem to matter to him what her feelings were about the place. It was his paradise, and therefore it must be hers.

But it was an unknown future that awaited her there, and it was the most alien part of her life

203

right now, peopled with strangers, except for Vincent himself. And despite all he said, the past was still a friendly memory, unchanging and constant. And even the dull and ordered life at Greystone Manor was at least familiar to her. She brought her churning thoughts up short, realizing she was in danger of turning into a feeble ninny even before they left the Greek mainland.

"Stop here, please," Vincent told the driver. Seconds later he had jumped down from the cart and was waving and calling out to a swarthy, tousle-headed man at the quayside. The man was lounging beside a boat that seemed to Lydia to be little more than a large fishing boat. She felt suddenly suspicious, and more than a little faint.

"Vincent," she spoke in a cracked voice, and he turned at once. "We're not getting into that thing, are we? It's surely not the craft to take us to Kurnios!"

If it was, she thought furiously, she would rather turn tail and march straight back to the ship and go directly back to England and throw herself on her family's mercy!

She felt Vincent's hand cover hers, and his voice was half-sympathetic, half-steely.

"We shall only be on the boat a couple of hours more, my dear. I agree that the transport may not be the most luxurious, but the welcome awaiting us will be warm. Trust me, darling."

The endearment momentarily stopped her indignant thoughts. She swallowed quickly, realizing that if this was the only craft available, then there was no help for it. And she was beginning to feel so weary, all she really wanted was to reach her destination. She nodded quickly, and Vincent's hand tightened over hers.

"Trust me" . . . she had no other choice, she thought weakly. She had come this far, and she had to go on. Besides, if she ran back to the ship like a frightened rabbit, demanding a passage back to England, her husband would only come after her, and the law would be on his side. It was his right to have her by his side, and to take her to his home.

Besides, she could never put herself in such a humiliating position. And where was her sense of adventure now? This was a new experience, and one to be savored. She saw the boatman come forward as he saw Vincent, his creased face breaking into a delighted smile.

"It's good to see you back, my friend!" the man spoke in a guttural voice with a strong accent, taking both Vincent's hands in a hearty grasp.

"It's a treat to the eyes to see you, too, Nikos. I've been away too long. Tell me, how are things on the island?"

"Good. Very good. The grapes ripen and the fish are plentiful. What more does a man wish for?"

Vincent laughed at the philosophical reply. "And Monty? Do you know how he fares?"

"Well enough, I'm told. But you'll see that for yourself very soon, my friend."

They continued to reestablish their links as the bags were unloaded from the mule cart, and then Vincent helped Lydia down. She brushed the dust from her skirt, aware that her hands trembled slightly. The familiarity with which Vincent and the boatmen spoke did nothing to allay her suspicions that he was not all he professed to be. Nor had she heard the man address him as anything other than his friend as yet, she remembered.

Why hadn't she denounced him long before this? she thought frantically. Why take the coward's way out, because in her heart she didn't want to believe that Vincent Montagu was a fraud at all? She realized the boatman was looking at her quizzically, and she saw Vincent give a broader smile.

"In answer to your unspoken question, Nikos, this is my wife." He turned to her then. "Lydia, this old reprobate and I have known one another a long time, and I'd trust him with my life. Which is what I frequently need to do when his boat gets the wind behind it!"

Nikos laughed at the easy camaraderie they obviously shared, shaking Lydia's outstretched hand vigorously.

"You'll be quite safe with me, Ma'am, so take no notice of Vincent. It's a real pleasure to meet you, and all of Kurnios will be rejoicing that our friend has brought home such a beautiful lady."

"Why, thank you," Lydia said, touched at the courtesy, and noting that Vincent showed no surprise at the man's use of his first name.

But as the two men led the way to the waiting boat, she gave up worrying and wondering, because very soon there would be no more chance for Vincent to hide anything from her. Once they reached Kurnios, he would be unable to keep the truth from her, whatever it was. And for Lydia, once they left this mainland, her last chance of turning back would be gone. But since such a possibility had never seriously entered her mind, she dismissed the thought as quickly as it had arisen.

Gingerly, she allowed Nikos to help her into the boat, aware that this was to be a very different mode of transport from the comfortable ship that had brought them to Greek waters. There was no deck on which to saunter and stretch the legs during long days at sea; no dining room where they could make pleasant conversation with other passengers such as the Fitzwarrens; no elegant cabin where the moon and starlight through the portholes could throw magical patterns across two bodies entwined, and enhance the sweetness of lovemaking.

"It will be a short crossing compared to the lengthy voyage from England, Lydia," Vincent said prosaically, breaking the spell into which she had momentarily been caught. "I can't promise you a highly comfortable one though. It all depends on the winds and the tides, but Nikos is an expert boatman."

"Is he also a clairvoyant, to know that we would arrive in Athens today?" Lydia said inconsequentially, as she sat down carefully on the wooden seating around the boat's interior. Her worst fears were confirmed by the strong smell of fish, and she had a job not to hold her nostrils together. This was definitely a fishing boat!

Nikos laughed, reeling something off in his own language in his amusement, before resorting to his careful English again.

"I bring fish to the mainland regularly, Ma'am,

207

and I know when the ship from England comes. Each week I check to see if my friend Vincent returns with his bride, and today is the happy day. There is no mystery."

He started up the boat's engine with a great roar, and conversation was lost for a few moments before Lydia got used to the noise. No mystery in Nikos's appearance, perhaps, she thought grimly, nor apparently, in the fact that he had gone to England looking for a wife! But as far as she was concerned, there was still a mystery surrounding Lord Vincent Montagu.

Two hours later, spray washed and dishevelled, Lydia ran her tongue around her salted lips and squinted to where Vincent pointed ahead. The water through which the boat plowed steadily was a deep turquoise blue, but all she could see ahead through the mist in her eyes was a great mound that seemed to soar sharply out of the sea. It looked gaunt and black and inhospitable, and her first thought was one of sheer panic.

"That's Kurnios," Vincent shouted back above the roar of the boat's engine. "We'll be there in about half an hour now."

She gave him a sickly smile. He and Nikos had spent much of the journey conversing in the bow of the boat, and she had been virtually left to twiddle her thumbs. It hadn't exactly endeared her to the approaching island and its inhabitants, where she would be the stranger.

But perhaps it would improve as they neared it, she thought optimistically. It would be less rugged and unfriendly, with its black rocks and jagged coastline with very few little bays of white sand to relieve the starkness. Lydia felt her heart sink all the same. As yet, she couldn't imagine anything less like the part of India she knew, lush and fertile and green.

Vincent was making his way toward her now. He took her cold hands in his.

"Don't be alarmed at your first sight of the island. I think the gods designed this side of Kurnios to deter visitors, jealously keeping the hinterland to themselves."

"It's better inland then, is it?" she said, through chattering teeth, though she was hardly cold in the soaring temperature. What she meant to say was, it could hardly be worse. She should have known that Vincent would read her thoughts perfectly well.

"Of course. There's a theory that the island may once have been a huge extinct volcano that rose out of the sea and simply burnt itself out. What happened then was that over millions of years the wide basin of the volcano, with its rich deposits of ashes, became like a storehouse for all the rainfall and windblown vegetation both from Kurnios and from other places. The basin itself is fertile and green and the island is completely self-productive."

"I can hardly believe it," she said skeptically.

"I know. Neither could I, at first. But you'll see," he promised, refusing to be put out by her lack of enthusiasm.

But how could she show the remotest sign of enthusiasm? She felt dirty and unkempt and thoroughly damp. Her back ached from the uncomfortable trip in a fishing boat. This was hardly the way Lord and Lady Montagu might be expected to arrive, she thought, with renewed suspicion. The relentless sun beating down on her neck had begun to make her feel light-headed, despite the shady sunbonnet she wore and the English parasol she held firmly over her until the wind nearly tore it from her hand. It was not an auspicious welcome to her new home.

"Is this the usual way you travel back and forth between here and Athens?" she asked Vincent crisply.

He laughed. "Not usually. I own much more sedate craft than this one, for all it seaworthiness, but there was no definite time for our arrival, as you know perfectly well. We could have asked Nikos to arrange for one of my boats to come and fetch us, but that would have meant staying overnight in Athens, and I saw no point when we're so near. I'm anxious to get home."

And to see this Monty, whoever he or she was. A dog, perhaps? Lydia was about to ask, when the boat rounded a headland of the island and they turned slightly northwards along the coast. Here, it was less rugged, although the black mountains still rose sharply from the coast. But there was a wider bay, and what would seem to be the only safe harbor on the island that Lydia had seen so far. It was filled with craft of varying sizes, but mostly with brightly painted fishing boats like the one they were in. There were several more imposing boats, which Vincent told her briefly were Montagu-owned.

"Is the whole of Kurnios Montagu-owned?" she said sarcastically, seething at his arrogance, and the undoubted queasy feelings she was experiencing now. The entire voyage from England had left her unscathed, but this fishing boat was doing all kinds of unsettling things to her stomach.

"More or less," he answered laconically.

He was impossible, she decided. But the truth would soon be uncovered now. There was a village set back from the bay which they were rapidly approaching, and she wondered if one of these houses belonged to Vincent, or if they had to go further into this hinterland of which he spoke, to the basin of the volcano. It might have sounded charming and romantic to Lydia a while ago, but now she was hot and cross and desperately near to being seasick, and all she wanted was to get off this boat and onto dry land.

"Is there any drinking water?" she asked faintly, as the sea and sky seemed to merge in her vision for a moment.

Vincent looked at her keenly, then shouted rapidly to Nikos in his own language. The boatman pointed to a container with a drinking cup attached, and Vincent quickly poured some water out of it and handed it to Lydia. She drank greedily, not realizing how dehydrated she had become, both with the heat and the salt spray she had swallowed.

"Perhaps we should have sent for one of the bigger boats after all," Vincent said, in some concern.

"Perhaps you should have. It would be a pity to get your prize home, only to find her half-dead

211

with exhaustion and delirium," she managed to retort.

She realized Vincent must have found a cloth from somewhere and had splashed the cooling water over it. She felt its wonderfully soothing caress on her face and neck as he bathed her with its dampness.

"I'm sorry, Lydia. In my eagerness to be home it didn't occur to me that you would be suffering. I took it for granted that the heat would suit you."

The old sweet nostalgia washed over her at his words as she remembered India.

"In the daytime it was always too hot to sit in the sun, and it was up to the *punkah-wallahs* to keep us cool with their fans. In the evening, when the sun went down, Mother, Father and I would sit on the shady balcony of the bungalow. Those were the best times, watching the Indian sunsets. It wasn't like this, being tossed about on a bumpy sea in a flimsy boat."

She stopped as she heard the growing singsong nuance of her own voice, and to her own ears it was as if she had assumed the persona of old Nadima. She must be slightly delirious already, she thought wildly, and then Vincent's strong hands were holding tightly onto hers.

"Hold fast, my darling, it will be just a few minutes more and then this awful rocking will stop. It's worse now, because Nikos has turned off the engine, but we'll be nudging into the slipway at any minute. Once you're on dry land again, all the floating sensations will go away."

She forced herself to speak sensibly. "And then

212

what? Do we rest for the night, or is there still more travelling?"

The look on his face confirmed her worst dread.

"It will be another hour or so, no more, once we've got a mule caravan organized. Meanwhile, we'll rest in Nikos's house, and his wife will give us some refreshment. It's the Greek custom to break bread and eat salt with a stranger."

She stared at him in horror, taking all this in. A mule caravan sounded to her like a trip to hell. And she wanted to be rid of the taste of salt in her mouth, not take more of it in. Though she knew the phrase was meant as a symbol of friendship, she found herself taking it literally.

"What sort of a place have you brought me to, Vincent?" she struggled to say, closer to tears than she would admit.

"I've brought you home," he said quietly. "Welcome to Kurnios, Lady Montagu."

He really meant it, she thought in some amazement. He thought this place was paradise on earth, and he just couldn't see that she was used to all the comforts of a gentleman's house, and always had been. She revised the thought. Of course he knew, but he obviously just didn't care. She had been the impoverished cousin at Greystone Manor, and therefore she was expected to be eternally grateful to him for taking her away from all that.

But to bring her to this! The man must be completely mad. She already knew he had delusions of grandeur. Why else would he parade himself as Lord Vincent Montagu, when she was becoming

213

increasingly certain he had no right to the title? Which meant that his use of her own title was nothing less than a mockery. . . .

Chapter Nine

As the small number of islanders apparently idling about the harbor greeted them, Lydia realized that Vincent was accorded every deference. But whether this was because he was the only Englishman in evidence at the moment or anything more, it was impossible to tell. She heard him call out to the Greeks in their own language, and assumed it was to organize the mule caravan. She noted how they sprang to do his bidding, but by then she was too uncomfortable and light-headed to do other than observe the alacrity with which they could move when it suited them.

Nikos informed her it was only a short step to his house, and she had no option but to walk across the hot earthy ground in her flimsy shoes to where he pointed to a small cubelike house, white-painted as were all the others scattered about in the small community. It all looked deserted, with surprisingly few people in sight, and Lydia commented on the fact. Vincent spoke easily.

"They take advantage of the early morning and the cool of the evening to do their work, and rest during the hottest part of the day. It's something we English can never get accustomed to, and see it as laziness, which it most certainly is not."

"The fish come out at night, and so do the fishermen," Nikos put in with his ready smile. "It makes sense, no?"

"I suppose it does," Lydia had to agree.

It had always amazed her how the Indian natives had seemed to work both day and night, and she'd always had every respect for their industry. She also remembered how her mother had taken a welcome lie-down in her shaded bedroom at the bungalow every afternoon to be fresh for the evening, so she could hardly argue with the sense of what Vincent was saying.

For a moment she tried to imagine the English government decreeing that shops and businesses should close every afternoon, and that work must continue into the evening instead. What a hue and cry that would cause, throwing ordered social life into chaos! But of course, such a necessity didn't apply, because the climate was so different.

"Does something amuse you, Lydia?" Vincent said, seeing her small smile.

"Just my own rambling thoughts. They're not worth sharing," she said quickly.

They were nearing the small house now, and she felt a wild relief. To be indoors anywhere was better than walking through this crunchy volcanic substance that was so hard on her feet. She shivered, trying to picture a time long ago when the volcano must have erupted, spreading its evil, insidiously burning lava even to the very edges of the sea.

"I think you're in dire need of a rest," she heard Vincent say as if from a long way off. If he hadn't been supporting her with his arm, she suddenly felt as if she would fall over as the bright rays of the sun seemed to dance off the white-painted house in front of her eyes.

"I do feel a little faint," she muttered, and then the door was opened and she was inside a small square room, in a dim interior of blessed coolness. A young woman came shyly forward.

"This is my wife, Anna," Nikos said. "Vincent has brought home a bride to Kurnios, my dear, and we rejoice with you both."

The little formal speech gave Lydia time to draw breath, and, gratefully, she sank down on the chair that was offered to her. The furnishings were simple but comfortable, and she was content to let the chatter wash over her for the time being. She was quickly offered a glass of grape juice, then hot dark coffee, while bowls of nuts, sweetmeats, fresh grapes and dark olives were handed around.

She felt decidedly better when she had drunk her fill and nibbled at the light fare. Anna was a plump, pleasant girl, but with very little English, so conversation was somewhat curtailed. In any case, Lydia was more than ready to move on when the excited shouting from outside told them their transport had arrived.

But although she had been warned what to expect, when she saw it, she almost reversed that idea. There were three mules in all, with a handler for each one. They pulled three narrow, open carts, and, horrified, Lydia was told that she and Vincent would be in the first, their baggage in the second.

"We have the third in case either of the others loses a wheel, or the mule refuses to budge, or any other minor incident occurs," Vincent said casually. Far too casually.

"You *are* joking, aren't you? You don't really expect me to sit for an hour in one of those idiot carts!" she spluttered.

Vincent looked at her coldly as the handlers began to mutter among themselves.

"Lydia, we have to cross the mountain. This is the best transport there is at short notice. We could go the long way round in one of the carriages, but it will be dark before one is available. We'd be obliged to stay here for the night. I thought you'd prefer to get home."

"Home!" she muttered bitterly. "That's a word that's beginning to have very little meaning for me any more."

Out of the corner of her eye she could see their baggage already being put into the second cart, and knew there was no help for it. Whatever she said, it was all going to happen just as Vincent dictated, and she could do nothing to stop it.

With the utmost dignity, she stepped forward to the first cart, ignoring the varying smells that emanated from it, and tried not to wonder what had been transported in it before. She allowed Vincent to help her inside, arranged her skirts as if she was in the most elegant of her uncle's carriages, and flicked open her parasol against the bright sun as she waited for her husband to sit beside her.

But her eyes blurred a little as the handlers began shouting to the mules to move, and the jerking, uneven movements began. She longed for a soft bed, where she could sleep and sleep and sleep, and never have to think about tomorrow.

She was obliged to cling on to the side of the cart with one hand, while determinedly keeping the parasol aloft with the other; a defiant symbol of her Britishness in this alien land. Even as the thought slid into her mind, Lydia was startled by it, and suddenly ashamed of the way she had so often disparaged her own roots.

"It's not the most comfortable of rides," Vincent conceded, when she had remained silent for the first part of the journey into the foothills on the intimidating mountain. The tracks of the many mules and vehicles that had gone before them did little to help her confidence.

"No, it is not. I didn't expect to be transported in a box on wheels, nor to be black and blue by the time I arrived. That's always supposing there's any kind of civilization to arrive at, by the end of this nightmare."

She felt his arm around her shoulders, pulling her close to him. If she might have expected anger at her outburst, she was mistaken.

"My poor sweet. It's so much less than you expected, isn't it?"

She turned her head to look at him. His face was very close to hers, and she could see nothing but concern and gentleness in his eyes. She swal-

219

lowed, wishing his compassion didn't always have the strangest effect on her, sapping all her resolve to remain detached.

"I didn't know what to expect. You told me so little," she mumbled, wondering if he was about to kiss her. But she should have known he wouldn't do that in public, not when the three Greek handlers were constantly calling to one another, whistling and nagging their mules to push forward over the stony ground. The handlers were obviously very interested in this lady from England who persisted in appearing so very *English*, no matter how high the temperature rose.

But she realized the heat was becoming less intense now. They were well past the hottest part of the day, and as the caravan went higher into the mountain area, the air was sweet and clean, and it resembled one of the welcome rare hot summer days in England. It was certainly no worse than anything she had experienced in India. It was late afternoon by now, the sun lower in the sky, and Lydia snapped her parasol shut with a decisive click. She looked at Vincent steadily, demanding that he tell her more about her new life, but he merely laughed, removing his support from around her shoulders and tucking her hand in the crook of his arm.

"But I wanted to surprise you," he teased. "I always knew you had the kind of spirit I admire most in a woman. You're not afraid to meet new challenges, and neither are you afraid to snap back when you feel you're hard done by. I even like that, my Lydia. God preserve me from a simpering female."

"You hardly married one of those," she commented, not knowing whether or not to be mollified by his words.

"Nor did I marry a coldhearted woman." His arm around her shoulders squeezed her more significantly, and Lydia felt the warm color rise to her cheeks. Right now wasn't the time to remind her of the way she inevitably responded to his caresses, however veiled the innuendo. Right now she wanted to keep all her senses alert for what was to come, and more pertinently, to keep clinging onto the side of this alarmingly rocking mule cart!

She tried to take an interest in the terrain over which they were passing. With a stretch of the imagination, she had conceded that the lower mountain slopes were semi-fertile, dotted with twisted and ancient-looking olive trees, tended by black-clad women who looked as if they had stepped straight out of a biblical setting. Used as she was to the garb of women of other races, it unnerved Lydia to see how they paused in their work to stand and stare as the caravan passed. It was as if she was an object of much curiosity in her pale-colored Western dress and the flimsy parasol she was suddenly glad she had snapped shut.

"I wonder how my cousin Audine would have viewed all this," she heard herself say without thinking. A small smile curved her mouth. Poor Audine would have fainted off long ago from the culture shock of it all. She heard Vincent laugh.

"I'm more than thankful she doesn't have to

221

view it. Your cousin had seemed a strong and capable woman to me, and offering for her hand was one of those ideas that seemed excellent at the time, but I know now it would have been a total disaster."

"So you think you got the better bargain?"

For the life of her, Lydia couldn't think why she had said the words, provocative as they were. Without even thinking, she had glanced at him out of the corners of her eyes, flirting, teasing. At once she knew it had been a mistake.

Vincent's arm was still around her shoulders, and she felt his thumb slide up to the side of her neck, gently caressing her soft skin. She resisted the urge to lean against it, capturing his touch, keeping him close.

"If you don't know that by now, then you're more insensitive than I thought, my darling. A passionate man who marries a cold woman is doomed to a life of misery. And I doubt that your cousin Audine would satisfy even the most unassertive man in that department. If you know what I mean."

His eyes were dark, looking deep into hers. And oh yes, she knew what he meant. Vincent Montagu was certainly not "unassertive" in the euphemistic way he described. He was the most virile, red-blooded man a woman in love could ever hope to marry. Already they had experienced things in the heat of lovemaking that she had never dreamed of doing, and which she was sure would scandalize her prim English cousin.

She swallowed dryly, and turned away from that

searching, knowing gaze.

"Is that all a man marries a woman for? I would have thought he could get all the lust he needs from other quarters."

Again, her tongue seemed to have a will of its own, she hadn't meant to sound so scathing, nor so condemning. But the long journey, the heat, and the distress at her surroundings, were all taking its toll. She felt light-headed again, as if she was journeying forever. This jolting ride would never end, and she would probably die of exposure and exhaustion long before they reached the utopia of Vincent's island home. She felt him remove his arm from her shoulders, and heard the chill in his voice.

"I'm sorry if my attentions mean so little to you. Lust is but a part of a man's feelings toward the woman he marries."

"Really? And what else is there?" she cried out in a low, choked voice. "You're not going to pretend that you love me, I hope! Please remember that I know very well your mission in coming to England was to find a wife. I merely suited your purpose better than my cousin."

"And you would do well to remember it," he answered, coldly angry now. "I'm sorry if my physical attentions offend your delicate sensibilities, but I'll brook no half-measures in our relationship, Lydia. I gave you my name and my protection, which is what most young women seem to require to raise their status in life."

They seemed to be in an isolated little world of their own. The Greek handlers had fallen silent, and whether or not they understood this conversation Lydia had no idea. She only knew she felt humiliated, frightened, and furious at his dismissal of a woman's place in the world. For the moment she overlooked his reference to giving her his name; the authenticity of which she had yet to investigate.

"You demean every woman by your high-handedness," she said choked again. "Without women, there would be no continuance of mankind."

"And without a man to impregnate your noble women, they would be barren. So let's not pretend that it's a one-sided operation, shall we? It's only the most narrow-minded of your sex who think God played a cruel trick on mankind by making men and women dependent on each other for the procreation of the species. Others prefer to think he gave us the enjoyment of each other as a bonus."

Lydia was stunned at this outspokenness. She had never heard anyone speak so bluntly on such matters before. It shocked her, even as it stimulated her senses. She had to admit there was a raw excitement in hearing him speak so. There was arrogant masculine pride in every ounce of the man, she thought. And whatever the circumstances of their being together, he was hers. They belonged.

"I'd rather we didn't continue discussing the subject, if you don't mind. Do we have much farther to go now?" she managed to say, hoping to divert his anger into something more constructive.

"It's not too far," Vincent said briefly. "We'll be

MORE PASSION AND ADVENTURE AWAIT... YOUR TRIP TO A BIG ADVENTUROUS WORLD BEGINS WHEN YOU ACCEPT YOUR FIRST 4 NOVELS ABSOLUTELY *FREE* (AN $18.00 VALUE)

Accept your Free gift and start to experience more of the passion and adventure you like in a historical romance novel. Each Zebra novel is filled with proud men, spirited women and tempestuous love that you'll remember long after you turn the last page.

Zebra Historical Romances are the finest novels of their kind. They are written by authors who really know how to weave tales of romance and adventure in the historical settings you love. You'll feel like you've actually gone back in time with the thrilling stories that each Zebra novel offers.

GET YOUR FREE GIFT WITH THE START OF YOUR HOME SUBSCRIPTION

Our readers tell us that these books sell out very fast in book stores and often they miss the newest titles. So Zebra has made arrangements for you to receive the four newest novels published each month.

You'll be guaranteed that you'll never miss a title, and home delivery is so convenient. And to show you just how easy it is to get Zebra Historical Romances, we'll send you your first 4 books absolutely FREE! Our gift to you just for trying our home subscription service.

BIG SAVINGS AND FREE HOME DELIVERY

Each month, you'll receive the four newest titles as soon as they are published. You'll probably receive them even before the bookstores do. What's more, you may preview these exciting novels free for 10 days. If you like them as much as we think you will, just pay the low preferred subscriber's price of just $3.75 each. *You'll save $3.00 each month off the publisher's price.* AND, your savings are even greater because there are never any shipping, handling or other hidden charges—FREE Home Delivery. Of course you can return any shipment within 10 days for full credit, no questions asked. There is no minimum number of books you must buy.

4 FREE BOOKS

TO GET YOUR 4 FREE BOOKS WORTH $18.00 — MAIL IN THE FREE BOOK CERTIFICATE T O D A Y

Fill in the Free Book Certificate below, and we'll send your FREE BOOKS to you as soon as we receive it.

If the certificate is missing below, write to: Zebra Home Subscription Service, Inc., P.O. Box 5214, 120 Brighton Road, Clifton, New Jersey 07015-5214.

FREE BOOK CERTIFICATE

4 FREE BOOKS

ZEBRA HOME SUBSCRIPTION SERVICE, INC.

YES! Please start my subscription to Zebra Historical Romances and send me my first 4 books absolutely FREE. I understand that each month I may preview four new Zebra Historical Romances free for 10 days. If I'm not satisfied with them, I may return the four books within 10 days and owe nothing. Otherwise, I will pay the low preferred subscriber's price of just $3.75 each; a total of $15.00, *a savings off the publisher's price of $3.00.* I may return any shipment and I may cancel this subscription at any time. There is no obligation to buy any shipment and there are no shipping, handling or other hidden charges. Regardless of what I decide, the four free books are mine to keep.

NAME _____

ADDRESS _____ APT _____

CITY _____ STATE ____ ZIP _____

TELEPHONE ( ) _____

SIGNATURE _____ (if under 18, parent or guardian must sign)

Terms, offer and prices subject to change without notice. Subscription subject to acceptance by Zebra Books. Zebra Books reserves the right to reject any order or cancel any subscription.

GET
FOUR
FREE
BOOKS
(AN $18.00 VALUE)

reaching the level interior soon. You'll be pleasantly surprised."

"Not unless you can promise me some kind of
civilization, I won't!" And she could hardly imagine it. The mountains where they were travelling
now looked completely hostile, and she shivered,
suddenly cold as Vincent said nothing. After a
short while he pointed ahead.

"Do you see the windmills?"

She blinked. It was as unbelievable as a mirage,
but there certainly did seem to be windmills
ahead of them, their sails huge and white against
the blue sky. There seemed to be dozens of them.
She realized how quickly the terrain had subtly al-
tered. The ground was no longer totally barren
and rocky. There were tufts of grass and foliage
springing up between the crevices, and in the distance there seemed to be hint of green shimmering on the stark horizon. There were even small
cubelike houses, she thought, similar to Nikos's
and Anna's. Or was that all part of the illusion,
too?

The more they travelled, the more the illusion
became reality. There were pockets of dwellings on
the outskirts of what seemed to be a huge verdant
plain, dotted with farms and larger houses. Domi-
nating the whole area was a large solidly built Eu-
ropean-sized house, though painted white in
traditional Greek-style, as if the building and its
owner were perfectly content to straddle two
worlds. The nearer they approached, the more Lydia could see the workers in the vineyards and or-
chards, and the abundance of fertile riches this

part of the island produced.

"Welcome home again, my lady," Vincent said softly, as she gaped, wide-eyed at the spectacle in front of her.

"Why didn't you tell me it would be like this, when I was so fearful of what I would find after travelling through the mountains?" she demanded, her self-assurance knocked completely off-balance.

Vincent gave a short laugh. "Why should I spoil this moment of pleasure at seeing the sheer amazement on your face?" he countered. "Besides, would you have believed me? You seem to believe so little of what I tell you."

His eyes and his voice challenged her, and she had the grace to blush. She wondered uneasily if he'd been aware all the time that she had doubted his identity. And if he was, and she had never questioned him, she wasn't sure whether or not that made her better or worse in his eyes. Or was he so withering of her need to get away at all costs from her uncle's house that her opinions counted for nothing?

"Well, you've got your way in one thing," she muttered. "I'm very impressed at all this. Who could help being otherwise? I think even Audine would be mollified by now."

"Lydia, can we forget about your cousin? I'm no longer interested in how she would have reacted to Kurnios. It's more important to me that it pleases you."

It was absurd for her to be so warmed by his remark. She was annoyed at herself for wanting these crumbs of approval from him, but she did.

226

"First impressions please me very much," she said quietly. "At least it looks like the home of a gentleman, and not as if I'm being abducted into the white slave market."

"Is that what you really thought?"

"It crossed my mind once or twice."

She spoke lightly, but there was more truth in her words than she'd even realized herself. The relief at seeing the normality of the big house, and the estate bustling with workers, was almost overwhelming. Even so, she remembered uneasily that they had had to cross mountains to reach this retreat, and that she would never be able to leave it without a proper guide. She would be as much a prisoner in this beautiful place as if she was in chains in a dungeon. It was a thought that she tried hard to dismiss from her mind.

The mules were more surefooted now than on their sliding trek through the mountains, and obviously eager to reach the end of their journey, too, where food and rest awaited them. No more eager were the two people inside the swaying cart, each for their own reasons. Vincent was returning home, and Lydia would have her suspicions brought out in the open at last.

News of their approach had evidently preceded them. When the small caravan finally reached the long entrance avenue of the house, there was a flutter of activity all along their route. It finally halted at the front door.

Almost immediately the large front door was flung open, and she saw an elderly, frail-looking man in a velvet blazer, unmistakably as English as if he wore the Union flag emblazoned on its pocket. He walked carefully down the flight of front steps to embrace Vincent, who had leapt out of the cart at once, leaving Lydia to be helped down by the Greek handler. The two men spoke rapidly for several minutes while she stood awkwardly alone. She saw the gladness in the old man's eyes, and the way he gripped Vincent's arm, and then at last Vincent turned to her.

She saw that he was smiling easily, behaving as if this was the most natural occasion in the world, while she still felt as if she was living through some sort of fantasy.

"Lydia, I want to introduce you to Monty right away—"

But the elderly man interrupted gently, and put a restraining hand on Vincent's arm.

"I think it would be best if we left the formal introductions until later, dear boy. The poor child looks exhausted, and I'm sure that something to drink and a soft chair to sit in would be far more acceptable than standing out here talking to an old man."

"I'm grateful to you for the suggestion," Lydia said, hardly knowing how to reply, or what his status was here. "It was not the most comfortable of journeys."

"And I'm not the most considerate of husbands," Vincent said dryly.

Since the comment produced no surprise on the old man's face, he had presumably been informed that she and Vincent were married. Was this the reason for the gladness in his demeanor? And if so, she had no idea just why it should be.

But she followed them inside meekly enough, and was surprised and pleased to find the house was every bit as luxurious as any of the best English houses. The furnishings were of the highest quality, the tables and chairs made of richly dark mahogany, exquisitely carved and moulded; the sofas soft and welcoming, and covered in finest silk. The carpets beneath her feet were thickly tufted, and servants came and went to attend every command. From such servitude alone, it was swiftly obvious to her that Monty, whoever he was, carried a lot of weight in this house. But so, too, did Vincent.

They had entered a beautifully appointed drawing room, their bags being taken upstairs to be unpacked later. Monty had called for drinks and biscuits to be served, and the three of them sat companionably now. At least, the two men were sociable, Lydia slowly realized.

The two were talking animatedly about Vincent's trip to England, and the people he had seen, and the vicissitudes of the voyage back to Kurnios. She sat quietly, thankful to relax while she sipped the very English cup of tea, and feeling nothing more than a rush of gratitude that this long journey was over at last.

But suddenly she felt a burning annoyance at being virtually ignored. And all her resentment toward Vincent and the circumstances that had changed her life so immeasurably welled up inside her in a raging anger. She clattered her cup down in her saucer, disobeying the etiquette of the day.

The two men paused in their lively talking and looked at her.

"I'm sorry to interrupt," she said, her voice more shrill than usual. "And I'm sure the two of you must have many important things to discuss. But I cannot keep silent any longer. I have suspected all along that my husband is an impostor. From everything I've observed in this house so far, I believe that you, Sir, are the real Lord Vincent Montagu. I wonder if you're aware that my husband has been masquerading under your name, even to tricking my uncle into accepting his courtship of firstly my cousin, and then myself."

After the words had burst out, she paused, her righteous indignation at the deceit causing her to breathe more heavily than usual. Her hands trembled, well aware of what an appalling scene she was causing in the gentleman's own house in denouncing a man he obviously thought highly about, but unable to keep her thoughts to herself a moment longer. At the same time she was so embarrassed she was hardly able to look at either of them.

But when she did, it dawned on her that there was no verbal outrage on Monty's part, and no visible humiliation on Vincent's. Instead, the two of them were chuckling, as if they had both been part of a great conspiracy, and she was the one caught in the middle. Startled, her glance flew from one to the other, and the truth about the collusion was obvious. The reason for it was mysterious as ever, but of one thing she was certain. She was a fly caught in some giant spider's trap.

"Lydia, my love—" Vincent began.

She leapt to her feet, hearing the endearment as some indulgent, patronizing way of placating an hysterical female. It only enraged her more. She rushed toward the door, hardly knowing what she was doing or where she was going, just needing to get away from the laughing eyes of the two men who had every advantage in this situation.

Vincent caught up with her long before she reached the door. His grip on her wrist was hard and cruel.

"Don't be ridiculous. You're tired and over-wrought. Come and sit down and we'll talk."

"Am I to hear more lies?" Lydia said shrilly. "Are you denying that you masqueraded as Lord Vincent Montagu?"

She saw him shrug.

"Since it pleases you, I won't bother to deny it."

"Of course it doesn't please me! Do you think I'm happy knowing I'm married to a charlatan?"

His voice was sharp. "But it pleased you to be married to a Lord, did it? I thought better of you, my dear. I wasn't aware that a title meant so much to you. I thought we were two of a kind, but obviously the conventions mean more to you than you led me to believe."

"How dare you throw that at me," she whispered, hurt beyond measure. "You've deceived me and my family, and now you dare to belittle me!"

She realized Monty was saying nothing at all while their battle continued. He sat impassively at the far end of the room, and Lydia couldn't even guess what he was thinking.

"And just how long have you been aware of my so-called impersonation?" Vincent was saying coldly.

"For quite some time," she informed him, unable to resist the small triumph of her exposure. "The people I lodged with understood that Lord Montagu was an elderly recluse, and not at all like the young man who came to England seeking a wife!"

"Then why have you not said anything before now?" he asked. "If I deceived you, then you deceived me just as much."

Too late, she knew she had been reckless in her ranting. And how could she say she hadn't wanted to expose him, because she wanted so desperately to believe that it was all a mistake? That he was truly who he claimed to be, and that she had fallen headlong in love with him . . . but that love seemed of little consequence now, she thought dismally.

"Well, Lydia?" Vincent demanded. "What do you have to say to that?"

Vainly, she tried to shake free of his grasp. "Don't try to turn the tables on me," she gasped. "You're the one who's taken another man's identity, and I won't stay here to be made a fool of. Please let me go!"

His reply was only to grip her harder.

"And where will you go, my dear?" he said, taunting her. "You belong to me in the eyes of the law, and by now, word will have spread that I have brought home a wife. The Greeks are very keen on family loyalty, and no one would help a

232

wife flee from her husband. Besides, there's not a boatman on the island who would aid any thoughts of escape, since all the boats here are Montagu-owned."

Lydia looked at him bitterly.

"Since you speak of escape, you do admit that I'm a prisoner here?"

"I admit nothing. You entered into a contract of marriage of your own free will," he said calmly. "You knew the prospects ahead of you, and that you couldn't expect to have an ordered English life. I understood it was one of the reasons your cousin Audine was so aghast at the thought of marrying me, and perhaps one of the reasons you accepted."

She was speechless at the audacity with which he spoke. That there was also a semblance of truth in his words made her even angrier. Out of the corner of her eye she saw their elderly host get to his feet and walk toward them.

"My dear, I think you are overtired and overreacting to the rigors of your journey," he said gently. "May I suggest that you are shown to your room and that you take a rest before dinner? I'm sure everything will seem different to you once you are rested, and we can all have a lengthy discussion later this evening."

Would she learn the truth even then? Lydia thought bitterly. She was truly beginning to feel dizzy and muddled, she wasn't sure she could take in anything more for the moment.

"Monty's right," Vincent said. "I'll ring for a maid to show you upstairs, Lydia, and I'll join you when it's time to get ready for dinner."

He rang the bell to summon a maid, who appeared almost at once. And Lydia had no option but to follow the dark-haired girl up the long curving staircase to the opulence of a huge bedroom.

When she saw it, she gasped. Even to her inexperienced eyes, this room could only be described as a bridal chamber. The lacy drapery over the large four-poster bed, and the satiny, pastel-colored furnishings, together with the fire already burning in the fireplace, were suspiciously inviting. She would have been denying her own nature if she hadn't felt a flicker of excitement at the thought of lying in such sensuous surroundings with Vincent.

"You must have worked very hard to get this room ready so quickly," she said involuntarily to the maid. The girl gave a slight smile, speaking in halting English.

"It no trouble, lady. Room has been ready long time waiting for young master's bride. You like?"

When she could speak, Lydia nodded quickly.

"It's very nice. Thank you," she said jerkily.

After the maid left her, she sat down heavily on the bed, her eyes staring unseeingly at the lovely decor, and registering none of it now. Suddenly it all seemed so clinical. All this . . . the ready-furnished bridal chamber . . . the welcome from the old man . . . the secret smiles of the Greek people she had met so far . . . it had all been prearranged. The only missing piece had been the identity of the bride herself.

For all her airy talk of arranged marriages to her English cousins, Lydia had never really imagined it happening to her. When she married, it would be for love, and nothing else. Now, all those finer thoughts seemed to mock her, because all the love was unrequited. Though even her love was being stretched to the limits now. She had been in the right place at the right time for Vincent Montagu's purposes, but the thought gave her no mystical pleasure as it had done previously. Instead, she felt degraded, as if she had been bought and paid for.

Chapter Ten

She had hardly moved by the time Vincent came into the room. She sat on the edge of the silk-covered bed, her face as cold as marble, despite the fire crackling in the fireplace.

She knew she was being completely irrational in feeling so resentful. She knew Vincent had come courting Audine. She knew he wanted a wife to bring back to Kurnios. What she hadn't expected was to discover his mission to England had been quite such a deliberate and calculating search, with the bridal chamber all ready and waiting. Apparently, anyone would have done. It hurt so much to know that, when she had really believed he wanted her. His eyes, his touch, and his lovemaking had all told her so, or was this the way any man could act when he lusted after a woman? A sob broke in her throat at the thought, because she had loved him so much, so trustingly, and so innocently.

She heard the door handle turn and open and then click shut, and she couldn't bear to look at him. But if she thought he was going to make some kind of apology, she was quite mistaken.

"That was quite a little scene you made downstairs," he said. "I began to wonder if I'd married a harridan after all."

For a moment she wondered if she had really heard him right. She was still numb with shock, but suddenly all the rage she felt blazed inside her. She leapt to her feet, her hands clenched tightly at her sides.

"How dare you accuse me of making a scene, when you've deceived me all this time! You called yourself Lord Vincent Montagu, when Edwin Claremont assured me that the real gentleman was elderly and a recluse. Fool that I was, I desperately wanted to think him wrong, and I took you at face value. But as soon as I saw this . . . this Monty . . . and heard you talking together, well, I presume he *is* the real Vincent Montagu?" she finished witheringly.

Vincent looked thoughtfully at her. She was flushed and trembling, and to him, very, very desirable. He folded his arms, resisting the urge to snatch her to him and smother the condemning words with kisses.

"To be quite accurate, he's the *other* Vincent Montagu," he said coldly.

Lydia stared at him, her thoughts whirling. She felt dizzy with all the strain of travelling, and now all of this to contend with. Her resolve suddenly crumbled, and she spread her hands helplessly.

"I don't understand," she said, her voice husky.

The huskiness of her voice and her apparent feminine capitulation unleashed something in Vincent. He crossed the room to her in quick strides.

He took her in his arms, even as she felt herself sway. Somehow they fell heavily across the bed together, and from its depths rose an aromatic scent of herbs and spices to tease the senses. Instantly, Lydia was transported back to India, where old Nadima had told her such things were always spread on the marriage bed as an added stimulant and aphrodisiac for new brides.

"Then understand this. The time for talking has ended," Vincent said roughly. "Now it's time for loving."

He could have said a thousand things more flowery and sentimental to persuade her. He could have made it sound less like a duty than the most sensual experience Lydia had ever known. He could have coaxed her, instead of pushing her clothing aside almost angrily, and entering her with a thrusting strength that practically amounted to rape. He could have done any of those things, and none of it would have filled her with such a response that was primitive and exquisitely exciting, and drew sobbing gasps of sheer pleasure from her when it ended. She had felt nothing like this before. It was as if she had enveloped the heart and soul of the man and truly become part of him.

"I'm sorry," she heard Vincent say raggedly, as he lay against her, his breathing tortured. "I didn't mean to hurt you."

"You didn't," she whispered, but the words were so lost in her dry throat he never heard them.

He moved away from her, adjusting his clothing, and she hurriedly covered herself, aware that he seemed deeply troubled. She longed to comfort him, but Vincent Montagu was a man always in control of his own emotions. Even now, when they had been as close as two people could be, she would hesitate to probe into his thoughts. But that last act hadn't really been an act of loving closeness, she reminded herself. It had been an almost desperate act. Her euphoria was quickly diminishing as he walked across to the fireplace and looked deep into the flames.

Slowly, Lydia sat up, wondering just what to say to this man who was her husband, and yet still an enigma to her.

"I think you owe it to me to answer some questions, Vincent." When he didn't respond, she plunged on. "I'd like to be clear about your relationship with Monty, for a start. And why did you come to England looking for a wife? Most of all, why did you choose me?"

He gave a short laugh. "I would have thought the answer to the last was obvious. You're a very lovely, sensual woman, Lydia, and from the moment we met I knew we were destined to be together. Don't deny that you knew it, too. The moment I looked into your eyes, I knew there could be no other, and your cold cousin couldn't hold a candle to you."

She wasn't sure whether to be flattered or not. He spoke in such distant tones, he might have been discussing the acquisition of a new horse or painting.

"Perhaps I did know it," she admitted. "But your

239

purpose has become very clear to me now. You would have married anyone to bring a bride back to Kurnios. It's hardly a pleasant discovery."

"It was necessary," he said coldly. "And a man needs to be married. Why do you question it, when you can have everything a woman could wish for here?"

Lydia moved across the room to stand on the other side of the fireplace. The wood sparked between them, filling the room with its pungent aroma. She shook her head.

"It's not enough. I need to know the truth. I don't deny that there's passion between us," she almost said love, but if all the love was on her side, she wouldn't humiliate herself by seeing the mockery in his eyes. "But a marriage needs to be built on trust. As yet, I don't trust you, Vincent."

She caught her breath, knowing she could be on dangerous ground in challenging him so. He was a man of strong emotions, quick to anger and probably slow to forgive. She didn't know him well enough yet to always be sure of his reactions.

"All right. You want the truth, and you shall have the truth." He was harsh now, yet she could sense pain in his voice, too.

He faced her, his face as set and controlled as hers had been earlier. "My name is Vincent Montagu, and so is Monty's. He's my grandfather, and the only deception was that I used his visiting card on my visit to England, elevating myself to Lord Montagu. I don't actually inherit the title until his death, at which time the estate and the island will

240

also be mine. And that time is drawing rapidly nearer."

He stopped abruptly, leaving Lydia to fill in the missing words herself.

"You mean he's dying?" she whispered.

"That's exactly what I mean. He has a year at most, and probably less."

Lydia ran her tongue around her dry lips. She was so taken aback she hardly knew how to reply. Condolences seemed out of place. She didn't yet know Monty, but she could feel compassion for the way Vincent already grieved for him. Yet she sensed, too, that he wouldn't want her sympathy. In the peculiar way of family loyalties and privacy, Monty's ills were his ills, and Lydia was still the outsider.

"I'm very sorry. But why was it necessary to use his persona?" she asked inanely, lacking anything more to say.

"It was a deliberate choice, my dear." She heard the hardness in his voice now. "Monty and I put our heads together, and decided that any young woman would far rather marry a Lord than a plain Mister, so we decided that I would use the title prematurely. It was the bait to catch the bride."

She stared at him, all her resentment rushing to the surface again at such male arrogance. Even though an old man was dying, and a younger one was grieving, they had no right to play on female emotions the way they had.

"I think that's the most insufferable thing I've ever heard," she said softly, not trusting herself to raise her voice for fear she would screech like a fishwife.

Vincent shrugged. "There are times when you have to use the only ways and means available."

"But you still haven't told me why." She was insistent, without really knowing why. Hadn't she been humiliated enough? Why insist, if there was still more deception to discover? But some devil inside her made her go on torturing herself.

"I thought your astute little brain might have guessed by now," he said dryly.

"Please don't patronize me, Vincent! What is it you want from me!" It wasn't love, she thought bitterly. Not the beautiful, flowering love of her girlhood dreams, which would seem to be totally lost forever now . . .

"A child, of course," he said brutally. "Monty's time is running out, and his dearest wish before he dies is to see an heir to carry on the Montagu line."

As she listened, Lydia felt as if she was reeling backwards. Her knees seemed to buckle, and Vincent was by her side in an instant, leading her to the chaise longue at the end of the bed. He sat close beside her, his hands imprisoning hers, no matter how hard she tried to pull away.

"You're despicable," she said in a choked voice. "I can't believe anyone would deliberately set out to marry someone merely to father a child. It's unscrupulous. I can hardly believe Monty would be agreeable to such a thing either!"

"Listen to me, Lydia. You don't know my

grandfather. He's been everything to me for most of my life, and I would do anything for him. And though this was initially his idea, I went into it willingly. If it would make his last days easier, and give him something to live for in the meantime, then no sacrifice was too great."

"So that's what I am? A sacrifice?" her voice was shrill and disbelieving. All her dreams of love were crashing around her. She felt sick and shamed.

"I'm sorry if I chose my words badly," Vincent went on tersely. "You must believe that I have the greatest respect for you, Lydia. I successfully caused your cousin to reject me, in favor of you, if you recall," he added arrogantly.

"She was less gullible than I," Lydia said bitterly.

He went on as if she hadn't spoken. "Monty was at a very low ebb a few months ago, and that was when we first thought of this plan. I would go to England and bring home a bride. He has a very strong gambling streak, Lydia, and it turned into a challenge. I was only too happy to agree to it, since it gave him a new interest. We put a time limit on it. We had to, because I had to be married and the wife produce a child, before . . . well, you see the reason for it, don't you?"

She was numb with shock. The more she heard, the more she despised the so-called plan, yet she could also see how much Vincent loved the old man. There was no need for him to marry quickly on his own account. He would eventually inherit all of this anyway, and could marry and produce children in his own time. But for Monty, there was so little time.

"It became an obsession for Monty," he went on when she didn't answer. "The conditions for the wager became more elaborate. He wanted an English heir, therefore it had to be an English bride, but the baby had to be born on Kurnios. And all this in the shortest possible time. The one thing we didn't do was put a time limit on it, because his own time limit was in God's hands. As long as the conditions were fulfilled that was all he wanted."

"And what was the prize for the winner?" she asked in a cracked voice. "A wager has to have a prize, doesn't it?"

He shook his head. "Not in the usual sense. It wasn't part of the bargain. You might say we're both winners. Monty had us both here, and I have my bride."

"You don't have the child yet, and perhaps you never will," she was stung into saying. "I feel hurt beyond measure that you married me purely in order to produce a child for Monty. How could you use any woman in such a way!"

"You see now why I didn't want to explain any of this," he said angrily. "Why couldn't you have taken everything at face value, instead of questioning it all?"

"Because I have a mind of my own, that's why!" she said, tugging her hands out of his grasp at last. "I'm not a simpleton, nor am I some kind of breeding cow, available at your convenience whenever you please to produce offspring!"

"But that's exactly what you are, my dear. At my

convenience whenever I please. As for producing offspring, it may be that you're already impregnated. I've enjoyed you often enough and thoroughly enough for it to be a fact already. And if not, make no mistake that I shall enjoy you whenever I choose until it happens."

"And what then?" she said dully. "Will I be left alone from then on?"

He looked at her strangely. "Is that what you want? Are my attentions so distasteful to you?"

The words trembled on her tongue to say that *no*, they weren't distasteful. He gave her the ultimate pleasure every time he lay on her and forged into her. She wanted him so much, even now, seeing the shadowed look on his face after his revelations about Monty, and she hated herself for her own bodily reactions. She waited too long before making any reply.

He stood up quickly.

"I see," he said, without expression. "Well, although it is against my principles to force a woman, you will do your duty just as long as I say you will. If it happens that I tire of you, I can always find an alternative, my dear. There are many diversions, even on so small an island as Kurnios. Do you understand me?"

She refused to answer, clamping her lips tight shut. He was impossible and hateful. How had she ever thought him remotely charismatic?

"Unless you've suddenly gone deaf, I would appreciate an answer."

She looked at him with utter contempt. "You

may think you own me, Vincent, but you do not. If I must provide you with a child, I will do so, and then may I be free of you?"

"Certainly. On certain conditions, of course."

"What conditions?" She fell into the trap.

"You would be rewarded handsomely for a start, and you would be free to go to England or wherever else you may wish. But you would leave the child here. He will be cared for as if he were a prince, so have no fears about that. When he's old enough, he will go to England to be educated, and then, of course, you would be permitted to see him occasionally."

She gasped, appalled at such conditions. They were nothing short of barbaric.

"You must be completely mad to think I would ever agree to give up my own child in such a way!"

He gave a slight smile. "I rather thought that would be your answer. So it seems we stay together."

If she was foolish enough to allow a glimmer of hope to enter her mind, she might even think he had engineered it this way, goading her into saying she would never leave her own child. As if he really wanted her here, but she wouldn't allow any such thought to color her anger.

Distantly, she heard the sound of a gong being struck somewhere in the house. Vincent heard it, too, and stretched out a hand to her.

"We're being summoned to dinner. Can you compose yourself enough to come downstairs?"

"If I must, though, I would like a few minutes alone to change my dress and tidy my hair," she muttered.

He said he would send a maid to help her with hooks and fastenings. Until the girl arrived, Lydia stood motionless and drained in the middle of the room, wondering just how disastrous this marriage was going to be. She had come upstairs to rest and calm herself after the journey. Instead, she felt more dishevelled and upset than ever, her nerves were raw, and cursed with the feeling that destiny had dealt her the cruellest trick of all.

At dinner that evening, she was able to study Monty with a different view. She recognized how frail he was, how transparent the pale skin, how the hands trembled. She saw, too, how the flashes of pure affection between the two men almost lit up the room, and could put a sparkle even into a dying man's conversation. She had to concede that there was love in every gesture Vincent made toward his grandfather.

It didn't excuse their plan, but perhaps in a small way, it helped her to understand it. But playing with peoples' lives in the way they had was a dangerous occupation. She couldn't punish or blame Monty for his desire for some kind of immortality in a great-grandchild, but she could still despise Vincent for the way he had gone about it.

Yet, what else could he have done? The reasoning part of her brain questioned even that. What

247

would her reaction have been if he'd come to England, stating brashly that he was looking for a wife solely for the purpose of bearing him a son, and then the wife could go where she pleased? No respectable woman would have agreed, no matter what the reward. And Vincent certainly wouldn't have wanted a slut for the mother of his child. So the subterfuge was clearly necessary, she supposed grudgingly, at least in his eyes.

"I asked if you would like some more wine, Lydia?"

She started, vaguely registering that this wasn't his first time asking, and that the jug of sparkling red wine in Vincent's hand was hovering over her glass. She nodded quickly, thinking it would at least dull her senses and lessen some of the hurt she felt. She watched as he poured, seeing several splashes of the deep red liquid spill onto the white cloth. Like spots of blood, she thought, and wished the analogy hadn't sprung so poignantly to her mind.

She had never before sat at a table with a man who was going to die. And the ridiculous thought that followed was that they were all going to die, every one of them. Vincent, with his stern face this evening, except when he spoke with Monty, and herself, depressed and mouselike, quite unlike her usual self. They were all going to die eventually. Only the timing was to be decided by forces beyond themselves.

"Are you always so quiet, Lydia, my dear?" she heard Monty say. She couldn't help noting how relaxed he seemed, despite the trembling hands. He was the most relaxed of them all, she thought wonderingly. How could it be, when he knew what fate had in store for him? Or perhaps that was the very reason, because he no longer had to fight against fate. His was assured. She forced a quick smile.

"By no means, Lord Montagu—"

"For pity's sake, girl, don't go lumbering me with my title! I'm too old to bother with such trifles from the people closest to me, and besides, it alienates me from a pretty young thing like yourself. The name is Monty."

"I'll try to remember," Lydia said, moved by the realization that there was still plenty of life in the old man yet, despite everything.

He gave a wicked chuckle, the faded old eyes twinkling. "Well then, you were going to tell me about yourself."

"Was I?" Lydia said, startled.

"You say you're not always as quiet as you appear this evening, and that's a good thing. I like young people with a bit of life around me. But apart from the brief snippets my grandson has told me about you, I only know what I see. Brought up in India, weren't you?"

He was obviously encouraging her to talk, and once started, Lydia didn't find it difficult to unbend toward him. Lord Vincent Montagu was a charming gentleman, she conceded, even though he had set in motion the chain of events that had brought her here. She would guess that in his youth, he'd been more than fond of the ladies, too.

249

A trait that was all too evident in his grandson.

"And you found it a trial, having to depend on your relatives' charity, I daresay?" Monty said sympathetically, when she paused for breath.

"Well yes. Although I didn't live with them; at least, not until Vincent and I became engaged to be married," she added, feeling the first blush of the evening come into her cheeks, not really wanting to refer to that episode at all. "I lived in lodgings with some very nice people, and I went to Greystone Manor each day to tutor my young cousins. It was all very different from my life in India when my parents were alive."

A bleak memory of her time at Greystone Manor came to her mind then. The sneers and carping manners of Audine, the irritations of the younger girls, the feeling of dependency on her family, when she was sure she was no more than a liability to them. Surely any escape was better than continuing in such a life. She caught Vincent's steady glance, and the blush deepened.

She wondered, too, if the reference to her parents' deaths was utterly tactless. She had already drunk too much wine, and her words had flowed too freely. But it seemed to be what Monty wanted, and she could hardly not respond to a man who had so little time left on this earth to talk to anyone. As if he could read her thoughts, he suddenly leaned forward, his thin hand reaching out to cover hers for a moment.

"My dear, you mustn't feel you need to indulge me in idle chitchat if you don't want to, nor feel you must cushion me from any talk of death. It comes to us all, and I'm perfectly well prepared for mine. I know Vincent has already told you that my time is limited, so you and I must make the most of it. Do you agree?"

"Oh, yes. Of course," Lydia said in confusion, not too sure just what he wanted of her.

"Good," Monty said briskly. "Then it will be no surprise to Vincent to know that plans have been well in hand for some time for a ball to celebrate his wedding."

Vincent laughed easily, his eyes laughing at Lydia, and daring her to betray any anger.

"You see how he organizes everything?" he said to her. "There was no doubt that I'd be bringing home a bride. And even his own funeral plans are well in hand, as he calls it."

Lydia was stunned at this frank comment. At any other dinner table, she would have thought such a remark in the worst of taste, but Monty merely smiled and said that if everyone was as orderly as himself, there would be less need for panic when the inevitable occurred. She had never heard anyone speak so easily about their own death before. It was a philosophy that she found hard to understand, but probably a very comforting one for those who could cope with it.

"I suggest that we hold the ball in a month's time," Monty went on. "That will give folk time to get used to the idea, and by then, Lydia, you'll have met a good few people on the island. You won't be a stranger for long, and you'll find that everyone is friendly here."

"You speak almost as if social occasions are as commonplace as in England," she ventured to say. "Are there many other Europeans living on the island?"

"A surprising number," Vincent put in. "I assure you you won't find it lacking in the social graces, and there are some very nice Greek families that you'll enjoy meeting, too. Like Nikos and Anna, for instance."

If she found it the strangest mixture of cultures and social strata she had ever come across, Lydia knew better than to say so. Brought up in India, where the social castes were very much kept in their separate layers, it was like a breath of fresh air to hear an English Lord and his grandson speak so highly of a boatman and his wife.

It was not the English way, either. She doubted that her Uncle Percival had the slightest idea of how a boatman made his living. There were some aspects of Kurnios she was definitely going to enjoy, Lydia thought.

"Do you play an instrument, Lydia?" Monty wanted to know next. "We have an excellent pianoforte in the blue drawing room, and it's been a long while since anyone played it."

"I do play a little," she said reluctantly.

"Good. Then when we've finished our meal, you shall entertain us."

Again, she caught Vincent's amused look. For a second, she wondered suspiciously if Monty really was under sentence of death, but one more glance at his waxy cheeks and those slender hands, and she was all too aware of it. But his amazing spirit hadn't faltered, and she was aware of her growing respect for the man. No wonder Vincent loved him. No wonder he was prepared to marry any suitable Englishwoman, to pander to Monty's obsession for an English heir.

The thought was in her head before she could stop it. Crossly, she reminded herself that she was caught up in this intrigue now, and she was the one brought here under false pretenses. But it was also dawning on her that somehow she couldn't find it in her heart to blame Monty. If anyone had to bear the brunt of her anger, it had to be Vincent. And his shoulders were broad enough and strong enough for that.

He came around to move her chair back for her when the meal was finished. His hands were light on her shoulders, and she felt them give her a gentle squeeze.

"Thank you. He adores you already," he said quietly.

For a few seconds Lydia's eyes blurred. It was a simple compliment, all the more emotive because of the simplicity of the words. But the irony of it was that it wasn't Monty's adoration she wanted. It was the love of the man she had married, and whose lovemaking she must endure as if under protest, until she produced the child this barren estate needed. And then presumably she would be free to go where she wished. It was irony indeed, when the only place she wanted to be was right here.

An hour later, she was becoming tired of playing the ditties on the pianoforte Monty clearly enjoyed so much. It had already been an endless day, and the old man's stamina seemed to last out longer than her own. Her shoulders drooped after the last piece, and she felt the tension between her shoulder blades, and begged to be excused.

As she turned around, she discovered that she and Vincent were alone in the blue drawing room.

"Where's Monty?" she asked at once.

"His valet came and took him off to bed," Vincent said. "You'll have seen that he has a remarkable attention span for an old gentleman, but when he needs to sleep, it's like turning down a lamp. It seemed a shame to disturb you, and in any case, he doesn't like to be seen to weaken."

"He's a very remarkable man," Lydia said slowly. She hadn't even heard the valet enter the room, nor the two men retire, but she had been totally absorbed in the music, and as so often happened, she had been oblivious to all else.

"He is indeed. The world will be the loser when he leaves it," Vincent said, his voice heavy.

"You love him very much, don't you?"

He spoke in short, sharp sentences. "Of course. He's been grandfather, mother and father to me, and so much more. I can never repay him for his love. I shall miss him."

Lydia could feel the brittle tension in the room, and didn't dare to anticipate how Vincent would be when the day finally came. She knew from her own experience the black emptiness of the day

254

when loved ones died, and the blackness didn't end in days or weeks. She switched her mind quickly from such dismal thoughts, flexed her aching muscles, and tried desperately to stifle a yawn, such a mundane thing seemed so inappropriate at this emotional time.

"You're very tired, and I shouldn't have allowed you to play for so long," Vincent said abruptly. "Incidentally, you play very well. Your fingers caress the keys as if you caress a lover."

She caught her breath. It was an extraordinary thing to say, and for a moment she wondered if Vincent was going to spoil what had turned out to be such a perfect evening with another brutal attack on her senses. Right now, she just couldn't bear it. She was too filled with the softness of the island night, with Monty, with the feeling of having come home after all, with everything.

"Don't be alarmed. It was just an expression of admiration," he said, as if alert to all that was in her heart. "I think we're both very tired tonight, and that we should both try to get a good night's sleep. I promise you won't be disturbed by anything at all until you hear the morning birdsong."

He held out his hand to her, and she reached out until her fingertips touched his. To her surprise, he turned her hand over and brought it to his lips, gently kissing the soft flesh of her palm. It was a gesture that moved her more than words. It spoke of tenderness and love, though she hesitated even to breathe the word in connection with his feelings for her.

255

But his arm rested lightly around her shoulders as they ascended the staircase together and entered the warmth of the bridal chamber. Foolishly or not, there was the smallest frisson of hope in her heart for the future.

Chapter Eleven

By the time Lydia had been on the island for several weeks, she had discovered more and more about this idyllic place. Far from the ruggedness of the mountains they had traversed to reach Vincent's home, there was a gentler, softer side to Kurnios.

It sloped away from the Montagu estate in a series of plateaus, on which families had built their houses and grew their grapes and olives in small, clustering hamlets and larger villages. The fruit flourished on stepped terraces to capture the hot beating sunshine, and just as importantly, to conserve every bit of rainfall. Going right around the island from the harbor and climbing the grassier slopes would have meant a much easier way of travelling to reach Montagu House on the day of their arrival. Lydia also accepted that it was far longer, and more meandering route.

And knowing now what she did about Monty, she could see why Vincent had been so anxious to reach home as soon as possible. In any case, the mountain route had probably not been as arduous as it had seemed to her, with well-worn trails gouged out by mules and donkeys and goats over the decades.

Lydia was also delighted to find that there were more European families living on Kurnios than she could have imagined.

"One day we shall probably become a summer escape for many more visitors from England," Vincent observed dryly as they approached one of the elegant new houses, built in a familiar English style, but white-painted in keeping with the island tradition, so that it conformed to both. It was one of a group of houses forming one of the villages.

"Would that worry you?" Lydia asked.

"It might, if they invaded our paradise and changed its character. The people here have a right to remain as they've been for centuries, living off the land and the sea, without foreign invaders disrupting their way of life, and attempting to improve it!"

"But isn't that exactly what you and your grandfather have done? And all the other English people living here?" She couldn't resist continuing the discussion, whether or not it turned into an argument.

"Not at all. Monty arrived here quite by chance, and the sailing vessel his parents owned was thrown off course, and they were obliged to put into a safe harbor. As you can imagine, there was very little here then to interest any kind of speculator. Just the fishermen, and the fruit-growers. The vessel had to remain for some weeks for repairs, and in that time the young Monty explored the island with his father, and for some reason he and the islanders took to one another like two halves of the same coin. He was mad keen on drawing and sketching, and he made a map of the island to take home, even then calling it his very own island. It was inevitable that he'd return here one day. When he did so, he was a young married man, and since my grandmother was related to a wealthy Athens family, it seemed like fate that they should end their days here and continue the Greek connection."

"But how did he come to own the island?" Lydia couldn't hide her fascination at hearing this romantic story.

"Mainly through encouraging the islanders to sell their produce to the mainland and overseeing all the business details, of which they had scant knowledge at the time. They were good farmers, but hopeless businessmen, and always being taken in by the cannier mainlanders. Anyway, the Greek government was impressed enough to make Monty an offer of the island, and remain as its nominal governor. In reality I suspect they were glad to be rid of it, since it had never paid its way."

"And now it does?"

"Now it does," Vincent agreed. "As for the other Europeans living here, Monty was very careful whom he approached with offers of a fabulous place to live and work, in return for an investment in the future of Kurnios. It's by no means a rich island, but a flourishing one, and it's certainly all worked out exactly as he planned."

"Except for someone to continue his line."

Lydia wished she could bite the words back, but they were out before she stopped to think.

While they had been talking, and during the last few weeks of comparative calm between herself and Vincent, she had almost managed to forget the cir-

259

cumstances that had brought her here. She had been welcomed by Monty's friends, and drawn into their social life, and everyone seemed to like Vincent Montagu's new bride.

She felt him squeeze her arm as their pony-drawn cart stopped now outside the elegant white-painted house overlooking green terraced vineyards.

"Except for that, but as you already know, I've not intention of failing him in that direction," he said meaningly.

She felt the heat in her face, and was tempted to say he had failed so far, since there was no sign of a baby, for all his passionate lovemaking. For a moment her head swam, remembering just how ardent he could be, and how willingly she had responded. For the life of her, she couldn't pretend she didn't welcome his passion. And he knew it.

The family she was introduced to that morning knew Bath slightly, so it gave them a mutual topic of interest. Lydia was more intrigued at how Daisy and John Brandon, and their two young children, came to be living here so far from home.

Daisy laughed. She was a fresh-faced, friendly girl, with a distinct English West Country accent.

"We came originally for John's health," she said, to Lydia's surprise, as they sipped orange juice on the shady veranda of the villa. The children ran around on the grass without shoes, enjoying the freedom.

"You wouldn't think it to look at him now," Daisy went on, smiling at her husband, "but two years ago he was diagnosed as consumptive, and no amount of money poured into medicines and cures did any good. Then we heard about Kurnios and dear Monty, who was inviting suitable investors to come here, and has turned out to be such a good friend."

"We're not farmers, you understand," John put in. "But we were able to employ our own workers and reap the benefits of the grape harvest. Our doctor said it might be the best thing for me, just to live in this sunnier climate, so we took a chance," he said in explanation.

Daisy reached out a hand for her husband's as they sat companionably together.

"It's worked out better than we could ever have dreamed," she said softly. "The complaint seems to have gone away, the children are thriving, and we simply love our new life here."

"And we owe it all to Monty," John added. "If he hadn't thought us suitable applicants—"

"Don't underestimate the considerable amount of money you've brought to the island," Vincent said crisply. "It's people like you who have helped shape the future of Kurnios."

Daisy laughed teasingly. "You won't wriggle out of our praise of Monty that way, Vincent! Nor of the way you promoted our cause. We're eternally grateful to you both, and even more delighted that you now have a happy marriage of your own. I hope we shall see much more of you and Lydia."

Lydia kept the smile organized on her lips. This thoroughly nice girl, with her traumatic worries over her husband, and her nice, stable life, could have no notion of the way Vincent Montagu had virtually bought his bride. And for one reason only, to give a selfish old man an heir. . . .

Lydia was shocked at the thought that ran around her brain at that moment, but in her most cynical moments she knew it was the way anyone else would see it. She had been bought and paid for, and in return for the idyllic kind of life this little family shared, she was required to produce a child, preferably a son, she supposed.

She realized Vincent was smiling steadily at her now, his look daring her to comment on Daisy's mention of their happy marriage.

"That's one of our reasons for coming here today," he said. "Monty wants to throw a ball to celebrate our wedding, and naturally, you're all invited. It's to be on the Saturday of next week. You'll come, won't you?"

"I should just say we will!" Daisy said, clearly delighted. "If I miss anything at all about England, it's the social occasions my family used to hold."

"Daisy's father is Sir Gilbert Armstrong, a prominent member of parliament," John put in for Lydia's benefit. "I can't imagine why she wanted to marry me and come to live on a remote island, when she could have had all of London at her feet."

But the confident way in which he said it, and the glances they shared, said it all.

By the time they left the villa, Lydia felt she had made two good friends. More than anyone else she had met, she could feel an empathy with Daisy Brandon. She said as much to Vincent on the way back to Montagu House.

"I knew you'd like her," he said somewhat vaguely. "She's a lot like you."

Lydia looked at him in surprise. In appearance they were totally different. Daisy was the typical English rose, pale of skin, despite living in a hot climate, with silky fair hair, rosy cheeks, and a deliciously plump shape that John obviously adored. The children were small replicas of their cheerful mother.

"I don't know how you can say that!" she said. "We look totally different."

"I grant you that, my sweet. But I was thinking more about your personalities. You're both survivors. You're strong as well as beautiful, and you bring out the best as well as the worst in men."

"Well thank you, I think! Is that supposed to be a compliment?"

"It is," he said tersely.

She opened her mouth to say something more, but began to realize she didn't have his full attention. They were returning to Montagu House by a different route, and it was a more populated area. There was one villa in particular that Vincent seemed to be watching. Even from this distance it appeared quite luxurious, with a fabulous view of the slow moving white sails of the windmills on the slopes of the terraces, and beyond them, the stunning blue of the Aegean Sea.

In fact, now that Lydia looked about her, while they travelled at a necessarily slow pace during the heat of the day, she saw that this area could definitely be called a town, even if it was as unlike any English town that she had ever seen. But there were roadways winding in and out of the dwellings, and a sugar-cake of houses on the hillside, whitewashed and cleanly elegant in their simplicity.

"Do you know someone who lives there?" she asked. "Are we making another visit today?"

She rather hoped not. She was feeling tired and in need of the afternoon siesta, and she didn't want any other conversation to spoil her enjoyment and memory of the delightful Brandons.

"It's the home of an acquaintance," she heard Vincent say. "But we shan't be visiting there."

He spoke casually enough, yet in a strangely guarded way. And all Lydia's feminine intuition bristled inside her, instantly alert, knowing at once that the whitewashed villa was the home of someone important to him.

It had to be a woman. It was inconceivable that a virile man like Vincent Montagu had lived all his life on Kurnios without knowing women. Knowing them and loving them. Her thoughts careered on, stabbing her between the eyes, as jealousy ripped through her breast, as keen as a blade.

"Will she be invited to the ball?" she said without prevarication.

Vincent glanced at her.

"I never said it was a woman."

"Isn't it?"

He gave an enigmatic shrug. "My dear, it's a little late in the day to be showing jealousy. You're my wife, and no one takes precedence over a man's wife."

And the most foolish thing a wife could do was to be jealous of an old love. As if he had said the words aloud, Lydia could hear them in her head.

Just as long as she remained an old love . . . her own

264

words added fiercely.

She had never thought herself a possessive woman, nor had occasion to be. And she was sensible enough to admit that friends of both sexes made any relationship healthy and open. But if she had never had cause to feel jealousy before, the pangs of it were more searing than she could ever have imagined. And it was all so ludicrous, when she didn't even know who lived in the villa.

But Vincent had never answered her question about whether or not she would be invited to the ball. And her pride wouldn't let her repeat the question.

All the same, it remained in her mind for a long time afterwards. She wondered just how deeply Vincent had become enmeshed with the woman at the villa or with any other woman on the island. Had he had a mistress who was dear to him? And was she still dear to him? Was she still confidently expecting his favors, even though he had a wife? He could explain to her that his bride meant nothing more to him than a means to an end for Monty. An English wife, who would bear an English heir.

As her maid helped her dress for dinner that evening, she pressed her hands to her belly, as if to will any such child away. The longer she remained barren, the longer she would keep Vincent. The shocking thought almost broke her heart, because it meant that already she was envisaging the time when she would lose him.

"Is my lady quite well?" the maid said, as Lydia continued to press her belly and gazed unseeingly into the long mirror.

"I'm perfectly all right, Coora," she answered quickly. "It's nothing, just a touch of colic, I expect."

The girl smiled uncertainly, not sure of the word, and continued fastening the necklace of pearls and emeralds around Lydia's neck. It was one of her father's last gifts, and one that she had always thought brought her luck, even though some people said that pearls meant tears. She dismissed such nonsense; the necklace was so magnificent and flawless, and she needed its reassurance tonight. It might allay some of her alarm at the memory of the way Vincent had looked as he gazed at the villa of the unknown woman that afternoon.

"My lady is very beautiful," the maid said shyly when she had finished her attentions.

The cream-colored gown Lydia wore was of a heavy water-silk, rustling with every movement, and complimenting every curve of her body. The jewels in the necklace were a blazing contrast to the absence of color in the gown, but only emphasized it more. Matching emeralds adorned her ears, and her dark hair was teased alluringly around them. Her blue eyes glowed vividly in her honeyed skin, and she looked the epitome of young vibrant health. No one could have guessed how vehemently she had felt compelled to make a statement on her own femininity that evening, as if to assure herself she could hold her own with any other woman in the world.

"Thank you, Coora," she said to the maid now, and dismissed the girl from the room just as Vincent entered it. He stared at Lydia's reflection in the mirror as if seeing her for the first time, and she felt a wild fluttering of nerves, echoed by the pulse-beat in her throat.

It was as if she was seeing him for the first time, too, seeing how darkly desirable he must be to all other women. In more vulgar terms, what a catch he must have seemed to the women living here. There must be many disappointed Mamas on the island, when they heard he had brought home an English wife.

"Have I missed something?" he said softly to her. "Is this some special occasion that I'm not aware of? Your birthday, perhaps?"

She shook her head. "Not for several months," she said politely. "But you must tell me if I've made a mistake. Am I too grand for a dinner at home with my two gentlemen?"

She didn't say it merely to please him. Already she felt as bound up in Monty's life as in Vincent's. She was a part of their lives, and she wanted Vincent to realize that she knew it.

He walked to her and drew her to her feet from the dressing-stool on which she sat with unconscious sensuality oozing from every pore. He pulled her into his arms and gazed into her eyes.

"You always look stunning to me. You could wear a fisherman's garb and still be the woman I desire far more than food at this moment. But I fear it must wait until later, my darling. Monty has invited people to dinner this evening, so your clever intuition must have warned you to put on your finery. I've only just discovered it myself and came to tell you."

His fingers ran around the curve of her breast as he spoke, and the tingling sensations his touch produced made her bite her lip. It took so little for him to arouse her, and any thought of remaining immune to him seemed doomed to failure. How could she, when she loved him so? She caught her breath at just how much she loved him, totally and for ever. But the very force of her love made her back away from him a little.

"It will be pleasant to have company for dinner," she forced herself to say. "Even the most normal of married couples can't exist on a diet of love alone. And that description can hardly apply to our marriage, can it, Vincent?"

He looked at her steadily for some minutes, and she felt the pulse in her throat beat more painfully. He bent and kissed her lips; a chaste, insulting kiss, more like that of a brother than a man to his wife.

"It doesn't become you to be sharp, my dear. As for normality, I hardly think you can find me lacking in a husband's duties, as it will be my pleasure, and yours, to discover later when our guests have gone."

Duties, Lydia thought bleakly. Was that all it meant to him, all the loving, the passion, the sensations he awoke in her that made her almost delirious with pleasure when he made love to her? She followed him silently downstairs to the brightly lit dining room, putting a bright smile on her face as Monty came forward to introduce her to their dinner guests, a man and two women. For a moment, Lydia's heart faltered, wondering if she was to come face to face so soon with Vincent's mistress. It would be a piquant occasion for him, she thought bitterly. His wife and his mistress at the same table. . . .

"My dear Lydia," Monty said smilingly. "I want to introduce you to some of my good friends. This is Milos and Athene Guistiani, and Milos's mother, Eida, whom I count as one of my oldest friends."

Lydia was angry with herself for automatically expecting the worst. For the three charming people with Monty were a complete family unit. The married couple must be already nearing fifty, she guessed. And the mother, Eida, whose creased and elderly features were of an age that matched Monty's own, could hardly be thought of as anyone's mistress, let alone Vincent's!

"I'm so happy to meet you," Lydia murmured, remembering her manners, and very aware that she was starting to let her imagination stray into dangerous areas. if she was going to see every woman on Kurnios as a potential rival for Vincent's affections, her life here was going to become impossibly stultified.

"We are most happy to meet you, too, Madame," the elderly Eida put in before either of the others got the chance to speak. Her English was heavily overlaid with a thick Greek accent and many flowery gestures. "For far too long we worry over our dear Vincent, and now at last he bring home a beautiful bride to Kurnios, and we all rejoice with him."

"Mother, give her a chance to catch her breath before you overwhelm her with compliments," her son Milos said mildly. "You will excuse my mother, dear Madame Montagu. She lets her tongue run away with her."

269

Lydia smiled, liking these frank people more and more.

"Then I understand her very well, for I'm often accused for doing the same thing myself," she said. "But please won't you call me Lydia? I hope that all the friends of my husband's and of Monty's are also friends of mine."

"Then we shall be delighted to do so," Milos said.

The customary pre-dinner drinks were handed round, and it could have been any English drawing room setting, Lydia thought, with some amusement. No matter where they went in the world, the English always had style, and never more so than when entertaining friends.

"You'll forgive me for saying so, but you speak beautiful English," she commented to both Milos and Athene, when they were all seated around the beautiful dining table. The sumptuous main course of roast lamb and vegetables had been enjoyed to the fullest, and delicately flavored fruit sorbets were being served.

"Ah, that is because both were educated in one of your fine universities," Eida interrupted, obviously never one for remaining silent for too long. "It is what you call the status symbol, even among we Greeks. That is the way you say it?"

"It is," Lydia said, smiling slightly. She refused to look at Vincent just then. His son, too, was destined to be educated in England, which was apparently the status symbol which people here held in high esteem.

"I understand you once lived in India, Lydia?" Athene asked. "It is not a country I would wish to see."

"Really?" Lydia looked at her in some surprise. "But it is one of the most colorful nations of the world."

"But surely there is great poverty there," Athene persisted. "I only know what I have been told, of course, and you must forgive me if I do not have your knowledge of the country. But are there not beggars in streets that are running with filth and animals in the houses?"

"Really, Athene, not at the dinner table," her husband admonished her, with an apologetic look at Monty.

"No, please," Monty said at once. "I, too, would be interested in which Lydia has to say about India. Surely it cannot all be as distasteful as Athene suggests?"

"Certainly not," Lydia said, mildly indignant. "I grant you there are beggars, and parts of the country are not always the most wholesome of places, but it's not all like that. There are also the fabulous palaces of the Indian princes, and the ceremonials that occur inside them. I was privileged to see some of them with my parents. The wonderful bejewelled elephants take part in these parades, and the princes sit on them in their *howdahs*, and the rituals and beliefs they enjoyed are simply fascinating . . ."

She became aware that everyone had gone silent, and she blushed deeply. "I'm sorry. I shouldn't ramble on so."

"Please don't stop, Lydia," Vincent said. "You've enchanted us all. Tell us something of these rituals."

But she was so embarrassed, her mind almost

271

refused to function. There were so many rituals, and right now she was finding it hard to remember even one. She swallowed hard, telling herself not to be so pathetic, and searching her memory.

"Well, you know of course that India is a Hindu country. The Hindu people revere light as something almost magical, or godlike. When the evening lamps are lit, they look on that moment as mankind replacing the light of the sun, and the true Hindu always places his hands together in a moment of reverence. It may sound foolish to outsiders, but it's just one of the things I found fascinating. I couldn't begin to tell you of all the wonders of that country!"

"You obviously still miss it very much," Athene said. "Even more than you miss England?"

Lydia felt almost startled by the question. She gave a short laugh.

"Oh, I don't miss England at all! I think I was always meant to live in a warm climate, and I feel far more at home where the sun shines most often. It always shone in India, except for the rainy season of course." She tried not to sound too nostalgic, thinking she was in danger of monopolizing the conversation, and tried to sound more prosaic. But they wouldn't let the discussion end.

"What about the animals?" Milos persisted. "You've already mentioned elephants, but don't they hold the cow sacred in India?"

"Oh yes. As for other animals, there's the tiger, of course. My father took me on a tiger hunt once. It was exciting to begin with, but in the end I hated it. I didn't like to see those magnificent animals being killed for sport."

272

"Well, I think we've heard enough about India for now," Vincent said, as her mouth drooped a little. "You'll gather that my wife is well travelled, but I hope she's found her true haven at last."

It was an odd way of putting it, but for some reason everyone raised their glasses to her at that moment. Lydia felt a moment of rare contentment, surrounded by these friendly, smiling faces. By the time the evening was over, and she and Vincent prepared to retire for the night, she told him how much she liked the three she had met that evening.

"And the Brandons, too," she said, remembering them. "You have some very nice people living here, Vincent."

"I told you. Monty was very careful whom he invited to share his island," he commented. "The Guistianis belong to a very old, established Athens family, and even when they became very rich and there was absolutely no need for it, old Eida still continued her practice."

She looked at him sharply, not quite liking the sound of this; thoughts of witchcraft flew high in her mind. "What practice is that?"

"She's a midwife," he said. "When your time comes, we have an excellent doctor here who will attend you, of course. Most of the islanders, though, still rely on Eida's ancient methods and potions to take the sting out of childbirth, and prefer to have a woman at hand."

Lydia gaped at him. This was all moving much too fast for her as was the unsavory thought that the old Greek woman might have been brought here this evening especially to look her over. She may have overtly been studying what Nadima used to call a woman's childbearing hips. It was suddenly all too much. She burst into great scalding tears.

"How could you!" she wept. "How *dare* you!"

She felt his arms close around her, rock-hard. She was in their warm circle, and they were about all that was holding her together, since her legs were beginning to feel like jelly now.

"What crazy ideas are going through your head now?" he said harshly. "God help me, Lydia, but you're the most fanciful woman I've ever known."

"And you've known so many, I suppose!" she flashed back at once, unable to resist the taunt.

"I have, as a matter of fact," he said, his voice still unyielding. "Which is why I took some time and trouble in choosing the right one to be my wife."

"One with apparent childbearing capabilities, you mean, don't you? Those were the only credentials she required, I believe?"

He swore an oath beneath his breath. He was breathing very heavily, as heavily as herself. She was already undressed and in her nightgown, while he still had some garments to remove. Her body was tingling with righteous indignation, and then with something else as she recognized the darkness of desire in his eyes as he felt the upthrust of her nipples against his chest. It was as if her anger only sharpened that desire, and before she knew what was happening, he had pushed her onto the bed and pinned her there beneath him.

"If that's what you choose to believe, then there's no point in our wasting any more time, is there?"

274

he said, almost cruelly. "I promised you a ravishing this evening that you wouldn't forget, my sweet, so make yourself ready."

She didn't move, She merely stared up at him, her blue eyes wide and breathtakingly lovely, even though they were blurred with tears. She wouldn't resist, but nor would she help him. Since he was her husband, she had no option but to submit to him. He could do as he would with her, and she would lay as still as a statue.

Her thoughts obviously transmitted themselves to him, for he gave her a sardonic smile as he swiftly rid himself of his clothes, scattering them where they fell. Her heart thudded at the sight of him, magnificent and proud, and potently ready for her. He spoke with soft seduction as he leaned over her.

"Very well. If you refuse to raise your nightgown for me, I shall just have to remove it for you."

With one swift jerking movement of both hands, he tore the soft fabric from neck to him, while she gasped in disbelief. This was a new and different Vincent. This was a man who wanted his woman and wanted her *now*, but without tenderness or loving words. This was a man who saw his maleness being thwarted, and was having none of it.

"Do you really think you'll be able to lie there and not respond to me, my sweet wife?" he said, in a soft voice edged with steel. "I think not, if only because I've already taught you too well."

She gritted her teeth, but the touch of his hands over her nakedness as he caressed her was more than she could take without showing some sign of response. Sheer abandonment washed over her as

275

Vincent bent his head and followed the path his hands had taken with gentle kisses, and soft little moans of pleasure left her parted lips. Her hands were in his hair, kneading it, without even realizing what she was doing. And when the kisses became more insistent, more penetrating, she gasped, aching for fulfillment.

And then all the waiting was over, and he was astride her, riding her with an energy that sent her senses reeling. Her arms clung to him, her very soul seemed to soar up to meet him, and the glistening of their entwined bodies was a potent aphrodisiac. It could go on forever and she wouldn't care, she thought wildly. If the whole world ended now, she would be complete here in his arms.

"Not yet, my dearest," she heard him say softly, as she recklessly gasped out his name. "Not yet."

She looked at him blindly, dazed with love, not yet sated by his lust. And then he was gripping her, pulling her into him and turning them both around, until he lay on his back and she was the rider. Her unpinned hair tumbled about his face, and she was momentarily numb with embarrassment, hearing his breath catch as her full breasts brushed against his chest. Then he captured the abundant strands of her hair, pulling her down onto him even more, and thrusting upwards.

Lydia hardly knew what was happening, but the sweet wild rapture of being part of him was dictating its own terms now. She rode with him into realms of ecstasy she had never known before. And then came the moment of twisting heat when he was the one to cling to her, to call out her name in

276

hoarse gasps, as if the life force gushing out of his body and into hers was an exquisite mixture of pleasure and pain.

And then it was finally over, and she was still wrapped in his arms, and somehow the coverlet was cocooning them. *Safe against the world.* This was Lydia's last drowsy thought as she drifted into an exhausted sleep. Safe against however many other women had once been part of Vincent's life.

Chapter Twelve

Over breakfast a few days later, Lydia begged the use of the small pony cart to explore by herself. She had already deduced that it was quite safe to travel on the leeward side of the island, away from the more jagged mountains and the remnants of the once active volcano. And the islanders were peaceful and friendly. She was sure she would come to no harm.

"That is, always supposing I'm to be allowed away from the house on my own," she said to Vincent, knowing quite well it would bait him.

"Of course you are, if you wish, and as long as you stick to the recognized routes. You're not a prisoner here," he said, as distantly as if he cared little where she went. But he must care, of course, she thought bitterly. She was his investment for the future.

"I think it's a good idea for Lydia to explore a little by herself," Monty championed her. "You should get to know your new homeland, my dear, and learn to see it through your own eyes. Both Vincent and I are biased about its charms, but I've no doubt you'll fall in love with it, too."

"I think I've already done that," she said, smiling back at him, and realizing to her surprise that it was true. She had found no difficulty at all in falling in love with the island. Its very ruggedness, and the native ingenuity of crop growing through their agricultural setbacks and still surviving against everything with which nature had savaged it, was something that touched her soul. And she liked the friendly, hardworking Greek people, especially admiring the women, toiling in the fields in their dark, dusty clothes alongside the men.

"Do you want to go this morning?" Vincent asked. "It might be a good time, since the doctor's coming to see Monty, and I want to call on our lawyer."

"Then that's settled. I shall go out on my own today," she said, nodding, and avoiding Monty's eyes.

He never seemed at all bothered by the doctor's regular visits, but each time the man came to the house, Lydia felt as if it struck another nail in the old man's coffin. She didn't want to think of him dying. Already she knew that Kurnios *was* Monty, and without him, the heart would be gone out of it.

But it was pointless to dwell on such dismal thoughts when the sun was shining brilliantly in a clear blue sky, and begging all humanity to be outside in the glorious, clear air. Especially as Monty himself took these routine medical visits as a necessary evil on the one hand, but also the gleeful excuse to inveigle the doctor into a mock-friendly game of poker on the other. The so-called medical checks rarely lasted less than two hours, and often more.

It was some time later, when she had been jogging comfortably along in the pony cart for a long while, that Lydia was aware of an unbelievable sense of freedom. At home in India, she had been too young and her life too pampered for her to wander anywhere on her own. Besides, it wasn't suitable for the daughter of an English gentleman to walk abroad anywhere in such heat. It wasn't until she went to live in England, beholden to her uncle's family as she was, that she had actually tasted the novelty of walking the streets alone, fending for herself, and realizing the sheer pleasure of being independent of other people, however well-meaning.

As the little grey pony plodded along ahead of Lydia's cart, she held the reins loosely, knowing for the first time how much she relished this sense of freedom. Of course, it was ironic to think she was really free. She was Vincent Montagu's property, just as these villas and fields indirectly all belonged to him through Monty. She was as much a prisoner on Kurnios as if she was behind bars. But there was never a prison cell that held as much luxury as Montagu House! Nor such an endearing inmate as Monty.

She refused to let herself think of Vincent in any context at all at that moment, concentrating instead on breathing in the mountain scents, and revelling in seeing the horizon dazzle in a heat haze ahead of her.

"Whoa there, Lydia! Are you coming to visit us?"

The sudden sound of an English voice took her by surprise. For a startled moment she had to concentrate quite hard, having been in an almost memeric state induced by the heat and the plodding gait of the pony. And then she relaxed as she saw John Brandon, incongruously perched on the back of a mule, and reining in alongside her.

"I didn't see you coming!" she began.

"Oh, I could see that. You were lost in a dream by the looks of you. But be careful the sun doesn't get to you, Lydia. Its strength can be deceptive at this time of the day, and you tend to think the cool air of the mountains is lessening its effect, but be warned. Daisy had a very bad attack of sunstroke when we first came to the island. Why don't you call in to see her for a cool drink? I know she'd be delighted to see you."

"Without a formal invitation?" Lydia said doubtfully.

John laughed. "You need to change your attitude now you're living on Kurnios, Lydia. Etiquette has its place, and we'll all be as formal as you wish at Monty's ball. But friends should be able to visit one another whenever they wish, don't you think? The children have gone back to school on the mainland and will be there for the next few weeks, so Daisy's feeling their loss. I know she'd love to have a friend call on her."

With one leap, he included her in their circle of friends, and she felt a great warmth toward him and toward his wife, who would have married for

281

love and for no less worthy reason.

"Then I shall certainly call on Daisy. I didn't even realize I was so near to your house."

Nor how far she had come, nor how long she had been outdoors. She could see the Brandon house ahead of her now, and it was truly a welcome sight. The sun had risen so insidiously fast she hadn't been aware of its prickling heat, but she could feel it beating down now, on the back of her neck and her lower arms below the sleeves of her morning gown.

She had seen people suffering with sunstroke, and had no wish to be one of them. Having lived in India for so long, she had never thought it would happen to her. But India had been a long time ago, she recalled with some unease, and she was probably no longer immune. Perhaps it was time she stopped clinging to so much of that past as well, she thought with sudden surprise, and faced the fact that whatever the future held, she had gone into it willingly. It was childish to keep holding India to her heart as some kind of talisman against all ills.

Daisy Brandon welcomed her into the cool interior of her home as warmly as if she were a confidante of long-standing. It cheered Lydia immensely. She had known many acquaintances in her life, but she had had few women friends over the years. She had made no close friends of her own age in Bath, where she had been too exhausted from coping with her small cousins each day to bother with too much social life. And she would certainly never have chosen Audine as a friend. But this girl was different.

"You must be a clairvoyant, Lydia," Daisy said in delight. "I was thinking this very morning how pleasant it would be if we met. I do miss the children now. But please sit down, and I'll fetch some lemon cordial. Would you care to sit outside? It's rather too hot for me, but we have a sun canopy on the veranda if you wish."

"I'd rather stay inside, too," Lydia said thankfully. "It's far hotter than I realized, and I can already feel the prickling on my skin."

Daisy looked concerned. "I have some soothing salve which will help to stop the discomfort. Everyone underestimates the strength of the sun when they first come to the island. We're so high up in the mountains here, you see, and the breezes give you a false sense of security. But you'll be fine with the salve."

Lydia hoped she was right. She told herself she was imagining things to feel so dizzy and lightheaded. By the time Daisy had brought the salve and she had put it on her reddened skin, she felt somewhat better. Added to which, the cool drink and the tidbits the two of them had nibbled on were restoring her a little. It had been foolish to stay out for so long without a parasol.

"So, how are you liking our island?" Daisy said, with the proprietary pride of one who had lived here longer than the newcomer.

"I like it very much. The people are so friendly, and to be truthful, I never expected there to be so many Europeans here. It's quite cosmopolitan, isn't it?"

"Oh well, that's all Monty's doing. Vincent will have told you the history of how it all came about, of course."

She spoke matter-of-factly, as if it was the most natural thing in the world for a man to tell his future wife all there was to know about her new home before she ever came there. It was sadly far from the truth. In any normal relationship, in the leisurely and delicious courtship that led to marriage, what Daisy said would certainly have been so. But theirs was anything but a normal relationship. Lydia forced a quick smile.

"Oh yes, of course. It was still a surprise to me though. I think Vincent wanted me to form my own impressions, rather than tell me every detail."

She drank deeply, realizing she had drained her glass of lemon cordial before Daisy had barely touched hers. She was thirsting for more. The other girl refilled her glass at once, as attentive as a good hostess should be.

"Are you sure you're quite well, Lydia?" Daisy spoke a little anxiously. "You do look very flushed."

"I'm fine," she replied. "Please don't worry about me, Daisy. Tell me instead about some of the people I shall be meeting at the ball. You must know all of them."

She tried to breathe deeply, and not to feel as if her skin was truly on fire. It would settle down soon, once the salve took effect, she thought desperately. A fine sight she would look at the ball with fiery, angry-looking flesh in the lovely, low-cut gown she intended to wear. She leaned back in her chair, and the coolness of the fabric covering blessedly soothed the skin at the nape of her neck. She heard Daisy give a small laugh.

"I wouldn't know where to start to describe some of them. We do have some rather autocratic English people here, and some of the jewels of Greek society, as well as what are termed the ordinary folk, like John and me."

"I wouldn't call you ordinary at all!" Lydia said, striving not to let the room swim in front of her.

"Oh well, you know what I mean. We're ordinary folk compared with the several rather stuffy old retired colonels and their ladies, to say nothing of a rakish English duke, and the daughter of one of Greece's richest shipping magnates—"

When she stopped abruptly, Lydia knew it was for a very special reason, and sensed that it was one that was vitally important to her. She wished she could grasp the importance of it, but the hazy, watery waves of the walls wouldn't keep still. She was slipping into their depths as if she were slipping into a swirling blue ocean. The last thing she heard was Daisy frantically calling out her name.

"Lydia . . . Lydia . . ."

She struggled to open her eyes, but they hurt too much. Everything was hurting, from the top of her head, raging with a stabbing headache, to the tips of her toes. She could swear that even her toenails hurt.

"Madame Montagu . . ."

"Oh, Lydia dear, please say something . . ."

Why on earth did they keep bothering her when

all she wanted to do was return into her twilight sleep once again? And whose voices were they? One was deep and familiar, another more guttural that she didn't know, yet another feminine, with a delightfully rural English accent . . .

"I suggest we leave her to sleep some more," the guttural voice said now, as she struggled to make sense of things. "When the body is ready to be awakened, it will awaken naturally. I beg you both not to be unduly alarmed. She's young and strong, and she'll recover from this very soon now. Sleep is obviously what she needs, and the sedatives are at least relieving her of some of the pain."

She wanted to scream at the unknown man that the pain was excruciating, but she seemed to have lost the power to open her mouth to say the words, or to lift her eyelids to let them know she was perfectly aware of what was going on. But that was a mere temporary illusion, because she wasn't fully aware of anything. Seconds after she sensed that the trio had left her, she drifted back into that nightmare world, where images came and went, and her skin felt as if it was on fire. She burned as if the hot lava from the volcano that had once devoured Kurnios was seeping into her flesh, and greedily eating it away until she, too, was reduced to ashes.

She became fully conscious then, uttering a small anguished cry low in her throat. Tentatively she opened her eyes, to stare at a ceiling she was sure wasn't her own. There was very little light in the room, and what there was was soft and rosy, and after a moment she realized it was no more than a small pool of candle glow. She concluded that it must be night. And somewhere in her brain came the ridiculous urge to applaud herself, for having the sense to recognize night from day! She felt the slow stab of tears in her eyes, and wondered if she had been very ill.

She lifted her head, and discovered that it was blessedly clear. The raging pains had gone. Her arms felt a little stiff, but she flexed her fingers and toes and found every one intact. No matter how she tried, she could remember nothing. She didn't know where she was, nor why she was wearing a strange nightgown that didn't belong to her. She felt suddenly very frightened.

The door opened, and for a second Lydia was tempted to burrow beneath the bedclothes, not wanting to face the reality of being in an alien place.

"Lydia, thank heavens you're awake at last! We've been so worried about you."

Lydia's eyes flew open, and she saw the small figure of Daisy Brandon approaching the bed, a relieved smile on her face. Relief washed over Lydia herself, just because she had remembered the other girl. Such a simple thing, but so vitally important to her peace of mind.

"What . . . what happened?" she croaked, her mouth dry and parched.

Daisy went at once to a pitcher of water and held a glassful to Lydia's lips, where she drank gratefully.

"You had too much sun. Doctor Stavros said it was a very bad case of sunstroke."

"Sunstroke! How was that possible when I've lived in India? I'm quite used to the sun."

Daisy shook her head. "Vincent says you haven't lived in India for a long while, and besides, the climate here is much dryer, and the sun burns more directly. I did warn you."

"Yes, you did," Lydia muttered. "I feel such a fool."

"There's no need."

"How long have I been here?" she asked next.

"Two days. John came home just after you collapsed, and sent for Doctor Stavros at once. He went to fetch Vincent then, and he's been sleeping on the sofa over there in case you wanted anything during the night. He's gone home to fetch some fresh clothes for you, but we expect him back within the hour."

Lydia was finding it hard to take it all in. Two days had gone out of her life! And Vincent had been sleeping here in this room and she hadn't known it. She saw the rumpled blankets on the sofa, and felt a great tenderness toward him for doing this.

She was feeling better by the minute now, and she sat up carefully, thankful that her head no longer felt so disoriented, and wanting to be up. But caution made her take it slowly, and apparently she should wait for Vincent to come back with clean clothes.

Daisy insisted she remain where she was for a little while longer, and remained to chat with her. As she grew stronger, fragments of a past conversation kept slipping into Lydia's mind. There was

288

something she needed to know, something she had almost learned, but which was still eluding her.

"Are you ready for something to eat now? Some broth, perhaps? Or some cold chicken? You've had nothing but the drinks we could force down you for two days, Lydia. You should eat something."

"Cold chicken then, please," she said, grimacing at the thought of the hot broth they gave to invalids. "And Daisy? I'm so sorry to have been such a trouble to you."

"Nonsense," the girl said cheerfully. "We were intending to be friends, remember? And we were having a good old gossip about some of the folk going to Monty's ball just before you collapsed. Now, you just lie there and I'll fetch the food, then you can have some washing water if you feel up to it."

"Oh, I will, and I'll also have to think about going home. I can't impose on you forever . . ."

Her voice trailed away because Daisy was already out of the room and clattering down the stairs. But the words had triggered off a nagging memory. She still couldn't quite catch it, but she was sure it had something to do with a Greek shipping magnate. Which was very odd, because she still couldn't connect anything else in her mind with such a person.

She lay back and closed her eyes for a moment, still puzzling over it. She must have dropped off to sleep again, because the dull buzz of voices was hovering around her again when she awoke. This time, she was perfectly capable of opening her eyes and seeing Vincent by her side.

"So you've come back to us at last, have you?" he said, his voice rough-edged. "Don't you dare do such a stupid thing like that to me again, do you hear?"

She stared at him; the brimming warmth in her heart dissipating fast at the abruptness of his tone.

"I didn't do anything to you," she said huskily. "I was the one who collapsed, and you don't have to tell me how stupid I was. I promise you I'll never do it again, but not because you demand it! I never want to feel that ill again."

She turned away from him, not wanting to see the derision in his eyes. He thought her stupid, and so she was. Then why had he decided to stay here with her, if she was so irresponsible?

The answer was obvious. He was protecting his investment once more because if anything happened to Lydia, he'd have to go searching for a mother to bear his child all over again. And if there had to be a suitable time of mourning, it wouldn't be soon enough for Monty.

She smothered the sob in her throat. She thought she heard Vincent swear softly, but Daisy brought her food into the room just then. If he'd intended to say anything more, the moment was gone.

"My wife seems to be out of pain now, and there seems to be no need for me to stay with her," he said shortly to Daisy. "So I propose that I go home and get a good night's sleep and come back for her in the morning."

"That's fine, Vincent. You can't have been very comfortable, sleeping on the sofa."

If the other two both knew that wasn't the true reason he wanted to be as far away from Lydia as possible, neither of them was letting on.

Lydia felt his polite kiss on her cheek, knowing it was more for Daisy's sake than her own. She felt like weeping at his implacable attitude, but nothing was going to let him see it.

After he had gone downstairs, with Daisy at his heels to bid him goodnight, Lydia discovered that she was famished, and that the succulent aroma of the cold chicken was waking up all her taste buds. She ate heartily, and drank the hot tea that accompanied it. When she was replete, she leaned back against the pillow.

Daisy found her with a speculative look in her eyes as she brought a jug of hot water and towels into the room.

"I feel so guilty, having you wait on me," Lydia said.

"Don't be silly. The girl who works for us went home for the night long ago, but I'm quite capable of carrying a jug and towels by myself. I'm afraid servants make you lazy."

"Daisy," Lydia said carefully. "Did I say anything while I was asleep? Did I ramble?"

The thought had occurred to her that she might have betrayed the truth about herself and Vincent, and it would be humiliating to think that anyone else knew. Vincent's loyalty to his grandfather might have been misplaced, but Lydia's own loyalty to Vincent and herself was never in question. She couldn't bear it if this wholesome girl knew how their marriage had come about, and especially the

291

conditions that went with it.

"You did mutter rather a lot, but I couldn't understand much of it. You kept calling for somebody with an odd name. Naddy or something. You kept asking this Naddy what to do."

"Nadima," Lydia supplied. "She was my old nurse when I lived in India. I depended on her for everything."

She smiled ruefully. India was a long time ago, and Nadima was long since dead. It was time for Lydia Montagu to stand on her own two feet, instead of depending on others. She could even vaguely remember thinking something of the sort on the way here. Now, it was all sharply underlined for her.

"I daresay you miss her," Daisy said. "But you have a new life here now, Lydia, and people who love you. I do hope you'll be happy on the island."

"I know I will."

How could she say anything else to this anxious-faced girl, who wanted to hear that everything was fine, and that no undercurrents were disturbing the serenity of a new bride's life?

She thought it would be hard to get to sleep that night, but in the end she slept well, fortified with the food inside her. And by the time Vincent arrived the next morning, she was downstairs, wearing the clean garments he had brought from Montagu House the evening before.

"You're looking better," he said coolly.

"Thank you."

They were like two strangers, polite, remote, and she saw the start of a frown between Daisy Brandon's eyes, as if just beginning to wonder if something wasn't right between these two. Lydia forced a smile to her lips and spoke to him more warmly.

"I'm looking forward to going home, Vincent, but Daisy has been kindness itself, and I can't thank her enough."

"We both thank you, Daisy," he added.

"Oh, for pity's sake, don't go on so. I only did what any friend would have done," Daisy answered in a fluster.

Impulsively, Lydia hugged her before she went outside on Vincent's arm, to where the pony cart was awaiting them. She gave a small shudder, remembering how foolish she had been, and then stepped determinedly inside it.

They had driven for some minutes without speaking, and then Lydia spoke in a small voice.

"You didn't have to make it quite so obvious that you were so displeased with me. I know I was foolish, and I deeply regret it, but believe me, I suffered for it."

She touched the reddened flesh on her arms, only just starting to fade from its angry color, thanks to the salves and lotions the doctor had prescribed.

"I can see that, and I'm not displeased with you. And I'm the one with the regrets, not you."

She looked at him sharply. The sun was not as strong as it had been the other day, for it was earlier in the day, but she still had to shield her eyes from its glare to look at him.

"You mean you regret marrying me, don't you?" she said slowly. Her heart may be breaking, but she had to ask, to know. There was no point in hiding away from the truth.

"Of course I do. I should never have married you," he said harshly.

She was consumed with a misery too deep for words. She couldn't have spoken then if her life had depended on it. How could he be so cruel, so vindictive? Condemning her to a life with a man who didn't love her, and who regretted ever marrying her? The one small salve to her pride was the fact that she had never told him she loved him. Thank God he didn't know, for that would be the final humiliation.

"Well, now we both know where we stand, don't we?" she said, consumed with misery. "I'm glad the pretense is over, and once I've done what's expected of me, I'll be more than thankful to get away from here and return to England."

She had to fight back the tears as she spoke, for it was a complete denial of the way she really felt. She never wanted to return to England's cold rainy climate. She blossomed in the sun. But neither could she spend the rest of her life with a man who didn't love her.

Right now, she didn't even bother mentioning that she had every intention of taking her child with her. That would be one of *her* conditions, she thought fiercely. Monty would see his English heir, and Vincent would see his son, but the child's life would be with her, wherever she chose to live.

"So it seems you're a fortune hunter after all,"

Vincent said coldly.

She drew in her breath, hurt beyond measure. But it no longer mattered. Let him think what he liked. He probably despised her for even accepting his proposal of marriage . . . his *devious* proposal. How dare he slander her, when he was guilty of the worst deception!

"If that's what you choose to believe, I can't stop you," she said. "So in view of all this, I'd prefer our marriage to be in name only from now on, but that would seem an impossibility, wouldn't it? It wouldn't suit your little plan."

She glanced at him. He was looking at her, a strange, enigmatic expression in his dark eyes. Those eyes, that could soften with tenderness in a moment, or surge with a passion that could take her to the stars. . . .

"Unless the child is already on its way," he said meaningfully, his gaze dropping down to where she twisted both hands in her lap.

"And if it is, you'll leave me alone until it's born?" she was conscious of her high, shrill voice.

Dear God, what was happening between them? This was the very last conversation she wanted with him. So cold and calculating, like two people striking a bargain. *And over a child.* Over what should have been one of the happiest moments in a couple's life.

"If that's what you wish," he agreed.

"Well, I'm sorry to disappoint you, but there's no child on the way yet," she said in a trembling voice. "Doctor Stavros asked me some very searching questions about it when I was so sick, and he assured me I was not pregnant."

"Then we shall just have to resume our nightly rituals until you are," Vincent said, as if it were some nuisance that had to be undertaken. Her heart was breaking, but she stared straight ahead and said nothing more until the welcome sight of Montagu House was ahead of them.

She couldn't guess at Vincent's thoughts, nor dare to look at him again. Nor could she think what on earth had made her tell such untruths about Doctor Stavros's diagnosis. The doctor had never asked her anything about a child. He treated her only for sunstroke, and Daisy had told her his very real concern about the vomiting was that she was losing far too much fluid, insisting that she had to keep drinking plenty of water.

No wonder she had fitfully woken out of her delirium from time to time, dribbling the water down her chin that others had pushed down her throat, and with the uncomfortable feeling that she was being blown up like a balloon.

But why had she been stupid enough to tell such a lie to Vincent? It would be so easy for him to question the doctor the next time he called on Monty, and to learn the truth. And if he did so, he would read into it only one thing. That Lydia Grey Montagu still wanted his attentions, for all her strenuous denials. She still wanted the warmth of his body at night, and the sensuality of his love-making.

Vincent told her that Monty had been very concerned for her welfare, and was anxious to see her. So while Vincent was stabling the pony cart, Lydia sought out his grandfather. He was in the cool library, among his books, and she hastened to reassure him that she was well.

From the depths of his comfortable armchair, he looked more frail than ever, she thought. She dropped onto a stool by his side, where she looked up at him. In so short a time, and despite the circumstances, she had developed a real affection for the old man, and he for her.

"I really am much better now, Monty," she said, suddenly guilty that in her mood of self-pity she had almost gone straight upstairs to her room and buried her head beneath her bedclothes. She knew how awful that self-pity was, compared with what Monty faced.

"Anyway, it was my own fault for not realizing the strength of the sun, and staying out in it for too long."

Monty was still doubtful. "That's as may be, but your lovely skin still looks very sore and angry, my dear. Has Doctor Stavros given you something to put on it?"

She nodded. "The salve he gave me works wonders. I'm to take a sedative each night as well, to help me sleep, and to prevent me from scratching. It itches appallingly at times, and if I scratch it without thinking, the pain soon reminds me."

A sedative at night was a very good thing, she thought. It would help dull her senses to the fact that if Vincent turned to her in the darkness, it was from duty, not love. She had known it for a while, of course. Yet far from feeling dulled, her senses right now were acutely sharp, noting everything with a new poignancy.

"I sincerely hope the worst of it will be over by the night of the ball," Monty went on. "Vincent will be anxious to show off his new bride, and I'm sure you'll be in demand from the other young blades for dancing. I only regret that I'm no longer able to take you around the floor myself. You may not believe it, but in my young days, I was quite nimble on my feet."

He gave a deep sigh. He so rarely showed distress at his deteriorating condition that Lydia felt some alarm. She noted how he slumped in his leather armchair, the pages of the half-open book on his knee fluttering a little, as if no one had pressed them flat to read them for a long time. They were merely a prop to pass the time. Lydia felt a deep sorrow for this brave-spirited old man who had given so much to this island, and whose life-span was ebbing fast.

"I'll dance with you," she said emotionally. "Even if the two of us can only shuffle in a corner, I promise you a dance. You'll be my favorite partner."

Monty smiled with genuine affection at her upturned face. He patted her hand with the waxy fingers that were thinning so fast now, careful to avoid her heated forearm.

"You must save that description for your husband, Lydia. But I'll be more than content to be second-best."

Her eyes blurred, and she leaned her head on

his arm for a moment, thankful that he couldn't see her expression. If only everything were as serene as Monty believed. He had organized this whole charade for his own gain, and she should hate him for it. But somehow she couldn't.

And because she and Vincent had agreed by silent consent to cushion Monty from their marital troubles, he had clearly assumed that she was happily resigned now to her new life. He assumed that she and Vincent were perfectly in tune with one another. But that wasn't so, Lydia thought miserably. There was very little harmony between the two of them; they only agreed on discord.

was for two days, and she was surprised to find
him much she had missed him. Even when they
argued, she was stimulated by him.

"You ..." he said ...

She th... trip is ... and ...

Chapter Thirteen

After a week, Lydia's sunstroke was nearly forgotten. She was young and healthy, and the skin
had healed remarkably quickly. She was still careful
to shield it from the sun, fearful that the dreaded
irritation would begin again. Doctor Stavros had
examined her arms and neck several times during
his visits to Monty, and pronounced her of a
strong and robust disposition.

"He makes me sound like a prize filly," she said
with a laugh to the two men of the house, after
the doctor had gone.

"But a very valuable one, my sweet," Vincent
said. "Sunstroke can be dangerous, so don't underestimate his concern for you."

But she knew only too well she was only valuable to him because she had yet to fulfill her obligation. She was beginning to hate the feeling of
being watched and pampered until she produced
the heir Monty wanted so badly.

A while later, as she was strolling in the grounds
in the cool of the evening, needing time to be
alone, Vincent caught up with her in one of the
rose arbors. He had been to the mainland on busi-

ness for two days, and she was surprised to find how much she had missed him. Even when they argued, she was still stimulated by him.

"You lied to me," he said flatly now.

She flinched, her grip on her parasol tightening. She turned to face him, pretending not to know what he meant.

"That's rich, coming from you, when my whole reason for being here is built on one of your lies!"

He took hold of her arm. A week ago she would have cried out at the pain, but there was only the pressure of his fingers to make her wince now.

"You know very well what I mean. Why did you tell me the doctor had asked about your condition, when he did no such thing?"

"Have you been discussing me with him?" she said, her face heated.

He led her to one of the long seats in the arbor and sat down abruptly beside her.

"Why should I not? It seemed a normal thing for an eager husband to inquire if his family doctor thought there was anything wrong in the fact that his wife hadn't conceived yet."

Lydia closed her eyes in embarrassment. It wasn't something that gentlefolk discussed openly. Sometimes a lady didn't even tell her husband she was in a delicate condition until well on in her time, and then it was polite of him to keep away from her until the event was over. Nadima had told her so. She swallowed hard.

"And what did he say to such a question?" she asked, nonplussed for a moment. "I trust he thought it was highly indelicate of you to be asking

301

such a thing when we've been married such a short time!"

"He did not. Doctor Stavros has been a friend of the family for many years, and we've always discussed things frankly with him."

She looked at him with growing suspicion, her voice sharp. "You surely aren't going to tell me he's aware of your reasons for marrying me? Of Monty's insane wish for a kind of immortality through my son?"

Vincent shrugged. "It's hardly an insane wish. It's normal practice among families to want to continue the line. Royalty insists on it, so why should we ordinary mortals be any different? And of course Stavros knows. He'll be the one to attend you when the time comes. He'll help to ease *our* son into the world, just as he helps to ease Monty's passage out of it, God willing."

"Dear heaven! Who else knows? Does the whole of Kurnios know I'm no more than a farm animal, to be mated and nurtured until I produce the fatted calf?"

She had leapt to her feet, her eyes blazing. Vincent stood, too. He was very close to her, but he didn't touch her. She could have run away, but neither of them seemed capable of moving right then. The moment was too intense.

"No one else has heard it from me," he said harshly. "I'm not in the habit of blabbing my business abroad, except to those most closely concerned."

"And what was I, if not the one most closely concerned? Yet those two old men knew long before I did, just what was expected of me."

"Well, I grant you Monty knew before you did, since it was his original idea. And we felt obliged to discuss it with Stavros for his professional opinion. We didn't know how long it was feasible for me to be away from the island, you see."

She was speechless. It had obviously been of the greatest importance for Vincent not to stay away too long. Monty's days were numbered, and Monty would want Vincent near him when the time came. But more than that, Monty needed an heir, and she was the scapegoat who had been seduced so readily by the charismatic Vincent Montagu. She was the biggest fool that ever lived, but the biggest joke of all was that she had fallen so wildly in love with him.

She was unaware that the tears had been trickling down her cheeks until she felt his fingers wipe them away.

"I'm sorry, Lydia," he said, so quietly she could almost believe he was sincere. "My whole concern was for Monty, to make everything as painless for him as possible. I never gave more than a passing thought to what the discovery might do to the woman I married. I assumed that living on the island and the luxury my wife enjoyed here would be enough. I see now that I should have thought more carefully before agreeing to Monty's plan. It was wrong of me not to have told you everything."

"Yes, it was," she said bitterly. "You should have been honest from the beginning. It would have been better."

"But then you probably wouldn't have married

me. You still had stars in your eyes whenever marriage was mentioned, whether or not ours was a conventional one with a proper period of courtship. And if I hadn't gotten you, I'd have had to settle for second-best, with someone merely willing to do her duty and be paid off."

She wouldn't be pacified by the oblique inference that she had been his first choice, when she knew that she had not been.

"Wouldn't that have done Monty's bidding just as well? You didn't have to make me—"

She bit her lips, knowing she had been in danger of saying he didn't have to make her fall in love with him, so that the heartache went on and on.

"I've already said I'm sorry. I don't know what else to say, except that you'll never want for anything as long as I live, Lydia."

She pulled away from him, hardly knowing how she had come to be in his embrace.

"You may mean well by saying so, but somehow it seems to me like the worst insult of all," she whispered, feeling as if she was being paid off in advance for a task she hadn't yet performed. She tilted her chin, blinking back the tears. "But I'll try not to fail you, Vincent. I'll do my best to accommodate both you and Monty with the goods you bought and paid for."

She swept away from him in the direction of the house. She kept her chin tilted high, trying not to show how upset she felt. Her hands shook on the silk parasol, and she held its slim bone handle as if it were a lifeline.

She was shaking inside, too, appalled by her own words. It was such a brutal, insensitive way to refer to a tiny baby, and one that would be so welcomed if it had been born out of love.

For a brief moment Lydia allowed herself to dream. She could almost imagine she held such a child in her arms; breathing in the sweet scent of him; marvelling at his likeness to Vincent, and loving him all the more because of that likeness. . . .

He caught up with her before she reached the house.

"I know I've hurt you, and I'm sorry. It was certainly never my intention," he said roughly. "But since we have to live together, can we not call a truce? Can't you even be a little happy here, Lydia?"

She knew that what he said was true. They had to live together or, at least, it would seem so. There was nowhere else for her to go. She wouldn't demean him, or herself, by admitting to anyone else that their marriage had been a mistake, and throwing herself on the hospitality of other people. Even as the thought flitted through her mind, it was an ironic one. The only other people she knew on Kurnios were Vincent's friends, not hers. They tolerated her, and were prepared to befriend her, because of him. And outwardly, at least, she would much prefer it if people saw them as a happy, loving couple.

She drew a deep breath. "I could be very happy here in different circumstances," she said in a muffled voice, not daring to say more. "But my feelings shouldn't bother you unduly. You have

305

everything you want, which I suspect is the way things usually happen. Does anyone ever say no to you?"

He smiled crookedly. "As a matter of fact, I don't have everything I want, yet. But I hope that in time that state of affairs will resolve itself."

She felt the heat in her face. He meant the child, of course. But the future was in the lap of the gods. If fate meant her to have a child, then it would surely happen. If not . . . her anger faded at the thought that she would still remain Vincent Montagu's wife.

She was instinctively certain he would still go on hoping, presumably even after Monty's death. He'd still want to carry out the old man's request. It put an enormous burden on him. Even she could see that it was too much of a burden for any man, to be obliged to marry a woman he didn't love, to father a child for an old man's whim. But it didn't lessen her resentment that she had to be the one, and she had been foolish enough to fall in love with him.

Lydia refused to let herself be swamped with self-pity at the role in which she found herself. Instead, she concentrated on her own preparations for the wedding celebration ball, now only a few days away. Monty clearly relished telling her how sumptuous and splendid it was going to be. No expense was to be spared. There would be musicians and caterers, the entire house and gardens would be decorated, and there was to be a lavish firework display to finish off the evening.

They sat companionably together in the drawing room one sparkling morning, going through the guest list together. From the length of the list, to which Monty seemed to add more names every day, it seemed as if the whole of Kurnios was being invited.

"It still amazes me to discover how many people live here. It seemed such an isolated and inhospitable place when I first saw it," she remarked.

"It will take more than an evening to get to know everyone, my dear," he agreed. "But we're doing our best to make you feel at home in our island paradise."

"And you're succeeding," she told him with a smile, already feeling a real affection for the old man, despite the treachery he had launched. Because of his illness and its inevitable end, which aroused all her softheartedness and pity, she had unconsciously transferred all her resentment to Vincent. She was managing fairly well to control much of that resentment now, but it could still flare up when she least expected it.

She studied the names on the long list of ball guests. Some of them were familiar to her now. There were those she had already met with Vincent, and those who had come calling at the house, eager to meet the English bride of their benefactor's grandson. There was no doubt that both Monty and Vincent were held in very high esteem on the island.

Monty laughed as she stumblingly read out some of the Greek names, begging him to put her right on the pronunciation, so she wouldn't make a complete idiot of herself when she was introduced to them.

"My dear, it wouldn't matter a jot if you called them all by the wrong names. Everyone will fall in love with you at first sight, just as Vincent and I both did."

She kept her eyes lowered as she gazed at the list of names. For Monty, falling in love with her was a gallant, grandfatherly gesture. In Vincent's case, it was so cruelly far from the truth. She was surprised that Monty could believe that this had been a marriage for love. Surely he couldn't really think so? Or was he just deluding himself, knowing the true facts, that she was no more than a pawn in his game? She should probably let it pass, but somehow she just couldn't.

"You don't have to pretend with me," she said slowly. "Vincent didn't marry for love, Monty, and we both know that."

"But you did, didn't you?" he said gently.

She looked up quickly, wanting to deny it, not wanting the embarrassment of admitting all the love was on her side. Even though, when she lay in Vincent's arms at night, it was almost impossible to believe that this strong, passionate man didn't love her . . .

But looking into Monty's understanding old eyes, she knew she couldn't lie. She gave a quick nod.

"Yes. I married for love," she was husky with the bittersweet truth of it.

"My dear, do you think it quite impossible that because an old man made a cruel wager and his

308

grandson took it up, that the marriage couldn't be for love as well as the gamble? Do you really think a man like Vincent could pretend so well, if he was repulsed by his wife? Or that he would have chosen one he couldn't love? He did choose you, Lydia, and he wouldn't have done so lightly. For the Montagu family, marriage is for life."

She could almost be persuaded by his words. She wanted so desperately to be persuaded by them. But always at the back of her mind was the thought of her cousin Audine, the girl Vincent had first pursued so coldheartedly. He would have married her, and that certainly wouldn't have been for love. What made Lydia's fortunes so different?

"I would really prefer not to talk about it," she said quickly now. "Just tell me again about some of the guests, Monty. Are there really some English dukes among them, or are they just honorary titles? I daresay you could call yourself anything here, and no one would be any the wiser!"

She tried to sound light-hearted, but she quickly realized what she had said, and hoped he wouldn't think she was censuring Vincent for his own masquerade.

In truth, she rarely thought of that now. It no longer mattered. What mattered more was the real reason she had been brought here. That still hurt. So much so that it often resulted in her reacting stiffly and unresponsively toward Vincent. Even while she loved him, she was overly conscious that he went through his marital duties as much for his desire for a child for Monty's sake, as for the fact that he was undoubtedly attracted to her physically.

309

She recalled one of her most recent bouts of doubt and resentment. She lay unresisting while he made love to her, and he finally thrust her aside in frustration.

"Have I become so repugnant to you that you can lie there like a piece of marble?" he had said angrily.

She felt the ready tears dampen her cheeks.

"You're not repugnant to me, Vincent. Only your reasons for marrying me. I can't forgive that."

"Then try to forget them, for pity's sake, and don't let them color the rest of our lives. I wouldn't have thought you could be so unforgiving."

"Neither would I," she had said, knowing she sounded petulant, and unable to stop it. "But sometimes it's hard to get it out of my mind. I feel as if both you and Monty are just watching and waiting for your prize to be fattened up."

The next moment she had felt the warm touch of his hand on her stomach. His fingers had moved slightly against her skin, soothing and restful. Without thinking, she had given a small sigh of pure pleasure, stretching a little, unconsciously turning toward him. She had become so tense of late, it sometimes seemed impossible for her to relax at all.

"We're doing no such thing," he had said, softly and persuasively as he gently palmed her flesh. "But would it be so odd if we were? In all families, Lydia, highborn or humble, the most normal and desirable sealing of a marriage is the birth of a child. Isn't it the true fulfillment of all women too? Don't let the miracle of it all be spoiled for you."

"But if you only—" she had begun raggedly.

"If you want me to say I love you, I'll say it—" he had said, anticipating what she needed so much, and couldn't quite bring herself to say. But hearing him put it so bluntly, she shook her head vigorously.

"*No*. I don't want to hear that."

Not in this mood, not just because it would please her, not when she realized she was deliriously succumbing to his caresses, and she knew very well he would be saying it only to pacify her.

She had realized something else, too. She had been holding out against him for too long.

And dear God, how she wanted him. She wanted him so much. With a small cry deep in her throat, she felt her limbs relax. As if it was out of her control, she felt her hand reach out for him, and heard the sharp intake of his breath as she held him and caressed him.

"You're right," he had murmured softly. "What need do we have for words, when everything that we are is saying it for us?"

She had resisted him before, but she was past resisting now. She felt the heaviness of his body cover hers, and she opened up to receive him, in what old Nadima had obliquely referred to as the joining. Why Lydia should think of that now, in the ecstasy of the moment, she couldn't imagine, but somehow the word was so exactly right. It was the joining of two bodies and two souls that could produce the miracle of another.

She gave a gasp as she felt the hot flood of his seed inside her. As his arms held her tight in the final twisting seconds, she hugged him to her. She wanted his child, she wanted a part of him to be growing inside her.

She had felt it with an almost primeval need. The joining of a man and a woman to produce a child was truly God's most stupendous miracle. She buried her face in Vincent's chest still needing him close to her. She was thankful he didn't speak, just as if he sensed something of her emotion.

He couldn't possibly have guessed her turbulent thoughts, but she had taken poignant comfort from the fact that he continued to hold her in his arms until morning.

The Saturday of the Montagu celebration ball dawned with a still, breathless heat. The sky, inevitably cloudless, was almost stark in its blueness, broken only by the glowing sphere of a hot, golden sun. Lydia felt she was somehow being stifled, and prayed fervently that by evening the shadows would have lengthened, and hopefully a cooling breeze would stir through the foliage of trees and shrubs that seemed as lethargic as herself.

The maid, Coora, prepared to help her dress that morning after her refreshing bath. But the very thought of donning constricting corsets and petticoats left Lydia feeling weak.

"I think Lady does not like the heat too well," Coora observed, pulling the corset laces into place. "The lovely English skin is still damp after the toweling. It needs some powdering to prevent the chafing, perhaps?"

312

"It would probably help," Lydia murmured, feeling beads of perspiration on her forehead as well as the rest of her body. The morning gown laid out on her bed was the coolest she had, made from softest sprigged cotton, and beneath it she would wear the least possible number of petticoats she could, but today she knew it was all going to feel as heavy as lead.

She stood patiently while the maid dabbed the scented powder on her skin, and then returned to her tugging on the corset laces.

"It's no use," Lydia said finally. "I shall simply expire if you do them up too tightly. You'll have to let them out a little, Coora. By this evening, when it's more important that I look my best, I can revert to my normal shape."

Right now, she hardly cared if she had a fashionably tiny waist or not. She felt too giddy with the oppressive dry heat to care. This evening was far more important, anyway. She would be on show, the rightful lady of the house, and she wanted to look as stunning as she could, for herself, for Monty, and most of all, for Vincent.

She realized Coora was looking at her thoughtfully, seeing the inch-wide gap in the corset laces.

"Is Lady quite well?" she said, with a snide glance. "Nothing is amiss?"

"Lady is perfectly well, thank you," Lydia said shortly.

It was no more than the life-sucking dryness of the mountain air that made her wilt. She had thought she should be well able to cope with it, after India, but the last two years in the rainy English climate had obviously turned her softer than she thought. She certainly didn't want this sharp-eyed girl putting her own interpretation on a small indisposition. She didn't want anything to tarnish the sudden buoyant feeling of well-being and hope that had come to her just recently.

Vincent had been especially tender toward her and she hadn't refused him anything. Why should she, she had finally reasoned, when they both wanted the same thing in the end? Her wishes had turned completely around, and she wouldn't think beyond that point. She wanted a child, too . . . just to hold Vincent's child in her arms was the ultimate dream. Lately it seemed, as if with some inner knowledge that neither explained to the other, their days and nights had been far more harmonious than before.

She spent the day quietly sewing in her room or reading in Monty's library. She had been told there was nothing for her to do, and that Monty was to supervise everything that morning before he went off for his rest after lunch.

It gave him a purpose, Vincent told her, and she wasn't to worry about him. As she tried to read a book on which she couldn't really concentrate, she could hear the vague shouts as Monty instructed the workmen putting up the lights and erecting the platform for the fireworks, and later, the teams of caterers arriving. But she saw how ready Monty was to take his habitually long siesta during the afternoon.

Vincent had suggested that Lydia, too, should take plenty of rest. There would be plenty of danc-

314

ing during the long evening ahead, and she should conserve all her energy. Where he went that day, she had no idea, but she saw very little of him until he arrived back at the house around teatime, to join Lydia and Monty in the little English ritual they always observed.

"You look rested," he said to her.

Although she had spent an hour lying on her bed with all the windows flung open, she didn't feel it. To her own annoyance, she felt fat and frumpish, although it was a term that could never be applied to her. But the appalling dry heat had really drained her, and said as much to Vincent.

"It'll be cooler once the sun goes down. A fair breeze was beginning to blow in from the sea."

"You've been down to the sea?" she said in surprise.

"I needed to see Nikos," he said. "He was bringing me something from the mainland. You'll remember that I had business there a few days ago."

"I remember," she said. She felt a small sliver of resentment. Business matters were obviously not meant to concern her, for he never mentioned them. Only slowly was she coming to realize that just about everything on Kurnios revolved around the Montagus. They owned property, land, the fishing industry and many of the elegant vessels that were leased to the wealthy British families. Only slowly did she realize just how influential was the Montagu dynasty, of which she was now a part, and which her child would inherit.

And as usual, he said nothing about the business that had taken him to the mainland until Monty had retired once again to his room, and there were only the two of them in the drawing room.

"I trust you haven't changed your mind about the gown you're to wear this evening," he said, startling her by the comment.

She gave a short laugh. "I promise I shan't let you down in front of your fine friends, Vincent! I shall wear the sapphire blue, just as I said. You did say you approved."

She was angry at sounding so anxious. She was independent enough to wear whatever she chose, but to her own irritation she knew how much she needed his approval.

"I do approve, and I've no reason to think you'll let me down," he said, sounding momentarily as irritated as Lydia. "Why must you always think the worst of me? Is it so impossible to take my words at face value?"

She bit her tongue, as instinct almost made her snap that he hardly deserved such trust from her! But she was weary of the arguments. They all seemed so pointless now, because she had married him for better or worse, and there was no changing that. And certainly he had given her a life-style that would be the envy of many women. She wanted for nothing . . . except what she craved the most.

"Very well, I hardly expected you to answer that, my darling," he said with dry sarcasm, when she remained silent. "But you needn't think that everything I say has a barbed meaning behind it. I merely wanted to be sure your gown would be the perfect foil for your wedding gift."

316

"My . . . my wedding gift?" she stammered. He had already been generous, in the way a rich man showered gifts on his wife.

"This is our celebration ball, so it seemed appropriate that you should have a special gift to mark the occasion. It's the reason I went to Athens a few days ago, but the engraving couldn't be done immediately, so Nikos was entrusted to bring it back today."

He drew out a long slim case from his inside pocket, and as he handed it to Lydia, he opened the lid. She gasped at the flawless necklace nestling in a bed of white silk, a fabulous creation of diamonds and sapphires that would compliment her ball gown perfectly.

The fleeting thought ran through her mind that Vincent obviously saw nothing incongruous in entrusting this costly item to the care of a fisherman. But she had quickly learned that Nikos was far more than a mere fisherman. He was a valued employee and keen businessman in his own right, who would probably give his life for the Montagus if need be.

"It takes my breath away," she said at last. "It's the most beautiful thing I've ever owned."

"Just as you are to me," Vincent said gravely.

She knew she should be affronted at the arrogance of the words, but this was not a moment for taking umbrage. This was a moment of sheer enjoyment as Vincent lifted the shimmering necklace from its case and fastened it around her throat. She turned quickly to see herself in the mirror over the mantel, and held her breath at the glittering

317

jewels. With her slightest movement the facets gleamed and shone, accentuating the color of her eyes, as bright as the sapphires themselves in her pleasure.

"It's fabulous," she said, awed. "And I hardly have words to thank you, Vincent. My only regret is that I have nothing to give to you."

His hands closed over her shoulders, and his head was very close to hers. She felt the touch of his mouth against her neck, and her eyes closed for a second at the ecstasy of his touch.

"What I want from you is something more precious than money can buy, my sweet one. We both know what that is, and just how much pleasure there is in the giving."

She felt her cheeks grow hot, hardly knowing how to answer at that moment. His words spoiled things, and yet they were so erotically true. When she was in his arms, in his bed, it was so easy to forget everything else. At such times she was simply the woman he wanted her to be.

"You never showed me the engraving on the necklace," she said in a quavering voice.

He gave a soft laugh, bending his head to touch the nape of her neck with his lips.

"Wait until later to read it, when you remove it for the night," he said teasingly. "It will have more meaning for you then."

She had to be content with that, though she couldn't see that there could be too much engraving on such a necklace. The gems were large, set in silver filigree work, and fastened with a heavy clasp.

Whatever the circumstances, Vincent didn't spare any expense when it came to his wife, she admitted. And for once, her pleasure in the necklace forbade the cynical little thought that it was one more payment he made for her services.

But she refused to let such a shadow spoil her enjoyment of this evening. She knew she looked her absolute best, and the necklace set off her gown perfectly. Monty exclaimed at the sight of her when she descended the long curving staircase on Vincent's arm, to where the older Montagu awaited them.

"My dear girl, I swear if I was thirty years younger I'd sweep you off your feet myself. It's a blessing it's not my heart that's in disorder, or I'd have it broken tonight at the thought of your belonging to some other man," he said, without bothering to disguise the mock-lustful look in the old eyes.

Lydia laughed, suddenly light-hearted at his nonsense, knowing that she could hold her own with anyone at the ball. Even more than that, she would probably be the envy of many of the younger women, because she was Vincent Montagu's wife.

"You're a wicked old rogue," she said softly, "and I'll bet you had your share of young ladies lining up for your favors in your day."

"That I did, my love," Monty grinned. "And not only in the daytime either."

Vincent laughed. "You'll have my wife blushing in a minute, if you carry on talking like that."

"Oh, I doubt it." He gave Lydia a broad wink.

319

"If she doesn't know by now what a lusty breed we Montagu men are, then you're not the man I think you are, Vincent."

For a moment, Lydia wondered if she was really standing there, taking part in this teasingly personal conversation between the three of them. She should be upset, angry, and at the very least, horrified. To her surprise, she was none of those things. She was almost exhilarated, as if she really belonged in this extraordinary household, and such free and easy talk was all a part of the tapestry of their lives.

"You see what he thinks of me," Vincent said, but there was real affection in his voice for the old man as they moved toward the great hall where the evening festivities were to begin, and where the guests would be arriving at any moment.

"I know what he thinks of you, and you should be honored that someone loves you so much," Lydia said quietly.

He looked at her in surprise. Monty had gone ahead now, and they were briefly alone outside the door of the great hall.

"Honored? Yes, I suppose I am, though it's an odd word to use, isn't it?"

Lydia shook her head slowly. "I don't think so. None of us has a God-given right to expect love from every quarter. It has to be earned, like everything else in this world."

She took an embarrassed breath, and continued quickly as he said nothing. "I apologize for that little piece of philosophy! I know this is hardly the time to start getting introspective. Shouldn't we be putting on our party faces and getting ready to greet our guests?"

His answer was to pull her roughly into his arms and press his mouth to hers. She could feel the jewels of the necklace between them, cold against her skin, and then she could feel nothing but the joy of being in his arms for one long sweet moment before they became the public property of their guests.

Chapter Fourteen

Monty had been determined to make it the island's most glittering occasion. The Montagus had many friends and acquaintances on the island, and it seemed as if each lady was determined to outshine the other in terms of jewels and silks and satins.

Lydia was introduced to so many people that she was dizzy with trying to remember them all, and in the end she gave up trying to remember names, and just concentrated on thoroughly enjoying the evening. Some of the guests she already knew, and it was a delight as well as a relief to be greeted by name by the Guistiani family, by Daisy and John Brandon, and a number of others, to whom Vincent had already introduced her on their visits around Kurnios.

She was delighted to see that Nikos and Anna were there, too, both darkly handsome in their Greek attire. She was even more surprised to see that the sprinkling of titled English people was in danger of becoming a flood before the evening was very far advanced. She'd had no idea there were so many of them living on the island.

"It seems as if everyone of note has come here to

retire," she said to Vincent, as yet another Lord and his Lady openly admired her necklace, her beauty, her good fortune in snapping up such a handsome husband. Although no one was indiscreet enough to actually say the words, every envious glance spoke them. And Lydia wouldn't have been human if she hadn't revelled in the adulation both she and Vincent received.

"Why should they not?" he said. "When you find your Eden, it would be foolish to run away from it."

She had the strangest feeling his words were not only meant for the Europeans who had discovered Kurnios, but for her. As if he were willing her to find this her paradise, too, so that she would never want to leave it. So that she would never want to leave *him*. She told herself not to be foolish enough to read meanings into his words that weren't there. But the moment was very sweet all the same.

Before she could think of a reply that didn't give all her feelings away, John Brandon had approached her, claiming a dance. She went into his outstretched arms with a mixture of relief and resentment for breaking the spell in which she'd been momentarily held. But she couldn't be angry with John Brandon for long. He was so genuine a person, head over heels in love with his wife, and clearly enchanted with his hostess.

"Lydia, I hope you won't think it impertinent of me to say, that barring myself, I consider Vincent to be the luckiest man here tonight," he said sincerely, as they twirled around breathlessly to the Viennese waltz tune the musicians were playing now.

She smiled up into his face, flushed with exertion and by the undeniable excitement of having so many compliments paid to her that evening.

"How could I ever think such a charming remark impertinent!" she said effusively. "I'm so happy tonight, John, and so grateful to Monty for arranging all of this."

He was thoughtful for a moment. "And you're truly happy? Despite . . . well, despite everything?"

Her spirits plunged downwards in a second. So he knew about the wager, or at least, that Vincent had gone hotfoot to England in search of an English bride. But then, of course he knew! Lydia reasoned. Hadn't she been welcomed to Montagu House, with even her bedroom prepared and waiting!

But she'd hardly considered the implications of the whole island knowing! If John knew, it meant Daisy knew, and who else in this room knew. Watching her, speculating, wondering just how much persuasion, or more especially baiting her with his wealth, the dashing Vincent Montagu had to bring to bear to make her his wife. *His wife.* The very word tasted so bitter in her mouth now.

"I'm happy," she said woodenly. And she had been terribly, until seconds ago.

"Good. Then continue to be so, Lydia. It will be a sad time for you all when it comes, but if you'll take a word of advice from someone who's known him a long time, you'll not let him see your distress. Monty being Monty, he'll want to go out in a blaze of glory, and never a whimper, and you've

324

already brought the sunshine back into his life to help him through. Anyone can see that."

Long before he had finished, Lydia was blinking up at him, her thoughts spinning as she grasped all he was saying.

"Monty?" she echoed. "Were you thinking about Monty's illness when you asked if I was truly happy?"

"Of course I was. What did you think?" She saw his good-looking face tinge with color. "Good Lord, Lydia, you don't think I was trying to pry into your marital affairs, do you? I would never do that. Besides, it's obvious that you and Vincent are happy. He adores you, and anybody can see you were made for each other."

She realized at once that of course he wouldn't pry into her marital affairs. It wasn't in his nature to pry into anyone else's marriage. She was in danger of becoming obsessed with this notion that everyone knew just why Vincent had married her, and the burden she carried in the necessity to produce a child before Monty's time came. She was ashamed of her own self-indulgence, and she squeezed his arm in real affection as the dance came to an end.

"I'm sorry if I was taken aback for a moment, and of course, Monty's illness is never far from our thoughts. I must confess though, I've had so many compliments this evening, it's making my head spin. I think I should go out on the terrace with a cool glass of lemonade to calm myself."

And if he thought she was a dizzy female, with her head turned by all the praise showered on her tonight, it hardly mattered. He was already pushing his way through the crowds of dancers leaving the ballroom, to bring her the required glass of lemonade as she moved out through the long French windows onto the marble terrace.

The night was softly warm, a myriad stars shimmering in a velvet sky, the moon a great yellow orb that seemed to hang suspended above the island. It was a night meant for lovers, Lydia thought, with a catch in her throat. A night for making love and exchanging vows; a night for pretenses to end.

She wandered through the abundant rose bowers, where the fragrant scent of the blossoms drifted into her nostrils. So English, and yet so erotic, with their heady, full-bloomed perfume. Behind her, the music and chatter seemed to fade into nothing. She relished this rare moment alone, drinking in the beauty that was Kurnios, knowing that John Brandon would come looking for her soon. She would have to return to the ballroom, but just a moment more . . .

Just then, her attention was rivetted by a man's deep voice, somewhere nearby in the shrubbery. The voice was speaking in low, passionate tones to someone. A woman, of course. It was a lovers' tryst, here in the gardens of Montagu House. Lydia couldn't help but be enchanted by the thought, continuing as it did her romantic illusion of this lovely night.

She heard the woman's response, in a rich, sensual voice that was surely not English. She couldn't hear the words, nor did she wish to, as she real-

326

ized she was an unintentional eavesdropper on an intimate meeting. She should move away at once, even though the man was speaking in the woman's language now, so she couldn't have understood a thing he was saying. She had not yet learned any of the Greek language, though she had begun to toy with the idea of trying to learn it.

Lydia's breath was suddenly caught between her teeth, and her heart was beating painfully fast. The man seemed to be remonstrating with the woman, who appeared to be pleading with him. She had no idea who the woman was, but the man's identity had become crystal clear to her. It was Vincent . . . *Vincent* and an unknown woman, trysting in the moonlight at his own wedding celebration ball . . .

She twisted around to go back the way she had come, her breath tight in her throat. At the slight sound she made, the couple moved from their arbor, and she dodged between the rose bushes, unable to bear it if Vincent knew she had seen him. It would be doubly humiliating. She merely saw the flash of a crimson gown before she reached the terrace again where others were milling outside to escape the heat of the ballroom, and John Brandon was seeking her out.

"I thought I'd lost you," he greeted her. "Will you come and join Daisy and myself?"

She saw Daisy seated on one of the many wrought iron seats on the terrace, and moved across to her at once. It was so good to see someone so nice and ordinary at that moment, and to rid her mind of the intrigues that undoubtedly went on around her. Lydia realized she was also more than glad to sit down. In fact, if she hadn't done so right then, she was sure she would have fallen down.

"Are you feeling quite well, Lydia?" Daisy said anxiously. "You're breathing very heavily."

"I'm still recovering from the waltz," Lydia told her, thankful to have a ready excuse. "Your husband is a very energetic dancer!"

Daisy laughed. "I know it. I've tried telling him that we ladies have difficulty swinging our voluminous skirts around to accompany him, but he continues to insist that a Strauss waltz must be done as energetically as possible to get the full effect of the music."

"Then I suggest he whisks you around with him next time," Lydia said, trying to sound as frivolous as her new friend.

She sipped at the cool lemonade John had brought her, hoping she didn't look as though her hands were gripping the glass too tightly. She needed to hold on to something, even a glass of lemonade, so that the world didn't feel as if it was slipping away from her.

"Oh!" Dimly, as she struggled not to disgrace herself by swooning away at her own ball, Lydia heard Daisy's soft exclamation at her side. "How dare she come here tonight!"

The words were said quietly, almost beneath Daisy's breath, and in an aside to her husband. Lydia knew instinctively that she was not meant to hear them, but her ears seemed to be acutely attuned tonight to hearing things that were not meant for her. She looked around her casually, and her heart almost stopped as she saw a beautiful woman in a crimson gown standing on the edge of the terrace.

For a moment she seemed to stand there alone, her hair a black cloud around her olive-skinned face, the black eyes and strong features that signified the Greek woman, quite stunning.

And then several of the older gentlemen moved toward her in greeting, their wives a step or so behind. There was no sign of Vincent, Lydia thought savagely, but she didn't need anyone to tell her that this was his mistress. It was as if the hated word shrieked the truth at her.

She hadn't seen Monty in a little while, but now she saw him coming out onto the terrace with a group of elderly friends, among them Doctor Stavros. The music had stopped temporarily, while they all took a breather. Rather to her amazement as well as chagrin, he caught sight of the woman in the crimson gown, and went toward her with outstretched arms.

"Marina, my dear, I'm so glad you were able to come."

So, despite what Daisy Brandon might think, the woman had been invited, and it had been Monty who invited her. She saw Monty kiss her on both cheeks, and then she linked her arm easily inside his. They were clearly old acquaintances.

And who knew? If the woman named Marina had been English born, she might well have been Vincent's wife now. If it hadn't been for this old man's whim to have an English heir for his kingdom, this woman might have been legally sharing

Vincent's bed and his life, as Lydia strongly suspected she had been doing already until Lydia herself came on the scene.

Intuition was doing all kinds of things to her self-esteem at that moment, and her hands twisted involuntarily around the lemonade glass in her hand.

She knew she was being cursed with the most violent attack of jealousy she had ever known, but she couldn't rid herself of it. This Marina had known Vincent long before she did. Lydia was certain Marina had shared intimacies with him that now belonged to his wife, and Lydia was desperate to know if those intimacies were still continuing. She wanted to know and feared to know the truth, not knowing which was worse.

"Lydia," Monty had turned to her now, drawing the crimson-clad woman toward her. For one reckless moment, Lydia wondered if she could possibly summon up the nerve to turn away, to publicly snub the smiling Greek goddess. She knew that she could not, it would be incredibly bad manners. And this was still Monty's house after all; the real and very present Lord Vincent Montagu.

"Allow me to introduce you two charming ladies to one another. Marina Delos, this is my lovely new granddaughter, Lydia Montagu."

"How do you do?" Lydia said coolly.

"*Kalispera.* Good evening," the husky voice from the garden said to Lydia.

She felt the touch of the woman's fingertips against her own and an aura of sensuous rose perfume wafted around her. The urge to snatch her hand away was almost irresistible, and then she caught the flash of something undefinable in Marina Delos's black eyes.

For a moment she couldn't think what it meant, and then she recognized it. It was the assessment of one woman for another. From the one who had lost, to the victor . . . at least, that was the way Lydia chose to interpret it right then. If she had not, she would have been in total despair.

She reminded herself forcibly that *she* was Vincent's wife. Whatever this woman had meant to him or still meant, he had married Lydia Grey. This was her home, her domain, she wore Vincent's wedding gift around her neck, she shared his bed. She lifted her chin in a small gesture of defiant propriety.

"I'm afraid I don't understand your language," she continued sweetly. "I'm sure I would never be able to learn it. But then, I've always thought it's very important to remember one's roots, don't you think?"

She listened to herself in a kind of horror. Was she really being so patronizing—so insulting—to a guest? Her liberally minded parents would have disowned her for such behavior. In their eyes, no one of another race was inferior. It was the code by which they had lived, and it was obviously the accepted code here. And she had broken that code in an instant.

Thankfully, Monty had turned to be greeted by more of his guests, and it seemed that no one but Marina herself heard the barbed words. The full red smile never wavered, but the eyes were cold.

And Lydia knew this was a woman of whom she might well have cause to be afraid.

"Oh, I agree with you, Lydia. May I call you Lydia?" Without even waiting for an answer, she went on. "But it never fails to surprise and please me how many of your countrymen do learn our ways . . . and enjoy them in full measure."

Lydia knew that in those few sentences she had shown her talons. In using her given name so freely, she had reduced the gulf of status between them. In the small emphasis on the word country-*men,* she had implied that it made no difference how Lydia Montagu regarded her. Her position in the eyes of one particular English gentleman was intact, and would remain so for as long as she chose. And she had made it plain that Vincent was hers for the keeping, and that he enjoyed everything she had to offer.

Lydia told herself angrily she was being oversensitive to read so much into so few words. But the smiling red mouth was triumphantly uplifted, and she knew that every instinct was telling her the truth. This woman was Vincent's mistress, and Lydia didn't know how she was going to bear it.

"If you will excuse me a moment, I must go and look for my husband," she said in a false, high voice. "I haven't seen him for some time, and he'll be wondering what has become of me."

"I believe I saw him in the garden some moments ago," Marina said casually, unwittingly turning the knife.

Lydia simply turned her back on her then, unable to stand there and see that knowing look any longer. Her hands shook, and she realized she was still clutching the glass of lemonade. She drained it in one swallow, whether it was ladylike or not.

"Lydia, you look very pale," Daisy Brandon was suddenly at her side, speaking in a low voice, concerned for her. "Did she say something to upset you?"

Lydia looked at her sharply. "No, of course not. Why should she? She's Monty's guest, isn't she?"

"Well yes, I know she is, but she sometimes has a sharp tongue, and says things she doesn't really mean." Daisy was clearly flustered now.

"Is there something you want to tell me about her?"

She didn't want to hear it, yet she felt compelled to ask. She knew it wasn't the done thing to start questioning this old friend of the family, whose loyalties might well be divided now, but as far as she was concerned, the niceties didn't come into it any more. Lydia had to *know* . . .

They were entering the ballroom again, where the floor was being prepared for a troupe of Greek dancers to entertain the guests. Lydia looked around despairingly for Vincent. He seemed to háve disappeared, after his meeting with his mistress. Couldn't he face either of them now? Unless he had gone to see her more privately . . .

"Who is she, Daisy?" Lydia said in a trembling voice now, under cover of the excited chattering. "And just how well does my husband know her? Will you tell me the truth?"

"I can't possibly tell you that, my dear, and nor would I, if I could. It's not my business," the other woman said, clearly unhappy at being drawn into this. "But everyone here knows Marina Delos. She owns considerable property and a prospering vine production, which was left to her by her husband. He was much older than she, and when he died several years ago he left her a wealthy woman."

None of this was what Lydia wanted to hear. It meant though, that there was no husband to interfere if a certain English gentleman came calling. Her vivid imagination was again taking her where she had no wish to go.

"Is she my husband's mistress?" she said flatly, her gaze unwaveringly on Daisy's face. She saw the other girl's hunted look, as if she wished herself anywhere but here.

"I really have no idea about such things," she said quickly, embarrassed and scarlet-faced, but to Lydia it was a reply that simply revealed everything she needed to know.

Vincent's sudden appearance at her side was enough to flood her own face with color. He looked so *normal*, she thought, as if he hadn't recently spent time in the garden with his mistress, obviously discussing their future and how they were to overcome the little encumbrance of a new wife. She felt a sob deep in her throat and willed it down. This was neither the time nor the place to have a confrontation. It must wait until later, until this spectacular evening was over. But already, much of its brilliance was dimmed for Lydia.

"Where on earth have you been, darling?" Vincent said easily. "I've been looking everywhere for you."

"Have you? I went for a walk in the garden. I'm surprised you didn't find me there. It's very pleasant in the rose arbors at night."

She looked at him closely, but his dark eyes didn't even flicker. He was obviously so adept at keeping his paramour separate from his everyday life, that the inclusion of a wife wasn't even going to ruffle it.

"It's no matter." He tucked her arm inside his. "I want you to sit with me to watch the Greek dancers perform. If you've never seen them before, then you're in for a treat."

She allowed him to draw her into his world. They moved among the smiling, glittering company who made way for their host and his lovely bride to stand at the front for the best view of the dancers. Everyone stood for this part of the proceedings, except for Monty, who declared that his old bones demanded a seat. Lydia could see how the evening was taking its toll, but he was just as determined to see it out.

She saw, too, how Marina Delos had positioned herself to the right of the room, so that she was in their direct line of vision. The crimson gown was startlingly visible among the mostly creams and pastels of the other ladies. And Lydia deliberately kept her arm inside Vincent's crook, as if to say *whatever he was to you, now he's mine*.

But she forgot all about Marina as the troupe of Greek dancers entered the ballroom in their strange garb, the men in loose white shirts and fluted skirts that reached their knees, the black-haired girls in long flowing white garments. But once the music began, and the dancers began swaying in the strangely hypnotic rhythms that were so typically Greek, she forgot everything but the fascination of watching and marvelling at the intricate movements.

But then the display was all over, and the musicians began to play music for the guests to dance to. And Vincent turned to her, his voice gentle, his hands holding hers.

"Are you aware that we've hardly had a dance together since the beginning of the evening?"

"I thought you were too busy with your friends," she said, hoping she didn't sound as petulant as she felt. She saw the small frown between his eyes, and forced a laugh.

"Oh, Vincent, I didn't really expect you to spend every minute with me tonight! I know there will be people you haven't seen for a while, and I've been perfectly happy, I assure you. I haven't felt neglected."

"I should think not, from the number of partners you've had all evening," he said, smiling.

"So you have noticed, then?"

So he had been in the ballroom for part of the time. Not all of the evening had been spent beneath a heavenly Greek moon with Marina Delos.

He steered her into the middle of the ballroom floor, where they danced a lively gavotte.

"Do I detect a hint of sarcasm in that remark?" he said, as they came close and then parted again in the movement of the dance.

"Only if you choose to," she said, and then she

was suddenly weary of the subterfuge. "Perhaps later, when we're alone, I can make myself clearer."

"Perhaps you had better," Vincent said grimly.

After the gavotte, he bowed, and handed her over to the next partner who had signed her dance card. She watched him move away in a kind of misery, and the next moment she was incensed to see him dancing with Marina Delos. He had gone straight from Lydia to her. At that moment it seemed hideously symbolic.

By the time the ball was nearing its end, Lydia could see that Monty had almost used up all his reserves of strength. Doctor Stavros was at his side constantly now, ever watchful, and no one could fail to notice the white lines of strain about Monty's mouth and eyes.

But he simply refused to acknowledge that the evening was getting too much for him, and by now Lydia knew better than to suggest that he retire to bed. And by then, something else was also demanding her attention. Marina had been openly flirting with Vincent at every opportunity, and it was beginning to needle her beyond endurance.

Admittedly, it was almost always in the company of other people. As if the little indiscretions could easily be taken as harmless and social, Lydia thought, with increasing rage. But the way Marina looked up into Vincent's eyes, with those black flashing provocative glances, and the pouting red lips that blatantly invited kissing, was too much for Lydia to bear. She pushed her way forward and linked her arm through Vincent's, clasping it hard to her side.

"I seem to have seen little of you for the last hour, darling," she said, forcing a note of flirtation into her own voice. "Are you neglecting your bride so soon?"

She saw the little dart of amusement in his eyes as she turned to him, effectively blocking out Marina with the wide hoop of her ball gown. But she didn't care if he knew what she was doing. Let everyone know that she was the lady here, the rightful and legal wife of Vincent Montagu, and that no former mistress was going to usurp her place.

She startled herself with the primeval passion of her own thoughts. But he was *hers* now, and he was going to remain so.

"Why, Lydia dear," she heard Marina's throaty voice saying. "You surely don't begrudge your husband a little time with his old friends? He's been away from the island for so long, and we all have some catching up to do. I'm sure you're unselfish enough to realize that."

The words implied exactly the opposite, and Lydia was certain she heard a faint titter nearby. Marina was adroitly putting her in her place for her pettiness in clinging to her husband, when Vincent was friend and squire of all his domain, and should be free to speak with whomever he chose. For a moment, she felt completely nonplussed.

Then, without warning, she felt Vincent draw her free hand up to his lips. He spoke softly.

"My wife is the most unselfish woman alive, Marina, and if a new bride doesn't want to spend every moment with her husband, perhaps there's something wrong with the husband!"

The implication was risqué enough to make his meaning quite clear to both women. Lydia felt her face flame, knowing there was certainly nothing wrong at all with Vincent in that direction. She glanced at Marina, expecting to see annoyance on her smooth olive face, and instead, she was sick with embarrassment at seeing the small smile playing around her mouth that meant only one thing. Marina, too, was quite certain of Vincent's prowess in the bedroom.

Other people were crowding around them now, and the Guistiani family was urging everyone to come along and see the firework display, which Monty was about to set in motion. Impulsively, Lydia moved away from Vincent's side, to link arms with the elderly Eida Guistiani, and assist her down the terraced steps to the expanse of ground where the displays were set up.

"You should not let her rile you, my dear," she heard the old lady murmur, to her surprise. "What's past is past, and she cannot harm you now that you have your husband's love."

Lydia felt the sudden rush of fullness to her throat at the kindness of this old lady, wise with her years, and seeing far more than most.

"Thank you, Ma'am, but I'm not sure of anything—"

She stopped, for she could hardly say in public that her husband didn't love her, that it was all a sham, and that the once charming idea of arranged marriages that grew into love matches seemed such a mockery to her now.

She felt the old lady grip her arm.

"Be sure, then. Believe what these old eyes tell me. You have Vincent's love, and none can take it from you."

Lydia felt the dampness in her eyes, and blinked it away. They walked slowly, due to the faltering steps of the old lady, and ahead of them she could see the group of young people circling the firework area. The men in their dashing dark clothes, the ladies bright as butterflies in their ball gowns; skirts rich with color; necklines fashionably low to tempt the gentlemen; Marina hugging Vincent's arm in excitement.

She drew in her breath and looked away. How wise was Eida Guistini now? As she stared, he turned around, shaking the other girl off and taking Eida's other arm as they approached.

"My wife does my duty for me," he said gallantly. "Did I not make a good choice, Ma'am?"

"An excellent choice. I'm glad you had the sense for it," she said, as frank as only a lady of advanced years could be. Above her head, Vincent smiled into Lydia's eyes. His own were warm and filled with desire, and she could only weaken and wish that she didn't love him so much.

The firework display was a sensation, filling the air with great streaming ribbons of light and exploding showers of colored rain. Monty must have spent a fortune on entertaining their guests, Lydia thought finally, when the acrid smell of powder and smoke overpowered the strongest scents of the exotic garden flowers.

After prolonged applause, the guests began making their way back to the house. The ball was now officially over, and people would be expected to start leaving immediately. And at last, Monty gave into his body's needs and requested that the younger couple make his goodbyes for him. So it was Vincent and Lydia who stood side by side at the great door of Montagu House, receiving kisses and many congratulations on their marriage, and on the success of the evening.

Daisy Brandon embraced Lydia tightly.

"You looked so beautiful tonight, Lydia, and I know you and Vincent will be very happy. Come and see us again soon."

"I will," she said, smiling at this nice, uncomplicated Englishwoman, who could have no idea of the undercurrents in Lydia's own life.

So many kisses and cordialities . . . Lydia was starting to droop, and longing for her own bed by the end of it all. Marina Delos was among the last to leave. Vincent leaned forward to give her a dutiful kiss on both cheeks. At least, Lydia hoped and assumed that was what he intended. But Marina twisted her face at the last moment, so that his mouth landed full on hers, and she was curving her body into him, her hands cupping his face.

The kiss only lasted for the briefest moment, but it was a scandalous embrace that had the few remaining guests staring wide-eyed at the woman's audacity.

She moved quickly away from Vincent, to kiss Lydia lightly on both cheeks, and thank her coolly for a wonderful evening. The difference in the farewells was so marked that she might as well have declared her love vocally for Vincent there and then.

It stunned Lydia, somehow stripping away all her newfound confidence in the way people had been making such a fuss about her during this farewell ritual. In a single moment, she felt as though the wedding band on her finger meant very little to the flamboyant Greek woman who had known Vincent before she appeared in his life.

Sickly, she knew that whatever had happened in the past would continue, if Marina Delos had anything to say in the matter. Marina made it very plain that it was what she wanted, and to Lydia she was the kind of ruthless woman who would always get her own way. And she and Vincent shared memories of which Lydia had no knowledge. They had a past together, while Lydia wasn't even sure what kind of future she herself was destined to have with her own husband. It all fell so far short of a young girl's romantic dreams of love.

Chapter Fifteen

In their bedroom, she undressed with shaking fingers. The maids had long since gone to bed, and besides, she hadn't wanted anyone's attentions. But she felt Vincent's hands on the back fastenings of her gown, and bit her lip, knowing this could be leading to something wonderful, if only she could ignore all that had happened this evening. But she couldn't, and there had to be a confrontation.

She moved away from his reaching hands as the shimmery gown fell to her feet. Ignoring his help, she removed the rest of her clothes herself, and slid her nightgown over her head with her back still turned to him.

"You have the loveliest spine of any woman on this earth," Vincent said, his voice thick with seduction.

"And you have known so many to measure me by," she said, before she could stop the words. She realized she still wore his necklace, and she tried desperately to unfasten the clasp, but his hands were there, covering hers and removing it quickly.

"A few," he agreed, not bothering to deny it. "But those days are gone—"

"Oh, really?" She whirled around, to see the beautiful necklace still draped over his fingers. His wedding gift to her . . . she swallowed the lump in her throat, but she couldn't stop now. There were things that had to be said between them, or they would fester in her mind and poison their relationship forever.

"And how many of those other women still remain on the island, still fondly hoping for your favors now and then? Or is it confined to only one woman now? And a very demanding woman, as she made no secret of demonstrating to me tonight!"

He went to the dressing table, replacing the necklace in its case and snapping it shut before he answered. She flinched at the sharp sound. It sounded too final for comfort.

"I won't pretend not to know that you're referring to Marina Delos, but Marina is a very old friend, my dear. And I assure you I've no intention of forgetting all old friendships just because I have a wife. In any case, this little display of jealousy is unworthy of you, and I always believed it to be considered bad taste in a lady's etiquette—"

"To blazes with etiquette!" she raged. "And please don't bother to patronize me by quoting the rules to me! It would be more in keeping to instruct your lady-friend on such behavior, since she doesn't seem to know the meaning of the word!"

"Marina is not my lady-friend, and you'd do yourself a favor by not making yourself ridiculous in seeing things that aren't there," Vincent snapped.

"I saw her flirt with you all evening, and I saw

344

the way she kissed you before she left. How much more do you think I need to see! Are you going to deny that she means something to you?"

Even as she spoke, Lydia seemed to stand outside herself, and knew she was handling this all wrong. She was forcing him to say what she only suspected, however strong that suspicion was. And she still didn't really want to know. In her heart, she knew she couldn't bear to hear him say the words that meant Marina Delos was still dear to him.

"Marina Delos once meant a great deal to me," she heard Vincent say deliberately. "But that was in the past—"

"Was she your mistress?"

Horrified, Lydia heard herself whip out the hated word. It had once been a beautiful and secure word, the lengthy and honored title for a man's life partner. The connotations for it now were very different, taking away all that rightly belonged to a wife.

She wanted to sink through the floor as she saw Vincent nod his head shortly.

"Yes, she was my mistress. Now are you satisfied? You didn't think I lived like a saint before I met you, did you?"

"And what about after you met me?" she whispered dryly. Because she just couldn't sanction living as his wife if the liaison were still going on. She couldn't bear to think of him going straight from their bed to Marina's.

"You're my wife," he said coldly. "I assure you marriage is sacred to me. And if it has to be said brutally and openly, then you must take my word that I've broken off all other relationships since we exchanged our vows."

And Lydia knew just where that last relationship had been broken off, if she could truly believe him. It was so very recent; right here in the scented rose arbors, where an unwilling eavesdropper hadn't heard the actual words of the conversation, and had merely seen the trysting place of two lovers.

She stood with trembling lips, hands clasped together tightly. She knew that her eyes were probably still accusing, and she was totally unsure what to say next. And as if he couldn't bear the sight of those huge drowned eyes, Vincent gave a muttered oath and turned away.

"Since you obviously prefer to believe the worst of me, I shall sleep in my dressing room tonight. And in case you're wondering about my movements, I promise you I shan't be leaving the house before morning. Does that satisfy you, Wife?"

The next minute he had left her standing alone in the bedroom. All the magic of this wonderful evening had gone. And all because of *Marina,* Lydia thought savagely, putting all the blame on her rival. Her own jealousy was only natural. Any wife who loved her husband would feel as she did. Any husband who loved his wife wouldn't have put her in this position.

With a strangled sob, she opened the necklace case, as if to draw comfort from Vincent's gift. It was so beautiful, so flawless . . . the gemstones were as clear at the back as at the front. She caught her breath as she looked at the ornate clasp, only now remembering that Vincent had mentioned an engraving.

Around the rim of the clasp, in the tiniest letters imaginable, but still plain enough to read, were the words, "To L. Given in love. V."

She was too bewildered to go to him that night. She couldn't beg, and nor could she easily forget the humiliation she had felt at Marina's hands. But, "given in love," the engraving said. It might mean nothing at all, but to her fevered mind she prayed that at the very least it implied faithfulness. Hadn't Vincent himself said that marriage was sacred to him?

Lydia read and reread the words a hundred times, until the room had grown cold, and she was chilled thoroughly. By the time she finally crept into bed to try and sleep, a pale dawn light was already beginning to streak the sky with pink and gold, and Lydia had come to a decision.

She was married to Vincent Montagu, for better or worse. If she had to live the rest of her life on this island, they were better friends than enemies. Besides which, she thought with a catch in her throat, she didn't want him as her enemy. He was her husband and lover. And he had said, whatever had happened in the past was over.

In any case, it would probably be very unwise to probe into things that had happened before she came here. In doing so, she might well be in danger of inadvertently reviving an old relationship. A man could only be driven so far, and if she wasn't careful, she could very well drive him straight back to the arms of his mistress. She had enough sense to realize that.

Lydia knew she couldn't even contemplate such a thing happening. He belonged to *her* now, and they had made their vows before God. Her normally buoyant spirit was rapidly asserting itself. She kept reminding herself that whatever had occurred between Vincent and Marina in the past, he hadn't married her. Even before Monty's illness, and that ridiculous and tragic wager that had resulted in Vincent finding an English wife, Vincent hadn't thought enough of Marina to marry her.

She had clung on to that thought all through the remaining restless hours of the night. Now she threw on her dressing robe over her nightgown and marched into the adjoining dressing room where Vincent had spent the night.

He was still asleep, lying on the narrow bed inside the bedcovers, looking younger and more vulnerable in sleep than when he was taunting her or railing at her. She felt an overwhelming surge of love for him, and had to turn away quickly as tears stabbed her eyes. If only they had met in other circumstances, and learned to love slowly and naturally, instead of having this marriage thrust upon them, with the need for a child like an albatross around their necks. It was a sad welcome for a child, she thought wanly.

Vincent's clothes were scattered around the room as if he had thrown them off angrily, and left them where they lay. Without thinking, she began to pick them up and fold them, laying them on the chair.

She held his shirt to her face for a moment, breathing in the scent of him that still lingered on the fabric, and it was as if she held the man himself to her heart. Her eyes closed momentarily, knowing weakly how easily her head could still be filled with dreams. But she had come here with a purpose, to apologize with some dignity for her show of jealousy, and suggest that they try again.

"Come here," she heard Vincent's voice say quietly.

Her eyes flew open. She was standing near the full-length dressing mirror, and she could see Vincent's reflected image watching her from the depths of his bed. He must have woken while she was stealthily picking up his clothes. He must have seen the way she held his shirt. . . . She hadn't intended coming here to make a declaration of love, only to try and keep their union on a sane and sensible footing.

"I wanted to say," she began in a cracked voice.

"Don't say anything. Do as I say, woman. Come here!" He still spoke quietly, but in a more demanding and arrogant way.

As she hesitated, he tossed back the bedcovers to invite her into his bed, and she could see that he was naked. And more than that, he was magnificently ready for her.

Without another thought, Lydia loosened the tie of her dressing robe and slipped it off her shoulders as she moved toward the bed. He stopped her when she was halfway there.

"Not like that, my lovely. You're far too overdressed."

She had never voluntarily removed her night-gown for him in daylight . . . the morning sunlight streamed in through the window now, where he hadn't bothered to draw the drapes last night. She registered all this in an instant, and felt a sudden sense of abandonment she hadn't known before.

She crossed her hands and bent to pick up the hem of her nightgown, knowing she was enticing him as she lifted it slowly over her head and let it drift to the floor behind her. She stood motionless for a moment, feeling the warmth of the sunlight on her body, and feeling his eyes feasting on her nakedness.

"God, but you're lovely," Vincent said, his voice oddly ragged now.

"Then I do please you, my lord?" Lydia said, consciously provocative at that moment.

She had no idea how a mistress behaved, but for some reason, she wanted to behave like a mistress now. Here in this little room, with the narrow bed that was really only meant for one, she felt the excitement of forbidden pleasures sweep over her. Hardly knowing that she did so, she moved her legs slightly apart and slid her hands upwards to cup her own breasts. She felt the sharp tingle of response from her nipples as her fingers brushed over them, and with it an unexpected pleasure that ran deep into her veins.

"You do, wench. And you will please me more by relieving this swollen affliction immediately," Vincent said, with a small note of amusement as he picked up the nuance in her voice and actions and proceeded to play her game.

350

"Then you must tell me how best I can pleasure you, Sir," Lydia said huskily, moving toward the bed, and wondering if this was really happening. Was she really behaving in this almost lewd manner? But hadn't old Nadima once told her that nothing that happened between a husband and wife was wrong?

She was close to him now, and he flung the bedcovers onto the floor. She expected him to move aside for her to lie down, and that he would waste no time in filling her with himself. Instead, he pulled her down onto him, pushing her legs apart, and almost immediately he was inside her, and she was straddling him.

She gasped at the suddenness of it, but the last few moments of titillation had more than prepared her for the sensual invasion of her body. She was moist and ready to receive him, and he was vibrant with passion. Vincent's hands caressed the lush softness of her breasts, and he breathed her name as if he really loved her. But right now, it hardly mattered, because she knew just how badly he wanted her. It was the same for her. Lust and love were mingled into a series of thrusting sensations.

"Look at me, Lydia," he commanded next.

She hadn't realized that her eyes had been closed, that even now her feminine coyness was trying to shut out the wantonness that gripped her as if in a fever. Some semblance of remembered instruction about the decorum that a lady should always keep uppermost in her mind, even in moments of passion, still lingered in her consciousness.

"Look at me, my darling," Vincent whispered again, more seductively now. "Look at *us.*"

For a moment she didn't know what he meant, and then she followed his gaze, to where the two of them were reflected in the long dressing mirror. Her face flooded with color at the imagery there. The two naked figures entwined on the bed, her bare buttocks flaring out, her legs straddled over him. Her hair was loosened and gypsy-wild, her eyes glittering like a wanton's, Vincent's hands were reaching for her breasts, while she watched as if hypnotized, cupping and caressing and tasting.

"Ride me, sweetheart," he whispered. *"Ride me."*

She felt him thrust into her, and she saw the movement of his muscles as he tensed and thrust upwards. She gave a soft moan deep in her throat, and then her body took control of everything. Her hands dug into his shoulders to support herself as she obeyed his order, riding him gloriously, and taking them both to the heights of ecstasy. And finally, when the hot, spreading sensation of release rippled through her, and she felt the spurt of his seed into her, she arched backwards with a cry of exquisite pleasure, and sank down on him, completely spent.

Dear God, what will he think of me now? she thought in despair, when they had remained still for some minutes and he hadn't spoken. Was this what he expected . . . or wanted? She felt him pull the covers over them both, wrapping them both inside, and then she felt his kiss on her mouth.

"I'm sorry," she mumbled against his chest. "But you did say —"

He lifted her chin with his finger. She had burrowed beneath the bedcovers, and she couldn't see him properly. But she could hear the gentleness in his voice.

"You have nothing to be sorry for. Nor do you need to feel shame, or embarrassment, or any of the other nonsensical things women imagine they have to feel after enjoying physical pleasure. And I'm inclined to believe that you did enjoy it a little, or am I mistaken in that flush of pleasure?"

He was laughing at her now. No, not laughing, but teasing, certainly. And to her own surprise, she didn't feel shame. She still felt slightly embarrassed, but it was more at seeing herself act in so abandoned a manner than at what they had actually done. In a curiously detached way, she had had no idea that the act of human physical love could look like that, so undignified and yet so erotic at the same time.

"Well, yes, I suppose I did enjoy it a little," she said nonchalantly. Then, as he leaned away from her to study her face, she couldn't resist her own gurgling laughter coming to the surface. It was the understatement of all time. She had been transported to the stars.

After a suspicious moment, Vincent laughed, too, and suddenly they were both laughing helplessly, his body rocking against hers as he wrapped her in his arms and held her tight. If he hadn't done so, she would probably have fallen out of the narrow bed, which only made her laugh more.

Any of the servants passing through the corridors of Montagu House might well have thought the young married couple were up to all kinds of tricks to be so lively so early in the day after such a late night.

"Thank goodness we've sorted out one little problem then," Vincent was saying calmly, once the paroxysm of laughter had died down. "We share the same sense of humor."

"Do we?"

"We do," he said. "And that's not a bad basis for a marriage, is it?"

Everyone knew that love was a far better basis, but for the moment, Lydia knew she'd settle for being in so much harmony with him. She wasn't going to risk losing that now.

"It's a far better basis than some people have," she said, thinking of some of the poor little Indian princesses who never even met their husbands until their wedding day. When Lydia had been young and impressionable, seeing only the pomp and glitter of the ceremonies, it had always seemed so romantic. It was only in her later years that it had dawned on her how frightened they must have been.

With her somber thoughts, her mood subtly changed. The time for loving, and for this sweet closeness between herself and Vincent, was temporarily over. It didn't matter, because Lydia was lulled by the passion they shared, and by the indisputable fact that Vincent had chosen her to be his wife, for whatever reason.

Later that day, a maid came to tell her there was a visitor for her in the library. She was upstairs resting in the latent heat of the afternoon, while Vincent had taken Monty to see some old friends. She had already acknowledged that there were times when the two men should be alone. She was still a stranger here after all, and undoubtedly Monty would need private times with Vincent to discuss the future.

As usual, her thoughts veered quickly away, knowing only too well that Monty's future was so limited. She went downstairs to the library, mildly annoyed that the visitor hadn't left a card, and that the maid hadn't waited long enough to inform Lydia who it could be. Someone for the men, obviously, who thought that perhaps the lady of the house might do.

The moment she entered the library, she knew who the caller was. This room was not usually as full of floral arrangements as in other rooms in the house, and the aura of old leather was always more prominent. But today it was filled with a strong scent of roses. Lydia recognized the scent at once from the evening before, pungent and sensuous, and worn by only one person at the ball.

Lydia saw Marina Delos rise from one of the deep leather armchairs as soon as she heard the footsteps enter the library. She was garbed in more formal day clothes now, but she was still immaculately beautiful. To her annoyance, Lydia knew she was slightly creased and dishevelled from her afternoon rest, and was therefore at a disadvantage.

"Forgive me for calling on you like this, Lydia," Marina said in her husky voice. "But it seemed a shame to waste such a lovely afternoon, and I thought you and I should get to know one another."

355

"Why?" The word was out before Lydia could stop it, and she bit her lip. By her sharp response, she appeared at once young and gauche, the complete *ingenue*. Besides that, she had committed an appalling social discourtesy. She heard Marina give a small throaty laugh, as if it didn't matter a jot to her.

"I see that we already understand one another fairly well, my dear. As to your question, it seems obvious why we should get to know one another. We have so much in common."

The sheer gall of the woman made Lydia draw in her breath. How dare she come here unannounced like this, trying to undermine all Lydia's confidence!

"I'm afraid I don't see that we have anything in common," she said tightly.

"Ah, but we do. We have Vincent."

His name came between them like an axe falling. Lydia visibly flinched as she heard the caressing way the Greek woman spoke his name. She spoke it with an intimacy that spoke of other times and other moments when she would have breathed the name into his ears and against his flesh.

Lydia sat down heavily in the opposite armchair, feeling for a moment as if her legs would no longer hold her up. But far from making her feel at a disadvantage at looking up at the other, it made her feel more in control of her own home as she spread her skirts around her. She was mentally as well as physically staking her claim here. Marina was the outsider . . . as if she read her thoughts precisely, Marina looked down at her with

356

an amused smile for a moment, and then seated herself again.

"You are mistaken, Ma'am," Lydia said deliberately. "*We* do not have Vincent."

Her legs were shaking beneath her petticoats, but she had no intention of letting this woman see it. She felt as if she was fighting for her rights, even for her life. Marriage to her was sacred too, and no usurper was going to come between herself and the man she had married. No past mistress, and no future one.

Marina laughed softly again. "I would have thought Vincent has the right to choose his friends. Marriage does not mean a man is in servitude to his wife, Lydia dear. If you think so, I can promise you it's the surest way of driving him into someone else's arms."

"You know that for a fact, do you? Is this a habitual occurrence in your world, Ma'am? I assure you it is not in mine."

Her laugh rang out louder this time. "For heaven's sake, why don't you call me Marina? And don't be so stuffy, please. If we're to be friends—"

"How can you think I would ever wish to be friends with you?" Lydia said, her own voice low and passionate, her heart beating with sick rapidity at the woman's cheek.

Marina sounded more sorrowful now. "I'm so sorry you feel that way, Lydia. I'm sure you've heard the old saying that it's sometimes more astute to make a friend of your enemy. Not that I'm your enemy! In fact, it would be my pleasure to show you something of Kurnios—"

"There's no need. My husband has already taken me around the island, and introduced me to many of his friends."

Pointedly, she made it clear that she knew Marina Delos had been kept well out of those visits. But then, Lydia thought with a sinking heart, what man would willingly take his new wife to meet his mistress? Her mind was in chaos again, and the early morning pleasures with Vincent had vanished as completely as if they had never been.

"I'm sure he hasn't taken you everywhere yet," Marina went on, quite unperturbed. "I have one or two little excursions in mind that I'm sure would appeal to you. Perhaps in a week or so you'll feel differently about things, and we can arrange something together. I shall call on you again when you've had time to get accustomed to the idea."

Lydia was quite sure she would never want to arrange anything with this woman, but she was saved from the indignity of telling her by the appearance of Monty and Vincent. She was certain Vincent looked somewhat embarrassed at seeing Marina here, but Monty exclaimed with delight at once. The woman was obviously a favorite with him, Lydia thought, and if she had fulfilled his wishes racially, he would have been only too happy for Vincent to marry her. If it had been Vincent's own wish, of course. . . . There were so many ifs, far too many for Lydia's comfort.

Once she had got to the truth of Vincent's reasons for his marriage, at least she had understood Monty's motives in a grudging way, though she still thought it a wicked thing to do to juggle with peoples' lives. But now, for Lydia, things had shifted again.

"Why are you two sitting here without any refreshment?" Monty asked at once. "And why here, in this gloomy room? Come into the drawing room, both of you, and we'll get some tea organized at once."

Marina gave him an affectionate smile. "Dear Monty. Everything stops for tea with you English, doesn't it?"

"Of course! Battles may rage and kingdoms fall, but the English afternoon tea ritual must still be observed."

"Stop teasing, you wicked old man," Lydia protested lightly, linking her arm in his, and unconsciously projecting the image of a special rapport between them. "People will start believing that we English are a lot of silly buffers who spend every afternoon drinking tea instead of taking on more serious pursuits!"

She managed to include Vincent in her smile, making the three of them a complete unit, and Marina the foreigner. And if the other three noticed that she hadn't brought herself to mention Marina by name, she didn't care.

"Oh, I don't think that at all," Marina said evenly. "I know just how serious some afternoon pursuits can be with an Englishman."

Her eyes flashed a blatant message at Vincent, and Lydia felt a shock of disbelief at this outrageous innuendo.

As if only just realizing the tension in the room, Monty cleared his throat, obviously searching for something to say.

"You'll stay to dinner, won't you, Marina? After the festivities of last night, we're going to have a very informal meal, so don't bother your head over any nonsense about going home to change or anything. You always look delightful to me, in any case," he added.

"Then how can I refuse such a gallant invitation?" she said sweetly, to Lydia's annoyance.

But it was true that they had all agreed on a very informal evening after the hectic night before, with just the three of them. Now all that was spoiled, and Marina the interloper was there in their midst. At least, she was the interloper as far as Lydia was concerned. She had hardly dared to glance Vincent's way for fear her jealousy showed too obviously, but as the four of them entered the drawing room together, she couldn't miss the polite smiles he gave the other woman. And in her imagination those smiles spoke of an intimacy that still burned as brightly as ever.

It was all true, she thought sickly. Whatever love was once between them was still there. Perhaps even Vincent's enforced sojourn to England had made them both realize how strong that love still was. As Lydia's self-confidence faltered, she asked herself hopelessly how she could ever hope to compete with it. She was a novice in the ways of love; while even to her inexperienced eyes, Marina was an expert.

"I'll order some tea at once," she said now, pulling the bell cord for the maid, and determined to assert herself as the lady of the house before her nerve failed her completely.

She was angry as well as nervous at her own ineptitude whenever this self-confident woman was around. But whatever else she had anticipated finding here on Kurnios, she had never bargained for someone like Marina Delos, and that was the truth of it. She realized she seemed to be almost on the periphery of the chatter now, as the two men and their guest prattled on about people she didn't know, about the vine production she didn't understand, about the importance of the cool cellars where the vintage wine was kept.

"May I give you all some tea?" she said loudly, when the maid had brought the trolley, and she had poured out the cups of dark brew. "And perhaps a scone and jam to keep off the pangs of hunger before dinner?"

She smiled at Monty, knowing his weakness for the traditional English fare. He accepted at once, but Marina almost preened as she said she didn't need any interim food, and could easily wait until the evening meal. When the other three were all settling down with their scones, she spoke sweetly.

"I don't like to put on too much weight. I know it's fashionable among Greek women, but I still think it's a little unfeminine to be obese, don't you, Lydia?"

Lydia had a bite of scone halfway down her throat at that moment, and almost choked on it. She swallowed angrily, seeing the way Marina was eyeing her rounded curves. She had certainly eaten rather well since coming to Kurnios, she admitted, and several of her dresses were becoming uncomfortably tight around her middle and her bustline, but it was the height of bad manners to make such snide remarks in company. And she simply didn't believe they had been said idly.

"I rather think the Greeks have a lot of common sense in preferring their ladies well-rounded," she said. "A stick-thin woman doesn't have a lot of femininity, in my opinion."

"You're so right," Marina said easily. "I'm thankful I could never be thought of in such unflattering terms."

If she didn't exactly caress her own shape with her palms to emphasize her own curves, the provocative way she sat forward to sip her tea made just as much impact on the others. And all Lydia could think of was how many times Vincent must have held her and felt those luscious curves pressed against himself. She almost banged her cup in her saucer, dismally sure that the evening ahead of them was going to be unending.

By the time they sat down to dinner, she knew she was right. She had a blinding headache, and the more she seemed to wilt after the exertions of the night before, the more Marina seemed to sparkle. Marina hardly needed the glitter of the night before to make her seem at home and comfortable in this house, where she had obviously been many times before. Whether it was as Vincent's guest or Monty's, she knew the house and its occupants only too well.

And if Monty hadn't gotten this dogmatic notion for Vincent to marry an English wife and produce an English heir at all costs, Lydia had no doubt that Marina would either have continued in her role as mistress, or eventually become Vincent's wife. It wasn't unknown for men to marry their mistresses. . . .

"Perhaps you and I could have afternoon tea one day soon, Lydia," Marina was saying casually now. "It would be my pleasure to show you around my house and vineyards."

To show you the rooms with which Vincent was so familiar . . . especially the bedroom. . . . Lydia could almost hear the unspoken words coming from that smiling red mouth, and sensed that Marina was waiting for her to make some lame excuse. She tilted her chin.

"That would be very agreeable," she said, just as coolly. "I'm sure there are many occasions when Vincent and Monty wish to be alone, and it will be interesting to see some of the other houses on the island."

But it would be a long time before she set foot in that woman's house, she was thinking savagely, and then she heard Monty's chuckle.

"Don't expect to see anything like your fishermens' cottages, my dear, nor even anything that resembles the Brandons' place. Marina's husband was a wealthy man, and her home reflects considerable style."

Well, she wouldn't have expected anything else, Lydia thought, with irritation. She couldn't deny that everything about the woman was stylish, even if it was far too brash and overdone for her personal taste. She supposed that together they must make quite a contrast, she thought suddenly. She with her dark titian hair and vivid blue eyes and delicate English skin, and Marina, as lush and vibrant as the brilliant foliage that grew in such profusion around every cottage and villa on the island. . . .

Chapter Sixteen

All through that interminable evening, she couldn't keep her mind off the imagery of Marina and Vincent together. All the secure feelings that had been with her during the idyllic hours of the early morning had vanished like will-o'-the-wisp, and all the hated jealousy was back. She kept wondering just how many regrets Vincent truly harbored because of the circumstances that had forced him into seeking out an English bride. It was obvious to her now, that he had had everything he wanted right here in the arms of the olive-skinned Marina.

Bitterly, she knew the truth of the old saying that love for a man was a thing apart, while for a woman it was her whole existence. For Lydia, it was everything, total and complete, but as for Vincent, how could she ever know if he still secretly hankered for an old love, while being physically satisfied with all that the new love had to offer? She didn't know him well enough to be sure, nor did she think she could ever be sure.

Without warning, tiredness overcame her while they were still drinking coffee in the drawing room after dinner. She stifled a yawn, knowing it was in very bad taste to display such a thing. To her chagrin, Marina was the one person who saw it.

"Are you tired, Lydia? It was such a very long evening yesterday, and you danced with so many young men it must have been exhausting for you. You're not accustomed to the heat and our energetic dancing—"

"Oh, I'm more than accustomed to the heat," Lydia returned quickly. "As to the dancing, I enjoyed it very much."

Monty got to his feet. "Well, I'm extremely tired, if you young people are not. I shall bid you all a fond good night, and Marina it was good to see you, my dear. You must come and visit me more often."

Lydia listened in a kind of incredulous disbelief as she heard the platitudes passing between the two of them during the next few minutes. Was Monty totally unaware of the brittle undercurrents between the two women all evening? Couldn't he see the sometimes amused looks Vincent tried to hide, and the occasional frown between his eyes when Marina went too far in her faint references to a past they had once shared?

To his credit, Lydia could see he didn't like the way Marina frequently tried to score over her rival by these references. If Marina was still to be part of his life, at least in Vincent's eyes it was obvious she was to be a discreet part . . . but that wasn't enough, Lydia thought with sudden passion. Marina shouldn't be *any* part of Vincent's life from now on. He belonged to Lydia, and to no one else. The wide wedding band on her finger was proof of that.

"It is getting rather late, and I think we could all do with getting to our beds," she said pointedly, uncaring now if it was considered bad manners or not to say so.

Marina had been here for hours, in what had begun as an uninvited visit for afternoon tea. The shadows had stretched and paled, and the daylight blue of the sky had already merged into night. The huge moon was low overhead, and the nighttime scent of dew-drenched blossom was heavy on the still air.

"Why, so it is," Marina said, as if startled to find how the time had moved on. "I do apologize if I've overstayed my welcome, Lydia. I quite understand that newly married couples find late-night visitors tedious, especially after such an occasion as last evening—"

"Don't talk rubbish," Vincent said roughly. "You're very welcome to stay and take more coffee with us, or a glass of brandy, if you wish." He drained his own brandy glass, and indicated the decanter.

"I think I should leave, Vincent." She gave him a warm smile. "I came in the little trap, and you know how rutted the roads are. It can be unnerving, travelling alone at night . . ."

Her voice trailed away, and Lydia felt as though she was listening to the inevitable as Vincent insisted on escorting the lady home.

Suddenly she knew that this was what Marina had been waiting for all along, and it was probably her sole purpose in coming here at all. She knew she'd be invited to stay for dinner, and the later the evening got, the more likely Vincent would be to offer to escort her home. Lydia's cheeks burned with fury at the realization, but there was nothing she could do about it, short of appearing as tetchy as a fishwife.

"Then if you're ready, perhaps we should leave," Vincent said, and Marina stood up with a sinuous movement. He was polite enough, but Lydia couldn't help wondering just how much he looked forward to this clever engineering by his mistress.

As Marina looked directly at her now, Lydia was certain she could detect a look of triumph in the dark, glowing eyes.

"I'm so sorry to drag your husband away from you, Lydia dear, but I'm sure he'll want to return to you as quickly as possible. I promise not to keep him away from you for long."

"Oh, but we have all night to be together, so I assure you I shan't fret unduly," Lydia replied as lightly as possible.

"Meanwhile, darling," she deliberately turned to Vincent, excluding Marina from their conversation, "I think I shall go on up to bed, even though I'm not as tired as I thought I was. Please don't be long."

To her surprise Vincent came to her, catching up her hand in his and bringing the palm to his lips. He folded her fingers into her palm, as if to enclose the kiss there. The sweet, unexpected caress sent a sting of tears to Lydia's eyes. She couldn't decide whether he did it as some kind of recompense for the time he was now obliged to spend with Marina, or if it really meant something very special for the other woman to see.

"How sweet," Marina's voice was edged with sarcasm. "Your bride is obviously touched by small pleasures, Vincent."

"And by bigger ones," he murmured, so that only Lydia could hear. It was a precious, private moment between the two of them, and she was certain he was remembering again the magic of that early morning. Just as she was . . .

Several hours later, Lydia lay wide awake in the big canopied bed they shared, wondering just how long it took for Vincent to escort Marina home. She wasn't certain how far away she lived, but she was fairly sure it was the elegantly built white-porticoed building she had glimpsed on one of their first outings on Kurnios. The house and its occupants that Vincent had carefully avoided commenting on at the time . . .

She turned restlessly in the bed, all her fine feelings dispersing fast. Why didn't he come back? And more importantly, what was keeping him away? She couldn't believe it would take so long to deliver Marina to her home and return to Montagu House. Unless, of course, the lady had other ideas, which Lydia was very certain she would have. But she had trusted Vincent. After those sweet private moments just before they had left, she believed in him implicitly. They shared their lives now, and there was no room in it for Marina Delos, or anyone else from Vincent's past.

She found herself curling up in a ball in the empty bed, misery washing over her. She had given up everything for this man: homeland, friends, family, no matter how irritating those family members were. Was it too much to ask that he should give up his old life for her? A wife had every right to expect fidelity, and right now, the erotic vision of Marina Delos in Vincent's arms was the only thing filling her mind. She gave a broken sob in her throat, willing him to come back to her.

But there was anger mixed in with the hurt. She knew that if he walked in through the bedroom door this minute she'd be ranting and raving at him, and probably throwing whatever she could lay her hands on as well. And that probably wasn't going to solve anything. It would be far better to keep calm and try to sort it out once and for all.

She would give him an ultimatum. Either he must give Marina up for good, or she. . . . She crumpled, hardly knowing what her side of any ultimatum could possibly be. She was trapped here. According to Vincent, most people either worked for the Montagus or owed them allegiance or loyalty in some way or another, so there was little hope of her escaping. Besides, it wasn't what she really wanted. She wanted his love, and she wanted it exclusively.

She closed her eyes, willing her heart to stop its erratic beating, and to will the unwanted pictures of her husband and his mistress away. She must keep calm, she must be soft and pliable for when Vincent came home, if only to show him that his wife was all the woman he could ever want. How could she ever bear to share him with another woman?

When Lydia awoke it was daylight, and the maid was drawing back the curtains, so that she blinked at the harsh bright sunlight streaming in through the windows.

"Vincent," she murmured sleepily.

"The young gentleman went out early this morning, Lady, but the old gentleman is downstairs in the breakfast room. Do you wish that I help you dress now?"

"No thank you, Coora. I'll see to it myself," she said woodenly. She didn't want anyone around right now. She didn't want anyone's sharp eyes to notice the smooth, undented pillow beside her in the double bed, and to surmise what Lydia already knew. Vincent hadn't come home at all last night.

"Are you going to tell me where you've been?"

She spoke accusingly the minute she saw Vincent riding in through the grounds of Montagu House during the late morning. By then she had taken breakfast with Monty, as calmly as she could while trying not to show her feelings. She didn't want to worry the old man further. She couldn't help noting his waxy pallor today, although he assured her he was feeling as well as could be expected. Lydia had no way of knowing just what that meant, and it seemed too much of an imposition to ask.

Vincent looked down at her from his seat on the horse. He was more dishevelled than usual, but that took nothing away from the sheer masculinity of the man. To her annoyance, she knew what an advantage he had over her at this moment when she was feeling so wronged. He sat tall and arro-

371

gant, his riding crop in his hand, his hair ruffled in a ruggedly handsome manner. The black riding boots that caressed his elegant legs normally gleamed against the heaving flanks of his mount, but right now they were dusty and dirty, as if he'd been riding for a very long time.

Lydia caught hold of the reins in a proprietary manner, and she was angered to see how her hands trembled on the leather and that he saw it, too.

"I've been busy with estate business, my dear," he said, his voice oozing with indulgence. "It's something a man needs to do, and something that a wife needn't concern herself with."

"That's not what I mean, and you know it," Lydia said tightly, in danger of losing all control at the aggressor confronting her. She saw his eyes flash more dangerously as he saw her heightened color and unsmiling mouth. He leaned toward her, and she was aware of one of the young estate grooms hurrying toward them to take the steed away for a good rubbing down. Vincent was as cold as ice now, and his voice should have warned her that she was already going too far.

"My dear, you may question me as much as you like in private, and whether or not I answer you will be between the two of us. But in public, you'll oblige me by remembering your place. A wife does not question her husband's movements in front of servants."

Lydia flushed furiously. Uncouth was the only word for him, she thought. However right he may be, it was undignified to speak so in the groom's hearing. The fact that the young lad didn't seem at all concerned by it only angered her more. She remembered how her parents had always treated their meanest Indian servants kindly, and without the arrogance of the so-called "white man." It shamed her to hear Vincent speak so, whether or not he thought he was goaded into it.

"Then I'll wait until we can speak in private," she said, turning on her heel. "As soon as possible, please," she threw back over her shoulder, and stalked into the house.

He was impossible, she raged. He was in the wrong, and yet in a few moments, he had made her feel the guilty one.

She resorted to the library, where she so often felt safe and secure among the leathery scents of the books and deep armchairs. For some reason, it was the very morning the housekeeper had decided to brighten up the room by placing a bowl of deep red roses on a low table. Their perfume was sensual and heady, reminding her instantly of Marina. Lydia had the strongest urge to gather up the blooms and hurl them out of the room.

While she was still wondering if she dared put such a childish urge into practice, Vincent came stalking into the room, slamming the door shut behind him. He strode across to her, caught hold of her shoulders, and physically shook her. She was so astonished she could only gape at him, wide-eyed and fearful at this unexpected treatment.

"What do I have to do to convince you that you have a special place here, on this island, in this house, and in my life?" he said harshly. "Your jealousy is making you paranoid, Lydia, and I'm fast losing patience with it."

"Oh, *really!*" Her voice was shrill and hurt. "Then perhaps you'll convince me that I've no cause for it, when I can only surmise you've spent last night with your—"

At the last moment, she knew she couldn't even say the word. It made it all too real, too painfully real.

"And especially after we—"

She couldn't mention the early morning hours of the previous day either, not without letting him see how desperately she was in love with him. Her heart yearned for a two-way love, not this one-sided affair, where all the emotion seemed to be on her side, and where all his tenderness was simply borne out of a man's natural lust for a woman. That, and the need to give Monty his heart's desire before he died, she reminded herself bitterly.

She realized Vincent's touch on her shoulders was less cruel than it had been moments before. His fingers caressed her tautness now, and his eyes were dark and unreadable.

"Do you think that what we do means nothing to me, my foolish one?" he said abruptly. "You are the most delightful lover any man could be fortunate enough to take to bed. Don't ever underestimate your power over me, Lydia, my sweet. In fact, you may test it for yourself right now."

Before she could react, he had grasped her hand and guided it swiftly to where the evidence of his words was aggressively proud against his breeches. She almost snatched her hand away. Her fury seemed to arouse him as much as his own desire, she thought angrily, and it didn't enchant her.

"And what about other lovers?" she said, her voice hoarse at the indelicacy of asking such a question. "Can you promise me that I am the only one, which is surely what a wife has every right to expect?"

It was threateningly fashionable for men, even those in high places, to take mistresses, and for wives to turn a blind eye while they did their saintly duty and produced heirs for family continuity, but that wasn't going to be the way for Lydia Grey Montagu. She wanted all of her man, solely and completely.

"There are no other lovers," he said impatiently, turning away from her and throwing himself down in one of the leather chairs. He still held his riding crop in his hand, and he tapped it impatiently against his other palm. From the frown between his eyes, Lydia was quite sure he'd as soon thrash her with it.

"Will you swear to it?"

He gave a short laugh. "I will not. If you can't take my word for it, then you may surmise all you wish. I'll not be browbeaten by a chit of a girl to swear an oath. I did that when I married you, and that should have been enough."

"You make it sound as if it were a hardship," she said, seething.

"I'm not pretending that the idea of marriage was mine by choice, you know that very well. I seem to recall that you went into it willingly enough. It was for Monty's sake that I took the step I did. Once the facts were known to you, I consider I have every right to expect you to stick to your end of the bargain."

She felt sick to her stomach. "Even though you tricked me into it in the first place? I never knew the truth of it until I arrived here, remember? And is that all that our marriage means to you, a bargain?"

"I can't think it means any more to you than it does to me. But since it pleases your ferrety little mind to dig deeper, then I will tell you that I did not spend the night with Marina, as you so charmingly think to accuse me. I did spend some hours explaining to her that our former relationship was finished, but that I still wanted to consider her a friend. It was not something that could be settled within minutes, for obvious reasons."

"They're not obvious to me!" Lydia said, shaken, and not quite sure what to think now.

"Marina was upset," Vincent said shortly. "And yes, she did seem to think we would continue our relationship as before, despite my bringing home a wife. I did not see things in the same light, and there were difficulties. And these are not things I ever wished to discuss with you, Lydia."

His terseness said more than a long detailed explanation. For a wild, reluctant moment, Lydia found herself imagining the scene, unwillingly putting herself in Marina's place. The longtime mistress, confidently expecting that when her lover returned to Kurnios with a paid-for wife, her presence would do nothing to touch the special relationship she and Vincent had shared. And now she had been rudely spurned . . .

376

She imagined Marina weeping, throwing herself at Vincent, as lovely and desirable as she had ever been to him, and his compassion overcoming his determination to do the right thing. She bit her lips, knowing they were trembling. How would she have behaved in the same situation? In a moment of total empathy, she knew it would be exactly as Marina had done.

"But you told her it was over?"

"I told her it was over. And in the end she accepted it."

"And you didn't stay there the whole night?"

She saw his grip on the riding crop tighten, and knew she was going too far, but seemingly unable to stop.

"I spent the rest of the night drinking myself senseless with John Brandon, to the complete disapproval of Daisy, who insisted I spend what was left of the night in their guest room. I'm sure she'll confirm the facts to you when you inevitably want to check up on my movements. Now, if the inquisition is over, I would like to bathe and change my clothes."

It all sounded so plausible, and there was nothing else Lydia could do but nod dumbly and stand aside as he made for the library door. As he put his hand on the doorknob, he turned, a half-smile on his face.

"I suppose I should be touched that you think so highly of me that you want me all for yourself, Lydia," he said, though his voice made a mockery of the words. "But perhaps you should have paid more attention to the vows we made, when we

377

both affirmed the sanctity of marriage. We each need to trust one another on that score, my dear."

He was gone then, and she was left feeling the guilty one again, instead of the wronged wife she had started out to be that morning. Marriage was a far more complicated state of affairs than anyone knew until they entered into it, she thought wearily, feeling suddenly sick and empty of all emotion.

She realized she had been feeling sickly ever since she awoke that day, and she had put it down to her anxiety over present circumstances. Now, for the first time, she wondered if it was anything more sinister. Was she ailing from something, perhaps? Or could it be something else?

Unthinkingly, her hand moved gently over her abdomen. Surely it was still as flat as it had ever been? Though her breasts were undoubtedly feeling a little strained and sore against the fabric of her gown.

She had put the reason for that down to Vincent's attentions, and felt a little shiver of pleasure at remembering how his hands caressed her curving shape, and his mouth teased her nipples so readily into tingling arousal.

But, perhaps, she was already in the state he wanted her to be. She tried to think back to normal bodily functions that should have appeared regularly and had been erratic lately. It was simply because of all the upheavals in her life, she had reasoned without undue concern. For some reason, she recalled her old nurse's words on the subject she had been so curious about.

"When a woman has a child growing inside her, she knows instinctively, my young one. There's a feeling of such well-being, of renewed closeness with all of nature, with the earth and with the sky. When in the fullness of time it happens to you, you'll know."

Well, she didn't feel like that now, she thought crossly, in one of her frequent mood changes. And for once, she was irritated by the memory of Nadima's mysterious, flowery explanations. She didn't *know*, and the euphoric feelings Nadima had described were certainly nothing at all like the waves of queasiness flowing over her now. She sat down heavily again, assuming that the past half hour with Vincent had disturbed her physically as well as mentally.

She had to trust him, she thought desperately. Marriage was nothing without trust. She had to believe that his association with Marina was over, no matter what suspicions the woman herself might put into her head in the future. Her own state of health was obviously going to suffer if she didn't put thoughts of his past behind her. Their marriage would be doomed, and that was the last thing she wanted.

Daisy Brandon came to call on her that afternoon. Much earlier Vincent had taken Monty out for a regular visit to some of his old card-playing cronies, and Lydia had declined to go with them for the ride, pleading a headache. The afternoon sun was hot, and she was surprised that the two men seemed to enjoy its heat as much as they did and also that Daisy should come calling during the siesta hours.

"I thought this would be a good time," Daisy said, removing her hat as the two young women sat companionably in the drawing room, awaiting a tray of refreshments.

Once it had arrived and Lydia had poured them each a cup of Indian tea and handed around the sweet English biscuits they both adored, Lydia looked at her quizzically.

"Why would you think this an especially good time to call, Daisy? Not that I'm not pleased to see you at any time!" she added hastily. Things were far less formal here than in England, where the stuffiness of visiting cards and prearranged meetings took half the pleasure out of seeing friends. And she already counted Daisy Brandon as a friend.

"I know Monty has his regular card-playing afternoon today, so I guessed you'd be alone, and I wanted to talk to you, Lydia."

Lydia felt her cheeks go hot. "If it's about last night, I'd rather not say anything. Vincent's already explained, and it's quite all right, really —"

"Is it?" the other girl said candidly, and at her obvious concern, Lydia felt her face suddenly crumple. She put her cup down quickly, feeling the dampness in her eyes. She hated feeling so weepy, and she hated this floating feeling of having so little to do. Even tutoring her wretched young cousins at her uncle's house in England was preferable to inactivity and having too much time to think.

She realized Daisy was handing her a clean square of white linen. She blew her nose into it noisily, murmuring something about having it laundered and returned in due course.

"Don't be a goose. Keep it. Now, why not tell your Auntie Daisy what's really wrong? I promise it will go no further, Lydia. Though I can probably guess most of it."

"I wonder if you can. I wonder if you know how it feels to know your husband only married you as a kind of childbearing machine! Sometimes when I think of it quite cynically, it makes me feel no more desirable than a prize *cow!*"

She heard the laughter coming from the other girl. It wasn't malicious laughter, but gentle and sympathetic, and Lydia gave a shame-faced grin, mopping up the tears again.

"I've never said it aloud to anyone before, not even myself! You must think I'm indiscreet and disloyal to my husband at best, and partial to gutter-language at worst."

"Oh Lydia, stop being so sorry for yourself, for pity's sake!"

Lydia paused in her snuffling, not expecting this.

"I'm not sorry for myself. Well, yes, I suppose I am, but only because I've got reason to be!" she said indignantly.

"I can't think why. You have a husband who loves you madly, for whatever reason you think he married you. If you can't see that, then you're an idiot. Everyone else can see it."

"You think so?" Lydia said, totally skeptical. "Then perhaps you had better try telling Marina

Delos, who still seems to think she has claims on my husband!"

"She may think so, but it won't get her anywhere. If you had seen Vincent last night as John and I saw him—"

"So he was with you. It's nice to know he had friends to confide in, even if he couldn't come home to his wife!"

Daisy looked at her sorrowfully.

"Lydia, I know how hurt you must be feeling, but we're Vincent's old friends. We've known Vincent a long time. He and John have shared many confidences over the years, and sometimes men need to talk things over with other men, that's all. I wasn't involved in the discussion. But by the time the two of them got too drunk and raucous to stop falling about, it seemed the only sensible thing to do to offer Vincent a bed for the night."

Lydia knew she must look shame-faced as this generous-hearted woman was telling her in the most tactful way that she hadn't eavesdropped on Vincent's revelations last night.

"I'm sorry," she mumbled. "I just feel so terribly confused lately." And the headache she had invented for Vincent and Monty's benefit was fast becoming a stabbing reality.

"If it's any comfort to you, Lydia, the affair with Marina Delos was over long before Vincent went to England," Daisy spoke firmly, as if with a sudden resolve to bring the facts out into the open. "John and I were certain of it, and it was only the lady herself who wouldn't seem to accept it."

"But she came here yesterday, and stayed all

evening, and Vincent was eager enough to escort her home. And then he stayed away so long. What else could I think but the obvious?" It was a cry from the heart now, seeking reassurance.

"But why can't you see what is so obvious to us? Vincent truly loves you. Believe me, his friends who know him can see the glow that comes over him whenever you enter a room. It's not imagination, Lydia. You have to learn to trust him, or you'll be in danger of spoiling everything that you have. And the surest way of turning him back to past pleasures is by being suspicious of his every movement. No man will tolerate that. And I don't mean to lecture you."

"Perhaps I needed a lecture," Lydia said. "But the circumstances of our marriage were less than straightforward, and even I didn't know all that he wanted of me until I came here. It was a shock. And it's hard to give your trust when you weren't trusted with the whole truth in the first place."

She was embarrassed at speaking so freely about things that should be private between herself and Vincent. But she knew instinctively that this girl could be a good friend, and she had needed so badly to confide in someone. She hadn't realized it herself until now.

"Well, I must leave you now," Daisy said at last. "John and I have been invited out to dinner this evening, and I fear his head is still a little thick from last night."

She smiled to take the sting out of her words, bringing the visit back to a normal chitchat between friends. She hugged Lydia as she left, and there was a lump in Lydia's throat at finding such a worthwhile companion here. She was mother, mentor, friend and Nadima, all rolled into one.

Later, Lydia decided she must lie down, as the headache became more of a reality. She rang the bell in her room for Coora to close the drapes at her window, feeling she hardly had the energy to get out of bed and do it for herself. The maid looked at her with some concern.

"Do you feel unwell, Lady? Should somebody be sent for? Doctor Stavros, perhaps?"

Lydia shook her head and felt it spin.

"It's no more than a wretched headache. You might ask Cook to prepare me a sedative powder though, and I'll try and have an hour's sleep. I shall be quite all right later on. Before you go, you can help me out of my gown, if you please. It's stifling me."

She stood up, feeling the room sway, and the maid unfastened the buttons on her gown and slid it over her head. After a few minutes Lydia decided she may as well remove all her day garments and slide into her cool nightgown until it was time to dress formally for dinner. When she'd done so she felt decidedly more comfortable and ready to face whatever was ahead of her. She resolved that it was high time she tried to be less sensitive to everything Vincent said to her regarding Marina Delos. But she hardly realized how she seemed to be looking on every new meeting with her husband as an encounter on a battlefield now.

Chapter Seventeen

It seemed a very long time before Coora appeared in the bedroom again with the milky sedative liquid. Lydia struggled on to one elbow to drink it down in one gulp, grimacing at the bitter taste, and then sank back on the pillow again. Coora put the coverlet over her, and looked down at her doubtfully.

"I told Cook you were white and sickly, Lady, so she say she make up an extra strong dose for you. Cook say it will send you off to dreamland for a week!"

Coora was clearly proud of her quaintly rehearsed English idioms, and hardly noticed the dismayed look on Lydia's face as she went out of the room. An extra strong dose!

That wasn't at all what she had wanted. She wanted to be alert, because there was something she needed to tell Vincent. Something about trust, and trying again, and keeping the magic of their marriage alive . . . providing the magic hadn't all been on her side. Only, she couldn't quite remember what it was she had to say to him that was so important, because the headache kept jabbing her between the eyes. Both the pain and the sedative were already beginning to take precedence over her consciousness.

She drifted in and out of an odd dreaming state. She kept thinking she could hear Vincent's voice, talking to her in a gentle, loving voice, but whenever she turned her head and tried to lift her heavy lids, he was never there. She was aware of how she thrashed about in the bed, and she often imagined she could feel Vincent's hands calming her, replacing the coverlet over her fevered limbs, and cooling her brow with his calming touch.

It was obviously her imagination playing tricks, Lydia thought in one of her saner moments. Yet it was all so poignantly like the time she had been badly burned by the sun and had been so dangerously ill.

She had been so sure of his presence then. But this time the illusion always faded as soon as she struggled to open her eyes. She knew it was all an hallucination, and there was a great well of unreleased weeping inside her. She ached for him to be beside her, for his gentleness as much as his strength.

When Lydia felt finally able to open her eyes properly, it was as if she had been in an unconscious state for a very long time. In fact, it was hours, not days. It was dark, and the bedroom was lit by soft candlelight that was easy on the eyes. She turned her head a little, to see Vincent sitting on the window seat, supposedly reading a book, but with his head nodding over the open pages.

Lydia felt a great surge of love for him. Although he was as strong and powerfully built as ever, he looked oddly vulnerable to her in his shirtsleeves and breeches now, the usual pristine necktie loosened. He was no longer the awesome lord of the manor, but her love, her man.

As if aware of her gaze on him, or as if he heard the small indrawn breath she gave then, he looked up quickly.

"Don't you know you'll strain your eyes, trying to read in such a dim light?" she said huskily. "It's very bad for you."

He closed the book and walked across the room to her. He was unsmiling as he looked down at her. Yet, she knew he had gentled the coverlet around her thrashing arms, he had smoothed her heated brow and kissed her tear-stained cheeks. It had not been dreaming after all.

"And you shouldn't let Cook feed you with her impossibly strong sedatives," he said abruptly. "You missed dinner completely, and I was so anxious about you that I missed it, too."

She looked at him in astonishment.

"What time is it then?" she asked inanely, as if it mattered. As if anything mattered but the glorious fact that he was concerned about her.

"It's about three in the morning."

"Good Lord! No wonder I'm so hungry! I'm surprised you didn't hear my stomach groaning across the room."

She seemed to be recovering with amazing speed. And this jocularity seemed a blessedly normal way to cross the gap they had recently created between them. Talking of mundane things, like hunger and time, and making a joke of it. She saw the ghost of a smile touch his lips.

"I wonder you didn't hear mine," he said dryly. "I'm ravenous too. I'd send down to the kitchen for some food, but the servants will probably think there's a fire if we start ringing bells in the middle of the night."

"Why can't we fetch it ourselves?" Lydia heard herself say without thinking. "It will probably outrage Cook if we invade her kitchen, but whose house is it anyway?"

A sense of recklessness was spurring her on. Besides, the thought of a clandestine feast was somehow more stimulating than anything else right now. The effects of the sedative were wearing off fast, and a new kind of ebullience was filling her. It seemed to be catching, because Vincent gave a sudden chuckle.

"You're damn right. It's our house, so why not? Sit up slowly while I fetch your robe and slippers, and we'll see what we can find in the pantry."

He was being very considerate at telling her to rise slowly, but she wasn't ill, nor did she need pampering. But she certainly wasn't foolish enough to object to it! She was beginning to feel her mouth water at the very thought of food, and she fancied something spicy and savory, the idea of which sent even more juices to her mouth.

Five minutes later they were creeping through the silent house to the underworld of the kitchens and sculleries. This was Cook's province, and she kept it strictly out of bounds to all but her helpers. The gentry were not supposed to know what went on below stairs until meals were produced at the dining table with all the aplomb of a conjurer's magic act. The proprieties that were followed were exactly the same as if they were in the house of an English gentleman somewhere in deepest rural Sussex.

Vincent held her hand tightly for a moment, pausing as they descended as a stair creaked noisily. She felt a violent urge to giggle, suddenly finding it all so ludicrous to be stealing about like two thieves in their own home! But it was exciting and endearing, too, to know that Vincent wasn't above acting like a playful conspirator when the time warranted it.

They entered the kitchen full of Cook's shining pots and pans and shelves, full of plates and dishes for every possible occasion. The huge pantry and cold store was in this room, and Vincent threw it open with a flourish.

"What would my lady prefer this evening?" he said, taking on the role of butler. "We have choice hams, or chickens in red wine, or smoked haddock—"

"I'll have a little of everything," she said recklessly. "With onions and red cabbage. I insist on having onions, my man."

He laughed at her sudden enthusiasm. They were never served onions at the dinner table, for fear it would upset the digestion during the night or cause offense to sleeping companions. But if Lydia wanted onions, then onions she should have. She wanted to assist, but Vincent ordered her to sit still at the kitchen table and be waited on, while he did the honors.

A short while later they were eating huge pieces of cold chicken and succulent ham, with a great bowl of pickled onions between them, garnished with helpings of Cook's best pickled red cabbage. A dish of custard trifle finished off the meal, aided by a long drink of Cook's freshly made lemonade. Lydia gave a deep, satisfied sigh when it was all finished.

"That was the best meal I've ever tasted in my life," she said sincerely. "Even though I have a horrible feeling I'm going to pay for it in the morning."

"It's already the morning," Vincent told her. "So if you've had quite enough, my lady, I suggest we go to bed and sleep off what's left of the dark hours."

"Are you suggesting that you sleep with me, my man?" she said roguishly. "Without even tidying up your kitchen?"

"I am. But if you think I'm going to take advantage of you after what you've just eaten, then you can think again."

"I'm not sure that I think you even capable, after what *you've* just eaten!"

They might have gone on jesting with each other in the same light-hearted way, had not the door of the kitchen suddenly flown open. A florid-faced Cook stood there in her long patterned dressing gown, her wispy grey hair bristling with curling rags, and brandishing a rolling pin from one of the other kitchens. She gaped in astonishment at seeing the master and lady of the house looking as though they'd gorged themselves almost senseless,

390

with the remnants of a feast still in evidence on the table beside them.

"Bless my soul, but I thought we had thieves in the place," she said indignantly. "What on earth can you be about, Sir and Madam, frightening good people half to death?"

"It would take more than a beggar in the night to frighten you, Cook," Vincent grinned. "And you know very well that my wife and I both missed our dinner, so I didn't think you could object to our helping ourselves. Especially when it was your sedative that put my wife unconscious for hours."

"I'm very sorry if we've upset your domestic arrangements, Cook," Lydia said, more meekly than Vincent's half-aggressive tones. "Let me help you clear away the plates —"

"You'll do no such thing, begging your pardon, my lady!" Cook said, scandalized at the thought of Lydia lifting a finger to do such menial work. "You'll be doing us all a favor if you'll return to your own quarters and leave me to mine while I attend to the clearing up. I'll say good night to you now."

She sniffed in dismissal, and as Vincent put his arm around Lydia, she felt herself being hustled out of the kitchen. She could tell he was almost bursting with laughter as he led the way back to their room through the silent house.

"I wonder how Cook can resist banging every plate in her fury. We've broken an unwritten rule, Lydia, and we'll suffer for it by reproachful looks for a week or more."

But he sounded totally unconcerned, and she

wished he could always be this way, so much in tune with her, and seemingly carefree. If only they had met in another time and place, without the shadow of Monty's wishes hanging over them, she thought wistfully. If only Monty wasn't doomed to die . . .

"It's our house," she repeated doggedly. As if she had said something excruciatingly funny, they started laughing again, so that she was holding her sides by the time they reached their room. She had a terrible stitch in her side, and the effects of the spicy foods were beginning to work on her digestion. She prayed that she wouldn't be afflicted with the wretched heartburn. If she was, it would serve her right for being so greedy, though it would still be worth it. It had been a simply scrumptious meal.

A couple of hours later, she began to revise her thoughts about whether or not it had been worth it. They had tumbled into bed, arms wrapped around each other, too replete to do anything other than fall straight into a deep sleep. She realized now that Vincent had already risen out of bed, and when she woke and stretched luxuriously, she could hear him moving quietly about his dressing room.

For a few moments Lydia lay still, remembering the delights of the nighttime feast. They had been two conspirators in a secret world of their own, childish and gleeful. It had given a new dimension to their relationship. Lydia stretched blissfully again, then swung her legs out of the bed with a renewed feeling of well-being, wondering why it couldn't always be like that, and resolving to try and make it so. No suspicions, no jealousy, just the two of them, sharing their lives . . .

The next second it seemed as though her whole body was about to erupt as nausea enveloped her. Her head spun, and she seemed to lose all sense of balance. There was nothing near at hand for her to cling to, and she pressed the palms of her hands hard on the bed and tried to stay calm. It was difficult when she was feeling so clammy all over as she fought to keep down the food she had consumed during the early hours, and lost the battle. She disgraced herself abominably, she thought, and she knew she must be scarlet with embarrassment as Vincent came into the bedroom to see what was wrong.

"Go away. Oh please, go away!" she managed to gasp. "I can't bear anyone to see me like this!"

He didn't answer. He merely strode to the marble washstand and brought a bowl and facecloth across to the bed. Lydia sat trembling on the edge, doubled over her knees, her long tangled hair hiding her heated face, and hardly aware that Vincent held the bowl for her while she heaved and vomited into it. It was the ultimate humiliation, Lydia thought wretchedly. No man should see a woman like this. No man could ever love a woman who produced such a disgusting mess in front of him.

"I'm so sorry," she managed to gasp between the paroxysms. "I think the onions and the red cabbage didn't mix too well with the trifle after all."

She tried to make a joke of it, but she shouldn't have mentioned the items of food in such detail. It reminded her of them far too vividly, and then she couldn't say anything more before she was leaning over the bowl again, aware that Vincent was gently wiping her face and mouth with the facecloth.

"Will you stop saying you're sorry, you ninny? And if you think my stomach isn't strong enough to see you like this, then you don't know me very well. But I think there had better be no more midnight feasts for you, my love," he said softly as she finally leaned against him, her stomach sore and empty at last.

Weakly, she closed her eyes, wondering for the first time if that was the only reason for the nausea. Perhaps it wasn't. Perhaps she should have guessed at another reason. But if she was indeed pregnant, she felt the most extraordinary fierceness to keep the knowledge to herself for the present.

Even now, when she felt ridiculously disgraced by the vomiting, she wanted to keep Vincent all to herself. She wanted his gentleness for herself alone, and not for any child that would be the answer to everything he really wanted.

Whether it was right or wrong, she was aware of a feeling of shameful jealousy toward the child she began to suspect strongly that she carried. The child that Vincent wanted so much was wanted simply to satisfy an old man's whim. It was not expected for the pure and wonderful reason of a normal marriage, being the truly outward seal between two people who had married for love.

It was tacitly understood by everyone at Montagu House that Monty's illness would progress with a gradual deterioration in energy and strength. Apart from any physical symptoms, there would be a general lack of interest in everyday things.

It seemed to Lydia to be such a tragic waste of a life, to gradually fade into insensibility, but Monty told her cheerfully there could be worse ways of dying. His illness was at least painless, if debilitating, and he didn't constantly need to be given drugs to ward off any pain. He obviously felt he had somehow cheated fate, simply by not having to go through an agonizing painful illness, despite the fact that it was still going to kill him in the end.

Lydia simply couldn't identify with such reasoning. But perhaps she might, if it ever happened to her, she acknowledged. Some days he got tired more quickly than others, and some days he was bad-tempered and best left alone. And there was little doubt in Lydia's mind that he was getting increasingly forgetful, wanting to hear about things they had probably discussed only the day before, as if he had completely lost touch with the telling.

There were times, too, when Lydia sometimes sensed a faraway look in the old man's eyes, as if he had already glimpsed the beckoning of another world. It was a world that Nadima used to call "the world of the idyllic beyond."

In her singsong, dreamy voice, Nadima had always spoken of it as something beautiful to be attained by the most fortunate ones. The young and impressionable Lydia had been charmed by the words, not realizing at the time that it was no more than a euphemism for death, and therefore something that no one could escape. Now, faced with the approaching death of someone she had learned to care for, it seemed neither charming nor palatable. It frightened her.

"You're very pensive this morning, my dear," Monty said to her, when the servant bringing them their morning tea had left them together in the library, where she was ostensibly reading aloud to him. She was finding it hard to concentrate on the particular book he was enjoying.

"I'm sorry, Monty. I lost my place in the book for a moment, and my mind started wandering."

"I often wonder where it goes to at such times?" he mused. "Does it go back to England, perhaps, and to your family home? Why do you never speak of it, Lydia? I seem to have heard very little about it, and it's good to be reminded of England now and then."

Lydia sighed. Monty had heard the tale so many times, but he had obviously forgotten. She told it again briefly.

"I assure you my thoughts don't return there! And there's not very much of interest to tell. After my parents died, I could never have been happy in my uncle's household in Bath, so I lived in lodgings with some very good people who were kind to me. But aside from that, it wasn't the happiest time of my life in England. I felt too beholden to a family who didn't really want me, and my cousins weren't the best companions."

She understated those times, remembering

sharply her cousin Audine's scathing tongue, and the way she had always belittled Lydia, constantly reminding her of her place and the debt she owed her uncle. Audine had been a dried-up spinster long before her time, Lydia thought, and felt briefly sorry for a girl whom she thought would never unbend enough to know love.

"Then perhaps you still dream of the other place. Of India?" Monty persisted, remembering the name of that country well enough, and noting the violet shadows beneath the lovely eyes of the girl he had grown very fond of in the time she had been here.

"India was a very long time ago," Lydia admitted. "Yet in many ways it's more real to me than England. A child's formative years are very important to its future life, don't you think? Those days should be full of sunshine and love, and I certainly had all of that in India."

She lowered her eyes. Was she talking about herself, or about the child she carried beneath her heart, of which no one but herself was aware as yet? The child that was to be eventually educated in England, a true Montagu, before taking up its rightful place on Kurnios. Its future uncrowned king, Lydia thought, with a glimmer of humor tinged with bitterness. The child would be as lovingly trapped as they all were on this paradise island.

And if she no longer wished to be part of that life, she would be paid off handsomely, having done her wifely duty to the Montagus. She would be as she was before. She felt her throat constrict

397

at the thought, knowing that to be a complete misnomer. Having been a part of Vincent Montagu, she could never be as she was before. Her love for him had changed all that.

"So Kurnios is halfway between your two other lives, at least in geographical terms," Monty said, with one of the very lucid and perceptive comments that could still take her by surprise.

"How odd that you should say that! It's exactly what I thought when I first knew I was coming here."

"It's not odd that we should think alike, my dear. When people know each other well, they have an empathy with each others' thoughts and feelings. And they say that when one knows one is dying, one is even more sensitive to such things."

"Please don't talk about dying," Lydia said, closing the book with a little bang, as if to shut out the word.

"Why not? It's a fact of life, the same as birth. It's just another stage, Lydia. It's nothing to fear."

"You and my old nurse Nadima would have got on very well," she said, without thinking. "You have the same candid philosophy on life and death and everything in between. I'm afraid I can't feel the same way. When my parents died, it was the end of everything for them, and also for me for a long time."

"But you shouldn't think like that, Lydia. Everything that was good in your parents lives on in you, and they would be very proud of you."

"Would they?"

For marrying a man who didn't love her? For

virtually ousting her cousin in his affections? For agreeing to this old man's selfish needs in bearing a child and then giving it up? In a sudden mood of self-censure, Lydia considered herself a most unnatural woman, and she wasn't sure she was deserving of anyone's pride.

But then she was caught by Monty's words. *Her parents lived on in her.* Now she saw where this conversation was leading. Despite her affection for the old man, it was Monty's own narcissism and a stake in immortality through Vincent and Lydia that had brought her to Kurnios in the first place. Any reminders of it always made her uncomfortable. She certainly wasn't going to discuss it baldly with him now. She had never done so yet, and she was in no mood for any more self-analyzing.

"Do you mind if I don't read any more this morning?" she said casually. "In fact, why don't we take our tea out into the garden while there's still a pleasant breeze?"

"Yes, let's do that," he agreed. "But you can't avoid facing up to realities forever, Lydia."

She didn't know she was guilty of that either. She had faced up to the presence of Marina Delos, and since the confrontation with Vincent about the Greek woman, she was satisfied that he meant what he had said. The affair was over, and Vincent was once more as attentive and ardent a lover as she could wish for. And the result of his passion was the child she was sure she carried . . .

She was careful now not to rise too quickly in the mornings, and to wait until Vincent had gone downstairs before getting out of bed. She had pleaded for the English pleasure of taking a drink of tea in bed before rising, and she could usually fight down the nausea by sipping the weak drink Coora brought her, before she moved about too much.

She still hugged the secret of the child to herself. As yet, it was hers and hers alone. She wasn't prepared to share it with anyone, even though she knew, practically, that this wasn't a situation that could go on for much longer.

Vincent appeared at the breakfast table as she and Monty drank their morning coffee and ate their thin toast and preserves. Monty enjoyed the morning ritual, and Lydia had gotten in the habit of joining him. At this rate, she would resemble a balloon long before the child was born, she couldn't help thinking. Awash with liquid and eating far more than she habitually did.

"Eating again?" Vincent asked her with an indulgent smile. "I've never known a woman with such an appetite."

Lydia blushed, knowing he wasn't only referring to her appetite for food. But however passionate she had become in their lovemaking, it was all due to his seductive teaching, she thought, tingling with remembered pleasure.

"As long as I can still fit into my clothes, I'm not too worried," Lydia said lightly, knowing there was more truth in the remark than the gentlemen might think. Some of her gowns were already too tight around the bustline to wear any more now, and she had already got into the habit of wearing her looser ones. Even one or two of the Indian saris that Monty and Vincent admired so much were seeing the light of day more frequently now, while she commented casually that they were more comfortable to wear in the heat of the island.

"You've no need to worry about putting on a bit of weight, my dear," Monty remarked gallantly. "You're very comely, and a man likes a woman with a bit of flesh on her, and good childbearing hips."

It was one of his favorite sayings when he was in this kind of mood, and Lydia quickly changed the subject.

"When do you have to go to the mainland?" she asked Vincent, knowing there was a shipping contract he intended to negotiate for some of the island's produce. Lydia also knew it included some of the Delos wines, but she was determined not to let that fact disturb her. She didn't intend turning into the kind of jealous wife who couldn't bear her husband to have the slightest social contact with any other woman. Even when that woman was Marina Delos.

"Tomorrow. I expect to be gone overnight, unless we conduct our business very quickly. If you feel like it, you can accompany me, Lydia. We could stay in a hotel and make a night of it, like we did in Spain, and I can promise you a smoother voyage than the one on Nikos's fishing boat—"

"Do you mind if I don't?" she said quickly. The very idea of even the sleekest vessel heaving beneath her was enough to give her a surge of nausea. Even the tantalizing thought of spending a night in a hotel room with him didn't quite compensate for that just now. "Besides, it will be nice for Monty and me to spend an evening together talking about you," she said, in an attempt to tease.

"All right," Vincent agreed. "It probably wouldn't be much fun for you to wait around in the hotel while the negotiations went on. Just as long as you promise to miss me."

"I promise," she said, sure that all her love for him must be in her eyes. She turned away quickly, a blush staining her cheeks at the curving smile on his lips. He would make sure she missed him. He never went away from the island without making love to her the night before.

The Kurnios night had deepened into darkness, and Lydia felt Vincent's hand gently caress her stomach. The firelight threw soft shadows around their bedroom, creating an even more sensual atmosphere as they lay together in their large canopied bed. And the knowledge of what was to come seemed to be making her extra sensitive to his touch.

"Why do you flinch, my sweet? Have you eaten too much dinner again?" he whispered, with a mock groan.

"Why do you say that?" she mumbled, because it would be so very poignant to tell him now, in these tender moments. Yet even now, something held her back, some perverse little devil of self-preservation that harked back to his reason for marrying her.

"You're getting a little rounded, that's all. Not that I'm objecting. I'm as old-fashioned as Monty in that respect I like my women well-covered."

402

"Women?" Lydia echoed, obliged to comment on the collective term, despite her resolution to remain unruffled at any reference to his past. Even though she knew it was probably just an innocent word, she could still be piqued by it.

He nestled his mouth more firmly into her neck, and arched in delight at his kisses. His voice was teasing against her skin.

"That was a mere slip of the tongue, my love. I should have said my *woman*. My only *one*."

"Oh, Vincent—"

She wriggled down in the bed until her face was beneath his and pulled his mouth down on hers. She held his face between her-hands and felt his kiss harden as he recognized her answering passion. Then her arms encircled his powerfully muscled back, and she was drawn up to him, secure in the knowledge that at least she was wanted and cherished, and maybe even loved, a little.

He had never told her in words that he loved her, but everything about him said that he did. Naively, Lydia forced herself to believe it as the erotic seduction of his lovemaking began. She longed to ask, but simply didn't have the courage. She couldn't bear it if he only said it during moments of great passion, just to please her.

"God, but you're so beautiful," Vincent said hoarsely against her breasts as his kisses moved downwards to all the sexually sensitive zones of her body. He knew them so well now; the way she knew him.

When it was over, they lay together, all passion spent and breathing heavily, but still in each others' arms. Drowsy with the aftermath of love, and feeling so secure and content, it was one of the sweet, tender moments Lydia cherished, until Vincent spoiled it all.

"God knows why two such passionate lovers as we haven't managed to produce an offspring yet," he teased. "But it's certainly a more enjoyable form of sport than any other kind."

Lydia felt coldness seep into every pore at his words. She was stung by them, as sharply as if by a hornet's nest. How could he degrade the wonderful act they had just shared by referring to it as "sport?" She felt the blurring tears in her eyes and dashed them back. But it sounded like the way a man might comment to a whore, not to his wife.

She caught the strangest look in his eyes at that moment, and wondered fleetingly if he was so emotionally involved that he had to make light of it rather than reveal his true feelings. But it was so unlikely, she dismissed the idea at once. Unable to bear it a moment longer, she turned on her side, and muttered that they had best get some sleep, since he was to be off so early the next morning.

He obviously didn't notice that there was anything amiss. So much for intuition, she thought dismally. He turned into her, folding his arms around her so that she rested against him. She could feel the even softness of his breath against her shoulders. It was the way they so often slept, the way a set of silver spoons nestled snugly against one another in a velvet case.

"You're probably right," he said quietly. "No midnight feasts for us tonight, my darling, nor any second helpings of anything."

She kept her eyes rigidly shut, not responding to his arch comment, nor wanting to remember that other night, when they had seemed at last to be so carefree with one another. She just wanted to sleep, and even to blot out the memory of a love that had seemed just a kind of "sport" to him. In her last waking moments she thought bitterly what a fool she was to imagine it had ever been anything else.

Chapter Eighteen

"There's someone to see you, Lady," Coora said blandly.

Monty had retired to bed straight after the midday meal, and said that if he required anything at all for the rest of the day he would send for some dinner to be sent up on a tray. It was one of his bad days. Everything tired him; the heat of the sun, the drone of the bees, conversation, company, the effort of eating or drinking.

It had appeared to be a long day without Monty's company, or Vincent's, and by the middle of the afternoon Lydia looked up eagerly from the shady terrace, sure that the visitor would be Daisy. It was a little surprising for anyone to come calling during the hottest part of the day. But the Brandons knew Vincent would be away all day, and probably until tomorrow, and Lydia wondered now if she was to have a belated invitation to their home for the evening. It would be a pleasant diversion.

She felt a jolt in her stomach when she saw Marina Delos step onto the terrace, a large sun hat hiding most of her features. She wore less flamboyant attire than usual, Lydia noted, almost as if she

406

intended to play down her dark sultry looks. She looked almost friendly, and her smile was quite unguarded as she approached.

"I do apologize for calling unannounced again, Lydia," she said, her voice sincere and natural.

"It's perfectly all right," Lydia said coolly, though her heart was beating sickeningly fast in her chest. No matter how friendly this woman appeared, Lydia could never forget what she had once been to her husband. Perhaps it would always be so when face-to-face with the woman who had once known Vincent as intimately as she herself did. So how could she ever fully trust such a display of friendship?

"If you wanted to see Vincent, I'm afraid he's not here today," she added now.

"But I came to see you, not Vincent! May I sit down?" She didn't wait for an answer, but seated herself on one of the terrace chairs opposite Lydia. As usual, a servant appeared at once with a tray of cool drinks. The hospitality of the house didn't take into account unwanted visitors, Lydia thought dryly. Marina took a glass of cordial, and smiled at Lydia again.

"I know Vincent's gone to the mainland today, and I thought it was a good time for you and I to get to know each other better. My husband and I both knew the Montagus for many years, and counted them as our good friends. I'd like to count you as a friend too, Lydia."

She was so smooth, so plausible, especially drawing the memory of her dead husband into the conversation. Lydia couldn't easily detect the slightest hint of mockery or rivalry in her eyes or demeanor.

407

On the surface, at least, Marina seemed all that she appeared, a caller coming to pay a friendly visit on a new neighbor.

All the same, Lydia dearly longed to say that she and Marina could never be friends. A wife didn't make friends with her husband's mistress, or perhaps she did in some circles. The situation was completely new to Lydia, but she was wavering now. If she were to exercise her rights and ban Marina from this house, it might create embarrassing difficulties as time went on, when Monty would want to gather all his old friends around him. Perhaps after all, there was a case for burying old hurts when you were sure they could no longer touch you.

"I'm sure that would be sensible," she murmured.

"Good," Marina said. "Do you remember my offer to show you around the island? I thought today would be a good day, so shall we make some definite arrangements?"

"I think I told you Vincent's already done that several times, and I've become well-acquainted with it now," Lydia said, as evenly as she could.

Did the woman think she'd done nothing but sit here twiddling her thumbs in all the weeks since coming to Kurnios?

"I'm sure he has, but he won't have shown you *my* island. My secret island is the one where legends of the past still linger, and the ancient ghosts can still control the elements," Marina said cryptically.

Lydia stared at her, hardly expecting this stylish woman to have such a feeling for mysticism. It was so like the way old Nadima had spoken, instilling that sense of shivering excitement in a young girl about things that were not quite of this earth.

"*Is* there a secret part of Kurnios?" she inquired, trying to sound skeptical, and not too eager for knowledge.

"Oh, there's far more to the island than a burnt-out volcano, and picturesque windmills, and native industry! The ancient Greeks built many amphitheaters and temples to the gods on the mainland and on all their remote islands. The monuments were their talismans, and also their appeasement to the gods for any desecration of nature. Do you understand what I mean?"

"Of course!" The interest was burning inside Lydia. It made no difference that it was Marina telling her these tales, because her interest was too strong to be denied. Any hint of something mystical would always intrigue her.

"There's a famous tale here of a Greek goddess who committed a terrible sin by falling in love with a human," Marina went on casually. "Some say the sin was committed on the Kurnios mountain, and that it may even have been the cause of the volcano when the gods revolted against her in anger. But it's said that the people from every other Greek island like to believe the tale belongs to them alone."

"And do you believe in such tales?" Lydia said, intrigued even more.

"Who is to say whether or not ancient tales are true? I prefer to think they must have had some substance, as I suspect you do, too. We're kindred souls, you and I, Lydia."

This was a little too much for Lydia to accept.

409

She didn't have the remotest desire to be a kindred soul with Marina Delos, and she gave a short laugh.

"I hardly think that's likely—"

"Why not? As I once mentioned, we have so much in common. Not least is a love of the island, and the hot climate. We both love dancing and merrymaking, and we have the confidence of knowing that we are beautiful in our different ways—"

Lydia knew she must break into this airy assessment, before the woman had the audacity to say that they also shared the love of the same man. It would mortify her if Marina dared to say as much, since Lydia knew full well that Marina had certainly enjoyed Vincent's love while her own presence was out of mere necessity and convenience.

"Tell me more about the Greek goddess who loved a human. What fate befell her in the end?" she asked quickly.

Marina obliged at once. "She fell from a mountaintop and broke every bone in her body with excruciating slowness, and it was anything but an accidental fall. Not that anyone pushed her, but it was said she had the strongest compulsion to walk to the edge of the mountain and plunge over while her lover looked on helplessly. The story is that he was then swallowed up in the burning lava flow that followed. I daresay it's no more than a fairy tale."

"A pretty gruesome one!" Lydia said, shuddering.

"Most fairy tales are. I can't think why they're even called fairy tales, can you?"

"And are you saying that this particular mountaintop is part of your secret Kurnios?" Lydia asked, half-wishing the woman would go, and half-wanting to hear more.

"Probably not," she shrugged. "Though I've always chosen to believe so. But who is to say after such a time? What's absolutely certain is that a volcano took place here, so anything is possible, and many legends grow out of facts.

"Many of the old relics I mentioned are still standing," Marina went on. "Some are almost intact where the wind and salt hasn't eroded them. There's a ruined amphitheater on one of the peaks. It's reputed that by standing close to the rim at sunset, and closing your eyes tightly while holding a handful of stones from the interior of the ancient temple nearby, you can make your every wish come true. It's a pity the old goddess hadn't wished to be turned into a human, then she and her lover could have lived happily ever after."

It was tempting for Lydia to ask why Marina hadn't made her own wishes come true by keeping Vincent Montagu for herself. But then, she had had him for a very long time already . . . and perhaps the gods had been prepared to smile kindly on an Englishwoman with honey-colored skin who was destined to fulfill an old man's dream.

Lydia brushed her hand across her eyes, wondering if she was going slightly mad to be thinking such fanciful thoughts. But she had been indoctrinated powerfully in old Nadima's mysteries to scoff at anything. India was in her blood, and so was the steady beat of history and all things inexplicable that had always held such fascination for her.

"Where is this place?" she asked, knowing she was already condemning herself to be taken there.

She had to see it for herself. She was even more intrigued because Vincent had never mentioned these relics of a past age on Kurnios. But then, he was too prosaic and practical minded to be enchanted by such tales. He was also English, without having had a part of himself steeped in old Nadima's Indian folklore.

"It's not too far away, but a little higher up in the mountains. All the ancient sites were in high places, to be nearer to the gods," Marina said easily.

She rose to leave, obviously not intending to outstay her welcome, and smiled down at Lydia. "I could show you the legendary place sometime, if you like."

She wasn't pushing her into anything, Lydia thought. There was nothing sinister about the visit. It was just a neighborly gesture. She made up her mind.

"At sunset, you say?"

Marina shrugged. "Well, you can view the sites at any time of day, but the legend is only supposed to work at sunset." She gave a rueful smile. "I almost wish I hadn't told you. A sensible English lady like yourself must think we Greeks are simpletons to give credence to such talk of magic."

"I think no such thing," Lydia said quickly. "And of course it must be at sunset. We must go tonight."

"Tonight?" Marina paused for a moment, staring, as if no such idea had entered her head. "Well, then, tonight it is! I suggest you take a stroll through the grounds after dinner, and we'll meet at the back of the estate near the stables. Lydia, I wouldn't mention any of this to Monty. He has little truck with legends. Besides, he'd only worry at the thought of two women out after dark, although naturally a driver will accompany us."

"I shan't tell him," Lydia promised, reassured by her last words. "It will be an exciting adventure just between the two of us."

But after Marina had gone, and she had had time to think, she felt a little uneasy at accepting the suggestion so readily. It might be a very foolhardy thing to do, to go higher into the mountains, accompanied only by a woman she had considered to be her rival, if not her enemy, and an unknown driver.

But the intriguing charm of the ancient legend that only wove its magic at sunset was irresistible. She thought suddenly how Nadima would have approved. It was the thought Lydia needed to smother her qualms.

Monty didn't appear for dinner, which was just as well. Lydia wasn't sure she could have contained her excitement at the coming excursion. Vincent hadn't yet returned home, and she assumed he certainly would have done so if his business had been satisfactorily concluded. She presumed he would be staying on the mainland overnight.

She left the dining room and went to her room to change into something more suitable for going up into the mountains, where it would be decidedly chilly by now. The evening itself was cooler than usual, so it didn't appear odd for her to don a slightly warmer gown than usual, with a high-buttoned neck, and to carry a light woollen shawl over her arms for her ostensible stroll in the grounds.

At the last minute, she hesitated at the small mahogany writing desk in her room. Not to tell anyone at all where she was going seemed to be extremely foolish. Supposing there was any kind of accident? Although she was not the type of woman to anticipate trouble, the urge to record her movements, and with whom, was suddenly very strong inside her. It was almost a compulsion.

She drew out a piece of writing paper, and dipped her pen in the inkstand. She realized at once that she had no idea of the location of this ancient site, and found herself chewing the end of the pen in frustration.

"Vincent or Monty," she wrote, using both their names, to cover all contingencies, "Marina Delos is taking me to see an old legendary amphitheatre at sunset. I'm sure I shall return long before either of you read this, but just in case—"

In case of what? She hardly knew why she was taking such precautions, but she shivered suddenly, signed her name quickly, and placed the note prominently on her pillow. She was ready.

The sun hadn't yet dipped low in the sky when Lydia reached the stables at the back of the estate. Sunset habitually lingered for some time over the island, bathing it in a glory of unearthly reds and pinks and golds, but once the sun had gone down, darkness came with frightening swiftness for those who were unaware of it.

Lydia was confident that Marina would have taken care to provide lights on the carriage for the return journey. When describing the amphitheatre, she had waved vaguely toward the more civilized side of the mountains, and not to the ruggedly steep climb that had first brought Lydia to Montagu House.

It was with a huge shock that Lydia saw the other woman approaching. She was perched in an awkward sidesaddle seat on the back of a mule, while a handler sitting on a second mule held the ropes of a third, which was evidently meant for Lydia.

"You surely don't intend us to travel on those beasts?" Lydia spluttered in disbelief. Her disappointment was sharp, because nothing on earth was going to make her mount a mule in such an undignified manner, and she had so longed to make her own wishes to the beneficent gods.

"I'm so sorry, Lydia," Marina slid from the mule's back, in apparently great distress. "I tried hard to persuade Izros to take the trap, but he was adamant that it wouldn't be suitable. This is the safest means of travel, and I promise you it's far more comfortable than it looks."

"But how can this be safer than a trap! And there are no lights to bring us back down again," Lydia almost wailed.

"Lady need not fear," the guttural voice of the Greek mule-handler put in confidently. "Izros know every inch of the mountains, and Izros provide light when time comes. There will also be light from moon and from villages. Izros will guide safely down, never fear."

There seemed no help for it. If she wanted to see the amphitheatre against the magical backdrop of the fiery sunset, she would have to take the only transport provided. She gritted her teeth, allowing the man to help her onto the mule's back, where she had to admit the heavy padding and the neck ropes made it less horrendous than she might have supposed. All the same, Marina might have warned her about this, she thought resentfully.

"How does it feel?" Marina said, smiling encouragingly. "Not too bad, is it? And remember that adventure you spoke about. It will be something to tell your grandchildren, Lydia!"

She spoke artlessly enough, and as they began to jog forward, the motion was not unpleasant at all. It was quite soothing, in fact, and Lydia felt a little more mollified as Marina began to point out different objects and artifacts, and to tell her a little more about the history of the island.

"The volcano was millions of years ago," she said comfortably, "so there's no more danger from such a thing ever happening again. The ancient Greeks who built their sites on its rim did so in thankfulness that the raging fire from the center of the earth was something far in the past, but which in itself had produced this fertile island."

"But it took men to work it," Lydia murmured, not quite prepared to give all the credit to the mystical gods. The people of Kurnios were a hardworking race, and she had grown to respect their resourcefulness in exploiting the abundant riches of the island to make it as self-supporting as possible.

"Of course," Marina said without expression. "Where would any of us be without men?"

If that was meant to be something of a pertinent remark, Lydia chose to ignore it. She didn't intend

416

to be drawn into any conversation of a more personal nature, especially one that might involve Marina's past relationship with Vincent.

"How much farther is it?" she asked now, seeing that the sky was already beginning to change color to a richly pink hue.

They had long since left the villages and the windmills behind them, together with the more luxurious European villas, and now they seemed to be in an isolated and silent part of the mountains. But the rough tracks they traversed were wide and reasonably flat, and Lydia was reassured by the mules' surefootedness and the presence of the capable handler.

"We shall be at our journey's end very soon now," Marina's voice was oddly breathless, as if she, too, could hardly contain her inner excitement.

Lydia studied her curiously. Marina rode ahead of her, and the voluptuous curves of the Greek woman and her proudly elegant posture on such an ungainly animal couldn't be denied.

She was a woman oozing with self-confidence and beauty and sensuality, and all the *savoir-faire* and influence from the wealth her husband had left her. Lydia guessed her also to be a ruthless woman, and she was perfectly aware how such a trait often held a strange fascination for a man.

Any healthy, virile man would desire her, Lydia thought. Any man would be a fool to give her up. And any man that Marina desired, she would want to possess forever, no matter what the cost. Lydia felt a small frisson of fear run through her veins, and realized that her mouth was suddenly dry.

"Look ahead of you now, Lydia," Marina said, as

they rounded a curve in the mountainside. "Isn't that the most wonderful sight?"

The knotted fear in her stomach seemed to unravel as the ruined circle of an ancient amphitheatre hove into view. It was on the very edge of a precipitous slope of the mountainside, and Lydia's first reaction was simply to marvel at how it had ever been built. It had surely been constructed by superhuman efforts.

But the very sight of it allowed her to relax a little, because at least she knew that this place hadn't all been a pretense on Marina's part, nor a ruse to bring her rival here where she was at her most helpless and vulnerable. The relic actually existed. As Lydia's breathing became easier, she was aware of how painfully fast her heart had been beating in her chest in these last few suspicious minutes.

They had slid down from the mules' backs now, and the handler had taken charge of all three animals. He stood silently some distance away from the women, as the two of them walked toward the amphitheatre, carefully lifting their skirts away from the snatching roughness of the stones underfoot.

"How beautiful it is," Lydia breathed involuntarily.

Marina gave a crooked smile. "I thought it would impress even someone like you, who has travelled so much. I understand there are very grand buildings in India also."

"Oh yes! If you had ever seen the purity of the Taj Mahal by moonlight you would know the meaning of true beauty and devotion," Lydia said dreamily, everything else forgotten for the moment

418

but the memory of the aesthetic curves and domes and perfect symmetry of what she considered the most beautiful building on earth. And all constructed because of a man's love for his wife . . .

"I have never seen the place, though I believe I may have heard of it. But you cannot compare it with what we have here, I think. The Greek remains go back much further in time."

Lydia spoke quickly, unsure whether she had inadvertently offended Marina or not by her reference to the Taj.

"It would be foolish to even try to compare, because each has a richness and a history of its own, and each is important to future generations."

"Ah yes. Future generations. Tell me, Lydia, do you mean to have children?"

The question put her completely off-balance. It was impertinent for Marina to even ask such a personal question, yet it told Lydia something very important. Whatever had gone between them, Vincent obviously hadn't revealed anything of the wager between himself and Monty, nor the real reason he had gone to England seeking a wife.

Intuitively now, the blatant question, in the barely disguised affronted tone, also told Lydia that Marina had probably known before Vincent left Kurnios that their affair was over, and that when he brought back a wife there must be no further intimate contact.

It told her that Marina would have been brooding and seething all this time, and that the longer the resentment went on, the more dangerous an enemy Marina could become. And yet she had bothered to seek Lydia out, to try and make a friend of her. Lydia felt her heart beat sickeningly fast, and with a great effort she resisted putting her hand across her abdomen in an instinctively protective way. If she had done so, she was sure she would have given away the secret of the child she carried.

And as yet, no one knew of its existence but herself. For some reason Lydia was quite sure it was a secret still best kept to herself. Even if Marina had never meant to harm her, she may want to harm the child. The alarming thoughts raced through her head, and she turned her eyes away from Marina, and concentrated instead on gazing at the ruins surrounding them.

She tried to answer quite calmly. "That's rather too personal a question, I think. Every married couple hopes for children, Marina, but it's something to be decided privately between a man and his wife, don't you think?"

The sun was setting low behind the ruins now, and all the weathered stones were bathed in a fiery glow that seemed not of this world at all. As if those ancient gods were really here, breathing their magic into any venturesome mortal who entered their domain. Beyond the amphitheatre, Lydia could see the tall, narrow columns of the temple, its capping amazingly still intact.

As if tired of this conversation, and realizing she would get no personal details from this irritating Englishwoman, Marina spoke sharply.

"We must hurry. We'll go to the temple first, and you must gather up some stones from inside it, if you want to make your wishes known to the gods. If you've changed your mind, and think it's all nonsense, we needn't go any farther, and we can merely watch the sunset from here. It doesn't matter to me, whatever you decide—"

Lydia brushed the words aside with a little laugh, both from her own needs to see the thing through, and an uneasy desire to placate Marina.

"Of course we must go on! I want to prove whether the legend is true or not. And I haven't come all this way just to admire the sunset, spectacular though it is!"

Marina smiled then, as if she had been quite certain of Lydia's response all the time.

"Come along then, but do tread carefully, Lydia. Many of the stones are loose, and some are still falling occasionally."

It was a relief to be moving about, and no longer seated on the back of the jogging mule, although with the generously padded seat, it hadn't been as uncomfortable as Lydia had expected. But now, she was glad to follow Marina around the amphitheatre to where the comparatively small temple stood against the skyline.

Through its ridged columns, the sun was a great crimson ball of fire. They seemed to be standing on the very top of the earth and in the presence of the gods, and to Lydia, anything was imaginable at such a time and in such a place.

Obediently, as if in a half-hypnotic state, she bent down to pick up a handful of stones from inside the temple. The stones were still warm from the heat of the day, and perhaps still with something of the power from the long-dormant volcano. It gave her an awesome feeling to realize it.

Still following instructions, Lydia followed Marina back to the rim of the amphitheatre, clutching the stones. She stumbled over the uneven ground, but walked on grimly, as if driven on by a mission she had to fulfill. It was as if destiny demanded this of her.

"Stand as close to the rim as you can, Lydia," Marina said in a hoarse, excited voice. "I shall move back so that your voice is the only voice the gods will hear, although you don't actually need to say the words aloud if you prefer not to. By now, the gods will be attuned to your every thought. Close your eyes and hold the stones tightly while you make your wishes, and then scatter them to the four winds. The time is ripe for you now, Lydia."

Slowly, she moved a few steps backwards, and Lydia turned away from her to face the rim of the amphitheatre and the yawning chasm below the mountain. She felt no more fear, for now she was bathed in that crimson glow from the heavens. She felt somehow enervated by the aura of it all, a child of the gods, loved by them and by all the ancient mystique of the ages. She closed her eyes and clutched the stones, feeling as if their heat was penetrating her very bones. She made her wishes, her very dearest, deepest wishes . . . that Vincent would love her, love her, love her . . .

There was a sudden roaring in her ears. She wondered for a second if this was the god's answer. An unspoken, unearthly way of the gods graciously telling her that her wishes would be granted, and then she realized the roaring was of a far more earthly origin. It was the scrambling of feet over the uneven ground, together with a human screeching as wild and heathen as if all the demons in hell were being let loose, and it was immediately behind her.

She barely had time to glance over her shoulder before she saw the two figures leaping at her. Marina and Izros, her henchman, the two of them with only one intention in mind.

The next instant she felt a mighty push on her shoulders. It was impossible to keep her balance, no matter how she teetered on the brink. But even as she screamed in utter terror, she had the presence of mind to twist on her heels, and clutch out desperately for anything that would prevent the inevitable.

The only tangible thing within reach was the wide billowing skirt of Marina Delos, and as Lydia grasped it in desperate self-preservation, the battle for safety was lost, and the two of them went hurtling over the edge of the mountain together. Sky and earth danced crazily in front of Lydia's eyes as she fell, a huge, vast kaleidoscope of vivid color, before the world went black.

Lydia came to her senses slowly. For a few disoriented moments, she had no idea where she was, except that she was certain she was living through some kind of nightmare. The gnawing fear in the pit of her stomach told her that, even before she could begin to ascertain the truth about her surroundings.

She heard her own voice whimpering Vincent's name, Vincent, her beloved. Why wasn't she warm in his arms, safe within their large four-poster bed

with the lacy canopy shrouding them, and the soft
firelight enhancing their love-heated bodies?

Why wasn't Vincent somewhere near? So that
she only had to turn her head to see him . . . so
that she only had to stretch out her hand to touch
him . . . she only needed to whisper his name to
hear his voice respond, gentled by love . . .

Slowly she became aware of the utter impenetra-
ble silence all around her. Fearfully, she moved her
hand and encountered hard stony gravel beneath it.
She winced, knowing she must be cut and grazed,
because her flesh smarted so much. As she
flinched, she dislodged some small stones and heard
their spinning descent to somewhere far below. She
closed her eyes tightly, not wanting to admit what
her recovering mind was slowly telling her. She was
somewhere on the mountain, alone, and in the
dark.

Trying desperately to keep the fear under control, Lydia knew she must ascertain exactly where
she was. She opened her eyes cautiously, and
moved her head a fraction. It hurt abominably,
and she knew that she dare not look down. So instead she looked up.

The moon was hidden behind scudding clouds,
and the night was virtually pitch black. But by
then, sharp recollection of a terrifying, slithering
fall down the mountainside came back to her with
a hideous jolt of memory. And with it the remembered treachery of Marina Delos, her husband's rejected mistress, whom she had been so appallingly
foolish to trust.

"Oh Vincent, please help me!" she whimpered
again, as if she could conjure up his presence by

her very desperation. Wasn't it what she had wished from the gods? To be loved by her husband? And where was he now, when she needed him the most?

Irrationally, Lydia felt anger and bitterness toward even Vincent now, unwilling to credit herself with all the stupidity of believing in old fairy tales. Even Marina had agreed that fairy tales were gruesome, and more often than not they were evil stories in disguise. And where was the aid of the gods now, who were surely meant to protect her on this night of all treacherous nights?

Chapter Nineteen

Lydia sensed she was in dire danger of becoming totally demented as all Nadima's futile teachings whirled about in her head like so much flotsam.

"Believe in the fates, my young one . . ."

But was this truly the end that fate had always had in store for her?

"Always keep calm, and think calm and beautiful thoughts . . ."

But that was hardly the easiest thing in the world to do in this desperate situation.

Even so, Lydia realized she had at least stopped breathing quite so raggedly in the last few terrified minutes, so perhaps Nadima's words were helping a little, after all.

She knew she must try to think practically. The first thing to do was to assess if any of her bones were broken. She shifted carefully, flexing her limbs. Miraculously, they didn't seem to be broken, although she was appallingly stiff all over.

Lydia knew that at best she was badly bruised and scratched. She could taste blood on her lips and feel the hot stickiness of it on her neck and arms. The heavy layers of clothing had probably assisted her legs in escaping the worst of the physical damage. She moved somewhat more resolutely, and as she did so, she felt the soft shale on which she seemed to be lying, go spinning downwards again to the abyss below. She was too petrified then to move a muscle, for fear she would end up in similar circumstances.

She was also terrified at the thought of having to lie here all night. She began to shiver uncontrollably, and was sensible enough to know she must be suffering from shock. She knew she could die of exposure up here in the mountains. She had no idea how long she had already laid there, and she felt renewed panic at the total silence all around her. It was the silence of death, and she pushed the thought away from her with a mighty effort. Madness lay with such thoughts.

Trying to think coherently about what had happened, Lydia remembered the sound of Marina's screams as she plunged over the mountainside with her, and wondered briefly what had happened to her. It hardly seemed to matter now whether the other woman was alive or dead, since both of them seemed destined to share the same fate.

Involuntarily, Lydia gave a cry of sheer despair. It was almost an animal howl of anguish, and then the human need of self-preservation came to her aid, and she was shouting and screaming for anyone to help her.

"Vincent, Vincent, anyone, please. Can anyone hear me? Oh, Vincent, *please*, help me!"

She heard the echo of her own voice, reverberating for a moment among the mountain peaks and the ancient ruins somewhere above her, and then the sounds dwindled away into silence. She had known all the time that it was useless, of course.

No one would be mad enough to go near the mountains during the night, and there was no village for some miles back down the track.

Slowly, Lydia realized there had been no answering cry from Marina, and no sign of the mule-handler, nor any of the beasts. She was entirely alone, and she had never been so frightened in her life.

After a few more futile moments of calling and screaming, Lydia tried to control her racing heartbeats. Her chest ached appallingly from her heart's pumping. But it would do no good to use up all her energy in pointless shouting. She needed to conserve what strength she had to instruct any rescuers to where she was. She felt the wild sobs welling up in her throat at the thought. *If* any rescuers were remotely likely to come her way . . .

Something stirred in her memory then.

"The note! I left a note on my pillow," she whispered, with a monumental feeling of relief. "Oh, *please* Vincent, read it quickly. Read it and follow me. Help me . . ."

Even as she remembered the note, she remembered something else. The wild brief hope that rescue would come quickly flared and died. Vincent had gone to the mainland on business, and wouldn't be back on the island until at least the middle of the following day. Even when the maid went into their bedroom in the early morning, she would take only a cursory look when she saw that the bed hadn't been slept in, and assume that the lady of the house had made other arrangements for the night. No one would even see the note until it was too late.

A sudden sound made her check her sobbing thoughts. It was the sound of labored breathing, followed by a kind of snorting, and then there was a furious scrabbling of feet, sending more shale spiralling downwards. Lydia froze, her heart almost stopping. It could be Marina after all, having heard her voice, and cunningly determined to finish the job she had started. The danger wasn't over yet . . .

Lydia was torn between the urge to scream that she was here, that she needed help, and the instinctive need for caution. But in the end she had no choice at all, because she was rendered dumb with fear. By now she had realized she was perched precariously on a ledge, and it was the only thing that had prevented her falling downwards to certain death. She had no idea how far the ledge projected out, and she was too terrified to experiment and find out.

The scrabbling and snorting continued, and then the breath was almost strangled in Lydia's throat as she felt something large and heavy leaning against her, something strangely wiry and none too sweet-smelling. Even as her scattered thoughts tried to make sense of it, she heard the odd bleating sounds of an animal, and realized that one of the mules had slid down the mountainside. It was now pressed tightly against her, almost knocking the breath out of her as it scrambled for a foothold on the narrow ledge. The animal pressed hard against her, its own terror very evident.

"Come here," she said in a choked voice. "Keep still, for pity's sake, or you'll send us both to Kingdom Come."

Somehow she managed to grasp the rope that still dangled loosely around the mule's neck, and she tried to speak as soothingly as she could to keep it calm. From its hawking breathing, she knew it was perfectly capable of lunging forward in a panic. If she still held the rope, it would be the end of them both.

But unexpectedly, during the last few terrifying minutes, Lydia had become conscious of her own sense of survival. She wasn't dead, and no bones seemed to be broken. She had survived the fall with apparently no worse than cuts and bruises, and this lowly beast had somehow managed to find her refuge. And as it gradually relaxed and slumped against her, its body was giving her all the warmth she needed to keep out the chill of night.

It had to mean something. It had to be a sign that she wasn't yet meant to perish. She blessed old Nadima's belief in omens that had penetrated Lydia's impressionable soul after all. If this was an omen, then who was Lydia Montagu to deny it?

She closed her eyes, then just as quickly she opened them again. She daren't sleep. To relax completely was to risk rolling off the ledge, whether or not the mule was leaning on her. She didn't want all his weight on her stomach though. At the sudden thought, a new and more urgent panic set in, and she slid her hand protectively between her torn gown and the mule's flesh.

Until that moment, Lydia had completely forgotten about the baby, and renewed sobs filled her throat. How could she have forgotten what was the most important thing in her life after Vincent! She wanted this baby so much. It didn't matter now what her husband's reasons were for its conception. It was a living, breathing part of herself and Vincent, and since she loved him more than she had believed it possible to love anyone, she couldn't bear it if she was to lose their child now.

"Oh, Vincent, why did we have to meet under such inauspicious circumstances?" she moaned aloud. In these stark and awesome surroundings, there was only the mule to hear, and she knew that just the sound of her voice was doing much to calm him.

"Why couldn't we have met in another time, without the shadow of Monty's wishes hanging over us? Why couldn't our child be born out of love, and not just to satisfy an old man's egotistical whim?"

She went on muttering and talking aloud, smoothing the animal's coarse hide at the same time. It was as much to keep it awake as to keep herself from going mad. She couldn't risk the mule slithering off the ledge in unconsciousness, and taking her with him.

But whether she wished it or not, there were times when she slipped into unconsciousness herself. Pressed tightly against the wall of the mountain and wedged up against the mule, there were times when her eyelids drooped, and it was more than human nature could do to deny her a few moments' respite from the terror. And in such moments, she dreamed . . . she was held close in Vincent's arms, and as he caressed her, he was whispering to her all the words she so longed to hear from his lips . . .

"How could you think I married you for any-

431

thing less than love, my sweet Lydia? I loved you from the first moment our eyes met. I knew then that I could never marry your cold cousin, and that no other woman would ever be part of my life again. From that moment on, it was only you, Lydia, only you."

"And it was the same for me. It was karma, Vincent. I'm not crazy to believe in such things, am I? Tell me you believe in destiny, too, and that we were destined for each other."

"Always, my darling. We were always meant to belong to each other, through time and space, in other lives as well as this. I would have found you again if it took a thousand years. And if you're crazy, then so am I, and it's the sweetest madness in this or any other world."

And then the words ended, and the loving began . . .

The dream faded as the mule grunted, and Lydia was instantly awake, the soft weak tears on her cheeks. Oh, if only the dream were true. If only she were safe and warm in her own bed, cherished by her husband, and all the hurts and anxieties between herself and Vincent were dissolved forever.

At times during the long anxious hours of the night, she imagined she could hear voices calling out. Sometimes she thought she could see lights dipping and swerving, when she knew it was impossible. It was all an hallucination, and she was becoming increasingly light-headed. Nor could she rid her head of the unsettling tale of the Greek goddess who had perished on a mountaintop for her sin of taking a human lover, compelled to walk right over the edge . . .

That hadn't been *her* fate, Lydia knew with savage certainty. Lydia had had no desire to die, nor any compulsion to plunge over the edge of a mountain. She had everything to live for. A husband she adored, and a child growing in her belly.

It had been no accident either. It had been a deliberate attempt to murder her. Marina Delos was a murderess. Strangely enough, the statement of fact seemed to settle Lydia's stomach into a kind of renewed calm. If she had been destined to die, she would surely have died at her enemy's hand. That she had survived, and that the mule had been sent to warm her, must mean that the gods were still smiling kindly on her. She deliberately twisted every thought to her advantage, for to do otherwise would have made her truly mad.

"What do you think, beast? Aren't we the lucky ones to be blessed with survival?" she muttered to the animal leaning against her body, trying to bolster up her own waning self-confidence.

It gave one of its habitual grunts in reply, and she shuddered, because it didn't feel at all lucky to be stranded here in the dark, with her legs starting to go numb and a definite feeling of dehydration weakening her.

Lydia was sure she must be hallucinating again, as flickering lights seemed to dance about in her head, or were they somewhere high above it? She could no longer be sure of anything. A huge noise seemed to be filling her brain, like a million humming bees, all buzzing against one another as if battling for each to be heard. It was a long distance away . . . and then it was very near, and then it was all merging into one sound . . . and then it was separating and shouting her name.

She drew an enormous breath, fighting for her cracked throat to utter a sound.

"I'm here!" she shrieked. "Below the amphitheater. Help me please. *Vincent,* help me!"

Even as she screamed and yelled, the animal that had been her comfort and saviour through the long hours of the night, jumped in startled terror.

She clung to the rope around his neck, but she knew only too well that if she clung on too tightly she would plunge over the mountain with him. His weight was far too heavy for her to hold him, and as he scrabbled to retain his foothold she had to let him go. Wild sobs racked her body in those seconds before she heard his animal anguish as he went over the edge, and she lost her only companion in her plight.

"Lydia. Lydia, stay quite still. We're coming for you."

She jerked her head upwards, dazzled by the lights of a score of lanterns now. She could see nothing beyond the lights, but she knew the voice, the beloved voice.

"Vincent!" she screamed. "I'm here. I'm here!"

"Stay perfectly still and don't move anything," he instructed again, as if she were a complete idiot.

Where did he think she would go? Did he expect her to jump up and down in delight, brush off the shale from her skirt and skip up the mountainside to greet him?

The craziest thoughts ran through her head now, as the euphoria of imminent rescue replaced the

434

terror. She glanced about her as the light from the lanterns revealed her landing place. It was a ledge, she saw, and a fairly wide one. She had been fairly safe after all. If it had been any narrower though . . . for a second she allowed her glance to drift downwards, and her head spun as she gasped. The side of the mountain was sheer, and it plunged far below in a dizzying descent. Her limbs seemed to turn to lead as she realized what her fate could have been, and she couldn't have moved for all the riches of Croesus.

"Vincent, hurry," she croaked, but her voice was so thin and weak now that he couldn't possibly have heard her. There was too much noise going on above her, too many voices, too much discussion, too many ropes being dangled over the edge. But there was no possible way she could hold one and allow herself to be hauled up, didn't they understand that? She just couldn't do it.

"Lydia, listen to me." She heard Vincent's voice shouting to her again, ordering her to be calm, trying to instill his own strength into her. She lifted her head a fraction and nodded dully. But it was all going to be for nothing. She couldn't move a muscle. She was finally too afraid.

"I'm coming down to get you," she heard him say next. "You'll be perfectly all right as long as you stay quite still. Once I reach you I shall tie a rope around you and we'll be hauled up together. Do you understand?"

She almost laughed out loud. Of course she understood. He'd be coming down to the ledge and then the two of them would die there together. They would never pull them both up. The ropes were too fragile, and they would weigh too much. All hope seemed to have deserted her, but she gave another nod because it was what he expected of her.

Lydia had no idea how many rescuers were above her, but it seemed to be a great many. It also seemed hours before she was aware of Vincent's dark shape descending down the side of the mountain. As she saw him, it seemed as if all the blood in her veins was suddenly coursing wildly through her again. This was her love, and he was in great danger because of her and her foolishness. All the fear for her own safety evaporated, and she was consumed with anxiety for him.

When he reached her, to a great cheer from above, she saw that he was well roped, but even so. . . . For a second, her eyes blurred at the danger she had put him through, and then he was holding her close, his voice harsh and angry.

"I thought I'd lost you. Don't you ever do anything so stupid again, do you hear?"

She jerked up her head. Was he censuring her, even now? Or was his anger simply out of relief for her? She just didn't know, and she was too weak to work it out. She was hoarse with dehydration and misery.

"I'm sorry. It would have been so irritating if you'd had to go to England to find yet another wife, wouldn't it!"

She couldn't imagine why they were acting this way in this precarious situation. It would have been laughable if it hadn't been all so damnably poignant.

By now, Vincent was tying ropes securely around

436

her body and under her arms. She wanted to beg him not to tie them too tightly around her middle, but she still remained dumb about the child, and she was succumbing fast to the shock of her ordeal. She wished she could simply slide into unconsciousness and let the entire rescue continue without her, but she knew she daren't do that. She still had to play her part in getting back up this hostile mountain.

"Hold on to me, and if you believe in the power of prayer, I suggest you start saying a few now," he said roughly. "We're not out of this yet."

She clung to him as he shouted to those above to begin hauling them up. She kept her eyes tightly shut and tried to lighten her own weight by breathing shallowly and not slumping against him unduly. It seemed like an eternity, but suddenly she was aware that there was cheering going on all around her. Soon, other hands were removing the ropes around her bruised and battered body. She was safe and alive.

She looked around her at the exhausted and weary faces of those who had come to rescue her, Greeks and Englishmen alike, and loved them all. She was placed carefully onto a litter, and Doctor Stavros was holding a container of water to her dry lips and taking her pulse, and Vincent was kneeling beside her, holding her other hand as if he would never let it go.

And then it became all too much for her. She burst into tears before blessed unconsciousness finally claimed her, and she knew nothing of the long careful ride back down the mountain to Montagu House and sanity.

437

* * *

Her first conscious thought was that her own bed had never felt so soft, nor the room been so sweetly smelling. As Lydia opened her eyes to the sunlight at the half-shaded window, she realized there were sheafs of flowers all around the room, scenting the air with their fragrance. Vincent sat near the window, gazing unseeingly out of it. Her throat thickened, loving him so much, and yet with the feeling that there was an even wider gulf between them now.

"Have I been here very long?" she said, in the husky voice that seemed more a part of her now than anything else.

He turned to her at once. "A week," he said.

She opened her eyes wide. She had expected him to say a few hours, perhaps a day . . . but a week! She struggled to remember all that had happened, and to be dignified and sensible. There were so many questions to be asked and answered, but in the end there was only one that she was burning to ask.

"Why did you come back from the mainland early?"

He shrugged. "My business was finished earlier than expected, and there was no reason to remain. It was no brilliant piece of intuition, my dear, no call from the gods or any such nonsense to draw me to your side in your moments of danger. It was simply fortuitous that I did so and found your note on your pillow. I guessed then what Marina was about."

Lydia felt her gut twist, both at his unconscious

sarcasm and his reference to Marina Delos. "So you suspected that your mistress would have dark plans for me, did you?"

He looked at her without speaking for a moment.

"Marina was not my mistress. Anything between us ended a long time ago."

"She did not think so!"

"And I can't be held responsible for the way other people think. Nor for what secrets they harbor."

Something in his voice stopped her from any more heated discussion about Marina. She felt incredibly weak, and not yet ready to do battle with him.

"What secrets?" she said huskily, not really thinking straight yet.

"Yours, my dear."

Slowly, he rose from the window seat and moved across the room to her. She could see that his hands were clenched, as if he were holding himself very much in check. As he neared the bed, Lydia was shocked to see how strained he looked, as if he, too, had gone through a great ordeal this past week.

"Mine?" she echoed stupidly. "I don't have secrets."

Even as she said the word, her hand flew to her belly above the bedcovers, and she felt the color rush to her cheeks. She didn't know yet if the child was still all right, or if she had lost something very precious out there on the mountainside.

"Why didn't you tell me you were pregnant, Lydia?"

"I . . . I . ." she couldn't think of a single answer at that moment. His own answer was the more important one. "Oh, please tell me it's all right, Vincent. I couldn't bear it if anything had happened to it—"

His eyes flickered for a moment, and then he gave a brief nod. "It seems you're a very strong woman, Lydia. How was it you once referred to yourself? As a breeding mare, wasn't it?"

She gasped, wounded by his words. They had once been said in anger, when she'd asked scathingly if that was all he wanted of her. He was cruel to throw them back at her in that way. They were insulting and humiliating.

"But the baby still lives?" she whispered, closing her mind to everything else, because this was the only thing that mattered after all.

He nodded briefly. "Doctor Stavros insisted that you remain sedated all this time, until there was no more danger of your losing the child. I take it that it pleases you then?"

He looked at her strangely, and Lydia closed her eyes weakly for a moment. No wonder she still felt so muddled, if she had been sedated for a whole week!

"Of course it pleases me," she said huskily. "What kind of woman would be so unnatural as to want to lose her own child?"

"Even one that was destined to be taken away from her?" he said deliberately.

She gasped again, wondering if she had heard right.

"Why are you saying these things to me, Vincent? Haven't I suffered enough at the hands o your . . . your—?"

"Marina Delos is dead," he said, as she had known must be the case. "You have nothing more to fear from her. But if I had not come back to Kurnios early and found your note, and if a half-crazed mule-handler hadn't come hammering at the door bellowing about an accident on the mountain-side—"

"It was no accident," Lydia said bitterly. "Marina meant to kill me."

"And instead she was the one who perished," Vincent said without expression.

Lydia thought she could see now just why he was being so harsh with her. *The wrong woman had died.* Suddenly all her hopes for a future with this man dwindled and died.

"I shall want to leave the island just as soon as possible," she said dully, her thoughts moving swiftly on, and not wanting to prolong this conversation any longer.

"But not until after the child is born. It was part of the marriage bargain, and you owe me that much," he said.

Her eyes suddenly blazed, a painful deep blue in her white face. Even from this distance, in her reflection in the dressing-table mirror on the other side of the room, she could see how scratches and bruises still marked her delicate skin.

"It was never a part of the marriage bargain, as you call it! Certainly not one that I was aware of before coming to Kurnios. And I owe you nothing!" she said, her low, passionate voice beginning to rise.

"You have already taken everything from me,

441

Vincent. My innocence, my love, and now you think you are going to take my child! Well, you shall not, because I refuse to agree to it. If I must, I shall stay until the child's born, which will at least allow Monty to see his grandchild. I have enough compassion for his wishes for that, and a genuine fondness for him, too. But then I shall return to England, and I intend to take my baby with me."

She almost choked on the words, unable to finish saying all that was in her heart, that she *must* take the child, because it would be all that she had left of *him*.

She had turned away from him, unable to bear the anger on his face at her words. Naturally, he would remind her arrogantly that she was wasting her breath in making such imperious statements, because there was no boatman on the island who would defy Vincent Montagu's wishes, and take her away from Kurnios.

She suddenly felt his warm breath on her face, and realized he was leaning very close to her. He cupped her face in his hands, and forced her to look at him. She winced, because the skin on her cheeks was still scratched and tender, and there was a deep cut beneath one ear, but he didn't even murmur an apology. She sensed that he had too much on his mind to even notice. He was as uncouth a man as she had ever known.

"I took your *love?*" he asked, his unswerving gaze demanding to know the truth.

"What?" Lydia flinched, unable to remember exactly what she had said in her impassioned moments.

442

Vincent's voice was slow and deliberate now, repeating the words to her as if she were a child.

"You said I took your innocence and your love. I accept the first, but is the rest of it true, Lydia? Do you love me?"

She looked at him bitterly. He wanted to wring every ounce of humiliation out of her, she thought. He wanted to think of her as a besotted female who had been dazzled by the stars in her eyes at the thought of marrying this handsome man, and sharing his title and his island paradise.

"All right!" she suddenly cried out in a fit of frustration. "So what if I was foolish enough to fall in love with you? What does it matter now? What does anything matter but the fact that everything's over between us? We could never go on now. I caused the death of your mistress, despite the fact that she did her best to kill me. I doubt that you'll ever forgive me for that."

It was impossible for her to say any more then. His arms gathered her up to him, and she winced again, being still so sore and bruised in places she hadn't known she had. But in a kind of daze, she realized Vincent was no longer angry and condemning. He was laughing softly, and his voice was very tender.

"My sweet, beautiful, aggressive little witch of a wife! When are you ever going to listen to me properly? Marina Delos was out of my life even before I went to England, and once I had found you, there could never be any other woman for me. I thought the unspoken link between us on that first meeting had told you that. From that first moment, you must have known that your pale cousin never stood a chance."

Lydia stared at him, her cheeks starting to fill with color as the heady words seeped into her brain. She could discount all the arrogance with which he dismissed Audine's chances to marry him. But there was something she had to know, something she had every right to know.

"Are you telling me you love me, too?" she said, her voice breaking with the urgency of the question, and needing to know the truth so badly. She looked deep into his eyes, unable to bear it if they flickered one iota. The thought of losing him now, hurt more acutely than all the wounds in her tender flesh.

"Good God, woman, of course I love you," Vincent said, with a rough sincerity that sent her spirits soaring. "Didn't you read the engraving in the necklace I gave you?"

"Yes, I read it, but I wasn't sure if it was just words, because of all that was at stake in this marriage," she said tremblingly, still not sure if she could take in all that he was saying. "You can't deny that it started on a lie, Vincent."

"I don't deny it, but if I had explained everything to you in England, would you still have married me? I think not, and by then, I already loved you so much, I couldn't take the risk of losing you. The charade had to continue. But this is the truth. I love you more than my own life, Lydia. When I knew what might have happened to you on the mountain, I wanted to die with you, and it wasn't the thought of any child that I was concerned with. It was you, my darling girl, only you."

Her throat was so thick, her mind so stunned as

she tried to believe that this was really happening.

"Lydia," he went on softly, "we both know what's going to happen to Monty, and it's going to be a cloud on our perfect horizon for the foreseeable months. But let it be the only cloud, my darling. Can't we start afresh?"

Lydia drew a deep breath. At any other time, she would have expected him to sweep her in his arms and overcome any resistance by the ardor of his lovemaking. But apart from the obvious pressure to her bruised and battered body, she sensed that these moments were too important for even passion to overcome.

"Oh, Vincent, I want to," she said in a little rush. But even now, how could she be sure he wanted her for herself alone? As if he understood her unspoken fears, his arms tightened around her a little, careful not to hurt her.

"Lydia, I realize the memories of Kurnios aren't the happiest in your life. So if it's what you wish, then when Monty is no longer with us, you and I and our child will return to England together. We'll buy a mansion in the country and be English gentry for the rest of our days."

"You'd give up Kurnios for me?" she whispered.

He shrugged. "There's no paradise in Eden without my Eve," he commented.

He gave a half smile. "Knowing your penchant for legends, my love, there's an ancient one that says if a woman follows her man over land and sea, then the gods smile kindly on her." Unable to resist a touch of male arrogance, he went on, "I'm sure they'd overlook the difference in gender if a man followed his woman home to England—"

445

Lydia put her soft fingers against his mouth, stilling the words.

"How can you talk so foolishly?" she said, half-teasing, and beginning to feel more alive with every moment. "Do you think I really want to return to England, when everything I love most in the world is right here? This is where I belong, Vincent, just as long as I can be sure I have your love."

"You have that, now and for always, my dearest one," he said fervently.

"Then my home is here, on our island paradise, my darling, and I never want to leave it," Lydia said, with a throb in her voice.

A shiver of pleasure ran through her at the gladness in his dark eyes. The vision of a future stretching endlessly ahead was as golden and fertile as Kurnios itself. Kurnios was her destiny, as she had always known it would be, symbolically halfway between the two worlds she had once known.

Warmed by Vincent's kisses and hearing the constant reaffirmation of his love now, the horrors of the night on the mountainside were already fading from her memory. Lydia needed no other reassurances now that Vincent, her *husband* and *lover* would always be by her side. She was quite certain that love would flourish and blossom even more strongly between them.

And for both of them, she thought humbly, the child growing in her womb was a living proof of that everlasting love.

DISCOVER DEANA JAMES!

CAPTIVE ANGEL   (2524, $4.50/$5.50)
Abandoned, penniless, and suddenly responsible for the biggest tobacco plantation in Colleton County, distraught Caroline Gillard had no time to dissolve into tears. By day the willowy redhead labored to exhaustion beside her slaves . . . but each night left her restless with longing for her wayward husband. She'd make the sea captain regret his betrayal until he begged her to take him back!

MASQUE OF SAPPHIRE   (2885, $4.50/$5.50)
Judith Talbot-Harrow left England with a heavy heart. She was going to America to join a father she despised and a sister she distrusted. She was certainly in no mood to put up with the insulting actions of the arrogant Yankee privateer who boarded her ship, ransacked her things, then "apologized" with an indecent, brazen kiss! She vowed that someday he'd pay dearly for the liberties he had taken and the desires he had awakened.

SPEAK ONLY LOVE   (3439, $4.95/$5.95)
Long ago, the shock of her mother's death had robbed Vivian Marleigh of the power of speech. Now she was being forced to marry a bitter man with brandy on his breath. But she could not say what was in her heart. It was up to the viscount to spark the fires that would melt her icy reserve.

WILD TEXAS HEART   (3205, $4.95/$5.95)
Fan Breckenridge was terrified when the stranger found her nearnaked and shivering beneath the Texas stars. Unable to remember who she was or what had happened, all she had in the world was the deed to a patch of land that might yield oil . . . and the fierce loving of this wildcatter who called himself Irons.

FEEL THE FIRE IN CAROL FINCH'S ROMANCES!

BELOVED BETRAYAL (2346, $3.95)

Sabrina Spencer donned a gray wig and veiled hat before blackmailing rugged Ridge Tanner into guiding her to For Canby. But the costume soon became her prison — the beauty had fallen head over heels in love!

LOVE'S HIDDEN TREASURE (2980, $4.50)

Shandra d'Evereux felt her heart throb beneath the stolen map she'd hidden in her bodice when Nolan Ellio swept her out onto the veranda. It was hard to concentrate on her mission with that wily rogue around!

MONTANA MOONFIRE (3263, $4.95)

Just as debutante Victoria Flemming-Cassidy was about to marry an oh-so-suitable mate, the towering preacher Dru Sullivan flung her over his shoulder and headed West. Suddenly, Tori realized she had been given the best present for a bride: a night of passion with a real man!

THUNDER'S TENDER TOUCH (2809, $4.50)

Refined Piper Malone needed bounty-hunter, Vince Logan to recover her swindled inheritance. She thought she could coolly dismiss him after he did the job, but she never counted on the hot flood of desire she felt whenever he was near!